MAXWELL'S ISLAND

Having had his retirement snatched from him by malfunctioning technology, Peter 'Mad Max' Maxwell finds himself facing yet another new year at Leighford High School. After having her hopes of a dedicated house husband dashed, his wife, Jacquie, is further annoyed when a family holiday quickly becomes an impromptu Year Seven trip to the Isle of Wight, families welcome. Less than a week into their trip the situation takes another turn for the worse when the wife of Tom Medlicott, the new Head of Art, goes missing, forcing Jacquie to play the role of woman policeman.

MAXWELL'S ISLAND

MAXWELL'S ISLAND

by

M. J. Trow

Magna Large Print Books
Long Preston, North Yorkshire,
BD23 4ND, England.

British Library Cataloguing in Publication Data.

Trow, M. J.
    Maxwell's island.

    A catalogue record of this book is
    available from the British Library

    ISBN   978-0-7505-3519-9

First published in Great Britain in 2011 by Allison & Busby Ltd.

Published in Large Print 2012 by arrangement with
Allison & Busby Ltd.

Magna Large Print is an imprint of Library Magna Books Ltd.

Printed and bound in Great Britain by
T.J. (International) Ltd., Cornwall, PL28 8RW

To Louise; following in Maxwell's footsteps.

Prologue

The body at the bottom of the stairs had had a favourite philosophical conundrum he aired when mildly drunk at dinner parties and the chatting flagged. It was an oldie, but nonetheless a goldie; if a tree falls in a forest with no ears to hear it, does it make a noise? If he was able to take part in the current proceedings, it would have given him a whole new conversational gambit. Does a house with only a dead body in it make a noise? Do the pipes still gurgle? Does the gas boiler still make a pop and a sigh as the thermostat kicks in? Does the fridge make that judder and clink as the hopelessly iced-up condenser tries one more time to stay down to the chosen temperature? Does the bottle of vodka in the freezer click in response as its almost-frozen heart feels a minuscule drop in degrees? Does the grumbling of the continuing digestion of the frozen meal-for-one in the dead man's stomach still sound as horribly loud as it always did in the quiet bits at the cinema with yet another failing date? Does the whisper of settling blood, the susurration of hair in the draught under the front door, the long, slow sigh of the last escaping breath; do these tiny things still make a noise, now that the ears of the careful murderer, tucked under a dark cap to make escape more likely, detection less certain, have, like Elvis, left the building?

11

Chapter One

Maxwell leant back in his steamer chair, the sun warming his face, and he felt that all was pretty good with the world. If he reached out slightly with his right hand, he felt a cool glass, condensation running down the side. If he reached out slightly with his left, he came into contact with the tousled head of his little boy, intent on a game involving a lot of muttering and clashing together of small plastic soldiers. If he stretched one toe, he could annoy the large black and white tom cat stretched out on the rug recently vacated by his other reason to be cheerful, his wife. He sighed and snuggled infinitesimally deeper into the cushion and prepared to rest his eyes for a while longer. A small metaphorical cloud passed over his head. His current situation had all the advantages of retirement, were it not for one thing. He hadn't actually retired. This was, in fact, the last day of yet another summer holiday, a time which seemed to stretch on for ever when it began but, when viewed from this end, was horribly short. It seemed like only this morning that he had been in the hallowed precincts of Leighford High School, with its smell of floral disinfectant, paper and feet. Oh, wait a minute; he had been there this morning, signing in the hopefuls and the no-hopers into the Sixth Form for another year.

'Good God, Dave, what are you doing here?' he had asked, assuming the lad in question had thought this was the dole queue. So, the recession had scotched all hopes of Abigail going off to private school after all and there she was, sullen but proud and ... two more years of Mad Lottie... 'Jesus, make it stop'.

'Max? Max, are you out there?' Jacquie's voice floated down from the kitchen window, one floor above.

'I am so out there,' he muttered, in his finest Moe Szyslak. Nolan giggled and turned his head. The two Maxwell men locked eyes for a minute, and smiled at each other.

Jacquie, as ever, read his mind and possibly even his lips. 'No, seriously, Max, could you come up for a moment? I've got to go in for the afternoon soon and I want to talk to you about October.'

'That sounds slightly ominous, old man,' Maxwell remarked to Nolan as he heaved himself inelegantly from his chair. 'I doubt she's talking about the Eisenstein film or the cataclysmic Russian events of 1917 that gave rise to it. So that can only mean your mama doesn't seem to be planning to let me have a September this year. Don't eat anything poisonous while I'm gone. Don't annoy Mrs Troubridge. Don't annoy Metternich. Don't play in the traffic.'

'Usual rules,' agreed the boy, offering a small and grubby hand for a high five.

'Usual rules. Now, let's see what I've forgotten to do about October.' Maxwell let himself in through the back door, along what he still liked to term the 'back passage', if only to annoy Mrs

13

Troubridge, who abhorred any phrase reminiscent of body parts, especially those she termed 'down below', and he sprinted up at least the bottom few stairs. Just because he still could. 'Hello, the house,' he called as he got to the landing, keeping alive the banal scripts of B-feature western scriptwriters long dead.

'In here,' Jacquie called from the sitting room.

He poked his head round the door and his heart fell. She was sitting in a positive welter of travel brochures. He had thought he had hidden them with some cunning. 'Ah.' It was all he could come up with at short notice.

'Ah. Indeed, ah,' she agreed. 'Look what I've found.' Jacquie Carpenter-Maxwell hadn't kept the double-barrelled thing because she was a snob. As a hardworking DS, she retained 'Carpenter' because that was how she was known to oppos and villains alike. As wife, she used 'Maxwell' because, hey, that was the name of the old duffer she'd married. Her red-gold hair was swept up that morning, businesslike but feminine, and in the harem pants and smock top she wore, she could still undulate for England.

'I've been looking for those,' Maxwell offered hopefully.

'They were in the large suitcase under the stairs.'

He struck himself on the forehead and rolled his eyes. 'Tchah! However did they get there? I expect Mrs B put them there. In an effort to tidy up.' Peter Maxwell could have been any age really, but he'd settle for Dark, historian as he was. He never went in casual to his place of work,

14

so the bow tie was in place from the morning's interviews and his shirt was only slightly rumpled from where he'd been wrestling with Nolan on the lawn. Yes, he had grass in his side whiskers and barbed-wire hair, but Jacquie wasn't going to tell him and Nolan thought that was usual. But Maxwell was in the last-day-of-freedom mode, his cycle clips discarded in what a more innocent age had laughingly called 'gay abandon'.

'Mrs B? Tidy up? Max, please.' Jacquie couldn't imagine life without Mrs B's weekly visit, when all the gossip, smell of old cigarettes and the occasional flick with a duster was visited on 38 Columbine, but as a tidier-up of trifles, considered or not, she left rather a lot to be desired. But still, arguing wouldn't get her a holiday booked. She patted the sofa next to her. 'Come on, you can't avoid this for ever, Max. You promised you would book us a holiday for October half-term and book us a holiday you will.' She quietly removed some of the grass from his hair.

'Can't you do it online?' he wheedled, snuggling up next to her and smoothing his head against her cheek. It was a phrase he had heard at the chalkface where he worked.

'No,' she laughed, pushing him off. 'Can you?'

Despite huge advances in Maxwell's IT knowledge, including being able to switch on his laptop unaided and send emails to random recipients worldwide, he was still not falling for that. He was not going to be goaded into booking a zorbing experience for twenty-seven in the Hindu Kush in 2020 when what he was intending was a week in Lido di Jesolo, fun for all the family but especially for a family with Maxwell in it, sun, sea and Venice. He might even pop in on the Doge. He conceded defeat grac'ously, as was always his way, eventually. 'Tell me where you want to go, heart, and I'll nip down to Messrs Thomas Cook and book it.'

She kissed his ear as the nearest available skin. 'I'll let you know when I've chosen somewhere. I fancy an island, for some reason. My special preference is for somewhere Greek.'

'That could be good,' Maxwell conceded. 'They filmed *The Guns of Navarone* on Rhodes, for example.'

'Well, not there, then,' she said.

'Does Venice count as an island?' he asked.

'No.'

'Well, it is one. There's a bridge and everything. Lagoons as far as the eye can see.'

'I don't want to go to Lido di Jesolo. It will be shut in October.'

'Venice isn't shut in October.'

Jacquie stood up and reached across Maxwell for her handbag and keys. 'I've just got to change and then I'm off to work. I'll give it a little think while I'm ploughing through paperwork and if anything really scrummy comes to mind, I'll ring.'

Maxwell kissed the air after her disappearing back and thumbed through the brochures half-heartedly. Once upon a time, he had been a bit of a traveller. Off for whole summer holidays with an open train ticket in one pocket and a passport in another. He had had the loss of a family to try to minimise for a while. Then he got a cat, who brought the art of guilt creation when he collected

16

him from the cattery to new heights. He could almost hear Count Metternich hissing, 'No, I don't want to talk about it,' at him. Then he got a new family, who had polished and honed the edges of sorrow for his dead wife and child so that he could go for sometimes hours at a time without the catch in his chest as he remembered that slick, wet road and the sound of the useless brakes screaming. And so now, though it was oh-so-nice to go travelling, it was so much nicer to stay home. But Jacquie was right. The Lido was pretty much closed in October, all those scrummy T-shirts locked away infuriatingly behind glass, and Venice had rather a lot of water, into which small boys and inattentive teachers could easily fall, taking the gloss somewhat off the holiday. So, where...?

Metternich's favourite gadget, the telephone, rang at his elbow. 'War Office,' Maxwell muttered into the receiver, trying to clutch the dratted thing against his shoulder.

'And before you ask,' said Jacquie, at the other end, 'I don't mean the Isle of Wight, the Isle of Dogs, Canvey Island, Barry Island. Nor am I thinking of Jersey or any of the Channel Islands. Don't even think of the Hebrides, the Orkneys or the Scilly Isles. Anglesey is out as well.'

'I'm very impressed,' he said, dropping the brochure he was holding and walking to the window and looking down at his wife and son in the back garden. Nolan waved and fell against his mother, giggling. He was a great ganger-upper, was Nole, but had no favourites. Love the one you're with was his motto and he spread his time

17

equally between them. Sometimes, he ganged up against both of them, with Metternich his stout ally, and then he was most devastating of all. 'I had no idea your geographical knowledge was so comprehensive.'

'I'm sure I've missed a few,' she said, modestly.

'I'm sure you have,' he agreed. 'But I get the general drift.' He waggled his fingers at her and blew her a kiss.

'Same back,' she said and rang off. He looked down as she kissed her little boy on the top of his curly head and tickled Metternich between the ears. Maxwell still marvelled that the Count didn't take her hand off at the wrist when she did that. The old statesman was getting soft. He turned from the window and looked again at the pile of bright brochures on the coffee table. Everywhere looked the same: white beaches, coloured umbrellas, laughing couples loping insouciantly along the beach. He silently hoped that as soon as the picture was taken one of them fell over a beach ball, trod on a weever fish, something to wipe those smiles off their faces. Then he turned his back on the lot of them and went downstairs to teach his boy how the Battle of Waterloo *really* went.

The next day, with the smell of feet even more all-pervading, Maxwell was following his usual First-Day-Back pattern. He was considering getting a badge to wear which would announce 'No, I haven't retired after all', which would save his vocal cords and his temper. He admired the new paintwork along the Sixth Form corridor which had already gained that strange grey smear at the average height of a seventeen-year-old boy's backpack. He sipped his coffee and sighed, letting his head loll on the back of his chair. There was a time in every day, but more welcome on this day especially, when everyone was otherwise engaged. They were in lessons, in Tutor Time, in the process of realising that the Sixth Form was not for them after all. The current record for the shortest Sixth Form career stood at a staggering fifteen minutes, but every new year brought a new sweep in the staffroom; the prize wasn't usually much, for example, this year it was a box of biscuits only slightly past their sell-by, but it was the kudos that counted. The Head of Science had stuck-up Abigail down for one hour eight minutes. *Everybody* was hoping Mad Lottie wouldn't survive the round sixty. Maxwell listened to the sounds of the school going about its business. The low murmur of voices, the distant slam of a door, the crash. He sat up, all senses humming. The scream. Somehow, his body was on its feet and running for the head of the stairs before his ears had stopped analysing the sound.

A gaggle of rubbernecking children had gathered at the top of the stairs leading down from the Sixth Form mezzanine level to the lobby. A similar gaggle of rubbernecking staff had gathered at the bottom of the stairs, and to as little effect. The Head of Sixth Form, using a combination of hissed threats, brute strength and guile, was soon at the top of the broad flight and was hurtling down, taking the stairs two at a time, not always by choice. Spreadeagled at the

19

bottom, head down, legs up the slope, lay Sally Greenhow, once a protégée of Maxwell's, now the occupant of a ludicrously titled job in the department he still thought of as Special Needs. Her blonde hair was spread across the already rather manky flooring of the entrance hall, some of it under the no-doubt well-meaning foot of Pansy Donaldson. He gestured her to step back and for once she complied. He didn't want Sally to be bald as well as bruised. It would be too embarrassing. How did that old rock anthem go? Long, bald Sally? Everything seemed to be pointing in the right direction, and as he came nearer the teacher groaned and tried to get up, collapsing back again when the pain shot through her.

'Max,' she muttered. 'I seem to have fallen down the stairs.'

He knelt by her side. 'Never mind, old thing,' he said. 'Don't move. Someone has sent for an ambulance.' Managing to avoid the moronic interrogative, the use of which carried the death penalty in all of his classes, he nevertheless made his statement into a question. Heads swivelled, eyebrows and shoulders raised. Eventually Thingie One, receptionist par excellence, tumbled to the obvious conclusion and trotted off to call an ambulance. As self-appointed first-aider in the absence of Sylvia Matthews, Pansy moved in, enormous biceps flexing to take the strain.

'I don't think we ought to move her, Mrs Donaldson,' Maxwell warned, his voice quiet but scary. 'Nurse Matthews will be here in a minute and I'm sure she will advise.'

'But all the blood is rushing to her head,' protested the woman.

'At least it isn't all over the floor,' Maxwell said. 'And I'm sure she won't mind a bit of blood in her head if the choice is that or a displaced fracture. Would you, Sal? Don't nod or shake,' he added, placing a hand on the top of her head, 'Just focus on all the noughts on that compensation figure.'

'I'm fine,' she whispered and closed her eyes.

Brisk footsteps along the corridor brought blessed relief. 'What's going on here?' Sylvia Matthews' voice could clear a crowd almost as well as Maxwell's. 'Everybody back to where you should be. Mr Maxwell doesn't need an audience.' She looked down. 'Oh, sorry, Mr Maxwell. I heard you had fallen on Mrs Greenhow.'

'That's a new record,' Maxwell remarked. 'A rumour in Leighford High usually takes a full thirty seconds to develop. No, Nurse...' He stood up and faced down a group of Year Seven girls who were quivering in unison behind the school nurse. 'Girls, I know this is a very exciting start to the year for you, new school and all. I would like to assure you that the staff don't hurl themselves downstairs for your amusement every day. And I have never knowingly leapt on Mrs Greenhow in her life. Now, could you please go back to your class? You're in the way.'

There was a minor bit of shoving and one girl popped out of the group like a cork and stood there with her hands twisting in front of her. 'Umm ... are you Mr Maxwell?'

The Great Man was brought up short. Of course he was. The child had been in the school

21

for getting on for two hours and still didn't know? How odd. 'Yes,' he said. 'I am.'

'You taught my gran,' she said, all smiles.

Maxwell's eyes nearly popped out of his head. 'Your *gran?*' he spluttered. 'How old do you think I am?'

'Don't worry, Max,' muttered Sylvia from where she knelt at Sally's head, absently stroking her hair. 'I'll explain.'

Maxwell looked down into Sally's face, always pale to go with her genuinely blonde hair, now so pale that it was almost green. 'Gran?' he mouthed, and she smiled, but only slightly, so as not to jar her head.

'Who was that?' she whispered.

'A new bug. Glasses. Fringe. Female.'

'That sounds like Paige.'

'Page?'

'Max, you're going to have to promise not to laugh or anything. I really hurt. All over, and your laugh is so catching.'

'Yes, Max,' Sylvia chimed in. 'You really mustn't laugh.'

'Why should I laugh?' He spread his hands innocently out to the sides. 'I'm the one who has been accused of teaching that child's gran. Move over, Sal, I should be lying down.'

'Well, you did teach her. But her gran had Paige's mum when she was fourteen and it turns out it runs in the family.'

Maxwell did the sums in his head and grunted softly to himself. 'Hmm. Right. Well, in that case, I'm surprised it doesn't happen more. Who is the lovely granny?'

'Sophie Turner.'

Maxwell was quick as lightning. 'Just as well that Paige has a different surname, then...' He saw their faces. 'Same name? Oh, dear. How cruel.'

'Max,' said Sally, as sharply as she dared. 'You promised you wouldn't laugh.'

He was crushed. 'I'm not laughing.'

'You're laughing on the inside, Max, and that's what counts,' said Sylvia. She cocked her head on one side. 'Is that a siren?'

And sure enough, it was. The green-clad paramedics were suddenly everywhere, checking Sally's vital signs and locking her head in a device which would have made Torquemada proud. They felt along Sally's gangly limbs and found the broken ankle which she could have identified from the first. That went into an inflatable splint and then they were good to go. But before they carried her into the ambulance, a self-important Pansy in attendance, she grabbed Maxwell's hand. By now, the pain was ebbing as the morphine in the drip took hold.

'Max,' she wheedled in a slurred sort of way. 'I was doing a Getting to Know You, week after next. Can you do it?'

He squeezed her fingers lightly. He vaguely remembered that it was a good idea not to cross someone heavily sedated. Or was it drunk, carrying a meat cleaver? He could never get that right. 'Of course, Sal. You just go off and get better.'

Her eyes widened. 'You'll do it for me, Max? You're so wonderful.'

'Can't argue there,' he chuckled. 'Off you go,'

and the stretcher was carried away.

Sylvia and Maxwell waved it off, rather fruitlessly they knew, as no one in the vehicle was watching, but somehow it seemed so churlish just to turn away. When they did turn back into the school, Sylvia patted his back and said, 'She's right, you are wonderful.'

A small light went on in the back of Maxwell's head. He felt that he needed to check his facts. 'The Getting to Know You week is that one where Year Seven are off timetable to mingle and mix, isn't it?' He looked down anxiously into Sylvia's eyes.

She snorted lightly. 'Oops, Mr Maxwell,' she said. 'I think that you should accompany me to my office, where you may learn something to your advantage. I've got to fill in the Accident Book anyway.'

'Sylv,' he dropped his voice to subterranean levels. He had been working on his Valentine Dyall, the actor who put the burnt umber into dark brown (although that was all so long ago, only Maxwell remembered him). 'Tell me straight. What have I agreed to?'

She raised an eyebrow.

'Oh, heavens to Betsy, I'm that flustered.' Vivien Leigh with just a tad of Frankie Howerd. 'To what have I agreed?'

The nurse put her hands on her hips and faced him squarely. 'I thought you had promised that you would read the e-memos this term?'

'And I will. But today hardly counts.'

'Max. Today is the most important day for that sort of thing, surely? It's when all the announce-

24

ments go out. But in fact, this memo went out last term.'

'Ah.' It was a strange noise, somewhere between a groan, a scream and an eldritch cry.

'Remembered?'

'"The Getting to Know You week will this year be off-site,"' he quoted as best he could, doing his Dalek impression. He tried a tentative smile. 'So, that's days out, is it? Chessington World of Adventure? Brighton? London Eye? Trips of that nature?' He looked longingly at Sylvia. 'Just nod. Please nod!'

'Sorry, Max. I only nod when the answer is yes, not being of the Polynesian persuasion.'

He grabbed her arm, then relaxed his grip as he realised he was cutting off the blood supply. His voice was a strangled whisper. 'It's a week on the Isle of Wight, isn't it?' he said.

'Give the man a candy floss,' she said, shrugging him off. 'Families welcome,' she added. 'I'm coming. It will be fun. Bring Nole. He'll love it.'

'Oh, yes,' Maxwell agreed. 'He'll love it. His brand-new Headmistress will not be so keen, though, I expect. His mother will be furious. She's planning a week in somewhere exotic in October.'

'Well, that will be nice, then. *Two* holidays.'

'Sounds like a good idea in principle. Except that she only has one week left until the end of the year. Her holidays are not as generous as ours, as I am constantly reminded.'

Sylvia pursed her lips and shook her head, then patted the Head of Sixth Form on the arm. 'Well, don't do it, then. Sally will understand.'

25

'But I promised.'

'But you didn't know,' she riposted.

'But I should have known,' he parried in sixte.

'Whose side are you on?' she asked. 'I'm trying to talk you out of this.'

'I know you are, Sylv,' he said, turning for the stairs. He stopped, with one foot on the lowest tread. 'Have you read *Horton Hatches the Egg* lately?'

'I can't say that I have.'

'Seen the film, *Horton Hears a Who?*'

'No.'

'Well, I'm sure you know that Horton is an elephant, mocked and harassed by the Wickersham Brothers, who are blue gorillas.'

'Ah!' The light dawned. 'Dr Seuss. Is Nolan a fan?'

Maxwell looked confused. 'Possibly. Are Dr Seuss books for children? But what I meant was I am that elephant.'

'It was Sally who hit her head, wasn't it?' Sylvia asked the world at large.

Maxwell looked seriously at Sylvia. 'We are all elephants in this context, Sylv, keeping the blue gorillas at bay. Horton is very loyal and his refrain when mocked for trying to hatch his egg is "I meant what I said, and I said what I meant. An elephant's faithful one hundred per cent." I promised Sally I would do her week, and do that week I shall.'

Chapter Two

'And why,' came Woman Policeman Carpenter-Maxwell's voice from the darkness, 'are you quoting Horton at me?' She snapped on her bedside lamp.

'Bright light, bright light,' Maxwell complained, hiding his head under the duvet. He had been perfecting his Mogwai voice for years and had recently found a new audience in Nolan. Metternich had long ago ceased to be impressed. He was somewhere out on the tiles now, butchering rodents.

Jacquie pulled the covers down and looked her husband in the eye. 'There has been unremitting cuteness and consideration from you ever since I got home. Nice, clean, tucked-up child, a meal on a tray in front of *Mamma Mia*, a film you hate only second to *The Sound of Music*. And now, when you think I'm asleep or as near as makes no difference, you quote Dr Seuss at me. I'm a detective, for God's sake. I have a nose for these things. What's going on?'

'Can't a husband be cute with no reason?' he asked plaintively.

'Of course a husband can,' she said, letting go of the duvet suddenly so that his hand flew up and he hit himself in the face.

'Ow.'

'You deserved that. Of course a husband can.

27

It's just *you* that can't. At least, not without telling me why.'

'I'm the elephant in the room?'

'The moronic interrogative?' She was now even more suspicious. Maxwell was almost suicidal. That was twice in one day. 'And management-speak as well.' She sat up and looked ready for business. 'All right, Max. Now you have my full attention.'

This had not been his intention. He had indeed been trying all evening to get round both Jacquie and to the matter in hand. The trip to the Isle of Wight actually looked quite fun. The staff signed up already were from the more amenable section of the staffroom and were bringing families, so there would be opportunities to bunk off or, as the rubric had it, 'have time away from the students by mutual arrangement'. The hotel was of the better kind, with a pool and gardens and ... but there wasn't any way that he could make it sound like a week in Corfu in October.

'I don't know how to begin.'

Her blood ran cold. Conversations which began this way were seldom happy ones. 'Try,' she said, and even to her own ears her voice sounded pinched and high.

Maxwell turned his head and looked at her, his lovely wife, with bed hair and wide eyes. He punched her lightly on the leg. 'No, it's not like that. It's not bad news. It's just that I really don't know how to begin.' He extended an arm and she slid down the bed and snuggled in.

'Well, what is it? You know it always makes me suspicious when you quote Dr Seuss.'

'Luke Luck likes lakes,' he remarked.

'Good for him,' she muttered into his chest. 'Out with it, Mr Maxwell, or things could get nasty.' It wasn't her best Clint Eastwood, but he'd walk over hot coals rather than tell her so.

'Sally Greenhow fell downstairs today.'

Her head jerked up and he got another smack in the face.

'Ow.'

'Sorry. You didn't really deserve that one. Is she all right?'

His reply was a bit muffled as he nursed his nose with his free hand. 'She is in hospital overnight, being checked for concussion and while her plaster dries out properly. She has a broken ankle but it wasn't displaced. Loads of bruises.'

'How on earth did she do that? And can you move your hand? You sound like Marlon Brando. So, what do you want to tell me?'

'I'm gonna make you an offer you can't refuse.' The Don himself could not have done it better.

'An offer of...?'

'A lovely island holiday.'

She reached up and kissed his cheek. 'Oh, Max, that's...' Pennies dropped and lights came on, simultaneously. 'That's got nothing to do with Sally Greenhow bumping her head and breaking her ankle.'

He reached round and pinched her cheek, shaking it roguishly. 'Nothing much gets past you, Woman Policeman, does it?'

'No.' She shook her head. 'Can you let go? Now *I* sound like Marlon Brando.'

'Sorry.' He let go of her cheek, smoothed it just

29

because he wanted to and tucked his hand back under the covers.

'No, it doesn't. What I would like you to tell me is that Sally had a holiday booked in Corfu in October that she can't do with a broken ankle. So you, kindly, have taken over the booking.'

'That would be nice,' he said, hopefully.

'But, instead, you are going to tell me that in fact you are going to run her week on the Isle of Wight.'

He raised himself up on one elbow. 'You're good,' he said, shaking his head. 'My word, you're good. However did you work that one out?'

'Low cunning.'

'Well, clearly that, but how did you find out?'

She slid further down until she was completely hidden under the duvet and rolled it round herself, to protect her ticklish bits. Her voice was muffled, but clear. 'I bumped into Sylv in Morrisons on my way home. She told me.' She spluttered as he made an attempt at the soft bit on the inside of her thigh. 'She made me promise not to tell you until you had spoilt me all evening first.' She curled up into a tighter ball. 'No, Max, no tickling. No. Look, you'll wake Nole. No. Stop it.'

Suddenly, he did stop and she peeped out from behind the quilt.

'Don't you mind?' he asked.

She emerged fully and kissed the tip of his nose. 'Of course I mind. No sun. Sort of sea, but we have that here. A hotel, but full of kids. But, it's a week more or less with you, Nole will love it and it is the week after next, not months away.'

30

He kissed her back. 'I do love you, you know. You're a woman in a million.'

'No,' she corrected him. 'In a squillion. And don't think you've paid me back yet,' she turned over, pulling most of the quilt with her and turned out the light. 'Because you haven't. Not by a long chalk.'

By mutual but unspoken consent, Maxwell and his good lady decided not to tell Nolan the good news about his unexpected holiday until they had to. Before they could share it with him, they had to broach the subject with his new Headmistress, who made Snow White's stepmother look mild and fond of children. Maxwell had drawn the short straw. And lost at scissors-stone-paper. And lost at coin-tossing. He suggested they cut cards, but Jacquie was already halfway out of the door, with Nolan in tow.

'Sorry, Max,' she called back up the stairs. 'Best of three is best of three. No more chances. I'll make you an appointment for this afternoon after you finish. Best of luck.' And with a slam of the door, she was gone.

It wasn't that Maxwell was scared of Mrs Whatmough. She was only a Headmistress after all and Maxwell had eaten better men than her for breakfast. But she did have a moustache, something which Maxwell always found rather disconcerting on a woman, especially when she seemed to use wax not to diminish it but to accentuate its curled ends. She also had a cunning way with feng shui, so that her office somehow had, without overt artefacts or artwork, the

31

look and feel of a dungeon, torturers for the use of. And bearing in mind that the oldest child in her care was eight, it did seem rather an expression of her personality, rather than an attempt at controlling the pupils in her school.

Maxwell gave himself a little shake and cleared the breakfast table. Nolan was taking Proper School very seriously and the Coco Pop spillage was now quite minor. No need to get out the Hoover these days; a wet cloth and a bin bag would usually suffice. How quickly they seemed to grow up. A week on the Isle of Wight, behaving like kids, would do them all the world of good.

But every time he tried to immerse himself in household tasks, Mrs Whatmough's face loomed like some terrible gorgon from the suds in the sink, from the chocolaty smears on the tabletop, from the cat food detritus in Metternich's bowl – though to be fair the detritus was on the meagre side, so her features were rather sketchy. But sufficient unto the day was the Headmistress thereof, so it was a sunny Peter Maxwell who wheeled White Surrey down the path a few minutes later. The old velocipede wasn't what he once was, but then, which of us is, Maxwell pondered. If he'd had to take the flyover at near-impossible speeds every morning with just a hint of WD-40 on his working parts, how would he feel? Maxwell was in mid-leg swing, not something that could be interrupted without serious tendon-twanging these days, when he heard the thing he most dreaded.

'Mr Maxwell?'

Could he ignore it? How would he feel if it

turned out she was calling with the last breath in her body and he ignored her? Fine, probably. He prepared to swing again.

'Mr Maxwell? Have you got a moment?'

Without turning his head, he answered. 'Not so's you'd notice, Mrs Troubridge, no. Off to school, you know how it is.' Since Mrs Troubridge had last seen a school when that nice Mr Nickleby was her form tutor, that statement was probably pretty wide of the mark.

'I only need a moment, Mr Maxwell.' She was beginning to sound testy. 'I have someone I would love you to meet.' She sounded so excited, like an incompetent magician who had finally managed to produce a rabbit out of his hat, that Maxwell gave in. He was a kind man and his neighbour, though annoying and physically reminiscent of something from a Rider Haggard novel, was, when all was done and said, his neighbour. She and Nole got on like houses on fire, and even Metternich kept the number of dismembered voles left on her front step to a minimum, ever since the incident of which they no longer spoke. So, Maxwell turned to face her. And swallowed an involuntary shriek.

Mrs Troubridge was standing halfway down her path, her little marmoset-like features split in a happy grin. All four foot eleven of her was swelling with pride but she was still, as always, tiny. Behind her, in the doorway, like some living optical illusion, stood an almost identical person. But this person was not, like Miss Troubridge, Mrs Troubridge's previously long-lost, then found, then lost again sister, as like her as two

33

peas in a pod. No, this person was as like her as one pea in a pod and one simply enormous pea, growing on a giant's allotment. Everything else was the same. The grinning face, the fluffy hair, the pink dressing gown clutched tightly at chest and waist, so as not to inflame Maxwell's passions so early in the morning.

Maxwell rearranged his face into an amazed and welcoming smile. 'Mrs Troubridge! A visitor; how lovely.'

'Not just *a* visitor, Mr Maxwell,' she trilled. 'This is my cousin Millie. She comes from the North, you know, but you mustn't mind that.' She came closer to Maxwell, and reached up slightly so she could whisper near his ear. 'Miss Troubridge found her for me.'

Maxwell fought down the sentences which were gathering on his tongue, ready to leap into the air. 'She must have been quite easy to find,' was the least offensive, but even so he preferred to settle for, 'How kind. Had you been looking long?'

She risked releasing her dressing gown for long enough to cuff him lightly on the arm. 'Mr Maxwell, you always make me laugh. Except about the Incident, of course.'

Maxwell tapped his nose wisely. 'Not about the Incident, no. I do understand.'

Mrs Troubridge's voice became shriller. 'I still wake up, sometimes,' she cried. 'It never really leaves me.'

He decided to bring her back to earth. 'Your visitor?' He gestured up the path. 'Millie.'

The giant woman waved her fingers coquettishly.

34

'Oh, yes, Millie.' Mrs Troubridge pulled herself together with a final quiver. 'Miss Troubridge is compiling our family tree and she has had quite remarkable success.'

Maxwell the historian rose to the bait. 'Having an unusual name like Troubridge must have helped her enormously,' he said.

'Only *our* branch is Troubridge,' said Mrs Troubridge sternly. 'There was just my sister and me and, of course, *Mr* Troubridge at the end. No,' she sighed. 'If Miss Troubridge or I should die, then that will be the end of the line, I'm afraid.'

Maxwell was stunned by the hubris of the little woman. To assume that death was an optional extra showed extraordinary optimism. Or pessimism, depending on the point of view. His innate politeness reasserted itself. 'I am remiss, Mrs Troubridge. How is Miss Troubridge, these days?'

'Gadding,' snapped the little woman. 'There's no other word for it. And since she became a platinum surfer, there's no stopping her. But putting pen to paper for those of us who are not so computer-oriented, nothing. But, no,' Mrs Troubridge returned to the thought before one. 'Millie's surname is Muswell.'

'Ah, like the Hill.'

Mrs Troubridge stepped back, amazed. 'No, Mr Maxwell. The name Muswell denotes a boggy or mossy place. Not a hill. You do surprise me, being a supposedly intelligent man.'

Doing his best to look fairly bright, Maxwell turned back to his bicycle. 'I really must go, Mrs Troubridge,' he said. 'I will be late for school,

35

else. But perhaps you would like to bring Millie round for tea this afternoon? I'm sure Jacquie would love to meet her, and anyway we have a favour to ask you.'

The little face lit up. 'Babysitting?'

'In a way.' Maxwell had managed to swing his leg over the crossbar and was finally on his way. 'We're going away and wondered if you would feed Metternich.'

As he swept away, up the slope and off to the left at the top of Columbine, he could still hear her plaintive cry. 'But Mr Maxwell! What if there's another Incident?'

Leighford High School was looking slightly more battered on its second day of term. It was staggering, Maxwell had never ceased to think, how the work of six whole weeks for a posse of cleaners, builders and decorators could be completely undone in less than a day. The students of Leighford were no different from those of any other school, averaging them out and chopping off the ends of the graph in that cavalier way statisticians have. And yet he had never visited another school, college or indeed an institution of any kind without remarking to himself how less dog-eared that place seemed compared to good old Leighford. He wondered if the hotel in the Isle of Wight was really quite ready for this influx. He wondered if they would hold him personally accountable. Whether he would have to do the washing-up to pay for all the broken bedside lamps, shower fitments, beds, windows and other sundries which he feared Year Seven would leave in their wake.

Only the Head of Sixth Form's office still maintained the old standards. Japanese Zeros snaked over the unsuspecting US Fleet in *Tora! Tora! Tora!* above his desk. An impossibly Sixties *McCabe & Mrs Miller* screamed 'beautiful people' from the poster of the same name. And Jon Voight and Burt Reynolds weren't enjoying orienteering very much in *Deliverance*. But as long as these *films memoirs* and others like them were there, Maxwell could drift off into fond movie moment, thanks to his wife's eagle eyes on eBay.

He reached for the phone, still depressingly County Hall kitsch though it was. 'Sylv?'

'Mr Maxwell. I can't really talk at the moment. I'm dealing with a rather nasty case of coccidioidomycosis.' There was a distant crash. 'Oh, darn. The wretched boy has done a runner.'

'It's your fault, Sylv. You will use the posh term. What is it, by the way, of which you have a nasty case?'

'Oh, nothing. Just a rash. How can I help you?'

'I'm just having a bit of a mull over this trip,' although he knew perfectly well that the Isle of Wight was nowhere near Mull.

'Cold feet?'

'By no means. No, no, heavens no. Jacquie is delighted. Not delighted as such, you understand. But she was surprisingly understanding. I'm sure Nole will be ecstatic and I will have a weight off my mind when I have passed it by Mrs Whatmough.'

Sylvia chuckled in a rather scary way, made worse by the slight reverb on the phone. 'She'll

37

be fine, Max, I'm sure. Rosemary Whatmough and I go back a long way.'

'You know her?' He could feel a load lifting from his shoulders. 'Oh, Sylv...'

'Oh, no, Max. I said we went back. I didn't say we were friends. In fact, I might go so far as to say the very opposite.'

'But you said...'

'Just trying to cheer you up, Max. She'll be horrendous. Absolutely, appallingly, uncompromisingly horrendous. Anyway, things to do. Is that why you rang?'

He was occupied for a moment in swallowing hard. 'No. I was just wondering if you had any paperwork about the trip. We must be quite near the deadline for Health and Safety Risk Assessments, that kind of thing.' He tried to keep the hope out of his voice, but he should have known better.

'Sally had everything signed, sealed and delivered in at least triplicate before the end of last term.'

'There must be some non-payers, then. You know the rule.'

'What rule is that?'

'That if everyone doesn't pay up, then the trip can't run.'

'Fund-raising, Max. All last term and over the holiday. Don't you remember Year Ten offering to wash your bike? The whole thing is free. All the kids need is some money for spending on drinks and things.'

Maxwell let his arm drop to his side.

'Max?' Her voice sounded very far away. 'Max,

38

are you there?'

With a huge sigh he brought the phone back up to his mouth. 'Yes, Sylv. I'm here. Who's got the paperwork, then?'

'I would imagine it would be Tom Medlicott. New chap in Art.'

'He's keen.'

'As mustard. I think Sally grabbed him at the end of last term when he was down for orient-ation. His wife is coming, too.'

'So, then. That's me and Jacquie and Nole. Tom and his wife. You and Guy.'

'We're looking forward to it. We don't see enough of you all.'

'Right back atchya. Umm ... anyone else?' Another light at the end of the tunnel. Could it be that there would be enough staff without him?

'Well, because Sally can't do it, we are light on women. So I believe Mrs Donaldson is coming along.' He could hear her smiling on the other end of the phone.

'*Pansy?* She's not a teacher, though.' Straws were there to be grabbed. The woman ran the school office. It would be like putting an officer of Engineers in charge of the defence of Rorke's Drift. Hang on, though, that had turned out quite well.

'Nor am I,' she pointed out, not unreasonably. 'Look, Max. Either bow out and no one will blame you, or come. Look, I must go. My coccidioidomycosis has just come back. Silly boy – a good swill in some calamine and he will be as right as rain. Bye.'

Maxwell stood for a minute, holding the phone

tightly. Then he exhaled and went off to teach Seven Emm Three something about the Civil War. He wondered how long it would take before some benighted child asked him when they would get on to the assassination of President Lincoln. The present record stood at eight minutes.

Maxwell's timekeeping was both legendary and immaculate. He was never late for lessons, except deliberately. He never needed to look at a clock. The bell never came as a surprise and the lessons never seemed too long. But the interview with Mrs Whatmough was hanging heavily over his head, her moustachioed face leering down at him. He felt as Prometheus must have done, chained to his rock, waiting for the eagle to resume snacking on his liver. The day alternately dragged and sped past until it was finally time to beard – almost literally – the gorgon in her cave.

Nolan's school was just down the road and along a bit from Leighford High. It hadn't been chosen for that reason; they had chosen it, and the Local Authority had kindly allowed them to send Nolan there, because it was a very good school. Ofsted inspectors reeled out wreathed in smiles, making large ticks in every box. Children from there romped gleefully home with carrier bags full of trophies from every music festival in the area. Those up for entry into public schools both major and minor were mentioned in despatches as they passed their entrance exams with flying colours. The whole place seemed to shine with a perfect gloss not seen since the

Wizard left the Emerald City. The reason for this gloss was Rosemary Whatmough. Thus she could be said to be both the ointment and the fly.

Centuries at the chalkface had taught Maxwell that the thing a child hates most is a parent in their school. So he waited a discreet half an hour after Nole's knocking-off time before he turned up at the hallowed door. He had remembered to remove his bicycle clips. He had smoothed down his hair as best he could and stashed the shapeless tweed hat into Surrey's basket. He had prevaricated by examining every rose bush in the flower bed outside Reception for greenfly. But now, he had to face the woman. He pushed open the door. A receptionist of startling beauty was the first thing he saw and his heart lifted.

'Mrs Whatmough,' he remarked. 'I have an appointment.'

She lifted a disbelieving eyebrow and checked her computer screen. 'And you are?' Her voice could have cracked diamonds.

He bit back his usual retort and smiled. 'Peter Maxwell. Nolan Maxwell's father.'

The other eyebrow shot up into her hair. 'I see.' She scrolled through a few screens. 'Yes, here you are.' She glanced up at the clock. 'Do you know you're late?'

He was flabbergasted. 'I am?' He also looked at the clock. It said one minute past four. 'My appointment is for four, isn't it?'

'Yes.' The tone mingled surprise and distaste.

'So... I'm not actually late. As such.'

She snorted silently. Parents! What a shame they were necessary. 'Mrs Whatmough is a

41

stickler for punctuality. However, I'll see if she's still free.'

How different from the sweet responses of Thingies One and Two who worked at Leighford High and ate straight out of Maxwell's hand.

He wanted to haul the cow over her desk and ask her if she'd like a proper job, in a school where anything happening in the right half of the day would be a bonus. He wanted to muss her hair, breathe on her glasses and generally make her look like a person rather than someone's very optimistic avatar, had he known what an avatar was. But he just said, 'That would be very good of you. I'll wait over here, shall I?' He took himself over to a row of chairs and picked up a magazine. It was called *Which University – Planning in the Early Years*. Nothing like looking ahead, he supposed. It was probably aimed at the pre-pre-schoolers. He had hardly sat down when the Devil's receptionist called his name.

'Mr Maxwell? Mrs Whatmough will see you now.' She gestured to a door behind her, which was standing open an inch or two. He gulped and went in.

Rosemary Whatmough was sitting bolt upright behind her desk, with a file open in front of her. There was one sheet of paper in the file and Maxwell realised that, though Nolan had only joined the school the day before, the file was his. She didn't get up but extended a hand over the desk towards Maxwell.

'Mr Maxwell. How nice to see you again.' She sounded as though she had learnt the sentence phonetically but didn't know what it meant.

There was certainly no warmth in the greeting. 'How may I help you?'

There was nothing to be gained by shilly-shallying. 'Due to staff illness, I am taking a school trip to the Isle of Wight soon. Jacquie ... er... Mrs Maxwell, is joining me and we would like to take Nole... er ... Nolan.'

She smiled with just the very edges of her mouth. 'Soon? That would be half-term, perhaps?'

'Erm, no. That would be next week.'

'For the day? I assume you would be pursuing some educational aims, as it is a school trip?' The smile was still in place, but barely.

'No.' He swallowed. He didn't dare look down but he was sure that he was suddenly in his junior-school uniform of short trousers, slightly too long blazer, slightly too big and grey jumper, rather inaccurately knitted by his mother. He felt about nine years old and he had been caught scrumping. 'No, it's for a week.'

She picked up a pen and for a moment he thought she was going to stab him with it. But no she made a terse note at the bottom of Nolan's virgin page. Then she looked up. The smile was now really, *really* gone. 'I can't stop you, Mr Maxwell. There is a fine, of course. The Education Welfare Officer will be in touch about that. And there will be, as you have seen,' she flipped the file closed and tapped it with a talon, 'a note on Nolan's file. Such a sweet child and very bright.' She sighed. 'Never mind.' She pulled another file towards her, opened it and began to write.

Maxwell sat in his chair in disbelief. Depending

on the point of view, it had gone surprisingly well and also amazingly badly. Nole had his week off, but he had been labelled as a subversive influence, who would be watched from henceforth for any small infringement of lunch queue etiquette or other heinous crime. Never mind – he knew his son and knew that he had been an anarchist from the moment of his birth, but with such a dose of charm that hardly anyone noticed. Still, he would have a chat with the lad and say his cover was almost blown.

She looked up. 'That will be all, Mr Maxwell,' she said.

He got up slowly, surprised that he could move at all. He had been pretty sure for a minute there that he had been turned to stone.

Still reeling from the Whatmough Experience, a précis of which he was planning to send to Alton Towers for possible inclusion as their next white-knuckle ride, Maxwell arrived home to find Jacquie's car already there. He heaved a sigh of relief and slid his key into the lock. He was naturally pleased that his wife was home, but there was the double pleasure to be gained from the fact that, if one of them had forgotten Nolan, it wasn't him. He was about to step through into the hall, when he heard it. A strange noise, deep and long-drawn-out, which seemed to bypass his ears and burrow deep into his brain. His reaction to it was buried deep in his bones, in the tiny bit of DNA that all men share with the first mammal, the reaction of a small and squashy piece of fur hiding from a large and clumsy reptile. As he was trying to find the source, Metternich shot down the stairs and out, ears back, whiskers streaming in the wind of his own speed, meow dopplering into the distance as he hid beneath Jacquie's car.

The noise stopped, and his hackles slowly relaxed, the hairs on his arms lay down again and Metternich peered out from under the bumper.

'What the hell was that, Count?' Maxwell whispered, but the black and white behemoth could only stare. As the Head of Sixth Form teetered in his own threshold, he heard a door open upstairs.

'Max? Is that you?' Jacquie was bending down at the top of the stairs, peering down at him.

He gave himself a shake. Metternich slunk out from under the car and tried to look nonchalant while washing his paw, but was fooling nobody.

'Yes,' he carolled and made for the stairs, but she waved him back again and crept down to join him. She grabbed his arm.

'Did you hear that?' she whispered.

'Yes. What the hell was it? Metternich has gone white all over. Look at him. He's quivering.'

'It's Millie.'

Maxwell was still feeling a tad whatmoughed and raised a questioning eyebrow.

'Millie Muswell. Mrs Troubridge's long-lost cousin.'

'Ah. Yes, we met briefly this morning.'

'Apparently, we asked them to tea,' Jacquie said, folding her arms.

'I did mention,' Maxwell faltered. 'We do want Mrs T to eff–ee–ee–dee Metternich, don't we?'

It was no good. Metternich's spelling was

sometimes a little ropey; for example, he wasn't too good at the eye before ee thing, but he knew the basics. He walked back into the house past Maxwell, on his way to the cat flap into the garden, and gave him an admonitory clip on the ankle with a well-turned claw for good measure.

'Well, yes, we do. And I know she will take a bit of buttering up, but couldn't you have waited until Millie had gone home? She's leaving the day after tomorrow.'

Maxwell was contrite. 'I didn't know how long she would be here, to be fair, Immortal Beloved. I only saw them this morning very briefly as I was leaving the house.' There was a repetition of the sound from above. 'What *is* that?' he asked his wife.

'It's Millie laughing. She has a rather robust sense of humour. Nolan is entertaining her, as only he can.'

'Farting or card tricks?' His son was an adept at either.

'A bit of both. Anyway, come upstairs and spread the load.'

So, hand in hand, like Hansel and Gretel approaching the gingerbread house, they crept up the stairs.

Maxwell's impression of that morning had not been wrong. That Mrs Troubridge and Millie Muswell were related was beyond all doubt. But whilst Mrs Troubridge looked rather like a small rodent who had just come through a bad winter, food-wise, Millie looked like a capybara which had had a darned good season foraging on the

46

pampas. She wasn't fat; she was just huge, with hands like plates and thighs like wardrobes. Nolan was leaning on one of them now, and had ample room to do his favourite card trick of Find the Lady. He was getting very good at it, Maxwell was glad to see. With the kind of reference he would be getting from Mrs Whatmough, he would probably need the money.

Maxwell advanced into the room, good public schoolboy that he was, with hand outstretched. 'Millie. May I call you Millie?' She cuffed him playfully in assent and nearly dislodged a rib. 'So nice to get to meet you properly. Mrs Troubridge had never mentioned you.'

'She didn't know about me until recently,' Millie rumbled. 'I started tracing our family tree and I'm afraid I was very lazy and started with the easy bit. Troubridge is such an unusual name.'

'Indeed,' Maxwell agreed. That wasn't the only thing unusual about Troubridge, but it would be unneighbourly to say so.

'So I went on to Genes Reunited, Ancestry, that kind of thing. And I found that Araminta was doing the same. Two heads are definitely better than one when tracing family.'

Mrs Troubridge leant over and hissed in a stage whisper, 'Mr Maxwell doesn't really know much about computers, dear.'

'Oh, I'm sorry,' Millie said, patting his hand as though tenderising a steak. 'Do say if you don't follow. I do love my computer.' Unbidden into the Maxwell heads came a picture of Millie holding a laptop and making it look like a pocket calculator. Jacquie knew from their stiffened

47

shoulders and averted eyes that they didn't dare look at each other. Three minds with but a single thought. 'Anyway, I googled the name and away I went. I found Araminta first, and then she put me on to Jessica here.'

'It's a great shame,' Mrs Troubridge added, 'that Araminta and I are where Millie's trail runs out as far as this branch of the family goes. Mr Troubridge was an only child, of course, as I may have mentioned. His father and my father were brothers. Although they had several sisters, only two had children and of course they weren't called Troubridge on their marriage.'

'Unlike you,' Maxwell smiled at her.

'We can't all be lucky enough to find our Mr Troubridge within the confines of the family,' Mrs Troubridge nodded complacently in his direction.

It was just as well, Maxwell thought. Otherwise by now everyone would be hopping around on a single webbed foot. What he said was, 'No, indeed.'

Mrs Troubridge looked at him as though she had momentarily been able to read his mind. 'My father's sister Margaret is Millie's grandmother, so I suppose that we are second cousins, rather than cousins. Even so, I think if you look closely you might spot a slight family resemblance.' The two women turned their faces to Maxwell and tilted them to the light. 'Just across the eyes, perhaps.'

Jacquie thought it was time she came to the rescue. 'It's very striking in the right light, I must say,' she told them. Maxwell was trying to land

48

back on Earth, having got a little giddy orbiting Planet Troubridge. 'Have you found many other relatives, Millie?'

'It's been fascinating,' she boomed. 'Sad as well, of course, because one does find that some people have died before I got to them.' She managed to make it sound like mismanagement on their part. 'Then, of course, there is the distressing habit of divorce these days.' She dropped her voice so as not to alarm Nolan. 'Co-habiting.' The next words weren't even spoken, just mouthed. 'Civil partnerships. Illegitimacy.' Her voice came back to its normal million-decibel level. 'It makes my job very difficult, but I am very determined. I estimate that I am almost halfway there.'

'Well done,' Maxwell said. The historian in him had to applaud her efforts. 'How far back have you managed to get?'

Millie's eyes lit up. She took a deep breath and embarked on a whistle-stop tour through the Troubridge line, via the Muswells and sundry side lines. Maxwell was impressed. She had got back as far as compulsory registration in the 1830s without missing a beat. Before that had been more tricky, but by going to parish records and the lucky find of some family papers, she had made the first few steps into the eighteenth century. 'We are lucky, really,' she said. 'As a family, we have always been rather drawn to unusual names. Araminta, for example, isn't something you find every day. And my name, of course.'

'Millicent? It is unusual now, I suppose...'

She became coy. 'No, it's not Millicent.'

'Er ... Mildred?'

'No – I'll tell you; no one ever guesses. It's Millamant, from Congreve, you know.'

'How unusual.' There didn't seem much else to say. The Congreve with whom Maxwell was most familiar designed rockets for the Horse Artillery against that boundah Bonaparte.

'Yes. I must say it wasn't much fun at school. Still, my brother came off rather worse. My parents called him Mirabell, from the same play.'

'Ooooh.' Jacquie was sympathetic. 'It's a bit hard to find a shortened form of that, isn't it?'

'Yes. We all called him David, in the end. Poor soul.'

Mrs Troubridge, Storm Crow to her friends, came galloping into the conversation with news of fresh disasters. 'Yes. He died recently. An accident at home. Very sad.' She mimed a lifted glass and raised an eyebrow.

Millie wiped away a gathering tear. 'He is the reason that I started the family search, really,' she said. 'So much gets lost, when people die. We hadn't been close and I'm afraid I have lost touch with his family altogether. There was a wife – ex, now, I'm afraid. And a child, I believe. I'm tracking them down as we speak.'

'Well, good luck with that,' Jacquie said, picking up the cups and walking into the kitchen. 'I'd love to be able to chat a while longer, but we have some packing to do, that sort of thing. I hope you'll excuse us.'

Mrs Troubridge jumped to her feet. 'Of course, dear. Nolan, do I get a hug?' For some reason, Nolan and the old besom were best friends, except when football met tulip, and he gave her a

50

ferocious squeeze that nearly toppled her over. Millie gave him an affectionate pat on the head and nearly changed its shape for ever.

'Lovely little chap,' she boomed. 'Very like you to look at.' She beamed at Jacquie and then down at his curly head. 'So that's nice, isn't it?' She smiled beatifically all round and shook hands with Maxwell. 'It has been so nice to see you all. Jessica has spoken so well of you. I'm glad she has you next door.' She dropped her voice to a yell. 'She's not getting any younger.'

'No, indeed,' Maxwell said. 'Which of us is, after all?' He found it difficult to think of Mrs Troubridge as Jessica. He wouldn't presume to call her by it and she would be horrified if he did so.

Millie looked him up and down. 'I'm surprised to see you so relatively limber, Mr Maxwell,' she remarked. 'After what Jessica has been saying. Still, children keep you young, don't they?' And with that, she was gone, momentarily blocking out the light at the top of the stairs. Maxwell and Jacquie held their breath until both women were out of the house and severally trotting and lumbering down the front path. Had Millie fallen and landed on Mrs Troubridge, the consequences didn't bear thinking about.

When his ears stopped ringing, Maxwell turned to Jacquie. 'We haven't really got to start packing today, have we?' he asked, rather tremulously. If there was one skill that he had never quite managed to master, it was the packing thing.

'No, no,' she said. 'That was just to get rid of them. My head was starting to vibrate. Why don't

51

you nip up to the loft and do a bit of painting? What with Mrs Whatmough and Millie, you probably could do with some R&R. I'll send Metternich up to get you when supper is ready.'

'Do you know, Mrs M,' he said, sketching a kiss towards the top of her head. 'You are a lovely woman.' He turned towards the stairs and then stopped. 'Why are you being so nice to me?'

'You suspicious old so-and-so,' she said. 'No reason. Except, perhaps, because Henry had a word with me today. He happened to mention how nice it has been over the holidays not to have seen you. No offence; he just meant there haven't been any horrible murders in your vicinity. He also mentioned that there might be a little promotional opportunity at the nick, soon.' She gave a little preen. 'I might be up for it.'

'Sergeant Carpenter-Maxwell! Congratulations!'

'Start practising the "I" word,' she said. '*If* there are no more ... well ... murders.'

He looked truculent. 'I don't *do* them, you know,' he said. 'They just happen alongside me.'

'Well,' she said, as he turned to go. 'Don't let them in future. Look away. Go deaf. Let someone else find the body.'

He muttered something as he disappeared up the stairs.

'What was that?' she called.

'Yes, dear,' he replied, peeping back round the turn in the stairs. But he had his fingers crossed when he said it because you just never know.

Peter Maxwell loved his family dearly, up to and

including his cat. But there were times when only his attic would do, the Inner Sanctum, the Holy of Holies where an unfinished diorama of the Light Brigade sat waiting for orders in the late afternoon sun. Jacquie hardly every climbed this far north in the house and Nolan could only just, now that he was a big boy, be trusted not to play with those particular toys of Daddy's. Only Metternich had unlimited access and he didn't know a Light Dragoon from his left elbow.

Coming under scrutiny that afternoon was Private James Olley of the 4th Lights. The man's horse was shot during the Charge and the man himself had lost the sight in his right eye. The Queen, God bless her, had met him at the Brompton Barracks in March 1855. Maxwell even had a list of his grandchildren somewhere, so eat your heart out, Millie Muswell. Actually, Jim Olley didn't look too chipper at the moment, as Maxwell peered at him through his magnifying lens. White as a sheet with Humbrol undercoat. And *could* Maxwell find the man's sword? It had to be on the floor somewhere and the great modeller settled down to finding it as one of those annoying preliminaries that keep getting in the way of life.

'Another fine mess you've got me into,' Maxwell said.

Chapter Three

Jacquie stood on the edges of the milling crowd that was the Getting To Know You group and wondered if she had ever seen such a level of hysteria reached so quickly before. It seemed to her that one minute she was standing there quietly, holding Nolan in one hand and a large bag of sandwiches, Year Seven for the use of, in the other, and the next she was up to well above her armpits in a screaming horde of children. Bearing in mind that the journey to the ferry would take less than an hour and, once on the Island, the coach would have them at the hotel in less than thirty minutes, Pansy Donaldson seemed to have overcatered. There were enough provisions to feed an army for a week.

She nudged Sylvia, who was standing nearby with a clipboard and a harassed expression. She indicated the bag. 'Isn't this rather a lot of food?' she asked.

Sylvia smiled at her. 'You haven't been on a school trip before, have you?'

'Umm, no.'

'Within ten minutes of setting off, the boys will be hungry. Then, just when we have fed them and put everything away, the girls will be hungry. The vegan – and there always *is* a vegan – will find that her sandwiches have been eaten by someone else and so all that is left is a ham baguette. She will start to cry. Then, one of the boys will be sick. I'm old enough to remember the words of the song, after all – "Getting to know you, getting to feel free and queasy".' It wasn't a bad Deborah Kerr, all things considered. 'Then all of the girls will feel sick... You're looking a bit pale yourself, Jacquie. You just have time to leg it back home, you know.'

Jacquie shook her head. 'No, no, I'm fine. Anyway, Nole and I are following in the car. Tom Medlicott thought it might be an idea to have a car with us, for emergencies. I volunteered.'

Sylvia patted her shoulder. 'You're a wise woman, Jacquie.' She chuckled and gave a final triumphant tick to her list as a car screeched up and disgorged a rather dishevelled child. 'Last one. They're never ready for the early start.' She raised her voice. 'Right, now, everyone calm down and make a queue next to Mr Maxwell. He will see you on to the coach and tick you off as you get on.' She lowered her voice for Jacquie's benefit. 'I'm sure he'll start as he means to go on.' Then, louder, 'Fill the seats from the back and no pushing.' She turned to Jacquie. 'We'll see you at Southampton, then. Don't rush. We've left plenty of time.'

Jacquie looked at her watch and raised her eyebrows. 'We certainly have. We're not on the ferry until eleven.'

'There's many a slip, believe me,' Sylvia said grimly. 'Don't worry if you lose sight of us and if we aren't at the ferry on time, don't wait. Just get on and we'll see you at the hotel.'

'But, surely...' Jacquie couldn't believe that the coach could miss the ferry. They had allowed so much time that they could do the journey three times. Her learning curve was going to be steep and painful in the coming week, Sylvia knew. But it was no point in letting her find out all the pitfalls at once. It was too depressing.

'Trust me on this. You have all the details?'

'Yes. I've got my ferry ticket and the hotel address.' She passed over the bag. 'Don't forget the sandwiches.'

Sylvia lifted the edge of the flap. 'I don't believe it. Egg!'

'Max will be happy. He loves egg sandwiches.'

'All adults like egg sandwiches. All kids hate them. Never mind.'

They both looked over at the coach as the last child got on. There were vague sounds of pushing and shoving from inside and occasionally an anoraked back was pressed against a window. Maxwell was standing on the lower step, waving, though whether in benediction or because he was going down for the last time it was impossible to tell.

'Well,' Sylvia said, squaring her shoulders. 'Time to be off.' The Medlicotts and Guy, Sylvia's husband, were standing off to one side. Pansy Donaldson was pacing the perimeter, alert for slopers-off. Jacquie had met the Medllicotts for the first time at the final staff meeting the night before. Tom was tall, late thirties. She was shorter, slightly younger and rather pretty in a weaselly sort of way. Guy she had known for ages – he and Sylvia were as mismatched in age as Jacquie and Maxwell, but the marriage had been just as successful as theirs. He was a classic toy boy – handsome, fit and, if not necessarily the brightest dumpling in the stew, he loved Sylv and made her happy and so all her friends loved him too.

The Medlicotts she wasn't too sure about. For an Art teacher he had a very good opinion of himself. He was a new broom sweeping not so much clean as unnecessarily. His department would – and could – run with or without him, but he hadn't realised that. He had given them all his mobile number, his email address, his backup email address and his backup-backup email address. He had printed them all out on small cards which he had placed in their pigeonholes in the staffroom, on their desks in their form rooms, in their pockets and under the windscreen wipers of their cars. The small and elegantly designed pieces of pasteboard were now propping up wonky tables throughout the school. It would be nice to say he meant well, but Jacquie was not too sure that was the case. He wanted Maxwell's job, that was obvious– 'Hi, Tom Medlicott, Head of Sixth Form.' He wanted Bernard Ryan's job – 'Hi, Tom Medlicott, Deputy Head.' He wanted James Diamond's job– 'Hi, Tom Medlicott, Head Teacher.' But most of all, he wanted God's job– 'Hi, Tom Medlicott, Supreme Being.'

His wife was a hard one to read, woman-policemanly people-watching skills notwith-standing. She wasn't so much aloof as disinter-ested. She had tapped away at her Blackberry throughout the meeting and Jacquie couldn't help but wonder why she was coming along at all. Her name was Izzy. Of course it was.

With a hiss of brakes, the coach pulled away. Nolan was in a sulk, because he had wanted to go with Daddy and the big children. He sat in his seat in the back of the car, muttering. Jacquie had decided to ignore him. It was a phase, she hoped. Although Maxwell could mutter for England, so perhaps not. Metternich had also ignored her roundly that morning. He could sense packing from a thousand yards and so had been rather curmudgeonly for days. His votive voles had been left not so much for the pleasure of giving as for the pleasure of hearing her scream as morning foot met headless rodent. Even Mrs Troubridge had given her short shrift. She was missing Millie, for some reason, and Metternich was scant recompense. Although, as usual, he would weigh another pound when they got back; Mrs Troubridge couldn't resist his doe-eyed begging and he got through the Whiskas at an alarming rate.

Jacquie fell in behind the coach, but soon overtook it going over The Dam. She didn't think that a journey punctuated by sick-stops would be the best beginning to her holiday. And this *was* her holiday. And she was going to enjoy it.

On the coach things were going well. The egg sandwiches had been broached and a few of them had been eaten. Maxwell and Sylvia were keeping their counsel; when they reappeared around about Chichester, it would be Pansy's pigeon. It never failed to amaze Maxwell that in these days of global communication, a fair proportion of the students at Leighford High had hardly left the county. Mostly, their experience was a taxi to Gatwick, en route for a family holiday in Florida or Lanzarote, depending on parental tastes and pockets. So, as they left Sussex and entered the no-man's-land that was Hampshire, they became quieter, sinking down in their seats and looking out of the windows wide-eyed with wonder.

It was an unfortunate coincidence that the coach driver seemed to be an old Sussex boy too, and they were soon hopelessly lost on an industrial estate just outside Winchester. No one knew quite how this had happened, though Maxwell silently blamed King Cnut's town planning, but Tom Medlicott came up trumps and steered the hapless driver back on to the M3 and suddenly all was well again. Even so, the eleven o'clock ferry was just a hopeless dream by now, so Maxwell decided to go to Plan B. He stood up and turned round to speak to the horde. Teachers are trained to stand facing backwards on moving vehicles. The lesson comes just after Board-Rubber Throwing and just before Resignation Letter Construction.

'Now, listen up, troops,' he said. Peter Maxwell rarely shouted. There was seldom the need. There was something about the timbre of his voice that went straight to the eardrum, no matter how much background noise he was battling with. 'I don't think we are going to catch the ferry we had planned, due to...' He paused. He knew that many descriptions of the driver would fill the silence and indeed they did. 'That's enough of that,' he admonished, while being secretly impressed by most of them. He made a mental note to particularly watch the little girl about halfway down the coach. She had the face of a Botticelli angel and the vocabulary of a docker. 'So, if we have time when we get to

59

Southampton, we will hopefully be able to have a look at the excavations of the city wall. It's been partly reburied now, but I'll find it. When we arrive, anyone who wants to come for a quick stroll and do that can come and see me.'

'Will we get tested on it?'

Maxwell looked around for the source of the stupid question and found that it was, not really to his surprise, the freckly ginger kid sitting more or less under his nose. He leant forward. 'Pardon?'

The boy removed his finger from his nostril. 'Are we gunna get tested on it? Y'know. When we get back to school.'

A light went on in Maxwell's head. 'Probably,' he said. 'In fact, you might get tested on any single thing that happens this week. From the moment you got on this coach until we give you back to your parents next Friday. So I hope you've all been paying attention. Taking notes. Things of that nature.'

Frantic eye met frantic eye the length and breadth of the bus.

The ginger kid spoke up again. 'But I en't got no paper.'

'Oh dear,' smiled Maxwell and sat down, smiling beatifically at the M27 rolling itself up under the coach's wheels. This week could prove to be a lot of fun.

Jacquie and Nolan had got to the ferry on time. In fact, they had got to the ferry so early that they had been offered a place on an earlier one. Jacquie was undecided; if by some remote chance the coach caught the eleven o'clock, they might wonder where she was. On the other hand, Nolan was leaping around like something demented in the back of the car, chanting 'Isle of Wight, Isle of Wight, Isle of Wight,' as though it was some mythical isle of Avalon, or possibly Atlantis. She opted for the earlier ferry and so was halfway across the Solent before the coach had emerged from the toils of the Winnall Estate.

Once on the ferry, up on deck, she relaxed. There was a lot going on at work – promotion, office politics – and for once she hadn't shared everything with Maxwell. Henry Hall had been unequivocal. If she got inspector, she would be on notice that if Maxwell so much as passed the door of Leighford nick, let alone went in, and especially if he got involved in a murder investigation, she would be demoted quicker than the proverbial rat could go up a pipe. And he wasn't talking back to sergeant. He was talking traffic warden. She and Henry Hall went back a long way and she knew when he was serious. And this was clearly non-negotiable.

She took a deep breath of sea air, laced with the indefinable smell of trees, grass and autumn that blew over from the Island. This was their holiday. No talking or even thinking shop. It could wait until they got back home. Even Maxwell had never found a body on holiday, look though he might.

She looked down at Nolan, standing beside her at the rail. He was leaning on his folded arms and the wind was ruffling his hair. His eyes were half-closed against the sun off the sea and the salty breeze. He managed to look like all small boys since the dawn of time rolled into one; *puer minimus* Mk I, planning a week of running about and shouting during the day, sleeping like a log all night, on a diet of candy floss, chips and sand. She smiled and stroked his head. She hoped it kept nice for him, although she had a feeling that the weather wouldn't really have much of an effect. A dim memory of making a sandcastle in driving rain came into her head, followed by regret that she and Maxwell had spent so few of Nolan's days playing with him on the beach.

The boy lifted his face and smiled at her, a grin that stretched from ear to ear. 'It's going to be really good, isn't it, this holiday?' he asked. But it wasn't a question, it was a statement. He could also smell the damp earth, the sand, the surf, the secret places he would find, all overlaid to his sensitive child's nose with a beguiling whiff of hot dog. His daddy had told him that this was Dinosaur Island and he was already up there with the archaeopteryx. He sighed happily. 'If only Metternich could be here,' he said. 'He never goes on holiday.'

'He's sort of on holiday, though, isn't he?' she said. 'He's got the house to himself, Mrs Troubridge to feed him and keep him company in the evenings.' Mrs Troubridge, whilst denying it hotly, liked to indulge in the Maxwells' Sky subscription when feeding Metternich. She didn't seem to realise that leaving the box tuned to Diva TV or CBS Reality was a bit of a giveaway and they had never had the heart to tell her. And if a little telly kept her mind off Incidents, then that was only to the good.

Nolan was doubtful. He was sometimes looked after by Mrs Troubridge and he had never found it desperately exciting, but he conceded that perhaps it was different for a cat. 'S'pose,' he said. He thought for a minute. 'I s'pose Mrs Troubridge is feeling lonely now that Millie has left.'

'Miss Muswell,' Jacquie automatically corrected him.

'Hmmm.' Maxwell and Jacquie had a fairly laissez-faire view of parenting along the lines that Nolan was a human being, just like they were, but smaller. Metternich's view was that Nolan was a human being, just like he was, but marginally bigger. But one thing on which they all were agreed was that only aunties got called auntie, only uncles got called uncle. Other small human beings could be called by their Christian names or any other nickname of their choice – Nolan's best friend almost since birth, chose to go by the name of Plocker, for reasons lost in the mists of time – but all adults were to be addressed formally, unless otherwise requested. But Jacquie had to agree with the 'hmmm' – Millie Muswell was definitely more a Millie than a Miss.

'Don't "hmmm" me, young man,' Jacquie said, nevertheless. 'It will be nice for Mrs Troubridge to have Metternich for company, though, you're right.'

'Mrs Troubridge doesn't like it when Metternich brings her voles,' Nolan volunteered.

'No, darling,' Jacquie agreed.

'Or mice. Or birds. Or those false teeth, that time. She really, *really* didn't like that.'

Jacquie fixed her gaze on the horizon and tried

63

not to laugh. It had been a wonderful moment, though. Mrs Troubridge had been quite angry at the Count when he deposited the teeth at her feet. Much angrier, though, when she discovered the hard way that they weren't hers.

Fortunately for Jacquie's parenting street cred, their conversation was interrupted by a resonating 'bing-bong'. They looked at each other in excitement. A disembodied voice rang out.

'Will all drivers and their passengers please return to their vehicles as we shall shortly be arriving in East Cowes. Please take care on the stairs and may we remind you that all car decks are no-smoking areas. Please refrain from using mobile phones on the car deck and drivers are requested not to start their vehicles until requested to do so. Thank you for travelling with Red Funnel, and the captain and crew would like to wish you a safe onward journey.'

'That's nice,' Nolan remarked.

'What is?' Jacquie asked him, shepherding him down the precipitous stairs.

'Wishing us a safe and ward journey.' It was anyone's guess what he thought a ward journey was, but he had obviously grasped the general goodwill. 'Are we going to go far, now?'

'No, sweetie,' Jacquie said. 'I think it's about twelve miles. The whole island isn't very big. It won't take us long.'

'I wonder where Dads is,' Nolan said, meditatively, as he buckled himself into his car seat. 'Will he be here soon?'

'I'm sure he isn't far behind,' Jacquie said, hopefully. A sudden jerk signified that they had reached land and engines started all over, requested or not. 'Anyway,' she added, 'we'll be at the hotel soon and then we'll go out for lunch.'

'*Lunch?*' Nolan wailed. 'I don't want *lunch!* I want hot dog and ice cream.'

'It's a deal,' Jacquie said and, engaging a tentative first gear, drove off down what looked like a Meccano footbridge and onto the Isle of Wight.

'Holidays!' Nolan called. 'Hooray!'

Jacquie smiled at him in the mirror. For a child who had completed all of one week at school, he must be ready for a holiday if anyone was.

'Holidays!' she carolled back and switched on the satnav, which was having a minor nervous breakdown, not having really understood the ferry.

Tom Medlicott was getting a trifle testy. Maxwell seemed to have mislaid a child. Count though Medlicott might, he couldn't make the numbers add up. Why on earth had the mad old bugger taken them for a walk anyway? Why didn't he just keep them on the coach? They could have sat still for half an hour, surely. He spun round, clipboard in hand as Maxwell and Sylvia watched him indulgently.

'Bless,' Sylvia muttered.

Maxwell smiled. 'He'll learn,' he said. 'Eventually. Until you grow eyes in the back of your head, you're always going to be one short. But enough of this tomfoolery.' He stepped forward and grabbed the child who had been circling with Medlicott by the back of his anorak. 'Right. You. Name?'

The child froze. Then the barrack-room lawyer which is inside every kid, fat or thin, rose to the surface. 'You can't touch me. I got rights.'

'Human rights, would they be?' Maxwell enquired in an avuncular tone. 'We've all got those, not least Mr Medlicott, who had been trying to do a headcount. I don't do headcounts. I just make heads roll. Now, stand still over there, but first, I'll have your name.'

'I got…'

'Name?' As usual, Maxwell didn't need to shout. The tone was one which went straight through the backbone and tingled up the spine, like biting on an ice lolly with a sensitive tooth.

'Nathaniel. But all my mates call me Nate.'

'Right, Nathaniel. Go and stand over there. And believe me when I tell you, I will be watching you. All the time. Now, apologise to Mr Medlicott for being an annoying little twerp and let's get on.' Maxwell inclined from the waist to the Art teacher, who was uncertain as to whether he was grateful or furious. 'As you were, Mr Medlicott.'

Marshalling his dignity, the man stepped aside and counted the children on to the bus.

'*Now* he learns how to do it,' said Sylvia and sighed. 'It's going to be a tough week.' She would look back on that phrase, on that moment in the car park in Southampton, as a haven of peace and normality before the world turned upside down.

Chapter Four

It seemed impossible but finally the grown-up element of the Leighford High School Year Seven Getting To Know You School Trip were sitting on the deck outside the hotel, drinking grown-up drinks and having a grown-up conversation.

The coach had finally caught up with Jacquie and Nolan and the hysterical children had been divided up into groups for the subsequent day's activities. All the girls had wanted to be with Maxwell, because of Nolan. Failing that, the rather more sophisticated girls had wanted to be with Sylvia, because of Guy. All of the boys wanted to be with Tom Medlicott, because of Izzy, except one rather precociously sexually aware lad, who wanted to be with Tom Medlicott because of Tom Medlicott. No one wanted to be with Pansy Donaldson.

Using the time-honoured method of 'one potato, two potato', Maxwell had sorted them out, using a system of sleight of hand and subtle winks to Sylvia, who was compiling the list. In the end, he had the bright ones, Sylvia had the nice ones and the Medlicotts and Pansy had the rest. Pansy also had the vegan. She also had the vegetarian and the vergetarian, who would eat fish and chicken which had lived a fulfilling life before dying of natural causes. Well, somebody had to. There had been mutterings, of course. But the beach cricket had gone down well, the evening meal had been surprisingly good and within an amazingly short time and with a minimum of whingeing, everyone was bedded down for the night. Nolan had conked out halfway through and halfway across his banana sundae and was lying across the double bed in the family room they would be sharing, sticky and sandy, but happy and quiet. There would be time enough tomorrow to hose him down.

So now, they were all making the most of a balmy late summer evening to unwind. The coach driver, invited to eat at the hotel with them, had pleaded an auntie nearby, so had absented himself. He was a nice enough chap but Maxwell had taken the precaution of relocating the satnav from the car; the man could clearly not find his arse with both hands, to quote Pansy's rather surprising but totally accurate summing up. She was getting outside her third drink and was loosening up to a rather worrying degree. Although there was an awful lot of her to absorb the alcohol, she was still putting it away at an alarming rate. Perhaps the coach driver had at least been able to see the way the wind was blowing and the auntie had been a bit of quick thinking on his part.

The season being almost over, the seafront was quiet by this time in the evening. The faint strains of live music wafted along from a pub further down, but it was underscored by the whisper of the tide coming in and the soft scrape of the shells being dragged over the shingle and sounded quite tuneful. Maxwell lay back in his chair, nursing his Southern Comfort, and felt so at home that he could almost feel the weight of Metternich, sprawled out in his favourite position along the back of the chair. He could even feel the brush of his tail against his cheek. He brushed it away but it was unusually persistent.

'Max! Max! Wake up. You're snoring.'

'Mmmm?' He tried to turn over, but met an obstacle so didn't bother. 'Soz.'

Someone shook him by the shoulder. 'Max. Wake up. You're asleep.'

There was a strange logic there with which, had he had a mind to, he could have dazzled them all. Instead, he thought he might as well just go to sleep.

'Sorry,' he heard a distant voice say. 'He does sleep quite deeply, sometimes.' For some reason, there seemed to be chickens nearby. He could hear them clucking. Then, suddenly, there was no oxygen. None at all. He surfaced, struggling for breath. He squinted along his nose to find that Sylvia had a firm hold of his breathing apparatus. He knocked her hand away.

'For God's sake, Sylv,' he gasped, rubbing the pinch point. 'You could have killed me, there.' He looked around and saw four amused faces and Pansy. He grinned. 'Sorry. I must have dropped off.'

'You looked quite cute,' Guy said. 'Apparently, I look like a fish when I'm asleep.' He turned his eyes up and the corners of his mouth down. 'You looked like the dog does when he's chasing rabbits in his dreams.'

Jacquie smiled at him. Not only was it hard to imagine Guy looking unattractive, but it was good

69

to feel that they were friends enough for him to call Maxwell cute. It wasn't a description usually applied to the grizzled old git. 'You were doing the leg thing,' Jacquie told Maxwell, shaking hers in the air to demonstrate. She looked around the group. 'I'm always amazed he can still do that.'

'Oh, yes,' Maxwell said, sitting up a bit straighter and trying to wake up properly. 'Dreaming's a young man's game, all right.'

Izzy stirred her drink with a plastic swizzle stick. 'Tom sleeps like the dead. Honestly, sometimes I think he actually has died and have to give him a kick. He's all over bruises.'

'That's true,' her husband agreed and reached down to pull up his trouser leg. Despite the muttered demurs of his colleagues, he pushed down his sock and there, true enough, were a series of small bruises, ranging in colour from recent to the back end of last week.

'Ouch,' Guy said, sympathetically. 'I think I'm glad I just look like a fish.'

Sylvia poked him. 'You'll wake up with half a lemon in your mouth one of these days and a sprig of parsley in your ear.'

'Do fish have ears?' Pansy suddenly asked, in the unexpectedly loud voice of the drunk.

'Pardon?' Tom Medlicott said, who had been rather startled by it. He had forgotten she was there, just by his right elbow.

'Do fish have ears? Sh'said she would put parsley in his ear. Sh'meant it would make him look like a f'sh.' She smiled beatifically around. 'S'peck thas what sh'meant.' She leant over Tom. 'D'you think thas whash'meant?'

His eyes widened as the gin hit him in an almost visible wave. Pitching his voice in the calming range commonly used to an unknown dog he said, 'How many G&Ts have you had, Pansy?'

She looked horrified. 'None!' she declared and drew herself up. 'I hate tonic. Yeurghhhh!' She pulled a face. 'S'very nasty. Jus' gin. Thas what I drink. Gin and a spot of gin.' She giggled and it wasn't a pretty sight. She leant forward to include them all in the joke. 'An' it looks like water, so Mr Donsal... Mr Donda... *my hubsband*,' she finally said triumphantly, 'doesn't know I drink *at all*!' And with that she fell out of her chair and lay at Tom Medlicott's feet.

Maxwell smiled sleepily at Jacquie. 'I knew this week was going to be fun,' he said, and closed his eyes.

'Wakey, wakey! Rise and shine. Hands off... Rise and shine!' Maxwell decided that the time-worn army call was perhaps not too appropriate in this particular context. He contented himself with, 'Get your socks on, those who wear them. Breakfast in fifteen minutes.'

He walked briskly along the corridor, knocking on doors as he went, to the disgruntlement of a salesman, travelling in underwear, whom Reception had inadvertently put between two cohorts of Seven Why Sea.

Back in the family room, Nolan had been destickied and de-fluffed and now was waiting with barely concealed hysteria, pink and sweetly smelling.

'Dads, Dads,' he carolled as Maxwell came

through the door. 'Where are we going today? What's on the itinerarararary?'

'That's a big word,' Maxwell said approvingly. 'Rather bigger than necessessessessary, in fact, but a good shot.'

Jacquie giggled in the bathroom and said, through a mouthful of toothpaste foam, 'A bit like banana. It's hard to know when to stop.'

At the mention of banana, Nolan looked around, puzzled. He licked his lips. 'What happened to my 'nana sundae?'

'You fell asleep in it, mate,' Maxwell said, holding out his arms for his son to jump up. He gave him a squeeze. 'Have you got a half-a-nana-sundae-sized hole?'

The boy nodded. 'What's for breakfast, d'you think?'

'Hmm.' Maxwell sniffed extravagantly. 'Full English, unless I miss my guess.'

'My favourite,' Nolan yelled, flinging himself backwards in Maxwell's arms.

'Not for every day,' Jacquie reminded him, coming back into the room. 'Just today.'

Nolan patted his stomach. 'I won't get fat, Mums,' he said. 'Not like Pansy.'

'That's Mrs Donaldson to you,' Maxwell said, tapping him softly on the top of his head. 'And she's not fat.'

Jacquie raised an eyebrow at him.

'She's just big-boned.' Maxwell grunted as he hefted Nolan higher in his arms. 'Are you going to walk now, sunshine, or are you so "on holiday" you don't have to?'

Nolan jumped down. 'I don't need a carry,' he

72

said. 'Not now I go to proper school.'

'Tell me that this evening after Blackgang Chine,' Maxwell said. 'Perhaps Mums can carry us both.'

'Ah,' Jacquie said. 'The famous Policewoman's Lift.'

'Woman Policeman's Lift,' Maxwell corrected, automatically. He cocked an ear. A sound had been growing outside in the corridor. It was as if an army muttered. And the muttering grew to a grumbling; and the grumbling grew to a mighty rumbling, as out of their rooms Year Seven came tumbling. 'Hey up, Maxwells. The kids are on the march. If we're going to get so much as a sausage, I suggest we get a wiggle on.'

Nolan flung open the door, to a chorus of coos and aahs from various girls. He was swept up into the throng and was just a tousle of curls at the head of the stairs as Year Seven took the corner on the lam and were gone. Jacquie and Maxwell stood in the sudden echoing silence for a moment. Behind them, a door opened and the ghost of Pansy Donaldson peered out, blinking.

Maxwell looked around for a wandering child and, seeing none, hailed her. 'Pans! How the devil are you?'

She winced at the sound and then winced at the muscular effort of the wince. She raised a hand and tried a smile.

'Excellent!' boomed Maxwell. Jacquie had often been impressed at his vocal dexterity. He appeared to have become James Earl Jones doing an English accent. He walked up to the woman. 'Come along with us,' he cried. 'Nice full English fry-up with all the trimmings, that's what you need. Nice runny egg. Black pudding. Fried bread. Yummy!' He swept her down the corridor, her slightly green face pressed firmly into his shoulder. Jacquie, stifling a giggle fell in behind. She could just hear Pansy's protestations and felt, not for the first time, that she was glad she wasn't her right now.

The dining room was like a madhouse. The hotel had decided that it would be a help if they set up a buffet instead of table service and so one end of the room looked like a rugger scrum. Some tables had occupants, heads down in their plates, elbows out for speed, tomato sauce the predominant colour. The Maxwells looked around for Nolan and saw him tucked between two girls, getting outside a cooked breakfast which consisted of his usual weekly intake of grease. Then they looked around rather more anxiously for a table out of the way of the flying bacon fat and were relieved to see Sylvia's hand waving from the safety of a table in the bay window at the far side of the room. Maxwell steered Pansy over as Jacquie peeled off to elbow her way into the melee and get them both some food.

'Mrs Donaldson,' said Sylvia brightly. 'How are you feeling this morning?'

'Not too good,' the woman mumbled. 'Bit of a ... headache, actually.' She swallowed with an effort. 'Coming down with something.'

'Never mind,' Guy smiled sweetly and leant across to her to pat her hand. 'Nice bracing walk along to the Needles and you'll be fine.'

She looked up, but moving her head very slowly. 'Needles?' she whispered. 'Bracing?'

Guy whipped out his list of activities and traced a finger along a line. 'Yes. Mr and Mrs Maxwell are visiting the fossil coast, followed by early evening at Blackgang Chine. Sylvia and myself are taking our group to Parkhurst Forest looking for red squirrels, followed by a town trail. Mr and Mrs Medlicott are taking their group sketching at Carisbrooke Castle. As you have the smallest group, you will be dropped off last and the coach driver will be your health and safety backup.' He turned his radiant smile on Pansy, with no effect. 'That's right, isn't it?' he asked Maxwell.

Maxwell had no idea. Lists were for other people, but he thoroughly approved of the fossil coast idea. What he didn't approve of was Guy's use of the word 'myself', but they were all on holiday and standards could be allowed to drop a little. He smiled and nodded, as if he knew what was going on. He looked around the room. 'Has anyone seen the Medlicotts, while we're listing people?'

There was general head shaking, except from Pansy, who was sitting as totally still as she could manage, with her eyes closed. A child on the nearest table who had been frantically earwigging hoping to hear something to her advantage leant over.

'Mr and Mrs Medlicott went out for a run,' she volunteered. 'I just saw them come back up the front steps.'

'Thank you, Jazmyn,' Sylvia said. She turned back to her colleagues. 'Ears like a bat,' she mouthed. 'Watch what you say in front of her.' She looked anxiously at Pansy and then at Guy. 'Do you have the group lists?' she asked him.

He foraged in his bag and handed them over. She looked down the lists and then handed it across to Maxwell, pointing pointedly at a name.

'Point taken,' he said. 'We'll move her. As long as she isn't the vegan.'

They looked across at the child, who was eating a sausage thick with brown sauce.

'Whilst allowing that a sausage isn't necessarily meat as we know it,' Maxwell said, 'I think we can assume she isn't. Move her, then.' He looked again at the paper and made a few changes.

Jacquie, a little rumpled, got back to the table carrying a tray. 'It's like ... it's like...' She was lost for words.

'And this is a woman,' Maxwell said, pulling out her chair for her and bobbing up as he always did when a lady joined the table, 'who arrests axe murderers on a daily basis. And even she is horrified by the shenanigans of Year Seven.'

She smiled modestly. 'I haven't arrested an axe murderer for days, Mr Maxwell. I've been concentrating on poisoners since August Bank Holiday.'

Maxwell patted her on the back. 'Keeping the streets safe,' he said proudly and he lapsed into the tag line of an old TV show he had almost forgotten. '"There are eight million stories in the Naked City. This has been one of them."'

The bat-eared child couldn't make it out. Was all that true or not? This Big School lark wasn't as easy as she'd been expecting.

The noise got less as more mouths got filled by food, then rose again in a slow crescendo, underscored by burping. Maxwell got to his feet and quietly cleared his throat. The noise stopped as though switched off at the wall.

'I'm going to read out the final lists for activities today. Remember the people on either side of your name and then you'll always know if you are with the right group. When I have finished, you have half an hour to get back to your rooms and into appropriate clothing and back down to the lobby, where you will wait in silence, in lines. You won't make a single sound while I am speaking or I will kill you. You won't argue, or I will kill you. Is there anyone who doubts that I will kill you?' His eyes raked round the room. Not a soul stirred, especially not the traveller in underwear. 'Good.' He read out the lists of names. They were met by silence. 'Right, everyone back up to their rooms. The clock is ticking.' The room erupted in bedlam. 'Silently!' He raised his voice a scary notch and the noise was muted to a dull roar. He sat back down and slurped his last mouthful of coffee. Nolan had appeared at the end of the table.

'Hello, poppet,' said Sylvia. 'Are you looking forward to today?'

Nolan smiled at her. She was his favourite babysitter of all. More fun than Mrs Troubridge. Not as strict as Grandma. 'I want to come with you to see the squirrels,' he said. 'Are they really red?'

'Well, more ginger, really,' Sylvia said. 'And you can see them later in the week with Mum and

77

Dad – all the groups are swapping round.'

He mulled it over. It was true that Blackgang Chine sounded all right, but his father had said that it was the oldest theme park in the country. Did that mean that all the rides were broken? Eventually, he nodded. 'OK. I'll go with Mums and Dads.'

'Why, thank you,' said Jacquie, bowing her head. She looked across at Pansy, who was swaying. 'Mrs Donaldson.' Then, louder, 'Mrs Donaldson!'

The woman's eyes flew open. 'What?' she cried, momentarily disoriented.

'Are you ready to go? For your brisk walk to the Needles? Blow the cobwebs away, hmm?'

Pansy Donaldson was not as other women. She took a deep breath and gave her hangover its marching orders. 'Brisk walk? Certainly.' She got up and walked steadily out of the room. The others watched her go, admiration written on every face.

Guy spoke for them all. 'Wow!' he said.

Out at the coach, Maxwell's worst fears were realised. The driver was leaning against the door, swathed in a map. Unfortunately, the map was of the Isle of Man. Jacquie, quick as always to detect the underground rumblings that were the precursors to Maxwell's rare bursts of temperament, scurried forward and gently removed the map from the man's confused grasp.

'I don't seem to be able to find Ventnor,' he muttered.

'I wonder if you would be happier with this

GPS,' Jacquie suggested, in the tone she had often used to convince drunks that sitting in the back of a police car and having a nice ride home would be a better idea than shinning up the war memorial.

He pursed his lips in a soundless whistle and then shook his head. 'I don't have much truck with those sort of things as a rule,' he said. 'Give me a good old map, every time. Except that,' he reached for the map again but Jacquie held it behind her back, out of his reach, 'I'm just having a bit of trouble finding Ventnor.'

'Yes, I can see that,' Jacquie said. Then a thought struck her. 'Why were you looking for Ventnor? I don't think we're going to Ventnor today, are we?'

'Not as such,' the driver conceded. 'But I went there once when I was a kid and we were staying with my Auntie Irene. I thought that if we got there, I might find my bearings a bit better.'

'I see,' Jacquie said slowly. 'Perhaps your Auntie Irene could help us.'

'Do you know my Auntie Irene?' the driver asked, perking up.

'Um, no.' Jacquie was looking at Maxwell desperately, but he just waved placidly at her and she knew she was on her own. 'But I thought you said last night that you were going to stay with her.'

'Oh, yes, that's right,' the man said. 'I couldn't find her house, though. Anyway, she might have moved. Or be dead, even. It has been thirty years. And she wasn't really my auntie. That's just what we called her. Auntie Irene. Or Julia. I can't really remember.'

79

Jacquie was not often speechless. Her years as woman policeman, in various ranks and trades under that umbrella, had taught her most quirks of humankind. But this man was something else. She sighed and tapped him in a friendly way on the arm. 'Wait here,' she said.

'Houston, I think we have a problem,' Maxwell drawled as she rejoined the little knot of staff on the steps of the hotel.

'I think finding Houston would be relatively easy,' Jacquie said. 'It's going to be anywhere on the Isle of Wight that is going to be a bit difficult.'

Tom Medlicott moved a little closer. Bat-eared Jazmyn was perilously near. 'I was never happy about having him as staff backup,' he said. 'The man is clearly an idiot.'

'He has his CRB clearance,' Pansy said, as if that solved everything.

'I don't care,' the Head of Art snapped. 'I'm not worried that he might steal a purse or attack anyone. I'm worried that he can't find his arse with both hands.'

'Ssshhhh!' everyone shushed him, and all the Year Seven heads snapped up.

'Well,' he continued, lowering his voice. 'He can't. It's a wonder we got here at all. I'm going to phone Leighford and find out what to do.'

'You'll be lucky,' Maxwell said. 'It's Saturday. And anyway, the Head Teacher is Legs Diamond.' It wasn't the most professional thing to say to a new colleague, but what the hey, it was time he was introduced to the real world.

Medlicott was stumped, but only briefly. 'I'll ring the county hall here, then,' he said.

'Still Saturday,' Sylvia pointed out.

'Out of hours,' Pansy butted in, with her admin-perspective hat on. 'County halls never close completely.'

'And if they do,' Medlicott said, 'then we'll just combine the groups until Monday.'

He disappeared into the hotel foyer, and was seen dimly through the glass doors, gesticulating at the receptionist. He was soon back, with a map and a broad grin. 'Apparently, they do close completely, unless we want to report a problem with roads, floods, or other life-or-death situation with children or the elderly. But,' he raised a finger before the chorus of 'I told you so' could gather momentum, 'Rachel, the receptionist, has a friend who is a teacher, who has a CRB certificate that he can show us today and who knows the Island like the back of his hand. He's on his way.'

'Isn't that rather ... unconventional?' Maxwell asked.

Sylvia, Guy and Jacquie all looked at Maxwell rather oddly. If he didn't know unconventional, then who did? Actually they were all pretty impressed by Medlicott's get-up-and-go. It usually took Bernard Ryan three weeks to find a supply teacher.

'Possibly,' Medlicott said, tartly. 'But frankly, we've wasted enough time already and I had to think on my feet.' He turned to the milling crowd of Year Seven, who were beginning to get testy. 'OK, kids. Line up in groups. Get on the coach in silence and sit down. First one to speak stays on the bus all day. We're on our way.'

81

He walked over to the driver, who was searching in the luggage compartment for another map.

'You won't need a map,' he said. 'We are about to be joined by an Islander who will direct you. If you would like to get on board and fire up your engine, we will be off.'

Izzy was explaining her husband to the other staff. 'He gets like this,' she smiled. 'He's very laid-back, but when he's fired up, there's no stopping him.'

'A bit like the engine, really,' said Pansy flatly. No one laughed.

And that seemed to be true. The kids were on the coach, silently waiting and clutching their bags of packed lunch. The driver was in place and, having finally found his keys, had started the engine, which thrummed softly. The staff formed a small and orderly queue at the door of the coach and Maxwell, as last man, was just climbing aboard when he heard the sound of trainers hitting pavement along the Esplanade. He looked along the side of the coach and saw a curly-headed man of about thirty jogging towards him. He slowed down as he got nearer and waved a piece of paper.

'Mr Medlicott?' he asked.

'No,' Maxwell told him. 'Peter Maxwell. But this is the group you are looking for, all the same. And you are?'

'Barton,' the man replied, extending his hand. 'How do you do?'

'Well, Mr Barton,' Maxwell began, 'Thanks for helping us out at such short notice.'

'No, my first name's Barton,' the man explained. 'My surname is Joseph.'

'That must cause confusion sometimes,' Maxwell remarked.

The man looked puzzled. 'No, not really. Anyway, here's my CRB. You'll need that for your records, I expect.'

'Thanks.' Maxwell took the document and put it in his trouser pocket. 'It really is so good of you to do this.'

'No problem,' Joseph said. 'I'm at a bit of a loose end as a matter of fact. I'm a supply teacher here and it's a bit quiet at the beginning of term. You know how it is, no one has had a nervous breakdown yet.'

Maxwell patted his shoulder. 'Quite. Still, early days, Barton. Early days. Shall we?' He gestured onto the coach and the supply teacher bounced aboard. Maxwell faced the sea of upturned faces. 'All present and correct?' All the faces nodded back. 'Then let's go.' He spoke to the local man. 'We need to step on it a bit, Mr Joseph,' he said. 'We're meeting the fossil walk in about...' he turned to consult the clock, '...ten minutes ago. So any short cuts would be welcome. Wagons roll!' It was an excellent Ward Bond, all things considered, but only Maxwell knew it.

And the Leighford High School Year Seven Getting To Know You Trip was finally under way.

The fossil walk was delightfully relaxing. The guide walked at the front, some lad in his gap year who was going to read palaeontology when he'd learnt how to spell it, and Year Seven were strung out in a line behind him, heads down scanning the sand. Nolan was holding hands with Sasha, one of the more trustworthy girls, and every now and then bent down and picked up something for her to stow in her bag. She was developing a slight list to starboard, but didn't seem to mind. About ten per cent of the rocks he presented her with were fossils. One was a crab, which she would discover later; sufficient unto the day is the crustacean thereof.

Maxwell and Jacquie walked at the rear, hand in hand, straggling behind with the stragglers.

'Do you know,' she said to her husband. 'This is actually rather nice.'

The September sun was warming the sand and was bouncing back from the reddish cliff which rose not very high to their right. The sea was lapping gently as the tide turned, the waves too relaxed to bother with foam, spume or any of the other natural phenomena that this particular piece of beach could come up with in less clement weather. In years gone by, the combination of deadly rocks and poor navigational instruments had taken their toll along this stretch of beach and the waters had rolled over dead men without number. Today, the very slight breeze could just about lift the feather fringe on their son's forehead. The seagulls were high and far away, just a wisp of white against the blue, their calls coming and going as they wheeled clockwise up on a thermal.

Maxwell smiled down at her and squeezed her hand. 'It is,' he said, almost keeping the surprise out of his voice. 'You're not disappointed, are you? Really? We can still go somewhere else later, if you want.'

'If I had any holiday left, we could,' she said. Was this the right moment to talk about her promotion prospects? Perhaps not; that conversation would be best kept until they got home. 'Never mind; my allocation starts again after Christmas. Perhaps we can get away in February.'

'That would be nice.' He dropped a furtive kiss on her ear. All the kids were looking down at the ground, and anyway, surely one could kiss one's wife's ear even on a school trip. 'You are a lovely woman,' he remarked.

'Indeed I am,' she said. 'And I must say, it's nice not to have the phone going all the time.'

Maxwell looked around, at the cliffs and the sea stretching away to the misty Dorset coast, hardly visible in the distance. 'As you may know,' he said, 'my name is not exactly a byword when mobile phone technocrats gather, but I would be surprised if you have a signal here.'

She pulled her phone out of her pocket and turned it, squinting in the sun. 'For once,' she said, 'you are right. Nothing. Not even one bar.'

'Never mind,' he said, releasing her hand and draping his arm across her shoulders. 'It's not as if anyone would be trying to get in touch with us. And don't mention "bar" to Pansy.'

Suddenly, the air was split by a scream.

Sasha had found the crab.

Chapter Five

At the top of the cliff path, Maxwell regrouped his troops and inspected them and their finds. One girl in particular had managed an amazing haul of fossil coral and was full of plans for a career as a palaeobotanist. So, thought Maxwell, if that's all that comes of this week, it has been a success. He remembered her from when she had visited the school in Year Six; it wasn't often a ten-year-old was so adamant that she wanted to be a nail technician. Onwards and upwards. Nolan had some good finds as well, even discounting the crab, from which he had been separated with a few tears on his part. The crab had been quite grateful to be put in a rock pool and didn't show any distress at the parting. Jacquie took the opportunity to edge away from the group and check her phone. Maxwell looked after her and stifled a sigh. Once a woman policeman, always a woman policeman was his guess. He saw her bend her head and put her finger in the other ear. He heard her say, 'Are you sure?' and, 'Is he all right?' His heart slowed and then sped up far beyond its usual rate. He had all he loved within sight, so the news couldn't be too bad – not for him at any rate. But he could never forget the loss of his first wife and his daughter; a siren, a flashing blue light, an unexpected phone call, the woman he loved with solemn face and a finger in her ear – any one of those things could make him feel sick with apprehension.

She turned back to the group, pocketing her phone, looking thoughtful.

'Mr Maxwell,' she called. 'Could I have a word with you?'

The distance couldn't have been more than a few yards, but it felt like miles. He cleared his throat. 'Certainly,' he said.

When he was by her side, she held his arm. 'That was Henry. He had texted me to ring him.'

'Do you have to go?' he asked. Relief flooded through him. No one was dead. It was just work. Annoying, but there it was; he had been half expecting it anyway.

'Well, it depends.' She looked over his shoulder. Nolan was playing happily with the others and was out of earshot. 'Mrs Troubridge has had an accident. It seems she fell down the stairs. The neighbours from across the road found her. Metternich was sitting outside her door meowing.'

'The Count? Meowing?'

'I think the term used was caterwauling. The neighbour went over to give him a smack round the head to shut him up. Then he realised that Metternich was outside the wrong door and got suspicious. He looked through the letter box and could just see Mrs Troubridge's foot on the bottom stair.'

'Is she all right?'

'She's in hospital. She is in quite a bad way, but stable.'

Maxwell felt awful about the next question, but he had to ask it. 'And the Count?'

'Ah, now that's the thing.'

'The thing?' Maxwell could hear his voice from a long way away. He and the great black and white beast had shared a lot. The lonely times and the good. He could see him now, a tiny scrap of black and white, foisted on him by a particularly persuasive pupil. The old chap wasn't getting any younger, but he wasn't ready to part with him yet. 'What thing?'

'He's in a cattery. It was done before Henry got there. Apparently he's furious.'

Maxwell smiled. Fancy old Henry caring about his cat. 'That's good of him.'

'No, Henry's not furious, although I expect he was a bit annoyed. No, Metternich is furious. Totally livid and giving them hell at Happy Paws. They've had to give him his own cubicle.'

'I should think so too. I think he's best there, though, don't you? He took ages to accept Mrs Troubridge feeding him. He'll take even more umbrage if he gets palmed off on the Other Side.'

The Other Side had never really gelled with the Maxwells. Or indeed anyone in Columbine. Something in their demeanour seemed to suggest that their other home was Windsor Castle. All of Metternich's little gifts had been left on the step in vain. Something suddenly occurred to Maxwell and he gripped his wife's arm.

'It wasn't Metternich, was it? You know, who pushed Mrs Troubridge downstairs?'

She shook him off. The ghost of Henry Hall rose up, reminding her not to let Maxwell get involved. 'Max! Firstly, she wasn't pushed down the stairs. She obviously tripped. She's old and doddery. Secondly, Metternich is a cat. They don't push people downstairs. But if I understand you and you are worried that she tripped over him, no, she didn't. He was outside on the step, remember? He couldn't have got out if she was unconscious at the bottom of the stairs.'

Maxwell blew out his cheeks. 'Thank goodness for that. Not that it makes it any better for the poor old soul. But ... you know. After the Incident. It would have been a bit difficult.'

'Indeed it would. Anyway, I've asked Henry to drop in some flowers for us.' She read his mind. 'To Mrs Troubridge, not Metternich. He asked if we had Araminta's address. Do we?'

'I'm not sure that Mrs Troubridge has her address. She flits about a bit, does Araminta. But, surely, Millie's address will be there somewhere? She only went home the other day.' It had been a happy day *chez* Maxwell. The dull booming noise coming through the wall as Millie chatted to Mrs Troubridge had become quite wearing.

'I told him that. They have been checking phone numbers from the log on the phone. Not too many, poor little thing. There's a mobile, but it doesn't answer. Henry's checking it out.'

Nolan wandered over and tugged at the hem of his mother's coat. 'Wassup, Mums?'

'Wassup?' Maxwell asked. 'Wassup? What kind of talk is that? Mrs Whatmough would be appalled.'

'I think they call it jive,' Jacquie said calmly. 'Don't say that, Nole, there's a good man. See how Dad's has gone a funny colour? We don't want that, do we?' She leant down and swung him onto her hip. 'We were just talking about Mrs Troubridge. She's had a bit of an accident.'

'Is Metternich all right?' Nolan's tone was anxious.

Like father, like son. 'He's fine,' she reassured him and gave him a kiss. 'He's gone on his holidays.'

Rather unexpectedly, Nolan burst into tears, burying his face in his mother's neck. Through the sobs, they could just hear, 'I don't want the Count to go on holiday, like Plocker's dog.' He gave a huge sniff. 'And his granny.'

His parents looked into each other's eyes and the light dawned. 'No, not *holiday*, mate,' Maxwell said. 'Actual holiday. Like us. He's got his own chalet and everything.'

The boy raised his head, pausing only to wipe his nose on his mother's shoulder. 'Real holiday?' he checked, with another resounding sniff.

'Definitely,' Jacquie said.

He slid down her to the rabbit-cropped turf and turned back to Year Seven. 'You'd better be right,' he said, truculently, standing like an ox in the furrow, legs apart.

They watched him go. Maxwell turned to his wife. 'I just hope he never wants to invade anywhere,' he said. He put his arm round her shoulders and gave her a squeeze. 'Right,' he said. 'Packed lunch and then on to Blackgang Chine. Don't forget you promised us both a carry if our legs get tired.' He looked down at her and gave her a kiss. 'Don't worry. She'll be fighting fit by the time we get back. She's a tough old besom. It was just a tumble down the stairs.'

She smiled back, but she wasn't so sure. She hadn't shared everything with Maxwell. She hadn't, for example, told him that Mrs Troubridge hadn't woken up properly yet. Although she did sometimes cry out in her sleep. She hadn't been very coherent, but one phrase had come through loud and clear. And it was 'Don't! Oh, please, don't!' which seemed to her an odd thing to shout as you fell accidentally down the stairs.

The ward was quiet in the early afternoon lull between the lunch delivery and the post-clinic consultants' rounds. All wards at Leighford General experienced this quiet period, but none more so than Lady Elizabeth Molester, named after a long-dead benefactress, and now full to the brim with little old ladies, broken and bent after some disastrous accident. Some, like Mrs Troubridge, Bed 7, had fallen downstairs and by some miracle lived to tell the tale. Others, like Mrs Fiddymont, Bed 6, had tripped on a bathroom rug and as a consequence of a fall of less than a few feet was hanging between life and death, with an increasing leaning towards death. To the untutored eye, they all looked much the same. Fluffy white hair. Softly lined faces, slack, snoring mouths and blank eyes. Even the ones who had arrived at God's A&E with all of their marbles intact tended to let them loose when left in Lady Elizabeth Molester for more than a few days.

It was fairly easy to spot Mrs Troubridge, because she had a policeman sitting by her bedside. Not just any policeman, but Detective Chief Inspector Henry Hall. Henry would have been

91

horrified if someone had told him he was caught in a time warp, but it was true. He still sometimes wore the three-piece he'd bought when he'd made inspector and that was so long ago he found himself nodding with approval at the less-than-PC antics of dear old Gene Hunt. He was tall and solid, with less hair than he used to have, and his glasses endlessly reflected his surroundings, hiding the eyes behind them. No one who knew him in a work capacity would have said that he was a particularly sensitive man. His wife and sons knew him as someone who had interred the boys' dead goldfishes with tears, who helped lame dogs over stiles to further order; but he more or less kept that side of himself hidden from colleagues. But they all knew that he had a soft spot for Sergeant Jacquie Carpenter-Maxwell. And Mrs Troubridge was Sergeant Jacquie Carpenter-Maxwell's next-door neighbour and he was sitting in the place he knew she would have occupied, had she been in Leighford and not gadding about on the Isle of Wight. He had a notebook on his knee, for the look of the thing, but so far there hadn't been much to write down. She seemed to be counting under her breath, but really big numbers, hundreds of thousands, millions even. She even shouted 'Count!' sometimes, but Henry Hall was fully aware that that was probably the cat, Metternich.

He let his mind wander back to his visit to Happy Paws just before his arrival at the hospital. He hadn't liked the look in Metternich's eye even though there was steel-reinforced basket between him and the curmudgeonly quadruped, and he knew deep down that his next visit to 38 Columbine was going to involve clawed calves at the very least. Suddenly, he jumped.

'Count!' yelled Mrs Troubridge. 'Nine hundred and ninety-nine thousand, nine hundred and ninety-nine! Don't!' She sobbed and a tear rolled down her cheek. 'Oh, please, don't.' Henry Hall, kind man, wiped the tear away and then held her hand, patting it as if it were a small, injured animal.

'It's all right, Mrs Troubridge,' he said. 'Don't worry. I won't let anyone hurt you.'

Jacquie didn't have to carry Maxwell and Nolan by the end of the day, but it was a near-run thing. From a childhood visit, Maxwell had fond memories of Blackgang Chine but the thing he had forgotten was that it was so steep. Clinging to the edge of a cliff, and losing more and more through rockfalls and slippage every year, the paths wound back and forth between the different attractions, twisting and turning so steeply that, as they descended, Leighford's finest in line abreast, the eyes of those at the front were on a level and with, and going in the opposite direction from, the feet of those at the rear. It was like taking part in a huge Escher optical illusion and it made keeping count very difficult. It was a relief to find when they all collected at the entrance that they still had the requisite number. There had been several school parties in the Chine and only time would tell if the correct number was made up of the correct children.

No one except Nolan had been scared by

Rumpus Mansion and only Ethan Whatsisface had got a nasty one negotiating turns in the Crooked House. What would stay with them all, in some cases until they had children of their own, was Mr Maxwell treating them to that shoot-out at the end of the *Magnificent Seven*. Luckily, leaping over bales of straw, fanning the hammer of his thumb-breaker behind the stagecoach and gunning them all down through the batwing doors of the saloon, he was doing it in Cowboy Town so they all saw the relevance. And little Nole was so proud of his Dads. Not a scratch on him and he'd shot them all! What was it the Big Children at the school called him? Mad Max? Why was that?

The coach drew up and the Maxwell party dragged themselves up the steps. The eerie silence paid testament to a busy day; all of the staff and almost all of the students were sound asleep. Barton Joseph alone was bright-eyed and bushy-tailed, sitting alongside the driver.

'Hello, Mr Maxwell, Mrs Maxwell,' he whispered, stagily. 'Have you had a good day?'

Jacquie rolled Nolan's sleeping head along her shoulder so that she could look at the supply teacher. 'Yes,' she whispered back. 'It's been lovely. What about you?'

'It was great fun,' he said. 'I must say, Mrs Donaldson sets a cracking pace. I don't think I have ever walked Tennyson Down so quickly. She'll be sorry in the morning, unless she does a lot of walking at home.'

'She's always sorry in the morning,' muttered Maxwell, his trigger finger giving him a little gyp now, then, slightly louder, 'Are you going to lead us home, Mr Joseph, or are we dropping you off somewhere?'

'No, no, I'm along for the ride,' he chuckled. 'I only live a few doors along from the hotel. And anyway,' he dropped his voice very low, 'I don't think the driver could find his arse with both hands.'

'That's quite a popular opinion,' Maxwell agreed, settling into the front seat across the aisle. 'I trust we will be having the pleasure of your company for the rest of the week?'

'Well, that would be lovely,' the man said, 'but ... erm ... this is embarrassing, but when I'm not teaching I tend to do bar work, that kind of thing and so I can't really afford...'

'My dear chap,' Maxwell said. 'Has Mr Medlicott not discussed remuneration? I'm sure we'll be able to do something. I'll ring Leighford first thing Monday morning and see what's to be done. Or, failing that,' he fixed the driver's ear with a basilisk glare, 'I'm sure we can find the money from somewhere.'

A dark blush crept up from under the driver's uniform collar and swept over his balding head.

Maxwell leant forward and patted his arm. 'Home, James, and don't spare the horses.' He leant back in his seat and before you could say 'Year Seven Getting To Know You School Trip', he was fast asleep and snoring.

In all his years of supervising school meals Maxwell had never before seen so many children eat so quietly. The loudest sound in the room was that of feet throbbing and calves aching. In the age of the couch potato, there were very few eleven-year-olds who were as fit as Maxwell had been when he was a boy. Cycling, walking, ad hoc games of football – although admittedly not so many of those – had filled his days. His father, elderly as fathers went, had nonetheless always been ready for a game of French cricket in the evenings with little Peter and, when she unexpectedly joined them, his sister, Sandie. When he recalled his mother, the picture in his mind always included her bike, basket at the front, kiddie-seat at the rear, even after the kiddie in question was doing his O levels. It might come in handy, she always said, and if not for a child then at least for a bag of potatoes or, on one memorable occasion, the Christmas turkey. His parents now were a long-time dead and still he missed them sometimes; they would have enjoyed their little grandson, although being a hundred years old and rising might make their interaction rather difficult. They had lived long enough to see his only daughter born, but not long enough to see her die, for which he was thankful.

But these kids, he thought, shaking himself back to the present, what memories would they have of their parents? Sharing a puzzle on a DS Lite somehow didn't have the same power as a memory of sliding down the slope of Kenilworth Castle, to be swung high in the air at the bottom; of cycling breathlessly up a Malvern Hill and then, the inevitable corollary, freewheeling screaming down.

He ate absent-mindedly, watching his charges eat. Even the ginger kid who had given him lip on the coach was quiet, jotting down, Maxwell was amused to note, every item on his plate, just in case he was getting tested later. Jazmyn sat listening; it was what she did best. The others just shovelled in the pasta salad, scarcely noticing it was good for them, followed by fresh-fruit salad, in some cases for the very first time. Five a day? Yeah, right. He had sent the rest of the staff to their rooms, to de-child themselves after a long and strenuous day. The Medlicotts had had the quietest time, sketching, but keeping a bunch of excited children from scribbling on each other was tiring in itself, not to mention endless 'not too near the edges' and keeping a lookout for telltale wisps of smoke from behind Federigo Gianibelli's bastions. Sylvia and Guy had been squirrel-watching, again not exactly a walk on the wild side, but it too had proved to be unexpectedly hard work. Fortunately, Sylvia was carrying a comprehensive first aid kit, as walking through woodland, no matter how manicured, whilst looking at the tops of trees rather than the feet, carried its own risks and she was now completely out of plasters and Germolene. The removal of dog shit remained the problem of the kid concerned. It was easy to identify Pansy's group: they were lolling insensible in their chairs and some had already been carried up to bed, their legs useless having seized up on the coach. Jacquie was upstairs putting Nolan to bed. This involved stripping off his clothes and replacing them with pyjamas. Washing is for mornings when on holiday, was a time-honoured Maxwell family motto.

When he judged that most of his charges had

finished eating, he moved in like a ninja. The main skill here was getting them up to bed before they got their second wind. The timing was vital – too soon and they were back to full wakefulness before they got into bed and then ran screaming like banshees round the hotel until the wee small hours. Too late and they had to be carried insensible one by one up to their rooms, which was a tall order for even a team of teachers and he was alone on this one. Taking each child on their own merits, according to various clues such as speed of head nod, degree of eyelid droop, he walked round the room touching them lightly on the shoulder and suggesting in the low voice he had cultured over the years that they were tired and might want to go up to bed. It worked on everyone except for the traveller in underwear who was somewhat surprised to get such a suggestion from a man no longer in the first flush of youth. He had taken a bit of a shine to Pansy Donaldson in the bar the previous night, but he was aware that you couldn't be lucky every time.

With everyone safely stowed away, Maxwell ensconced himself at what he already considered to be 'his' table out on the decking and relaxed with a large Southern Comfort to the sound of the gentle waves lapping far out on the shingly beach as it turned at low tide. The air was still warm, and as he turned his head the most enormous harvest moon crept up out of the sea, reflecting in the still water. Someone came and sat beside him, and stroked his cheek to say hello. He assumed from this that it was Jacquie, but since seeing the gleam in the traveller's eye, he preferred not to turn his head.

'It's beautiful,' she said. Thank goodness; it *was* his wife.

'I don't think I've ever seen the moon so big.' He turned his head to look at her, 'Unless they cheat, like in *Bruce Almighty*.' He widened his eyes. 'You don't think there's anything in this Nostradamus thing, do you? Twenty-twelve, all that?'

She gave him a light punch on the arm. 'No, idiot.' Her face grew serious. 'But if there is, I'd be OK. My men are here, except the Count and he is needed at Happy Paws, to organise the evacuation.'

He blew her a kiss. 'I must say, I can't take the number 2012 very seriously. Do you remember when Nole used to count like that? Twenty-eleven, twenty-twelve, twenty-thirteen?'

'Yes, Max, I can,' she said. 'It was last week.'

'As recently as that? I suppose Mrs Whatmough knocked it out of him as being too darned cute.' At the mention of her name, a shadow passed across the moon.

One by one, the staff trickled down and joined them on the deck. They all sat transfixed by the enormous satellite and sipped their drinks in silence. They were all content that the day had been a success, that everyone had seemed to have had a good time and, as Izzy Medlicott remarked, nobody died. Only she knew that she was quoting a song by Nickelback. In the weeks to come, everyone would remember where they were when she said it.

Chapter Six

It was amusing to watch Year Seven straggle down to breakfast that Sunday morning. There was not so much as a single spring in any step – some were only making due progress by holding on to furniture or less crocked-up friends. It was, as Sylvia Matthews remarked to her husband, a very good way of getting to know each other, when you would fall over without the other person. Apart from the slow pace, it was pretty much a carbon copy of the previous day. Pansy had a hangover. The Medlicotts weren't there. The ginger-headed kid was taking notes. Nolan was eating enough fried food to last him a week, for the second time in two days. Ethan Oojah had walked into a bedside lamp. Just one thing was different; they had been joined by Barton Joseph, tracksuited and ready for the fray.

'Were we expecting him to join us for meals?' Sylvia asked Maxwell out of the corner of her mouth.

'I think he's getting his money's worth,' he told her. 'In case we don't come up with funding.'

And it certainly looked that way; why else would he be eating three Weetabix?

Then, suddenly, two things were different. Tom Medlicott appeared in the dining room doorway, not sleekly kitted out in running gear, an immaculate Izzy beside him, but in pyjama bottoms and skin. He stood dramatically with a hand on each side of the door frame, as if to stop escapees.

'Has anyone seen Izzy?' he asked.

The kids looked at each other and made various 'Idunnow' noises. One or two of the girls sniggered – sir with his top off. Coo.

He remembered himself. 'Mrs Medlicott, I mean.'

The answer was the same. Maxwell slid out from his seat in the bay window and went up to the man, shepherding him from the room. Maxwell was no stranger to behaving strangely, but he knew for a definite fact that he had never appeared before a room full of pupils in just his pyjama bottoms. It didn't result in very good discipline in future, he had been taught during his teacher training. It was around about Rule 400, just before exposing yourself, but important, nonetheless.

'Come on, Tom,' he said quietly. 'Let's go through here. Or,' he looked again at the man, wild-eyed, barefoot, 'better still, let's go up to your room. Bit more private there, don't you think?'

Tom Medlicott struggled in his light grasp, but found that it wasn't quite as light as he had thought. 'I must ask them... I can't find Izzy.'

'Has she gone for a run?' After all, they clearly did that as a habit.

'No. She wouldn't go without me. Or without at least saying she was going.'

Maxwell could understand that. He and Jacquie told each other if they were changing rooms, let alone that they were going out. But he had always rather thought that was because they both led

rather dangerous lives, she as a woman policeman, he as a nosy bastard.

'She did say that you sleep quite deeply. Perhaps she couldn't wake you to tell you she was
going out.'

'No, that's only in the middle of the night.
Anyway, she *can* wake me, if she really tries. It's
just that I don't wake up at external noises,
things like that.' Medlicott allowed Maxwell to
guide him gently to the stairs.

'Do you snore, Tom? I know I do and Jacquie
often changes rooms, just to get a few hours
sleep. Might she have done that?'

'In a hotel?' Medlicott was dismissive. 'Wouldn't
that be rather unusual?'

'Yes, but shall we ask?' Maxwell had to prevent
him from turning round and making straight for
Reception. 'Better still, I'll ask, you go up and get
dressed. I'll see you in the lounge in a few
minutes.'

The Head of Art turned reluctantly and headed
up the stairs, turning every few steps to make
sure that Maxwell was doing as he promised.
When he had turned the corner on the landing,
Maxwell walked quickly into Reception. He
knew he only had a limited time before Medlicott
was back down and kicking up a fuss.

The girl at Reception looked crisp and effi-
cient. Her name, on her badge and on the lamin-
ated sheet on the desk, was Lorraine.

'Hello, Lorraine,' he said, whilst mentally filing
her in his brain as Thingie Three. 'Can you help
me? Do you have a night porter or receptionist
here?'

She looked at her watch, somewhat ostentatiously. 'It's eight-forty-nine, Mr ... Maxwell.'

He was impressed and annoyed in almost equal amounts. 'Yes, I know. But *before* it gets to be eight-forty-nine, or,' he pre-empted her as she drew in her breath to speak, 'any time classed as day in this hotel, do you have a night porter or receptionist?'

'Yes, we do.'

'Thank you. Do they keep records?' he asked.

She looked at him in the way that reception staff are specially trained to do, mixing polite subservience with total contempt. 'Of course,' she said. 'We have a complete record of everything that goes on on night shift here, on the computer.'

'Well then,' Maxwell leant closer, aware that Tom Medlicott might come back at any minute. 'Can you have a quick look and tell me if Mrs Medlicott changed rooms last night?'

She smiled up at him. 'I don't have to,' she said. 'We are completely full. Thanks to *you* and your school party,' she added, with a twinkle. The staff of the hotel had a book going as to when the first window would get broken. The chef had had 'in the first hour' and was sulking. She had 'hours of darkness, Wednesday' and so still lived in hope. 'Delightful children,' she added.

'Indeed,' Maxwell said, keeping the surprise in his voice to a minimum. He'd have to see whether he could get that in writing. 'Well then, in that case, could she possibly have gone out for a jog or anything? Early, before you came on duty.'

'This isn't a prison, Mr Maxwell,' she admonished him. 'Guests can come and go as they please. The doors are locked, of course, at night and into the early morning, but the push-button to the left of the door opens it from the inside, so she might have gone out and not necessarily been seen.'

'I see. Well, thank you, Lorraine. You've been most helpful.'

'Do I understand that you have lost Mrs Medlicott?' she asked.

'We do seem to have temporarily mislaid her, yes. But I'm sure she will turn up soon.'

'I don't want to alarm anyone,' the receptionist said, in an alarming way, 'but the cliff paths are a little treacherous sometimes and if she went for a jog ... well, I think it would be wise to go and have a look, perhaps. Is Barton here?'

Maxwell had forgotten that the supply teacher had come highly recommended. 'Yes, he has joined us for breakfast.'

The receptionist made a note on a pad and smiled. Maxwell read it upside down. It said 'Breakfast x 6 @ £12'. Maxwell chuckled when he pictured Bernard Ryan's expression when the bill came in. 'Well, you couldn't do better than send him to look. He knows all the paths around here like the back of his hand.'

'What a useful chap,' Maxwell murmured and, smiling, turned away back towards the dining room. As he reached the door, Tom Medlicott came down the stairs, dressed but still looking strangely unkempt and confused.

'Her jogging things are still in the room,' he

said. 'In fact, I can't find anything missing at all.'

Maxwell forebore to say what he was thinking – *except your wife.*

'Except for Izzy, of course.' Medlicott tried a weak smile.

'I shouldn't worry about it too much,' Maxwell said, clapping him on the shoulder. 'Did she do her own packing?'

'No, I packed. That's how I know what we brought. She had been away a lot, sorting out some family stuff, so I have been doing all the laundry, that kind of thing. She just trusted me to bring what she needed.' He was looking puzzled. 'Where is she, Max?' He grabbed the Head of Sixth Form and stared into his eyes. 'Where has she gone?'

Maxwell gently moved his hands and held them, down at waist level, and spoke slowly and clearly. 'Tom, I know that you're worried. But we have a roomful of kids in there who are in our care. Before you say anything, yes, I am aware that they are not as important as your wife. But that's only how important they are to you. To other people, they are the most precious thing in the world. Izzy is an adult. They, despite what they think, are children. They get upset easily. They want their mum. They ring home. Then every-thing blows up in our faces.' He gently shook the man. 'Do you understand what I'm saying?'

Slowly, Tom Medlicott nodded, but his eyes were flicking from side to side as though his wife would appear like the genie of the lamp from behind any piece of furniture.

'I want you to wait out here. I'll send Jacquie.'

'That will be nice.' Medlicott sounded rather dubious and Maxwell remembered that he was new to the school.

'She's a woman policeman. A sergeant, in fact, soon to be inspector, we hope. So, she will take you up to your room and help you have a proper look.'

'I've made a bit of a mess, you know, in suitcases and things.'

'Never mind, she's used to that kind of thing. Then, I'm going to get Guy Minter and Barton Joseph to go along the paths from here and see if she has ricked her ankle or something. I'd send the driver as well, except that we can't waste time looking for him when he gets lost. What's his name, by the way? The driver.'

Medlicott looked at him rather oddly. 'You used it to him yesterday. I heard you.'

'I don't think so.'

'Yes you did. James, his name is, although I think he prefers Jim.'

Maxwell looked thoughtful for a moment and reran the conversation on the bus back through his head. He nodded as he remembered. 'Right. Well, the fact remains, he probably wouldn't be much help.' He leant over and stuck his head round the door. 'Mrs Maxwell,' he called. 'Could I just have you for a moment?'

Gales of laughter met his query. He shook his head. How could he possibly have fallen into that trap, after so many years at the chalkface? And how could so many Year Sevens be so quick on the uptake with the double entendre?

Jacquie walked through the dining room, head

106

high and elbow low, causing a few minor injuries in her flight path.

'Good elbow work there, heart,' Maxwell commended her. 'Now, we've done a bit of preliminary work and can't fathom out where Izzy might have gone. Could you pop up with Tom and have a look at the room? Woman policemanly stuff, clues and so forth.'

She looked at them both standing there, the husband of the missing woman, hopeful that she could magic his wife out of the wardrobe with a cry of 'Abracadabra'. Her own husband was looking rather sheepish. She knew that he was dying to mention that, since this wasn't a murder case, he could get involved, especially since they weren't even in Leighford, but somehow even he couldn't manage the 'm' word at the moment. She sighed and gestured Tom Medlicott up the stairs. With a muttered promise to Maxwell that she would speak to him later, she followed.

Maxwell watched them go and then went into the dining room and spoke quietly to Guy and Barton. They sloped off, sadly not looking in the flesh as cool and undercover as they did in their imaginations. Maxwell slid into Guy's vacated seat and gestured Sylvia and Pansy nearer. He filled them in on the plan and suggested that, even if the search was successful and the result quickly achieved, the whole brouhaha was taking up time which was pencilled in for travelling. Therefore, the morning's trip to Carisbrooke Castle would have to be shelved.

'We'll have a few beach football tournaments,' Sylvia suggested. She smiled at Pansy. 'We can each umpire a game.'

'Can we?' Pansy asked, weakly.

'Of course.' Sylvia produced a whistle and blew it sharply. Pansy covered her ears. 'Do you have a whistle, Mr Maxwell?'

'Indeed I do, Nursie,' Maxwell smiled. Sylvia Matthews had been his rock through the years, and they knew more about each other than was really decent, as their spouses often remarked. She wouldn't ask him for a whistle if she hadn't already known he had one in his trouser pocket. 'One whistle, umpires for the use of.'

'Excellent.' She handed it to Pansy, who groaned. She stood up and faced the still-masticating children. 'Finish eating asap, Year Seven,' she said. 'We have a slight change of plan this morning. Beach football.' A cacophony of groaning met her remark. 'Come on, now, you're all young and fit. Mr Maxwell is going to join us, aren't you, Mr Maxwell?'

Pansy looked round, an evil grin on her hung-over face. 'Yes, Mr Maxwell!' she cried, with enthusiasm. 'Do join us!'

'Hooray!' the room exploded. 'Come on, Mr Maxwell! You can be on my team!' and similar scary cries. Maxwell could do nothing but grin like a victim of strychnine poisoning and stand there, wishing Sylvia Matthews, Pansy Donaldson, Year Seven, but most of all Izzy Medlicott into the Seventh Circle of Hell.

'I'll go up and get changed, then, shall I?' he muttered, through clenched teeth. Maxwell was not the owner of much sporting apparel. What would be the point? When he cycled, he was

108

usually going somewhere where flannel trousers with a permanent cycle clip crease and a tweed jacket would be perfectly acceptable. On holiday, or on a school trip, which was of course a completely different thing, he wore a slightly toned-down version of the same, the jacket tending towards blazer, the trousers linen, the footwear a deck shoe in place of the usual brogue. But in any case, he would be seriously hampered in a game of beach football.

'You have football kit?' Sylvia asked in hushed tones.

'I had a whistle, didn't I?' he replied insouciantly and left the dining room, Nolan casually riding a hip.

'*Do* you have a football kit, Dads?' Nolan asked in amazement when they got to the door of their room.

Maxwell put his son down and hunkered lower to look him in the eye. 'What do you think, mate?' he asked the child.

Nolan lengthened his upper lip and placed it carefully over his lower, his thinking expression. He made a small sucking sound through his teeth. He looked at his father and announced, 'No, Dads, I don't think you have a football kit. *And* I think you have a plan so's you won't need one.' He smiled at his father, who stood up, swung him in the air and landed him neatly with a kiss plonked on his curly head.

'That's my boy,' he said.

Year Seven made their way across the Esplanade and milled mutinously on the sand. Some of

them could still hardly walk – they mostly repre-
sented Pansy Donaldson's group from the day
before. The vegan was nearly dead. The ginger
kid was burnt by yesterday's sun to an unattractive shade of magenta. Ethan Thingummy had
tripped over a pebble. Pansy's head hurt, not
again, but still. Sylvia Matthews blew a shrill
blast.

'Face this way,' she called. After some shuffling
she saw just faces and no head-backs. 'What we
are going to play,' she announced, 'is knockout
beach football. We will start with two games,
numbers divided in half, then half again by me,
so no team picking at this stage. Anyone who
fouls more than once is out and that team will
play a man down. Anyone seen fouling on purpose just to be sent off, stays on no matter what.
My decision, or that of Mrs Donaldson is final.
Now then...' her voice faltered as she sensed she
had lost her audience and she looked over her
shoulder.

Coming along the Esplanade were her husband
and the by-now ubiquitous Barton Joseph.
Between them, limping a little but otherwise in
perfect health, was Izzy Medlicott. She muttered
an imprecation under her breath; she had been
rather looking forward to Carisbrooke Castle.
She pinned on a smile and went towards the little
group.

'Izzy,' she said, when they were in earshot.
'You're limping. Can I help at all?'

Izzy looked meltingly at Guy and Barton who
blushed to the roots of his hair. 'I've just twisted
my ankle, Sylvia. Nothing much. I was having a

sit-down along the cliff path to rest it when these lovely men came looking for me.'

'Well, we were worried,' Sylvia said briskly.

'I left a note,' Izzy said.

'Tom didn't notice it,' Sylvia told her. 'Where did you put it?'

'I typed it on his PalmPilot. It's always the first thing he checks, every morning.'

'Perhaps it isn't the first thing he checks when he wakes up and finds his wife is missing,' Guy ventured, with a wry glance at Sylvia.

'Oh. No, perhaps not. But surely he noticed my running clothes were missing?'

'Apparently not,' Pansy Donaldson had also joined the fray. 'He and Jacquie are up searching your room as we speak.'

'Searching? Why? I'd only gone out for a run.'

Before Pansy could clock her one, a shout came from the top of the hotel steps. 'Izzy!' Tom Medlicott was dodging the light Sunday morning traffic and was suddenly on their side of the road, enveloping his wife in his arms. 'Where were you? I've been worried sick.'

'She'd left you a note, apparently,' Pansy said abruptly. 'Now then, Sylvia, gents, let's get this football game going.' And with a brisk toot on her whistle, she jogged back to the sand.

'She really does have remarkable powers of recovery,' Guy muttered.

'Either that or the hair of the dog has just kicked in,' said Barton, rather cynically. They bowed to his judgement; he had after all been her backup man the day before and he probably knew where the nips were hidden about her person. And when

111

it came to Pansy's person, there was a lot of person where nips could hide.

They fell in behind their leader, as Tom led Izzy back to the hotel as if she was made of china.

'Quite a lot of street cred lost there, I would imagine?' Guy mused to his wife. 'With the kids, I mean.'

'You have no idea,' she muttered. 'And, speaking personally, the staff are pretty pissed off, too.'

Chapter Seven

After the excitement of Sunday morning, the rest of the week couldn't help but be an anticlimax. Year Seven were preternaturally good. The ginger kid had a small wobble on the Tuesday when he found he had filled his notepad, but a quick visit to Staples with Jacquie in the car soon put him right and all was well again. Ethan Doodah stayed remarkably upright all week. Pansy proceeded to get drunker each evening and more hung-over each morning, until soon her recovery time almost met the time when the staff met to unwind in the bar. But since, as usual, the kids already knew she drank, it didn't really matter. Nolan had a whale of a time; spoilt rotten by staff and pupils alike, he thought that school trips were the best holidays in the world. Henry Hall kept Jacquie up to speed on Mrs Troubridge's recovery – slight – and Metternich's takeover of the cattery – total. In short, the Leighford High School Year Seven Getting To Know You School Trip was a resounding success. All of the plans were in place for the remaining days, groups sorted; even James the driver could finally find his arse with both hands and was almost as good at finding Ventnor.

When, on Thursday morning, Tom Medlicott appeared in the dining room doorway, not sleekly

113

kitted out in running gear, an immaculate Izzy beside him, but in pyjama bottoms and skin, standing dramatically with a hand on each side of the door frame, as if to stop escapees, everyone knew what he was going to say.

'Has anyone seen Izzy?' he asked.

Maxwell sighed and put down his knife and fork. 'Don't get up,' he said to the room at large. 'I'll get this.' And indeed, no one did get up, or even react much. He walked up to the Head of Art and gently manoeuvred him to the foot of the stairs and then on up to his room. He waited politely to be asked in.

The room was neat, no clothes strewn around, just one side of the bed flipped back, the other side neatly made. Tom Medlicott's PalmPilot was glowing faintly on the dressing table. There was no message on the screen.

'Tom,' Maxwell said, with a sigh. 'I don't know what's going on between you two, but you seem happy enough together. If there's something you would rather discuss with ... well, anyone else, I'm sure Sylvia could be a big help. Or Jacquie. They've both had counselling training.'

Medlicott was horrified and looked it. 'Counselling? Why should I want counselling? Izzy has disappeared. I just need help to find her, that's all.'

'But...' Maxwell wasn't used to being lost for words, but what could you say to a man who seemed intent on rerunning crises over and over? It was like *Groundhog Day*. It was déjà vu, all over again. He started afresh, hoping that the words would come. 'But, last time, when you thought

114

she was missing, she was just out for a run.'

'Yes.'

At least he isn't denying that, Maxwell was happy to note. 'So, do you perhaps think she might be out for a run now?' Colour him obvious.

'No. All her things are here. *All* her things. Except her pyjamas, which she went to bed in last night. Her slippers are gone, as well.' He was rummaging through them all again, as though to be doubly certain, patting the material in disbelief.

'Last time, Tom–' Maxwell began, but Medlicott cut him short.

'Look, Max,' he turned to face him, intensity in every pore. 'I know what everyone will be thinking and I don't blame them. On Sunday, Jacquie and I went through every piece of clothing in this room and I have just done it again. Everything that was here then is here now, I'm sure, plus her running things, which, as I know you remember, she was wearing on Sunday. *Where is she, Max?*' He slumped down on the bed and buried his face in his hands. 'Where is she?' It was a desolate whisper.

Maxwell patted him on the shoulder. He was stuck for an answer other than, 'Having a jog along the cliff top.' Apart from being worried that the man might be having some kind of breakdown, he also knew how he would feel if Jacquie was suddenly not there with no explanation. But he kept it in mind that 'not there' was not necessarily the same as 'missing'. He bent down, and said quietly, 'Tom, you wait here. I'll send Jacquie up and you and she can have a chat. She

115

will take some notes and she'll also be able to give you some help on how long we ought to wait before we ... well, take other steps.'

'Steps? What steps?' He was looking up at him in terror. Somehow, as long as only *he* was panicking, it was all right. Now Maxwell seemed concerned, it must be real.

'Tom, you're saying that Izzy is missing. If she is, we'll have to contact the police. You know that, surely.' Maxwell was confused. Either the man wanted his wife found, or he didn't.

'Well ... all right. But she won't like it. She's had a lot of involvement with the police lately, family stuff, won't bore you with it. But she won't want the police.'

'Let's be logical, Tom.' Maxwell was always rather dumbstruck when people couldn't see a simple piece of logic when it was plonked in their lap. 'She won't see the police, will she? Because, if she comes back ... we won't need the police.'

'Oh, right. Yes. I see. I would like to see Jacquie, please. If I can.' He looked at Maxwell, desolate and frightened. 'She was very good last time.' He sniffed. 'Don't spoil everyone's day, though. Just carry on without us.'

And without Jacquie, Maxwell thought. That left them at just over half-strength, but he thought they should be able to manage. As he left him briefly to fetch Jacquie, he tried hard not to show his concern to Tom Medlicott. While it was almost certain that Izzy had just popped out for a run again, there was a niggling little itch at the back of Maxwell's head that was tickling the bit of his brain that stored the information that lightning

116

doesn't strike twice in the same place. Crying and wolves didn't necessarily go hand in paw. Izzy was not particularly friendly and, despite the best part of a week in her company in the evenings, he wasn't much further forward in working her out. But one thing did seem to be the case and that was that she didn't seem to be the sort of woman who would mess her husband, or indeed anyone, around unnecessarily. She would have left a message somewhere and probably in capital letters after last time.

But meanwhile, Maxwell had a school trip to rescue and he went to break the news to his remaining team. It wouldn't be so difficult; the sketching party had been the smallest group all week, with the extras being spread between the others as the changeover happened. He and Jacquie had been due to do the Tennyson Trail up to the Needles and his feet and legs weren't sorry to be able to pass that one up. It might have been all right for Tennyson but he was a) barking and b) usually running away from the insufferable Julia Margaret Cameron. So their group could happily coalesce with the squirrel cohort. But what would be best of all would be to mass into one group and visit one poor benighted attraction, preferably a free one, to save Bernard Ryan completely combusting when the final accounting was up for consideration; although, clearly, when that great day came, there was no doubt where Bernard Ryan was going – he already, it was rumoured, had the handcart. Maxwell gestured Barton Joseph over – why keep a dog and bark yourself?

The local man came up trumps. A visit to the Newtown Nature Reserve would tick all the necessary boxes. A bit of history, a bit of botany, a bit of zoology and rather a lot of walking the kids all over the estuary until they were so covered with mud and the sweat of exhaustion that nothing would matter.

Maxwell left him to muster the troops while he went up to the Medlicotts' room to do a final liaise with Jacquie. The door stood open and through it he saw Jacquie sitting on the bed, opposite Tom Medlicott who had his head in his hands; Maxwell hoped that was again, rather than still. He gave a small cough and Jacquie turned to face him. She gave Medlicott a final pat and tiptoed over to Maxwell and ushered him back onto the landing.

'He's in a bad way,' she whispered. 'I must say, I'm thinking that he's overdoing it a bit. She's a grown woman, with no known illnesses, weaknesses or anything. She's not anyone we can report as missing at this early stage, but he's desperate to contact the police.'

'Aren't you the police?' Maxwell asked, confused about that not for the first time in his life.

'Not here, I'm not. Here, I'm just a woman trying to have a few days' break with her husband and son. But I suppose I can make a few calls. Just to chat, see how the land lies. I certainly don't want to call out the coastguard and the land and sea rescue, like Tom wants.' She reached up and gave him a kiss. 'Clear off with the kids. I'll catch you up later with Tom and Izzy when she turns up. Where will you be?'

'We're going to Newtown. That's up at the top bit, along to the left.' Maxwell would have no truck with geography; let others teach in a Humanities Department, he was a historian through and through. 'It used to be Francheville, the capital of the Island, in what Barton likes to call the "old days".'

'I didn't know there were any more big towns. Is it easy to find?'

'It's not what you'd call big, any more. There's a town hall and about six houses, from what I remember. But it is well signposted and the satnav will find it, I'm sure.' He returned her kiss. 'See you soon.'

Jacquie felt she had to ask the next question, just to be polite. 'I'll phone you, shall I?'

'Sweet,' he muttered. 'If you like, but I'll only hear it ring if I happen to be in the bedroom at Columbine. Try Sylvia. You'll be almost certain to have more luck.'

'Thought so,' she said, and crept back into the bedroom, where Tom Medlicott didn't appear to have moved a muscle. She stuck her head back round the door and crooked her finger to beckon him nearer. 'I'll give the local lads a ring,' she said. 'I'm sure there's more to this than meets the eye.' She blew him a final kiss and was gone.

As Maxwell made his way down the stairs he was trying his best to damp down his murder vibes. Like Jacquie, he was finding Medlicott's reactions a little over the top. But his relief at finding that his wife was all right on the Sunday morning had seemed genuine enough. But perhaps that was just because he hadn't been the one who had made her disappear. Or did he get the idea on Sunday to dispose of her completely? It was all rather sub-Hitchcock. He found the dining room disconcertingly empty and was disoriented for a moment until he glanced to his left and saw a row of faces pressed to the windows of the waiting coach. He trotted out and jumped onto the lower step and, checking only to make sure that Nolan was present and correct, halfway down the coach being fed Maltesers by two doting girls, cried, 'Chocks away, chaps! Tally-ho, Red Bandit Leader!'

It was a perfect Richard Todd, but it took James a few minutes to realise that this meant they should be on their way, but when he finally tumbled to the general idea he let in the clutch and they were off.

Jacquie had crept out of the Medlicotts' room to make her phone call to the local police station. She had the direct number, but thought it would be good politics to use the one that was accessible to the general public. In the same spirit, she began the conversation as a member of the public, too, but found that got her precisely nowhere.

Finally, she got to the point in the conversation when she thought a tiny bit of rank-pulling might not come amiss.

'Yes, thank you,' she firmly interrupted the nice-sounding but stubborn clerk on the other end of the phone. 'Thank you, but I wonder if you could put me through to a police officer?'

'I'm sorry, Mrs er ... Maxwell, but using our

checklist, I'm afraid that I am unable to log this case as a missing person. My guidelines...'

'I'm aware of the guidelines, but I am also aware of the whole picture in reference to this case. I am Sergeant Jacquie Carpenter-Maxwell of Leighford CID and I really must insist that you put me through to a police officer.'

'Is this a case we are working on with Leighford Police, Mrs er ... Maxwell?' the plodding voice asked.

'No, but–'

'Then, I'm afraid that, using my guidelines, I'm afraid that I can't log this case as a missing person.'

Jacquie sighed. 'Thank you, then. Goodbye.' She rang off and stood with her phone hanging limply in her hand while she cooled her fevered brow on the wall. After a slow count of ten, she brought the phone up again and dialled another number.

'Hello? Frank?' Good old Leighford. You knew where you were with the front desk there. 'Can you put me through to the Isle of Wight main police station? Newport, it'll be, I should think.' She listened to the man at the other end and gave a quiet laugh. 'Yes, I am on holiday, but a bit of a crisis ... yes ... yes, if you would, that would be brilliant. Thanks. See you next week.' She tapped her foot and hummed quietly under her breath as she waited for the connection. At least they didn't play music while you waited. Maxwell would have expected the *Z Cars* theme. A voice in her ear made her jump.

'Newport Police.'

'Hello...' A light lilt to the voice had alerted her. 'Is this Newport Police on the Isle of Wight?'

'No. This is Newport, Gwent.'

'Thank you. Thought so. Are you able to re-direct me, please?'

'I'll certainly try,' sang the voice, Welshly. 'Where would you like me to redirect you to?'

'Er ... Newport, Isle of Wight?' She knew that Maxwell would forgive the interrogative – it certainly wasn't her that was the moron on this occasion.

'Of course. I often have to do this, for some reason.'

'Well,' Jacquie said, with minimal irony, 'what an odd thing.'

'Isn't it, though? Putting you through.'

The echoing silence had a slight ping to it, indicating that she hadn't been cut off, so she waited, until, suddenly, 'Hello. Newport Police.'

Oh no. Another Welshman. 'Is this Newport, Isle of Wight?'

'Yes.'

'Not Newport, Gwent?'

'No. I can put you through if you like. We get a lot of this.'

'No!' Jacquie was immediately contrite. 'Sorry. I've been on the phone quite a while waiting to get through to you. No, it's you that I want. I'm Detective Sergeant Jacquie Carpenter-Maxwell, from Leighford CID.'

'Hello, how can I direct your call?'

'I'm not really sure. I just want to discuss a possible missing person.'

'May I just take a few basic details? Just to see

if we have anything already on The System.'

All police forces had The System, anything that worked for them in the first instance, before they started to call on HOLMES. In the bad old days, known to Peter Maxwell as the good old days, there had been the shoeboxes, then cross-referenced record cards, then, tentatively, computerisation. Nowadays, there were myriad powerful programmes, run from cooled rooms in basements with tentacles that circled the globe. But before all that, there was The System.

'You won't have. We are here on holiday.'

'Is it a child?' asked the clerk.

'No, an adult. We are here as a school party and she is one of the adult helpers.'

The clerk was embarrassed. 'She hasn't just, umm, perhaps...?'

'Sloped off for a rest? No, although I understand the question. No, she seems to have disappeared in the night or very early morning. I understand that her husband sleeps very heavily... Look, to avoid repetition, could you put me through to someone?'

'May I ask how long she has been missing?'

'Well,' Jacquie craned round to look at her watch, whilst still holding the phone to her ear, 'assuming she went around sixish ... about three and a half hours.'

The silence thrummed and twanged in her ear. She could picture the gestures the clerk was making to her colleagues in the office. Boiled down, they amounted to 'we've got a right one here'. Finally, she said, politely, 'I'm sorry, but we can't consider her missing before...'

'There are extenuating circumstances which I think would be simpler told straight to a police officer. Is there one available?'

'I'm not sure...'

'Look, I know you think I've gone mad, reporting someone missing so soon. But I *am* a police officer myself, and I *do* understand that it sounds ridiculous. But if you could just put me through to someone, then I can explain. If they think it isn't a case, then I'll just leave it. OK?'

'Well, the trouble is, we've got the Bestival coming up...'

'Good for you,' Jacquie tried to keep the acid out of her voice.

'...so we've a lot of people using up their leave, before then. We're rather short-handed.'

'I'll just be a minute.' Jacquie was now reduced to wheedling.

'Oh, all right, then. I'll see who's free.'

The line went dead, and Jacquie could only hope it was the dead of transfer rather than the dead of having to beat your brains out on the wall because you'd been cut off.

'Hello?' Thank goodness. It had been the dead of transfer; still, not one of George A. Romero's best, Maxwell would have assured her.

'Hello. Thanks for agreeing to talk to me. I'm Sergeant Jacquie Carpenter-Maxwell. I'd like to chat about someone who may be missing.'

'How long?'

A man of few words. Jacquie wasn't at all sure how this was going to pan out. 'Since early this morning.'

'Carnelpyew,' the man drawled. 'Sgorrerbe-

124

twennyforours. Sleast.'

'Yes, yes,' Jacquie said. 'I understand that. But this is a bit different...'

'Snot.'

'I beg your pardon?' Jacquie had learnt bridling from Maxwell.

'Snot diff'rent. Just cuz y're a p'licewoman.' Jacquie sensed she was making progress. Separate words were beginning to emerge from the sludge. 'Stoo soon. Ring back tumorrer.'

'I think that–'

'Tumorrer.' And the phone went down. Jacquie could have wept. In fact she did, just a little, out there on the landing. Then, she squared her shoulders. She could go back in there and explain to a distraught man – possibly a rather *too* distraught man – that they would have to wait another twenty-four hours at least. Or, she could ring Henry Hall and get some arses kicked. In times like these she asked herself – what would Maxwell do? And the answer was, nose about, irritate people, get half-killed by some maniac, then solve the problem.

Turning her back to the door, she raised her phone again and pressed one button.

'Hello. Henry. Is this a good moment? We need to talk.'

Chapter Eight

'Yes, it's fine. I was just finishing a meeting.' Henry Hall waved away the last stragglers from the briefing. How gripping could budget estimates be?

'It's just that... I don't really know where to begin.' Jacquie began to pace back and forth along the landing. She always thought better when she was on the move. 'As you know, I'm still on this school trip, and one of the staff has gone missing.'

There was a silence, broken eventually by a deep breath from Henry. He assumed from her moderate insouciance that it wasn't Maxwell. Damn. 'How long?' he asked.

'Well, that's the thing,' Jacquie admitted. 'Only since early today, but we thought she was missing on Sunday, and she wasn't. She seemed really sorry and she had left a note, only her husband hadn't found it, and ... ooh, guv, I feel as if I've got one hand tied behind my back, not able to do anything.'

'It's a bugger,' Hall agreed. 'Do the locals know you're with a school party? Because that really should make a difference. In a perfect world, there should be a Children & Youth Protection report on every one of the little dears.'

Jacquie shuddered, just thinking of the paperwork. 'Yes, I know. That's probably why they're

126

trying to put it off. Not that they know, but we're on our way home tomorrow. Twenty-four hours give or take and she'll be missing on her own. We won't be able to postpone; the hotel are booked solid for weeks. They specialise in school trips, at the end of the season.'

'Well, tell them that, then.' Henry Hall was running out of ideas. 'It will be a nightmare if she's still missing and you all come home. Think of the paperwork *then*.'

Paperwork. The ultimate threat. Or bribe, depending on the point of view. 'The thing is, guv, I've pretty much shot my bolt down here. I went through the public number and got nowhere. I went through the direct number, via Frank at Leighford and after a little trip to Gwent, ended up speaking to some jobsworth who seemed to be worrying about a pop festival.'

'Yes. They still have them there, by all accounts. Part of the time warp that is the Isle of Wight.' There was a puff of air on the speaker and Jacquie could picture her boss blowing out his cheeks and looking a little like a hamster in glasses. 'OK, Jacquie. I'll tell you what I'll do. I'll give someone I know a quick ring; it won't be on the Island, but it will do the trick. Meanwhile, get as much together as you can, interview staff at the hotel, that kind of thing. Did you say she was married?'

'Yes.' In fact Jacquie could still hear Tom Medlicott's soft weeping through the cracked-open door.

'Interview him then, obviously. Then the other staff on the trip. Is ... umm ... is Max...?'

127

'I'm fighting him off, guv, and to be fair he's so busy trying to keep the trip together, being three staff down.' Jacquie had felt this question coming for a while. She was surprised he hadn't asked it first.

'*Three?*'

'Don't panic. I haven't been breaking it to you gently or anything. I just mean the missing woman, her husband and me. That makes three of us out of action.'

'Of course. Sorry. I just always expect the worst when Leighford High School is involved. How have the kids been, by the way?' His men had blue-lighted it to Leighford High often enough for him to be wary. It *had* been fairly quiet for the last few days.

'Do you know, guv, they have been angels. There are one or two you have to watch, of course, mainly Max and Nole, but by and large they've been great; they haven't broken anything, except wind, probably, and everyone has had a whale of a time.' She was surprised to hear herself say it, but it was true.

'Except that one of the staff has gone missing. What does she teach?'

'Oh, she's a wife, if you know what I mean. Her husband is Head of Art at Leighford.' She waited for him to speak, but he didn't say anything. 'Guv?'

'Oh, sorry. I just had one of those moments, you know, when something just came into my head. Gone again now, though. Getting old.'

'Not you, guv. Mind like a razor. Just like Max. I think I'll be old before either of you.'

128

She suspected he might even be smiling when he replied. He hadn't smiled since March 2003, so one was just about due. 'I remember you when you were a little thing fresh off traffic. So please don't tell me you're feeling old. It was bad enough when the boys started shaving. Anyway, don't get me started on that,' he cleared his throat. 'I'll make my call, so you won't be treading on toes. Ask a few questions. If you get anything that we can go with, let me know. And, Jacquie...'

'Yes, guv?'

'Don't worry. I'm sure she'll turn up.'

'Yes,' she said with a confidence she didn't, in the pit of her stomach, feel. 'I'm sure she will. Before you go, any news on Mrs Troubridge?'

'Still sleeping, but they've at least ruled out any permanent damage now. She has a broken hip, of course. I'm not sure you're allowed on Lady Elizabeth Molester without one of those. She looks fine. I've ... popped in a few times. Keeping an eye.'

'But it was just an accident?' Jacquie detected a slight tone in Henry Hall's voice, one which she recognised of old.

'Ha ha.' It wasn't a laugh. It was Henry Hall saying 'ha', followed by 'ha'. 'Yes, of course. Old ladies fall downstairs. She should be in a bungalow.'

Or a straitjacket. Jacquie suddenly felt quite bereft. She couldn't imagine life without a lurking Mrs Troubridge behind every fence. 'Thanks, anyway, guv. You know ... for visiting. I know she appreciates it, even if she is still asleep.'

'You're welcome.' Henry Hall's mind was already well on the way to elsewhere.

'Bye, then. Thanks.'

'As I said, you're welcome.' Henry Hall rang off and sat back in his chair, tapping his mobile gently against his chin. He closed his eyes and tried to remember his fleeting thought, but it was no good. Never mind. It would come to him in its own good time, he had no doubt.

Jacquie turned back to the door of the Medli-cotts' room. She pushed it open, making sure that by the time she was in front of Tom, she was wearing her special woman policeman all-is-well smile, as taught at college and every workshop since.

His head snapped up at the sound of the door brushing on the carpet. 'Any joy?'

She sat next to him and widened the smile. 'I didn't get anywhere with the local police,' she said. 'But my boss from Leighford is going to make a few phone calls and get me cleared so that I can have a bit of a poke around myself. The only reason I hadn't already suggested it is that I know how easy it is to tread on local toes.' She looked up and scanned the room. 'Look, Tom, it's a bit depressing in here for you, isn't it? Let's go and sit outside, get a bit of a blow of air?'

He shook his head. 'What if she rings?'

'She'll have to come through the switchboard, these aren't direct-dial phones. As we go out into the garden, we can tell them where we are.' She patted his hand. 'Come on. What do you say?'

'It's not as though we need the sea air,' he said,

sulkily. 'We can get that at home.'

She smiled her agreement, but said, 'I know. But speaking for myself, I can't remember the last time we were on the beach at Leighford. And you've only just moved there, haven't you? You must have years of no sea air to catch up on.'

He stood up, as though on strings. 'All right,' he said, in a lacklustre voice. 'I suppose I could do with some air. We come from Northampton, which isn't known for its miles of golden sand, I'll grant you.' His smile was weak, but it was there. 'And anyway, I suppose if we are out in the garden, we'll be able to see Izzy. You know, from a distance. When she comes back.'

'That's the spirit,' Jacquie said, and put her hand on his shoulder. As she fell into step behind him, she squeezed her eyes shut and wished a wish. There were no magpies, no wishbone, no cherry stones, no last bite of pie to wish on, so she wished as hard as she could, instead. She tried to conjure up some of Nolan's blind faith in faeries, both tooth and godmother, as she wished as hard as she could that Izzy Medlicott was all right.

They chose a table that gave an uninterrupted view along the Esplanade in both directions but which was also within calling distance from the hotel door should a phone call come in. Jacquie tucked the notepad down on her lap, under the edge of the table. Tom Medlicott must know that it was there, but she just hoped that, without it being too obvious, he might forget about it and let go a little.

'Right,' she began, sipping the coffee which he had bought her while she chatted briefly to the girl on Reception, who even she, who knew the names of both Leighford Thingies, and the names of their dogs and husbands, thought of as Thingie Three. 'Right, now, I know this will probably seem a bit strange, as we have been together almost a week now, but just pretend we're strangers. Tell me all about you and Izzy. How long have you been married, for example?'

'It was our first anniversary on the fifth of September,' he said, baldly.

She jotted down a note. The next question would be quite a sensitive one. They were both mid-thirties; it was likely that at least one of them had been married before. She didn't have to ask it.

'We'd both been married before,' he said. 'My marriage had been over for years when we met. I have two children, eight and ten, but ... well, let's just say we thought it would be easier if the break was clean.' He looked into her eyes, challenging her to speak. She had been called out to enough domestic incidents involving custody to know that sometimes 'clean' was the best way, if you had the balls for it.

'I see,' she said, looking right back at him. 'And what about Izzy?'

'Yes, well, it wasn't quite like that for her. She well, she and her husband were still together when we met. He was a ... colleague.'

'A teacher?'

'Yes. My Head of Department, in fact. He was a few years older than Izzy. We ... well, I don't really want to go into details, but it wasn't easy. I got another job – *this* job – as soon as I could, but it was a difficult year, as I'm sure you can imagine.' Medlicott looked down at his hands, fingers interlaced, thumbs whirring, as if he had never seen them before. 'He started drinking, rather a lot. Coming in drunk, that kind of thing. He was suspended, for a bit...'

Jacquie could think of nothing she could usefully say, except, 'I see.' It seemed to be all he needed, because he was soon back in full flow.

'Izzy is a freelance motivational psychologist, as I'm sure you know.'

Jacquie didn't know. She had had her down for a PA, something like that. Perhaps motivational psychologists were less likely to go missing than secretaries – she didn't know, having never knowingly met one before. 'Yes, of course, she did mention it. Had she had much work since you got to Leighford?'

'She's having a career break. She had a family bereavement and was left a little money. Well, a reasonable amount, actually. She was an only child and her parents had divorced, so she's been busy, selling the house, that sort of thing. Getting things straightened out.'

'Oh, I see. So, no money worries?'

'None. She had quite a good settlement from her ex, as well, so...' His voice trailed away. She felt as if he could read her mind; no money worries, easy to run away. She did it once, she could have done it again. She tried to make her face more blank. 'It's in a joint account and in the house. I had been renting, so we had to start

133

from scratch. We don't have much cash, if that's what you're thinking.'

Jacquie shook her head. 'No, no, Tom. I'm not here to judge you. I just need to know some background. Anything might be the clue we need. Now, you say she had a bereavement. Does she still have family?'

'I'm not sure. We had such a quiet wedding, well, what with me not seeing the children and having no parents myself, I think she just thought it would be nicer with just the two of us, so we went to the Seychelles, got married on the beach.' He gave a small laugh and a shrug of one shoulder. 'Bit of a cliché, perhaps, but it suited us. We only really needed... I mean, *need* each other to be happy. We had a few cards, a few small presents, toaster, that kind of thing. But I never really asked who they were from. Izzy dealt with all that at the time. But now,' his face crumpled and he began to cry quietly, 'now I realise I don't know anything about her.' He leant forward and nearly knocked over the table, their coffees slopping into the saucers. 'What was I thinking? I was so selfish.'

'No,' Jacquie said, gently. 'Sometimes, there's no need to know everything.'

He looked up at her again. 'You and Max seem to be able to read each other's minds,' he said. 'You start a sentence, he finishes it, or the other way round. Even Nolan does it. You're like one person with three heads.'

'Hmm, I'm not sure I like that analogy,' she said, with a smile to take the sting out. 'We're actually very different. We both have jobs that take up every thought in our heads, for hours at a time. Poor old Nole gets shifted around from pillar to post; I don't think there's a child in the county with more minders than he's got.'

'Even so,' Medlicott said. 'When Team Maxwell swings into action, I don't suppose much can stand in its way.'

Jacquie smiled at him, but in her head, drowning out the here and now, was Henry Hall, telling her that if Maxwell so much as went near a murder, no, not even murder, if he was in the High Street when someone was caught shoplifting a jelly baby, then her promotion was a dream. She shook herself slightly to bring Tom Medlicott back into focus. Was being inspector worth breaking up Team Maxwell? She would have to think this one over. 'That's true,' she said. 'We're a bit like a juggernaut.' And it suddenly occurred to her that she wasn't thinking of the lorry, but of the procession to celebrate the god Krishna; could she be turning into Maxwell? 'Anyway,' she tried to get this conversation back on track, 'what I'm hearing, Tom, is about a happy couple, with any problems behind them. Don't overthink this one; hindsight is notoriously twenty-twenty.'

He sighed and ran his hands through his hair, so it stood up in tufts. She couldn't square this distraught man with the controlling box-ticker she had met just a week ago. Could it be that there was more than one side to Tom Medlicott? Including a wife murderer?

She tapped her pen on her pad. 'So there's no one she would have gone to?' No, she wasn't turning into Maxwell. Look at that preposition at the end of the sentence.

'No. It's just us.' He broke down again.

She stood up and walked round the table, bending down to put her arm round his shoulder and lean her cheek on the top of his tousled head. There was probably not more than six months between them, but she comforted him as though he were Nolan. 'Come on, Tom. Let's put you to bed. I've got some herbal sleeping tablets in my bag. They're not miracle workers, but they'll take the edge off, let you get a few minutes, perhaps.'

'You take sleeping pills?'

'I'm a policewoman. My husband lost his first family in a car crash, plus, he's a teacher who wants to look after the whole world. It's a wonder we don't use a sledgehammer.' She gave him a squeeze. 'Come on, you'll feel better after a nap.'

'If I hadn't been sleeping so soundly, perhaps–'

'"Perhaps" is silly. And anyway, she'll be back before you wake up, I bet.' This would mean a lot to some people, Jacquie knew. A bet was almost a guarantee. But Jacquie never played so much as Snap for money. She didn't play the Lottery. The National had never struck her as being particularly Grand. But it perked him up and she was soon tiptoeing out of his room, having tucked him under the covers like a child. She closed the door with exaggerated care and went downstairs to question Thingie Three.

But this got her nowhere. People could come and go almost invisibly; well, they could go. Coming back in tended to draw more attention. The CCTV cameras were for show only. They weren't linked to anywhere and there was no hard drive. Maxwell would have said there was no glass negative installed, had he ever given CCTV more than a cursory thought. There were some on the Esplanade, but only in one direction, where the pubs were. Turning left out of the hotel, onto the cliff path, could be done completely invisibly. Why was it that Joe Public was photographed clearly three hundred times a day going about his boring, innocent business? Dick Dastardly never was. The most heinous of crimes was always carried out by a pixelly blob. The doors stood open until midnight and anyone could enter or leave. After all, as Thingie Three said, it was a hotel, not a prison. Jacquie forbore to point out that it was a prison, beg pardon, hotel, full of children. She knew the point would go right over the girl's head. But, to cut a short story even shorter, no one had seen the woman after her husband closed his eyes the night before. And Jacquie hoped that this was literally true. Because, if it was, there was a chance that she was sitting up on the cliff path, nursing a sore ankle and swearing because no one went to look for her. Even, in a worst-case scenario, she might be sitting on a ledge halfway down the cliff, waiting to be spotted by a windsurfer. Because if someone else *had* seen her after Tom had kissed her goodnight, they might be looking at another outcome altogether. One that she felt like iced water, trickling slowly down her spine.

Jacquie Carpenter-Maxwell turned slowly from the reception desk and walked to where she had parked the car, along a bit from the hotel. She wanted a drive, on her own, with some music blasting out so loud it drove the trickling ice away. Meat Loaf would be nice. *Bat Out of Hell*. She foraged in the glove compartment and sighed. Nolan had prepared well for the journey, tossing out her music CDs to make way for *Charlotte's Web, Flat Stanley,* and finally, and so very appropriate, a complete set of *A Series of Unfortunate Events*. Somehow, nothing really appealed, so she just got in and drove in silence, broken only by the occasional confused musings of a strictly mainland-oriented satnav having its own nervous breakdown, accompanied by the unwelcome thoughts jangling round in her head.

Chapter Nine

Last-night hysteria had touched Year Seven and getting them to bed that night was a job for the A-Team, the Watchmen and the Untouchables rolled into one. And even then, they would have had a hard time. It seemed to the Leighford staff, minus, naturally, Tom Medlicott who was palely loitering in his room, that no sooner had they got one sector covered, than someone would make a break for it further down the corridor. It was like trying to catch a fart in a colander, as Barton Joseph so colourfully put it. Doing a headcount was impossible; it was always at least ten per cent out and, on one memorable occasion, they came up with double the required number. Pansy, whose drinking time was being seriously cut into by these shenanigans, tried to persuade Maxwell that too many was good enough, but wiser words prevailed and the count began again. Also, she had been pestering Maxwell for a while now on the need to inform the Senior Leadership Team at Leighford High of the disappearance of Izzy Medlicott. Maxwell ripped off Sean Connery's great line from *Indiana Jones* by telling her she might as well contact the Marx Brothers.

Eventually, everyone was in bed and, if not exactly tied down with actual ropes, they had taken Maxwell's threats seriously enough to behave as if they were. Soon all was peaceful, save for the weak-wailing threnody of the girls who had somehow forgotten that they would all be seeing each other again in school on Monday.

Jacquie was intrigued. 'Why are they crying like that?'

'Oh,' Sylvia dismissed it as she sipped her drink gratefully, 'ignore it. They're always the same. Last day before the holidays from school, first day back, birthdays, exams; the girls all cry and the boys go around punching each other. It's a puberty thing. Just you wait.'

Jacquie was still waiting for Nolan to go through all of the dread phases of toddlerhood; the Terrible Twos, the Thoughtless Threes, the Foul Fours and so on. Like his father, Nolan didn't ever do what was expected. He was probably limbering up for a biggie in the Nauseating Nines or something. She also sipped her drink. She felt the presence of Izzy Medlicott as clearly as if she had been sitting at her elbow. And yet, here they all were, making small talk. Someone had to bring her absence up, but who?

Maxwell, returning from the last round-up, flung himself into his chair and said, 'So, what's the next move on the Medlicott situation?'

Everyone breathed a sigh of relief. The elephant had left the room, leaving only minimal damage and a pile of steaming poo behind.

'We'll be able to go to the police tomorrow, surely?' Guy Minter suggested. 'They said twenty-four hours, didn't they?' Everyone looked at Jacquie, as the resident expert on police procedure.

'Yes,' she agreed. 'That's true. Twenty-four

hours is the standard, but a lot depends on the circumstances. Izzy is a healthy woman with adequate funds at her disposal. She and her husband have not been married long and she has a broken marriage behind her already.' A chorus of prurient muttering broke out at this point and she hurriedly tried to repair her indiscretion. 'Please don't let Tom know that I have told you any of this,' she begged them. 'While I wasn't told it exactly in confidence, it was while I was taking notes, possibly for a police investigation, so it isn't really for publication.' They all nodded furiously, except for Pansy, who was beginning to feel the need to hold her head on. 'What I mean by this is that the police will not be ready to mobilise air-sea rescue for this case. Not until we have established that Izzy has not simply gone home, for example, or back to her ex-husband. Stranger things have happened.'

'And often on school trips,' Maxwell added darkly. 'They bring out the bizarre in people.'

'Indeed. So, I think it would be quite helpful if we all just had a bit of a think overnight and per-haps jotted down anything that springs to mind. Tom and I will obviously stay and follow in the car when we've seen the police. They may want him to stay, but I'll try to discourage him. He can't do anything here, and she might have gone home for some reason. But tomorrow is an early start, for you at least, I expect.' Jacquie was planning ahead.

'Early start?' Pansy cried weakly, putting down her gin sloppily, perilously near the table's edge. 'How early?'

'Well,' Maxwell said, a gleam as near to vicious

141

as he ever came in his eye, 'it's breakfast at seven. Assemble at the coach at eight-thirty. Ferry at ten.'

'Home by half past five in the afternoon,' Guy put in in an undertone. Although James had ended up, in the absence of his Auntie Whatever, staying in the hotel, his hob had not nobbed with the staff. He was usually drinking his orange juice quietly at a pub down the road. Despite his obvious deficiencies, no one wanted to hurt his feelings, and anyway, it was never a good idea to piss off the man who was going to drive you home.

Maxwell chuckled. 'Hopefully, home by one-thirty. At any rate, that's when the parents come to get their little darlings.'

'Except The One,' Sylvia added.

Maxwell inclined his head in acknowledgement. 'Of course,' he agreed. 'Except The One.'

'The One?' Guy asked.

Sylvia turned to her husband. 'In any school trip, there is always one kid whose parents don't turn up, usually for about two hours. They claim to have written it down wrong on the calendar, got caught up in traffic, at a meeting, something like that. But usually, they just can't bear to have their kid back after a lovely week without them.'

'Which reminds me,' Maxwell said. 'We haven't done the sweep.'

'How true,' Sylvia said. Before Guy could ask, she explained. 'We all choose someone to be The One. If everyone is wrong, the money goes to charity. The winner gets it, if there is a winner, obviously. Right, me first ... fiver, is it?' She looked round; everyone nodded. 'Right, I choose Jazmyn.'

142

'Oh,' Barton Joseph complained. 'I was going to have her. In the nicest possible sense of the term, of course.'

'You're very trusting, Barton,' Jacquie said. 'If you win, we might fib and keep the money.'

'You all seem quite honest to me,' Barton said, loftily. 'And don't forget, I'll be on your case till I get paid for this week.'

'True,' Maxwell said, sombrely. He still had that interview with Bernard Ryan to come and it wasn't going to be pretty. Still, he'd left the man's balls on the mat often enough for it to be a near-formality.

'Choose another,' Sylvia encouraged him.

'Whatsisname, you know, the kid with the wall eye.'

'Che,' said Maxwell, delighted by the man's lack of political correctness. He could see a lot of himself in Barton Joseph.

'Yes. Him.'

'Right,' Sylvia said. 'Jacquie? Guy?'

They both had their own *bêtes noires* and chose them. Pansy had gone to sleep, head back and drooling in what was probably the best Homer Simpson impersonation the group had ever seen, so they chose for her; the nicest-natured child in the party, who had been phoned regularly by her mother every night at exactly six-fifteen. It was generally agreed that the doting parent was probably pacing Leighford High's car park already, in anticipation.

'Max?'

There was no contest. 'I'll have that ginger kid.'

There was a silence. Two names were missing

from the sweep, but no one wanted to approach Tom with such a frivolous thing, and who knew who Izzy, wherever she might be, might have chosen. Five-pound notes were handed over to Sylvia's safe keeping, including the one extracted with frightening stealth from Pansy's purse by Barton. Well, if you couldn't trust a member of the Royal College of Nursing...

'Were you trained by Fagin?' Jacquie asked, watching the expert removal.

Barton laughed. 'Possibly,' he said. 'After all, you don't know anything about me, really, do you? I could be a master criminal, for all you know.'

'You have a CRB,' Sylvia said, with a slightly nervous laugh.

'That only means I've never been caught,' the local man said. 'And anyway, Max just shoved it in his pocket. It could have been a CRB on Mickey Mouse for all he knows.' He looked at their stricken faces and laughed again, poking Guy in the ribs. 'Just joking. I'm as clean as the proverbial whistle. I just happen to be very good with my hands.' He waggled his fingers in the air, as if in proof.

Although he had meant well, and everyone believed him to be just what he said, clean as a whistle, it somehow cast a pall on the party and, heaving Pansy reluctantly to her feet, they all rose to make their way to their rooms. Barton Joseph hugged the women and then, after a slight pause, the men. He took the opportunity to make sure that Maxwell had all of his bank account details, for the payment.

Slowly, and for the last time, the staff of the

144

Leighford High School Year Seven Getting To Know You School Trip wended their way up to their rooms, Maxwell in the rear, shepherding them like a rather grizzled sheepdog. He wasn't exactly snapping at heels or worrying anybody, but he carried on making encouraging noises from the bottom stair until they had turned the corner of the stairs. He made his way quietly to the bar, bought himself a Southern Comfort and Jacquie a gin and tonic. He went back to their table outside and waited.

'You might have let me know what you were planning,' Jacquie complained as she plonked into the chair next to him. 'I was in my 'jamas before it dawned on me.'

'Good heavens, Woman Policeman Carpenter-Maxwell, you're slipping,' he said calmly.

She looked into her glass. 'My ice has all melted,' she complained.

He stretched luxuriously in his chair and collapsed back, smiling. 'Yes, it is a warm night.'

'I'm going to get a fresh drink,' she said, getting up and marching off.

He waited patiently until she returned and sat down again, with a rather perkier drink in her hand.

He raised his glass to her. 'Cheers, my favourite woman,' he said.

'And cheers to you, my favourite man.' She chinked her glass against his.

They sipped thoughtfully. 'Penny for them,' he said.

'They're not even worth a penny,' she replied.

145

'You know what they are.'

'Yes,' he said, quietly, 'I'm afraid I do. But shall I tell you anyway?'

'Why not?' she said, adding a tad more tonic. The hotel measures erred on the side of generosity, as Pansy had failed to realise, despite the events of the week.

'Well, I think, and you'll have to excuse me here, because I usually chat things over with the Count, and he sometimes needs me to explain things. So don't be offended, Granny, if I seem to be teaching you to suck eggs.'

'OK, Granddad, but just be warned that a smack round the head often offends.' Jacquie had often overheard Maxwell's musings with Metternich, and had frequently learnt quite a lot about a current case by her gentle eavesdropping. Even if there was nothing to be learnt, there was something quite special between the man and his cat; more correctly described as the cat and his man.

'Right. I won't be offering you a cat treat, or anything,' Maxwell reassured her.

'That will be because you don't have any,' she said, wryly.

'*Au contraire*, Blackadder,' he said, in his best Lord Melchett. With a flourish, he extracted a pack of sardine-flavoured treats from his pocket. 'I am never without them. I may need to calm an infuriated feline at any moment.' From the other pocket, he drew a bag of fruit pastilles, for calming infuriated children. He had only got them mixed up once and Metternich had taken some time to forgive him for the lapse.

'Off you go, then,' Jacquie said, settling back in

her chair, nursing her drink.

'I think that we can take it as read that Izzy Medlicott has definitely disappeared,' he began. 'What we have to discover is whether it is by foul play or just a decision on her part to fly the coop. Oh, perhaps at this point, I should explain that if Metternich has anything to add, he attracts my attention by licking his bum. You don't have to do that if you don't want to. You can just cough, or raise a finger in the air, something of that nature.'

'You're so good to me and I do appreciate it,' said Jacquie. 'But what's good enough for the cat is good enough for me.'

'As long as you're sure,' he said. 'Where was I?'

'Foul or coop,' she precised.

Maxwell found this confusing for a second and then was back on track. 'The next question applies to either situation. Did she go with someone from the trip?'

Jacquie made a slurping noise and half-heartedly lifted a leg.

'That's not going to do it, Miss Pfeiffer. Catwoman, you ain't. Shall we take it as read?'

'Please,' Jacquie said. Her admiration for cats had gone up a notch. 'No one else on the trip has disappeared.'

'No, not *yet*. But what if they do later?'

'Oh, I see. You mean, they have been planning it and this is the first phase.' She thought for a moment. 'That won't work, Max. There's no one she knows; the Medlicotts have only been in Leighford five minutes. And anyway, there aren't enough men to choose from. There's only you and Guy.'

'Both of us fine examples of our sex, if you don't mind my mentioning it.'

She smiled at him and was quiet for a moment, trying to imagine either of them playing away from home. 'You're both lovely,' she conceded, perhaps a little too slowly for Maxwell's liking, 'but out of the frame for more reasons than I can possibly give, in the time available.'

'I'll overlook your obvious cynicism there, Mrs Maxwell. But you're wrong about the numbers. What about Jim? Or Barton Joseph?'

'*Jim?* Jacquie was incredulous. 'He's as old as the hills and as thick as a plank.'

'I think I could give him a few years,' Maxwell said, quietly. 'Thick I will grant you.'

'For goodness sake, Max,' she relaxed into crossness to hide her confusion. 'You know what I mean. He is old; a million years older than you. He can't remember ... well, anything. Izzy's first husband was older, from what I can gather, but unless she has a really bad case of gerontophilia, then I can't see that Jim would attract her.'

'Gerontophilia. Coo.' Maxwell was impressed; it wasn't a word one had much opportunity to use. 'I'm so proud.'

'Look, you old git,' she said tartly. 'It's something I could easily be cured of, so watch your step. But Barton Joseph, now, that is interesting.'

'Yes, I agree, in that they are more of an age. But they don't seem to have had much to say to each other. And he is an Islander and I don't think she is.'

'Tom said they had come from Northampton,' Jacquie volunteered. 'But that might just mean most recently. But surely, he would have known if she came from the Isle of Wight? Wouldn't it have been mentioned, for example, when Jim was getting lost?'

'Yes, it would, but not if she was trying to hide it, prior to running off with Barton.' Maxwell clutched at an invisible straw that blew past on the light wind from the sea. 'I agree it sounds a bit improbable.'

'The whole thing is improbable,' Jacquie said. 'On a school trip, isn't it more usual to lose one of the kids?'

Maxwell sat bolt upright and cocked his head, as if to listen. 'Don't even say it,' he whispered. 'It's bad luck. Like saying "Macbeth" in a theatre. Just say "lose a Scotsman", anything but ... what you said.' He shuddered. 'Ooh, I can practically hear the wolves in the undergrowth. Dhuh!' He shuddered again and settled back in his chair. 'Again, I must ask. Where was I?'

'Improbably running away with Barton or Jim,' she again gave him the gist.

'You know, you're almost as good at this as Metternich,' Maxwell complimented her. 'Yes, I think it is too unlikely. But that doesn't mean to say she hasn't run off.'

'No.' Jacquie had intended her tone to convey agreement, that of course she had just run off, to buy time to empty the current account at least before clearing off with her new love, for a life of idleness in Brazil. But somehow, she didn't quite pull it off and Maxwell was on it like a dog on a bone.

'But you don't think she has run off.' In the

149

dark, he couldn't read her face in detail, but if ever a man knew his wife's body language, that man was Peter Maxwell. 'You think she has been abducted.'

'Or something like that, yes,' she agreed.

'Something like being abducted? Is there anything else like being abducted?'

'Yes.' Jacquie's reply was blunt, short and to the point. 'I think that the thing like being abducted is being set upon whilst having a bedtime stroll and being killed. It just remains to find out where it happened, who did it and where the body is. And if you think I'm being melodramatic...'

'Which I don't, by the way,' Maxwell thought it wise to add.

'Thank you. But if you did, I would reply that I have been in the police for a very long time. I think I can recognise a fishy situation when I see one.'

'As always,' Maxwell said, 'I bow to your experience.' He suited the action to the words.

'Also,' Jacquie said, 'I've got a bad feeling about this. That's talking as a woman now, not a woman policeman. Something just feels wrong, somehow. Like a dream.' She finished her drink in one. 'And now I'm going to bed.'

Maxwell stood up and pushed back his chair. Southern Comfort was not for chugging back in one; he raised his glass to her to show how much he had left and waved it to the edge of the decking. 'I'll just watch the sea for a minute, in case it does something exciting,' he said. 'Then I'll be up.' He leant down for her kiss and watched her pick her way through the tables to the door. Somehow, he just wanted to see her safely inside.

He wandered over to the rail and, leaning on it, watched the waves lap the sand. Very few people were still out and about; those who were were walking to their cars or watching the sea, like Maxwell. In the light from the street lamps and the moon, he could see half-submerged sandcastles, soft and blurred by the action of the water. Dotted along the Esplanade were booths which during the day sold candyfloss, ice cream, buckets and spades. In the daylight, they were brightly coloured, flags flying from their roofs and every possible beach commodity hung from the walls. Now, in the dark, their colours were bleached and the shadows they threw across the sand were black as pitch – a small army could have hidden there, having crept along in the lee of the sea wall, and they could be ready to leap any moment at an unsuspecting teacher finishing his drink all alone.

Or there could be a body concealed there, wrapped in canvas, under a pile of waiting deck-chairs. Or it could be curled up, stiff with rigor, in a cardboard box which had once held several gross of brightly coloured buckets, spades or inflatable ducks.

A spiteful little wind came dancing along the Esplanade, driving discarded chip wrappers before it. Sand devils rose and fell as it passed. It reached Maxwell and lifted his hair and raised goosebumps on his arms. He shivered and muttered to himself as he turned for the shelter of the hotel.

'Something wicked this way comes.'

Chapter Ten

As Sylvia Matthews boarded the coach outside the hotel on Friday morning, all boxes ticked, all kids stowed, all luggage present and accounted for, she couldn't help but scan the sky for signs of showers of frogs, pigs flying in tight formation or other unnatural phenomena. True, a member of the party had disappeared. Twice. But it wasn't a child; it wasn't even an actual member of staff. And Sylvia comforted herself with the thought that the woman was probably no better than she should be and had simply taken herself off because she wasn't getting on with her husband. She settled into her seat and leant forward to tap the driver into action. Beside her sat an excited Nolan, travelling with the big children at last. He had scarcely acknowledged Jacquie's goodbyes as he took his place in the queue to get on the coach and was solemnly ticked off the list by Sylvia.

Maxwell had finally cracked and told Pansy to ring Leighford High. He was fully aware that James Diamond, Bernard Ryan and their small army of flying monkeys couldn't organise a piss-up in a brewery, but at least he could say, hand on heart, 'But I *did* inform you of the missing staff member, Headmaster, technically while we were still on the Isle of Wight.' He gave Pansy clear instructions that, should the Headmaster wish to speak to him personally, he was incom-

152

municado, as they called the toilets on the Red Funnel ferry service.

Without Barton Joseph riding shotgun, Jim the driver wasn't quite so confident, but even so, they reached the ferry in plenty of time and suddenly Year Seven, tired of being angels, scattered from the coach like ants from a poked nest, and so the leaving of East Cowes was not the sophisticated affair they had planned, involving as it did running, shouting and threats. The crossing was no better and it was only after Maxwell had held them and assorted passengers spellbound, if a little queasy, with his graphic reconstruction of keelhauling that order began to be restored.

And all too soon, for Year Seven, but not half soon enough for their minders, the coach was on its way to the paradise that was Leighford, no doubt, to paraphrase G.K. Chesterton, by way of Kensal Green. Maxwell looked around for the ginger kid. Although his money was on him for the last to be collected, he would have chosen Jazmyn, given first pick. He must therefore pounce now, while the pouncing was good. He ambled up the coach, making random small talk with various Year Seveners until he got to his target, his sunburn now beginning finally to subside in a riot of freckle and peel.

'Budge up,' he said in a friendly tone and the child and his seat companion squeezed as far in towards the window as they could. 'So,' Maxwell said, chattily, 'have you enjoyed yourselves?'

'It was great, Mr Maxwell,' the non-ginger kid said, breathlessly. 'I had a brilliant time. I never knew red squirrels were real, but I saw loads.'

'I saw one squashed on the road,' said his carroty companion. 'It was...' he leafed through his trusty notebook, 'on Thursday.' He held the book out to Maxwell. 'Look.'

And there, in glorious Technicolor, was a drawing of a red squirrel, tongue and giblets lolling out, a tyre mark across its little white chest. Beside it was written, 'Red sqiruel. Sqassed nere our hotel. 15.45.'

Maxwell smiled and took the book from the lad. Accurate,' he said. 'I like that. Can I have a look?' and he flicked through. Not everything was illustrated in quite such detail, but almost every event of the holiday was there. Including, right at the beginning, something that made his knuckles whiten.

'Wensdy. 23.04. I had chips and a baterd sosage today for my lunch and I shud hav et my sandwiches becuz it disagred with me. I got up to the toylit and wen I looked out uv the windo I saw Mrs Medlycoat in the street. She wuz talking to sumbodi and was pointin.'

Maxwell turned the book over to read the name on the front. He raised an eyebrow. 'Your notes are very thorough, Gervaise,' he said, smiling.

The ginger kid looked frantically from side to side. 'Don't call me that, sir. Not doing vat "jjjuuurrr" thing at the front. It's gay, vat is. My mum calls me Jarvis. Like Cocker, you know what I mean?'

Obviously, Maxwell had no idea what he meant. To him, Cocker was a spaniel, but he gave a small mental salute to Mrs – he turned the book over once again – Potter, to hear the name

154

'Jarvis' and spell it the way she had. The woman had class, to go with her basic illiteracy. 'All right, Jarvis. Sorry. My mistake. So, as I say, your notes are very thorough.' He flicked through a few more pages. 'But I notice you don't say anything about where Mrs Medlicott went next.'

'Well, I wen' back to bed, dinn' I?'

'You weren't curious, at all? Wondered why she was there?'

'Na.'

And that was it. A simple denial. All adults were boring and that was the way of the world. Gervaise went back to his other hobby of investigating his nostril.

'Do you have your other notebook on you, Jarvis?'

'Yeah.' The child foraged in his bag and brought out a woefully stained and crumpled book. He handed it over trustingly to Maxwell, who tucked it into the other and rose to go.

''Ere,' Gervaise complained. 'I need vat. For ve test.'

Maxwell leant down. 'Well, I'll let you into a little secret, Jarvis.' The child looked up so trustingly that Maxwell suddenly didn't have the heart to tell him that the test had always been a work of fiction. 'I have been so busy, what with one thing and another, I forgot to take any notes. So, if I may borrow yours, to mark the others' work, if you see what I mean, I'll let you off the test. Is that all right?'

'Yeah!' Gervaise bounced in his seat, nudging his companion. Then his brow furrowed. 'I get a mark vo?'

155

'My dear lad, of course,' Maxwell said, patting his shoulder. 'An A, I shouldn't wonder.'

Gervaise Potter was completely happy. He sighed and sat back in his seat. An A! His mum would be so proud. If she remembered to pick him up this time, his day would be complete.

Maxwell made his way to the front of the coach. He really had to let Jacquie know this development as soon as possible. It would make a huge difference to what she had to tell to the Island police. He went and sat next to Sylvia, hoisting Nolan, to his chagrin, onto his lap to make room.

The boy wriggled down. 'Dads,' he hissed. 'Don't forget I'm a big boy now.'

'Sorry, mate. I forgot. Why don't you go along down the coach and sit with one of the girls. Camilla, she's a nice girl, isn't she?'

Nolan wasn't that sure, now that all of the Maltesers had been eaten, but he was an amenable child and trotted off down the coach to cries of delight from the more maternal little girls. Sylvia craned round the side of the seat to watch him safely stowed.

'That child is a delight, Max,' she said. 'If you could have put in an order for what you wanted, you couldn't have done better.'

Maxwell allowed himself a small preen before giving Jacquie all the credit. 'Genetics, Sylv, and a sensible mother. That's all it takes. But, look at this.' He gave her Gervaise's notebook and pointed to the relevant bit.

She read it incredulously. 'We must let Jacquie know at once,' she said. "Where's your phone?'

'Don't be silly,' he said. 'It's at home. Why

156

would I carry a phone when I'm on holiday with Jacquie?'

She looked at him with her eyebrows raised almost into her hair. 'How about because you are running a school trip? For goodness sake, Max. You don't surprise me often, but, when you do... Never mind. Use mine.' She leant over and pulled hers from her pocket. 'Oh.'

'Oh?' Maxwell was intrigued. She sounded at a bit of a loss and that wasn't like his Sylvia.

'I've never seen that before,' she said and held out the instrument. The screen was cracked clear across the middle. Above it was a swirling pattern resembling the Northern Lights. Below it was just plain. She leant across again. 'I think I know what caused it,' she said, holding out a small pebble with one perfect ammonite, tiny as a baby's fingernail, embedded in it.

'I suppose they aren't built to withstand fossils,' Maxwell said knowledgably, and not only because he was one. He couldn't help but feel a touch smug. 'I expect Guy has a phone?' he asked.

'Well, yes,' Sylvia said. She called down the bus to her husband and he made his way towards her, hand over hand as the coach racketed along the A27.

'Yes, Ms Matthews,' he said, formally. 'Can I help?'

'Have you got your phone?'

He held it out. 'What's wrong with yours?' As he spoke he caught sight of it in her hand. 'I've never seen that before,' he said. 'What did that?'

'A fossil,' Maxwell said, happily. 'We need to get in touch with Jacquie urgently. Can you give her

157

a call?'

'Sure.' He raised the phone to prepare to dial. 'What's her number?'

Maxwell looked blank. 'I have no idea? Sylv?'

She gestured helplessly to the phone in her hand. 'It's in here,' she said.

'Oh, Sylv,' Guy said. 'How many times have I told you to write them down as well. Do you remember when you lost it and–?'

'Yes, yes, that's enough.' Sylvia, famously organised school nurse as she was, could see her reputation being in tatters by the end of this episode. 'Never mind, I expect I have the number here, on my list.' She scanned down it. 'No. Just yours, Mr Maxwell.' She turned to glare at him as if it was his fault.

'What about Tom Medlicott?' Guy was definitely on song today.

Maxwell clicked his fingers. 'Of course. Do you have his number?'

Again, Sylvia scanned the list and slammed her hand down in frustration. 'No,' she sighed. 'Just the dratted school mobile number. And I know the battery on that old piece of rubbish died on Tuesday with no hope of recovery.'

'So,' Maxwell said, just to be clear, 'We can't get in touch with either of them?'

'Looks that way,' Sylvia said. Then she suddenly held up a finger. 'Darling,' she turned to Guy with a wheedling smile. 'Will your phone take my SIM?'

As far as Maxwell was concerned, she might just as well have started to recite 'Baa Baa Black Sheep' in Turkish, for all the sense it made, but

Guy seemed to understand.

'Sorry,' he grimaced. 'Locked to any other provider. I said when you took out that new contract–'

'Yes, yes,' muttered Sylvia. 'Is there anyone more annoying than the person who says they told you so?'

Both men knew better than to reply, so stayed silent.

'Phone the police station?' Guy suggested at last.

'I want to talk to Jacquie personally,' Maxwell explained. 'It's not the kind of thing I can leave as a message.'

'Well,' Sylvia said soothingly. 'We'll be back at Leighford shortly. Guy can take you home while I count them off the premises and you'll probably catch her before she gets on the ferry. I'll hang on to Nolan, if you like. I know you of old and you can't gallivant off after white elephants with a little boy with you. Though, I suppose Jacquie would say that would be a good thing.' She looked round at him. 'It's no good pulling that face, my lad,' she said, to the joy of Jazmyn, earwigging from the seat immediately behind them. 'We'll have to make the best of a bad job, that's all.'

Maxwell knew she was feeling cross with herself for letting him down, even though none of it was her fault. So he smiled and squeezed her arm and they sat watching the road getting more and more familiar until, with a triumphant and slightly surprised squeal of brakes, Jim pulled up outside Leighford High School.

Had the plan of Jacquie's morning been laid out alongside that of Maxwell, Sylvia and the rest, hers would, on first glance, have appeared to be much easier. Get Tom Medlicott up and dressed. Encourage him to have breakfast. Go to police station to report his wife missing. After that, the plan consisted of a row of dots. Getting Tom up was not so difficult. She had shoved him into the bathroom and firmly shut the door. She had sorted out one complete set of clothes, packed the rest and removed the suitcase to the car before he came out, rightly guessing that making a decision on what to wear might be a bridge too far. She had then gone back up the stairs to meet him and get him down for breakfast. All this was carefully timed so as not to coincide with the movements of the mass of Leighford High School. It would be bad enough for him to go back to school anyway, as go he must, without the memory for Year Seven of him being led by the nose by Mrs Maxwell.

He ate a good breakfast, everything being taken all in all. Whether he tasted any of it or not was another matter, but as far as Jacquie was concerned it was fuel, and it would come in handy later on if he could go through an interview with the police without fainting.

It seemed strange to walk out of a hotel without checking out and Jacquie briefly felt like a con-man as she walked Tom Medlicott down to the car as though walking him to the gallows. He sat beside her, silently. It wasn't that he was thinking deeply, or sulking, it was just that he could no longer be bothered to speak. She tried small talk. She tried the radio. In the end, she relied on the

160

satnav for conversation.

'In one hundred yards, bear left. In fifty yards, bear left. Correcting route. Please turn round when it is safe to do so.'

Poor thing, it had never really recovered from apparently driving on water. She almost replied to it, just to comfort its poor little silicon brain.

Suddenly, he spoke. 'Is that the police station?' he asked.

'Yes,' she said, reversing deftly into a parking space. She glanced up at the sign. 'Have you got any change? It's pay and display.'

'Surely I don't have to pay,' he said, in dead tones. 'My wife is missing.'

'Well, yes,' Jacquie conceded. 'But that might be a little difficult to convey in a note to the traffic warden. Never mind, I've got some.' She put in the maximum amount, although surely, she thought, this won't take two hours.

And she was right. Filling in the forms took a matter of minutes and, with a promise that the details would be passed on to the Missing Persons Bureau, they were back on the street. Here, Tom Medlicott seemed to come to life.

'That's it?' he asked. 'That's *it?*'

'I don't know what else you were expecting, Tom,' she said. 'They filled in the forms. Izzy is an adult, with no learning difficulties, medical problems, mental issues, financial issues or anything that makes her high risk. You saw that they had a note on file from my boss, Henry Hall, telling them that I would be doing preliminary work on the case, and I have. I know that DCI Hall will have been round to check your home address.' She could hear herself becoming pompous, but it was unstoppable by now. 'Now, we're getting on the ferry and we're going home.'

'No!' Tom shouted and made several startled shoppers turn and stare. 'I'm staying here.'

'And how will that help, Tom?' Jacquie was beginning to get, if not angry, then at least very frustrated. 'You can't stay at the hotel, because it will be filling up with a new school party within hours. You don't have a car, because, whether you are with me or not, I'm going to be on the first ferry I can squeeze on to. As far as I know, you have no real influence with the RNLI or the coastguard, so a trip round the Island looking at cliffs isn't on any real agenda as far as I can see. And finally...' Jacquie had run out of steam and she leant her forehead on his shoulder, 'I don't know what is finally, but I do know we've done all we can.'

He sighed, a sigh that seemed to come from a subterranean cavern deep in his soul. He leant his head on hers and almost whispered. 'You're right. Let's go home.'

She hugged him tight and could hear his heart beating fast. A mother pulled her toddler out of the way. Honestly! The way people behaved in the street these days. And they weren't kids either. They ought to know better, and just out-side the police station as well. The woman made the noise that can only be spelt as 'Tcha!'

'Come on, Tom,' Jacquie said, pulling gently away. 'We're making people go "Tcha" and that will never do. Come on,' and taking his hand as though he were a child, she led him over the road to the car.

On the ferry, Jacquie feigned sleep to distance herself from Tom Medlicott and felt as low as a worm for doing so. Tom Medlicott meanwhile was feigning sleep to get away not just from Jacquie but from the world, which had suddenly become very big and hard to take. He couldn't bear to look back. He had done that for hours the previous night, trying to identify that microsecond when Izzy chose to leave him. He couldn't look forward, because that meant facing getting in the car which they had left parked at Leighford High, moving the seat back to accommodate his longer legs – Izzy had driven them to catch the coach. It meant driving back to the house, the house they had only lived in for a few months but which already bore Izzy's traces; the smell of perfume in the bedroom, the pack of her favourite tea on the worktop in the kitchen. The tears squeezed past his closed eyelids and rolled down his cheeks and ran on, unheeded, until they soaked into his collar. He didn't think he could still have tears, he had shed so many. He tried to tell himself that he was mourning a woman who was almost certainly alive and well and laughing at him with some other man somewhere. But even thoughts can ring hollow and the tears still fell.

Izzy Medlicott lay across a huge boulder which, despite its size, had been tossed up by the power of the tide long years ago. Its lower edge where it met the dry, sandy mud at the bottom of the cliff was blurred with moss and it felt warm in the sun. It hadn't been lapped by the sea for months; only a winter storm would reach it now. She was curled up, apart from one arm that was lolling off the edge of the rock, the palm upturned, the fingers slightly bent. Caught in the fingers, trapped under a broken nail, was some grass and one flower of the sea pink which flowered all around and above up to the cliff edge. She seemed to be examining the tiny posy she held out for the bobbing gulls to see. She lay neat and tidy; Izzy Medlicott was always neat, always tidy. Her hair lifted slightly in the breeze, but always fell back, each lock in its appointed place. She could have been resting, taking in the still-warm rays of the late summer sun. She could have been sleeping, were it not for her eyes, which were wide open. She could have been alive, were it not for her neck, which had been broken, neatly, by a single blow, back there, up on the cliff top.

Chapter Eleven

Maxwell and Guy Minter were almost back to Columbine before Maxwell remembered a vital fact. He had no door key. To be fair to him, he had had no reason to bring one. He was with his wife and child. Mrs Troubridge was feeding Metternich, and as this had to be done in his own bowl in its designated corner of the kitchen, she had a key. The 'other key', as Maxwell knew it. Now she was in the hospital and Metternich was in the cattery, there was no way of getting in the house.

'I'm sorry, Guy,' Maxwell apologised. 'I just didn't think. Mrs Troubridge never goes anywhere. I've never really had to bother.' Another reason to miss the mad old trout, Maxwell thought to himself.

'Hold on, though. Don't you have a cleaner? From the school?' Guy was proving that he *did* listen to what Sylvia said.

'We do, yes, we do. Mrs B. Wonderful woman. She also picks up the key from Mrs Troubridge.'

'Ah.' Guy pulled in to the side. 'I wonder if there is any reason to go any further if you can't get in to your house?' he said, quite reasonably.

'My dear chap, of course. You're right. You can drop me off here.' Maxwell prepared to get out of the car, albeit a trifle puzzled; it really wasn't like Guy to be so inhospitable.

'No, no.' Guy restrained the Head of Sixth Form by hanging on to his arm. 'Don't be daft, Max. It's just that it would be a waste of your time to be delivered to a house you can't get in to – would you like me to take you somewhere else?'

Maxwell pondered. They had more friends now that Nolan was in the social whirl, but there was no one he would choose to go to in a crisis. Except Sylvia and Guy, and obviously they weren't a choice on this occasion. The others all had several children at least and their houses seemed to Maxwell to be in a state of barely controlled hysteria. They made the couple in *Outnumbered* look like model parents. 'No, not really ... wait a minute, though.' He broke off. 'Has Sylvia explained about the notebook?'

'Briefly.' Guy was always cagey when it came to the passing on of possibly confidential information. He had learnt the hard way it was better to say nothing than the wrong thing. In fact, he knew as much as either Maxwell or Sylvia about the notebook, but could always listen again.

'Well, it is clear that Gervaise – pronounced "Jarvis", by the way, if it ever crops up – saw Izzy outside the hotel on the Night In Question, late. And, as you know, I don't have Jacquie's number to hand. But Henry Hall will have it, won't he? He also knows a bit about Izzy's disappearance. So, the cop shop, if you would be so good.' Maxwell settled back in his seat and did up the seat belt once more.

Now Guy was in a major dilemma. He knew that Jacquie had been warned about Maxwell getting involved. People who confided in Sylvia were often confiding, all unknowingly, with Guy as well. Sylvia was Jacquie's hole in the ground, her confessional, her all-hearing ear when Maxwell was the issue. She had loved him before Jacquie came on the scene, before Guy had turned her life upside down. She was the only person Jacquie knew who loved Mad Max as much as she did, warts and all, and was Maxwell's listening post too, and so she often knew more about what was going on than either Jacquie or Maxwell did themselves. But Guy also knew that Maxwell could no more help getting involved than breathe. Plus, it was important that Jacquie got the information from the notebook as soon as possible, preferably while she was still on the Island. But, a visit from Maxwell to Henry Hall could seriously jeopardise Jacquie's promotion. As in, cancel it, pretend it never was born. He sighed. Decisions weren't his forte. He let the handbrake off and eased back into the traffic, on his way to the police station. When all other decision-making tools let you down, there was always one on which you could rely. Peter Maxwell would do just precisely what he wanted, so you might as well save your breath.

'So, Henry,' Maxwell said, after filling Jacquie's boss in on the situation, 'that's about it, really. Oh, thanks for visiting Metternich, by the way.'

'You're welcome,' Hall said. 'How did you know I've visited him?'

Maxwell pointed to his wrist, where a pair of parallel scratches disappeared under his cuff. 'His calling card.' It was an excellent Basil Rathbone.

167

Hall rubbed his arm reminiscently and said, 'He has a way with him, that's for sure. Still, I think he was grateful.'

'I'm sure he was. As are we all. And thanks for looking after Mrs Troubridge as well.'

'That's a bit different,' Hall said and Maxwell waited for details, which he knew deep down would never come. 'So you want to borrow my phone to call Jacquie?'

'That would be very good of you,' Maxwell said. 'I'm hoping to catch her before she gets on the ferry, that's all.'

'Yes, I do see.' Hall was being even less scrutable than usual.

'I mean, I wouldn't have got involved, as a rule.' Maxwell tried an ingratiating smile, strength 4 on the Rictus scale. It got no response at all. 'We have agreed, after all, that an investigation is no place for me.' Looking at Hall's poker face he could feel the hysterical laugh massing its forces behind his tonsils. 'But ... as sometimes happens, I ... came upon a clue...' He gave up. It was like pulling teeth.

Hall silently handed him his mobile. 'It's ringing,' he said and swung round in his chair, so that Maxwell had to pretend he was alone whilst looking at the back of someone's head.

'DS Carpenter.' The background noise was appalling, but Maxwell couldn't work out quite where Jacquie was.

'Darling?' he said. 'Jacquie? Where the devil are you?'

'Darling?' Jacquie held the phone away from her head to check on the incoming number. 'Guv, are you all right?'

'Guv? No, no, sweetness. It's me. Max. I'm using Henry's phone.'

'I can see that. Or hear, perhaps I should say. Why are you on Henry's phone?' A small creeping sense of foreboding made its way down Jacquie's spine. 'Where are you, Max?'

He tried to make his tone light and playful. He knew what he had done wrong, but, like a puppy who has weed yet again on the floor, hadn't been able to stop himself. 'I'm in Henry's office, precious. But I had to get in touch with you, it's really important, and I couldn't get in to the house and ... well, it was very difficult. I needed to get in touch with you before you caught the ferry.'

'Too late,' she said, shortly. 'As you can probably hear from the combined noise of about a dozen school parties, all worse than ours, and a million old ladies complaining about the cost of tea and a cake, I am on the ferry. I'll speak to you when I get home.' And she cut the connection.

Like most people who have been hung up on, Maxwell carried on the conversation. 'Righty-ho, dear,' he chirped. 'See you later.' He pressed what was almost certainly the wrong button and handed the phone back to Henry Hall, who had twirled back to face him across the desk. 'She'll see me later,' he explained.

Hall's face was still poker. 'I expect she will,' he said. He reached for the desk phone and raised an eyebrow. 'Coffee? There's something I would like to chew over with you, if you have a minute.'

Maxwell looked around him for the candid camera. It wasn't often he heard those words from any police person, even the one he kept at

169

home for his own amusement. To hear them from Henry Hall was quite disorienting. 'Coffee would be ... no, hold on. The coffee here tastes of tea, doesn't it?'

'When it doesn't taste of cocoa, yes,' Hall agreed.

'Cocoa it is, then,' Maxwell said and sat back, waiting to be amazed.

When it came, the cocoa, not absolutely un-expectedly, tasted of Oxo. But Maxwell was parched, so any old beverage in a storm. He sipped it, put down the styrofoam cup and leant back, arms folded. Henry Hall did exactly the same. *Mano-a-mano*.

'First of all,' Henry Hall kicked the convers-ation off, 'I want to make something totally clear. That by having this conversation, you are not involved in an investigation of any kind. Not that this is an investigation. It's just a chat.'

Maxwell inclined his head, somewhat regally. 'Absolutely, Henry. A chat.'

'So anything that I tell you is just for infor-mation for helping you to understand what I say. You are not to remember it, repeat it, use it to your own or anyone else's advantage, in any shape or form.'

Maxwell was getting a little testy. He had never forgotten anything in his life, so telling him not to remember something was like telling him to fly out of the window; totally impossible. 'Henry, let's just take it as read. What's it all about?'

'Well, Mrs Troubridge.'

Maxwell slumped. He had thought it was something exciting. 'What about her?'

'Well – and I have to tell you, Max, I'm on my

own here – I don't think she fell. I think she was pushed. In fact, I'd go further–'

Maxwell felt obliged to intervene. 'Henry, she has been a broken hip waiting to happen for years. There isn't ten penn'orth of her and she dashes around like something demented in slippers made for a much, *much* bigger woman.'

'And has she ever fallen over before?' Hall raised an eyebrow.

'Well, no, but, as I say, she's a broken–'

'Granted, old ladies break bits and bobs every day. She has a broken hip, as you know. She also has a rather good collection of bruises, quite literally from head to toe. And they all fit in with the fall, the doctors tell me.' Henry Hall started to fiddle with a pencil on his desk, rolling it back and forth.

'But?'

'But I think she was attacked and then thrown down the stairs to make it look like an accident. Whoever did it showed great attention to detail. One slipper on, one at the top of the stairs, that kind of thing.'

'The kind of thing you find after a fall?' asked Maxwell, gently.

'Again, granted.' Hall leant forward, rolling his pencil before him like some tiny siege weapon. 'Have you ever sat at a bedside?'

'Certainly have,' Maxwell said, smiling ruefully.

'Boring, isn't it?'

Maxwell nodded and smiled. 'Yes. And you feel really guilty about being bored, too.'

'Yes,' Hall said. There was a moment of silent shared memories, then Hall continued. 'I got

171

chatting to a nurse. You know, to break the silence. Lady Elizabeth Molester is a very quiet ward.'

Maxwell didn't doubt it.

'The nurse happened to have been the one who got Mrs Troubridge ready for her bed when she was admitted.'

Maxwell was leaning forward now as well. It wasn't so much that Henry Hall was a great story-teller as that his timing on a punchline bordered on Maxwellian in its precision. 'Yes?' he breathed.

'Her slipper,' Hall said, leaning back triumph-antly and throwing his pencil in the air, 'was on the wrong foot.' He missed the pencil and it rolled away under his desk, but nothing could steal the moment as the two men's minds sud-denly met in the middle.

'Henry, have you ever seen an absolutely terrible film starring Robert Mitchum called *One Shoe Makes It Murder?*' Maxwell asked.

'I can't say that I have.'

'Well,' Maxwell said, sadly, 'I have, and that's an hour and a half I'll never get back. But, that said, it's right, isn't it?'

'Well,' said Hall, '*I* think so. It's getting anyone else to agree with me that I'm finding difficult. It's not just the slipper, of course. I've seen Mrs Troubridge skipping around like a two-year-old myself and she just doesn't seem the type to go base over apex down a flight of stairs. And it's not as if she doesn't know the house like the back of her hand. How long has she lived there?'

'Since they were built,' Maxwell said. 'Some-times I think that perhaps she was there even

172

before that. Living under a hedge, cooking up potions.' He paused, fingers to lip. 'But who would want to hurt her? I mean, *I* do, regularly, but that's just because ... well, just because she's Mrs Troubridge, really. She loves us, that's why she's always there, waiting when I go in, waiting when I go out. Having Nole in for chocolate biscuits ten minutes before his tea... She is going to be all right, isn't she?' Suddenly, a Troubridge-less Columbine seemed a bleak prospect.

'She's had her hip pinned,' Henry told him. 'She comes to occasionally but she seems very shocked. She counts a lot, in her sleep. And cries out.' He saw Maxwell's stricken expression. 'She's on a drip, though, morphine, so that might have something to do with it.'

Maxwell reran the earlier part of Henry's remarks. 'Counts a lot?'

'Yes. Very high numbers. Quite garbled. Does she have money worries, I was wondering? Bills preying on her mind.' Henry Hall was clutching at straws.

'Do you know, I have no idea. She never seems hard up, but how can you be sure? I would imagine she has pensions, from Mr Troubridge. Plus her father, Mr Troubridge...' Maxwell looked up and saw the startled question starting to form in Henry Hall's mouth. 'No, Henry,' Maxwell held up a hand, 'don't let's go there or we'll never come out the other side. Her father was, or so I believe, quite successful in his day.'

'Well then, that might remain Mrs Troubridge's secret,' Hall said. 'But even so, I think someone gave her a shove ... at least.'

173

'Why "at least"?' Maxwell was pretty sure why, but he wanted Henry to say it first.

'Because of the slipper. Why would she be wearing just one on the wrong foot? And if it was intended as a sort of clue to why she fell, how could the person who shoved her make sure she was wearing the slipper before she fell? It had to be put on afterwards, when she had been chucked down the stairs.'

'I agree,' Maxwell said, slapping the desk and making the scummy cocoa, undrunk in their cups, jump inside its skin. 'So...' He got up. 'What next?'

'Next,' said Hall, not moving, 'is that I say thank you for your time and you go home. How did you get here? Would you like a car back to the house?'

There was so much more to be said, so many words and ideas massing in Maxwell's head that, for a moment, he just sat there. There must be something that would whet Henry Hall's appetite. To fill some time, he said, 'Wouldn't you like to know why I needed to get in touch with Jacquie?'

'I'm sure that's your business.' Hall's tone was wintry. Maxwell had heard it before. It was the tone usually employed by people who suddenly realised that they had told Peter Maxwell far more than they should. Most of them needn't have worried. Maxwell didn't waste his time in idle gossip, so if, as was usually the case, the things they told him had no bearing on anything important, they may just as well have whispered the words into a hole in the ground, safe in the knowledge that the world would never know that, like King Midas, they had ass's ears. But some of them, as in the current case, had told him something important, something he would worry at and dissect until the last useful bit of substance had been found and applied to the problem at hand, sometimes to their own disadvantage.

Maxwell soldiered on. 'I had found something out about our missing person,' he said, and paused, trying to read Hall's face. He might as well have been trying to read *Ulysses* translated into Sanskrit, for all the help that blank collection of features gave him. 'One of our kids saw her in the street on the night before her husband found her missing.'

Hall leant forward. His voice was quiet. 'You questioned a child?' he asked, incredulous. 'Without parental permission?' This wasn't the worst sin, on a scale of one to ten, but it was certainly ranked quite high. In the course of things, however, it was what Peter Maxwell did every day. How else can you gauge the little buggers' grasp of historical knowledge?

'Of course not!' Maxwell was careful to keep his indignation down to a dull roar. Hall could recognise too much protestation at a hundred yards and the distance today was just a couple of feet. 'He had a homework notebook and I happened to glance at it.'

'Useful,' Hall remarked, drily. 'Do the other kids' notebooks contain anything useful?'

Maxwell realised he was in the trap just as the door clanged shut. 'No,' he tried a chuckle, but it sounded hollow. 'Gervaise was the only one who was keeping a diary.'

'Hmm.' Hall was impressed. 'Keen student, is he, this...?'

'Gervaise pronounced "Jarvis",' Maxwell realised that Hall already knew this. 'I mean Jarvis, spelt "Gervaise", Potter. Very keen student, yes. Ginger.' The last word popped out without Maxwell's permission.

Hall knew his Maxwell. 'I see. Having fun with the ginger kid, Mr Maxwell? Jacquie has mentioned your hobby.'

'Painting model soldiers?' Maxwell asked, hopefully.

'No.' Hall inclined his head slightly, his version of a friendly smile. 'It's people with mullets, for me. It's becoming quite difficult, though, as they get rarer. Makes it more fun.' Maxwell was struck at how Hall seemed to have difficulty with the word. 'However, it still sounds to me that you may have compromised evidence.'

Maxwell chewed his lip briefly, then said, 'It doesn't need to be evidence as such, though, does it? Isn't it more in the way of being a clue? You know, to help us pinpoint when she disappeared. What she was wearing, that sort of thing.'

Hall agreed and said so; that was one of his most endearing traits, as Jacquie never tired of telling Maxwell. One of his least endearing was that he then minimised its impact. 'We won't need clues, though, will we, when her husband gets home and finds her there?'

Maxwell's heart did a little flutter. 'You've checked? She's home? Why on earth...?'

Hall silenced him with a flapped hand. 'No, no, we haven't checked. I'm just outlining the most likely scenario. More missing people turn up safely than stay missing.'

Still Maxwell stayed sitting. 'I really have a bad feeling about this one, though, Henry.'

Hall changed the subject, although only slightly. 'Has Jacquie told you about her promotion prospects?'

'Umm ... yes,' Maxwell knew where this was going and didn't like the view from the bridge.

'Good,' Hall said, getting up. 'That's very good. So, I think we're done in that case, Max, aren't we?' He advanced on Maxwell in a kind of one-man pincer movement and had his man at the door in commendably few moves. Maxwell was impressed. He used the same technique himself, daily, and knew a master of the art when he saw one.

'But, Henry...' Maxwell found himself talking to the door. Gathering his dignity about him and hoping that it had become a cloak of invisibility, he swept down the corridor, down the stairs and out into the car park, where Guy Minter was sitting, faithful as an elephant. And he hadn't even been in the room.

In his office, Henry Hall sat pensively for a moment behind his desk. Then, he seemed to come to a decision and picked up the phone. 'Bob? DCI Hall. Are you busy?'

'Well, guv, I–'

'Good. Could you just go to the file and bring me the incoming faxes and emails on national suspicious deaths for the last ... let's say, month. Don't worry about weeding out the ones they solve later. I want everything, as they were sent out.'

'That's huge, guv! I'm in the middle–'

'Bring a trolley, then,' Hall said shortly. 'Don't want you to hurt that back again, do we? And don't forget your glasses.'

Sergeant Bob Thorogood sighed and went to do his master's bidding. The sooner Jacquie Carpenter got back the better. This job was too much like hard work without her to do the guvnor's little bits and pieces. And what was he up to now, anyway? Surely not anything to do with the visit from Maxwell, the Copper's Curse? He reached up and paused, hoping for a twinge from his dodgy disc, but nothing doing. Piling the files onto a trolley he announced to the world in general that he was off to do some special work with DCI Hall.

'Good luck with that,' muttered a PC, up to her armpits in paperwork, having been unlucky enough to be the nearest beat officer when some underage drinkers had kicked off in the shopping centre. Roll on promotion, she thought. There was still paperwork, but it had to be more interesting than this.

'Good Lord, Bob,' Hall said as the sergeant rolled his trolley into the office. 'How many files have you got there?'

The sergeant ran his finger along the spines. 'About twenty, I should say. I brought this month and all of August, to be sure.' Thorogood was about to add another 'to be sure' but could never remember where Hall stood on Irish jokes, although it was a reasonable assumption that it was in the same place as his position on jokes in general. As far away as possible.

'Hmm.' Hall was casting his mind back, using visual clues, as taught by Derren Brown, Hall's secret vice. 'I don't think we'll need the ones from the first two weeks of August and I don't think we'll ... no, I know we won't need last week's. So that gives us the very first week in September and, let's say the last two in August.' He stood up and came round the desk. Henry Hall was always prepared to muck in, especially when the files were newish and not too dusty. 'Which are they?'

Thorogood bent down and turned his head sideways. The bottom ones, of course. Weren't they always? He lifted the top ones and Hall slid out the files he wanted. There were five of them.

'Is there anyone at a loose end in the ops room?' Hall asked the sergeant.

'No one is ever at a loose end, exactly,' Thorogood replied. 'There's always something to do.' He sounded like a weird fusion of Job and Confucius. He also wanted to remind the guv'nor what it was like back on the ground.

Hall glanced up at him and Thorogood was treated to a rare view of his eyes, over the top of his glasses. They were cold as ice and almost the same colour.

'But I'll go and check, shall I, guv?'

'Good idea,' Hall congratulated him, sitting back down behind his desk with the file in front of him. 'When you get back, I'll tell you what I'm looking for, shall I?' Hall looked steadily at him until he was out of the room. Only then did the DCI mutter, 'At least, I would if I knew what it was.'

Before Henry Hall had really had time to gather his thoughts, Thorogood was back with the WPC who had been wrestling with boring paperwork. He had told her that she was being redeployed to do boring paperwork, but she couldn't believe that it could be as boring as the stuff she was doing already.

'Hello, Fran,' Hall said, for him, very cordially. 'Thanks for the offer of help. Now, if you take this file and sit over there if you can clear a space and you, Bob, if you can use the top of the trolley? Just pull up a chair. Is that the right height for your back?'

Bob Thorogood's back was the running nick joke. It threw itself out for the European Grand Prix, the Six Nations final weekend and Wimbledon. Now that the football season was well under way, it needed extra tender care. It wasn't that keen on cricket. He grimaced at his boss. 'Fine, guv, yes. Thanks.' He opened his file.

'Now we're all comfortable,' Hall said, 'I'll tell you what we're looking for.' There was a very long pause. 'The short answer is, I don't know. But something is niggling me and it needs to be found. I'll tell you what has set it off and perhaps that will help us. If you find anything that seems to fit, just sing out and we'll discuss it.'

Fran Brannon was agog. She really didn't see how Thorogood could find this boring. This was *detecting*. A future in plain clothes stretched enticingly in front of her. She'd be up there with

180

Jane Tennison and that woman in *Wire in the Blood*. And the other one in *Trial & Retribution*. She was, after all, blonde and that seemed to be their only qualification. Then she realised that DCI Hall was still speaking.

'So, I'll just recap.'

Thank goodness, Fran thought. Wouldn't do to go out in the first round. Could be Community Liaison for ever.

'Falls down stairs. That's the first thing to watch for. Old ladies, I suppose, though that might be too big a group. We'll see. Mispers, but not youngsters, I don't think. We're not talking fed-up teenagers here. And...' he tapped his teeth with his pencil, 'I know this sounds silly, but ... teachers. Either working or retired. Supply as well, I suppose.'

Bob Thorogood snorted. 'Maxwell,' he breathed. At last, he might be sussed.

'No, Bob,' Hall said stiffly. 'Not Mr Maxwell. Just teachers in general. Not necessarily the victim or suspect, just any involvement. Right? Let's go,' and he suited the action to the words and scanned down his first document, running his pencil down the margin. 'Oh,' he added. 'Perhaps if we mark a document we've checked, just a small tick in the top right-hand corner. Then, if any of us should suddenly die or go sick or something,' he glanced here at Thorogood, his face impassive, 'the replacement won't have to duplicate any effort.' He bent his head again and the two others did likewise.

For quite some time the only sound in the room was the distant hum from the rest of the building, going about its business and, overlaid on it, the soft susurration of turning paper, the occasional 'da daaa', quiet and on the edge of hearing, that signalled another tick on another useless page. Sometimes, Bob Thorogood forgot to close his mouth and the click of his drying tongue grew in volume until he remembered, closed his mouth, licked his lips and started the whole cycle off again.

Fran Brannon was the first to find something. 'What about this, DCI Hall?' She wasn't quite in the 'guv' clan yet. She snapped the file open, extracted a page and passed it to him. He took it from her and speed-read it to the bottom.

'Hmm. Old lady. Stairs. Dead at the bottom, so not much else ... no bruising. No visible injuries, just the usual broken hip.' He passed it back. 'Dehydration and exposure. The usual suspects. Not quite there, but well done.' He looked at the files in front of his staff. At least the left-hand pages now numbered more than the right. But was that a good thing or not, bearing in mind that no one had found anything yet?

Then, suddenly, Thorogood shouted, 'Yes!' and punched the air.

Hall, not given to such gestures, merely looked up and said, quietly, 'Yes?'

Thorogood didn't bother with the niceties of opening the file. He just tore the page out and handed it over. He stood, quivering in front of Hall's desk like a gun dog which has unaccountably found a hippopotamus in the undergrowth.

Again, Hall scanned the page. 'Bob,' he said, 'I think this is it.' Fran Brannon's shoulders slumped. Community Liaison it was. Hall ran his eye down the page again. 'Yes. Death from a fall. Teacher.' He thumped the desk. '*Art* teacher! That was it!' He looked up at them and any other man would have given Thorogood a high five. Instead, he decided to share information. 'Do either of you remember my mentioning the missing person on the Leighford High School trip?'

Fran nodded enthusiastically. Thorogood shrugged and gave a single nod.

'Well, Jacquie Carpenter rang me because she wasn't getting anywhere with the local boys, and fair enough, I suppose – the woman was only discovered to be missing yesterday morning, but other circumstances ... anyway, she was in touch. Something Jacquie said touched a nerve and I couldn't put my finger on it. But what it was, was that the husband is an art teacher.' He splayed his fingers on the desk and pushed back till the chair was against the wall. The other two looked amazingly underwhelmed and the room filled with a silence you could have cut with an axolotl.

Fran fell head first into the trap. 'But, isn't that just a coincidence, sir?'

Thorogood closed his mouth, he was that shocked. Hall narrowed his eyes and said, without turning his head, 'Explain, Bob.'

Bob was only too happy. 'DCI Hall, and in fact all of the detective plain clothes,' and he managed to put just a tad more emphasis on the last two words, 'force, don't believe in coincidence, Fran.' He had been on his man management course and knew that adding a Christian name at the end of any kind of reproof softened the blow.

But Fran Brannon was still crushed.

'But ... I don't understand,' she said. 'Just because this man who fell from ... where did he fall from, sir?'

Hall consulted the paper. 'Umm ... a ladder. Apparently, he was repairing a window.' He looked again at the page. 'Do you repair a window from the outside?' With unconscious sexism, he directed the question at Thorogood.

Fran was single-handedly renovating a six-teenth-century cottage on the coast road out towards Brighton, but suddenly felt no need to help them out. Men!

'Anyway, yes,' Hall continued. 'He fell off a ladder.'

Fran picked up her point. 'So he fell off a ladder in...?'

'Adstone, it says here. Not sure where that is...' Hall turned the page over, hoping for more details. 'It's from Northants police, so presumably Northamptonshire.'

'So,' Fran was so scared she could practically see her life flashing before her eyes, but she soldiered on. 'So, a man fell off a ladder and died in another county.'

'Yes.' Hall was smug.

'And he's an art teacher.'

'Yes. Like the husband of the missing woman.'

'So,' she was scared and confused now. 'So, that makes it important?'

Bob Thorogood took up the tale. 'It is import-ant because of the total. He fell from a height and died. This links with Mrs Troubridge, and scores one. She is a neighbour of the Maxwells, who were on holiday with a woman who goes missing who is married to an art teacher. That scores two. That isn't much, but Jacquie Carpenter, who is a darned fine detective, thinks that her disappearance is suspicious. The missing woman is not local to here, so she may come from somewhere in the vicinity of where the man died. If so, that would give us three...'

Hall held up his hand. 'The score just went into the high double figures, Bob,' he said.

'Why?' The detective tried to screw his head round to read what the DCI was reading. He had never quite mastered the upside-down reading knack and this had slowed down many an investigation. It also quite possibly ended any hope of promotion.

'Because here it links next of kin.'

'Not bloody Maxwell?' Thorogood exploded.

Hall sighed. 'It isn't *always* Maxwell, Bob,' he said, patiently. 'It just sometimes seems that way. No, the man had no family. It took the locals a while to find anything out about him. Finally, they went to the school and got some bits out of his file. But the gossip was most useful and that was that his recently ex-wife remarried a colleague. Another art teacher. An art teacher called Tom Medlicott.'

The other two looked expectant, waiting for the punchline.

'Tom Medlicott is the new Head of Art at Leighford High School. He has just come back from a school trip to the Isle of Wight, though, sadly, without his wife.'

185

Chapter Twelve

It was while she was still on the ferry that Jacquie remembered another large fly in the increasingly sticky ointment. Maxwell didn't have a key to get into the house. The only one with them was the one on her key ring, currently on the grubby, stained table in front of her along with her phone and a cup of rapidly cooling coffee.

She was just running through a silent list of imprecations, some of which would have made even whiter the hair of the little old ladies who seemed to surround her on every side, had she said them out loud. Tom Medlicott sat slumped in his seat like a puppet with its strings cut. She could tell by the condescending looks and nudges that the old dears had decided she was his minder. And, in a way, she had to admit that she was. She turned to check the view out of the window, which wouldn't have helped her much as she had no idea of how long Southampton Water was or whereabouts the ferry terminal was. But it beat staring at Tom Medlicott.

Her phone rang, the jaunty tones of what Maxwell chose to call 'The Bum of the Flightlebee' making the witches' convention shudder and bridle.

'DS Carpenter.' She couldn't quite make out who was on the other end, but he seemed to be calling her darling. 'Darling?' Jacquie held the phone away from her head to check on the incoming number. 'Guv, are you all right?' Henry Hall didn't use endearments, even *in extremis* and he didn't sound as if he was *in extremis*.

The voice identified itself as her husband, and added, 'I'm using Henry's phone.'

'I can see that. Or hear, perhaps I should say. Why are you on Henry's phone?' A small creeping sense of foreboding made its way down Jacquie's spine. 'Where are you, Max?'

'I'm in Henry's office, precious. But I had to get in touch with you, it's really important, and I couldn't get into the house and ... well, it was very difficult. I needed to get in touch with you before you caught the ferry.'

'Too late,' she said, shortly. 'As you can probably hear from the combined noise of about a dozen school parties, all worse than ours, and a million old ladies complaining about the cost of tea and a cake, I am on the ferry. I'll speak to you when I get home.' And she cut the connection.

She threw the phone down on the table and, true to form, the back fell off and the battery dropped out. She picked it up as it was and shoved it into her pocket. Tom Medlicott gave her a look but said nothing. She knew he would be worrying about being out of contact, but she was tired of communication. She just wanted to go home and have a nice quiet weekend with just her family, no phones, no missing people popping up all over the place. Although, a nice popping-up Izzy would be a good thing, she supposed. Glancing out of the window again, she spotted a distant white building with once-

187

golden lions on the parapet. The ferry terminal was in sight and without speaking to Medlicott she stood up and made for the stairs. She sensed rather than saw him follow her. At the head of the stairs their progress was barred by a red rope, which she promptly undid.

'You can't do that,' someone said in truculent tones.

She looked down to see a child of about ten, snot encrusting his nostrils, glaring at her accusingly. According to his shirt, his name was Beckham, but she somehow doubted that. On the other hand, with some of the names she had had to learn in the past week, perhaps it was.

'I'm a policewoman,' she snarled. 'I can do what I like.' Stepping down a step, she let Tom Medlicott through and then rehung the rope.

As she went down the short flight to the car deck, she heard the little herbert say to an invisible parent, 'She's a p'liceman and she's arrested that man.'

'Disgraceful,' came the reply. 'Letting criminals on public transport.'

'Hmmph,' Jacquie heard another voice. 'Criminal? I'll tell you about criminal. Did you try to buy a cup of tea on your holiday? What a price? Isn't it disgraceful?'

How lovely, Jacquie thought. What fragrant memories the collected coven will be taking back to Wigan. She smiled briefly and a hand squeezed her heart as she heard Maxwell's voice correcting her 'Wigan' to 'Wiccan'. He just wouldn't have been able to stop himself.

Jacquie had attended all of the first aid courses

and had reasonable recall of most of the main points. She knew what to do in cases of electrocution, falls, breaks, choking, heart attack. She was finding herself a little stumped by Medlicott's complete shutdown. She couldn't help but feel that she ought to get him to a hospital, but knew that he would cut up rough at the mention of any delay, so she just got herself onto the motorway and headed east. He sat next to her but only his body was there; his soul was far away and she could tell, by the fleeting snatches of expression that scudded across his face, that he was reliving the best bits of the time since he met Izzy. She reached out and squeezed his hand. It felt like a glove full of jelly and sticks and he gave no answering squeeze.

The journey was a whisker under fifty miles, on a good day an hour, hour and a quarter. But Jacquie had known from the start that this was not a good day. There were roadworks just before they got in to Chichester and from then on the journey was a nightmare. It didn't help that when Tom saw the first road sign to Leighford, he began to whimper, a tiny, desolate sound somewhere in the back of his throat. Jacquie was a compassionate woman and had discovered wells of patience since marrying Maxwell that she never knew she had. She loved him dearly and every day was a new pleasure, but sometimes she, like everyone else who knew him, had to fight down the urge to hit him round the back of the head with a spade. What she would have given for that spade to be in the boot now.

Before she spoke to Medlicott, she tried each

sentence in her head first. She knew that he could go critical at any moment and someone deep in stress, as he was, could do anything – lash out, try and leave the moving car – she had seen all the options, often from the sharp and bloody end. As they reached the outskirts of Leighford, threading through the one-way system on their way to the Medlicotts' home on a new development in Tottingleigh, she had to finally speak.

'Do you want to go home, first, Tom, or to the police station?'

He turned hollow eyes on her and stared disconcertingly. She wished that she had paid more attention to the zombie movies which made Maxwell laugh so much; she might know what was coming next.

'Home?'

'Yes.' She only just stopped herself from calling him 'dear'. 'Just to see if, well, you know, if Izzy has come back early.'

'She hasn't got a key,' he said, as though turning home the final screw in the lid of a coffin.

'Don't you keep a spare?' she asked. She felt she had no room to talk, with her son and husband wandering homeless throughout Leighford. At least, she hoped just her husband. Surely, he hadn't taken Nolan sleuthing with him? She felt the little knot of frustration and annoyance unravel just a little and start to cast on and knit a few rows.

'Under a pot,' Medlicott said.

'Well, there you are, then,' she said, with false bonhomie. 'She'll have used that.'

'It's not there,' the man said, infuriatingly. 'Her

190

mother took it with her when she went back the other week.'

Mother? Had he mentioned a mother? 'Did you mention a mother, Tom?' Jacquie knew she sounded like a playgroup leader, but couldn't help herself.

'Well,' he said, after a long pause. 'They're not close. When her parents divorced, Izzy floated a bit, but when her dad died and she had to deal with the house, her mother was in touch. She just wanted a few things, you know, from the house.'

I bet she did, Jacquie thought. She still had nightmares over the appalling behaviour her relations had shown at her grandmother's funeral. She just said, 'I see. So, she won't have gone to her mother's then?'

'Doubt it,' he said, leaning his head against the window. Suddenly, he sat up and pointed. 'Number 6, Craftcarn Avenue. This is us.' He gave a dry sob at the use of the objective personal pronoun, ungrammatical as that use had been.

Jacquie drew up outside a detached house, standing neatly at the rear of a square of paved drive. There was one car on the drive, but this gave no clue as to whether Izzy was inside or not; she had driven them both to Leighford High to start the trip and her car might or might not still be there. Jacquie made a mental note to ring and check as soon as possible. Before she could so much as pull on the handbrake, he was out of the car and running across the drive, rummaging in his coat pocket for the key, which he then tried to get into the lock, but his trembling hand out-smarted him. Slowly, Jacquie got out of the car and joined him, gently taking the key from him and turning it. The door swung open and before they even stepped inside, Jacquie knew that the house was empty.

She would not have classed herself as a sensitive woman, although Maxwell would have argued that one. But she was very aware of the spirit of places, and this place had had no one in it since the Medlicotts had walked out of it, probably hand in hand unless she missed her guess, just over a week ago. She imagined Tom taking the suitcases to the car and stowing them carefully in the boot. She could see Izzy giving a last wipe round the sink and spreading the cloth to dry over the tap. She knew without asking that Tom would have got in the car and then immediately got out again to check that the gas was turned off properly. She could see Izzy pop her head round the sitting room door, to check that the SkyPlus was set to record all their favourite shows. The house made her feel sad, as it rose about her, holding its breath, waiting for its heart to come home.

She turned to face Tom Medlicott and quickly turned away. The naked hope, followed by grief on his face, was not for public consumption, not even for her, who had shared so much in the last twenty-four hours and more.

'She's not here,' he whispered. 'She hasn't come back, has she Jacquie?'

'No,' she said, and took him in her arms and held him as though he was her child. 'Let's go and sit down for a minute, then I'll phone my boss. He will know what to do.'

Henry Hall did know what to do, but he wanted to tell Jacquie face to face. He wanted to make it clear that this could be bigger than a missing wife, it could be a conspiracy, or a suicide, or a politic disappearance, depending on who turned out to be the murderer of Izzy Medlicott's first husband, the choices on the table being a cunning murderer, Tom Medlicott or Izzy herself. Not knowing the woman, he was tempted to put Izzy in pole position.

'So, where are you, Jacquie?' he asked.

'I'm still at the Medlicotts',' she said, as quietly as was compatible with being heard. 'Tom is in a terrible state, and I don't really want to leave him. But I must get home; Max and Nole are locked out with Mrs Troubridge in the hospital. I've got to get Metternich, before he takes us to court for wrongful imprisonment.' Her voice wobbled a little. 'I'm quite tired, Henry, to be truthful. This last day and a half has been quite full-on, plus I had absolutely no idea how exhausting a million kids can be.'

'A million?' Henry asked. 'That was a very big school trip.'

Jacquie smiled at the phone. Humourless bugger he might be, but he understood her almost as well as Maxwell did. 'OK, thirtyish. But it felt like a million, most days.'

Henry Hall tapped his pencil decisively on the desk and then jotted down a few notes. 'I'll tell you what,' he said. 'If you can stay a few more minutes, I'll get a car out to you. Address?' She gave it. 'Then, Mr Medlicott can choose to answer a few questions at his home, or come in here.'

There was something about his tone which made the hairs stand up on her arms. 'That sounds a bit serious, guv. He's in no state for the third degree.' They both knew, of course, that he could request his lawyer to be present, but, unless he was an actor par excellence, Jacquie didn't think he was thinking straight enough for that.

'Perhaps not. That may turn out to be a good thing. I can't tell you now, Jacquie, but this thing has blossomed a bit.' Hall was good at the teasing statement.

Jacquie dropped her voice even lower. 'Oh, God, guv, they haven't found her, have they?'

'No,' he told her. 'I really can't tell you any more while you're standing feet from the man but, trust me on this one, won't you, Jacquie? Someone is dead, but not, as far as I know, Izzy Medlicott. As soon as the car gets there, get off home, let yourselves in and have a cup of tea. Get Metternich, give him my regards and tell him I'm healing nicely. Then, when we've all had a rest and a think, I'll give you a ring. Or I might pop round later. Margaret's at her mother's, mad old trout has broken her arm.'

'Not another one falling downstairs?' Jacquie asked. There seemed to be some kind of epidemic.

'No. She was out on a quad bike with the Over Seventies Friendly Club. There is talk of a breach of Health and Safety, apparently.' The incredulity was evident in his tone. 'They were on an activity weekend. She'd already done the zorbing and the artificial ski slope, but the quad proved the last straw.'

Had Jacquie not been standing only a few yards

194

from a weeping man, she could not have helped adding, 'The straw that broke the camel's arm.' As it was, she would have to save it for later, when telling Maxwell about her day. 'Thanks for the car, guv. I'll be off home as soon as it's here, then I'll see you later, shall I? Takeaway all right? My Tesco delivery won't have come without Mrs T to let them in.'

'Takeaway's fine. Thanks. And, Jacquie ... about Max...'

'I'll send him out for a ride on his bike or something. Don't worry, Henry. He's not getting involved in this one.' She cut the connection, with fingers crossed to cancel out the lie and leaned against the immaculate cream-painted wall in the Medlicotts' hall. She closed her eyes and wondered where this one would end. Living with Peter Maxwell meant, almost by default, that some cases came very close to home, but not as close as this. She felt so sorry for Tom Medlicott, without really liking either him or his missing wife particularly. It was something about sharing breakfast, and gin and tonic on a darkening evening, and hauling Pansy to her feet and counting heads and...

A sudden knock on the door made Jacquie jump and she crossed the hall to open the door to the looming blue shape through the dimpled glass. The Seventh Cavalry, here at last.

Had David Attenborough had the foresight to set up a hide at Leighford High School that afternoon, he would have got loads of footage on the stalking behaviour of that dangerous pack of

195

predators, the Senior Leadership Team. They came out of their various lairs and spread out to close in on the small gaggle of pupils left waiting for parents in a corner of the car park.

The coach and driver had gone as soon as the suitcases were unloaded. Jim was incandescent, as far as his virtually comatose personality allowed, at the complete lack of tip which had been forthcoming as he waited ostentatiously by the door of the coach. That mad old git had driven away with the rather handsome bloke, leaving the fat drunk and the scary nurse behind. The scary nurse had glared at him and the fat drunk had looked him up and down as if he might be a welcome snack, and he had eventually given any cash up as unlikely and had driven away, crashing the gears and turning left instead of right out of the school gates.

But the prey had smelt the SLT on the wind and by the time they got there, thirsting for blood – Maxwell's blood for preference, anyone's at a pinch – Sylvia had very cleverly brought in reinforcements and a rather nice and inoffensive member of the Science faculty was in place with the clipboard, ticking off for the use of. Of Pansy and Sylvia there was no sign. As the SLT snorted and pawed the ground in frustration the final parent drew up and collected their child. The charity box would be gaining this year, as the temporarily abandoned offspring was none other than the delightful Camilla, whose mother had been held up tending to a wounded blue tit brought in by the cat, thus proving that nobody is ever quite perfect.

'Can I help you, Mr Diamond?' the chemistry teacher asked, clipboard stowed neatly under his arm.

'No,' Bernard Ryan snapped, before the Head Teacher could so much as open his mouth. 'We were looking for the staff who took this trip.' The years had not been kind to Bernard Ryan. He had expected a headship long before this, followed perhaps by the papacy and then a godship. Somehow, it just hadn't happened and he was too old now. Instead, he'd just take it all out on hapless young teachers his boss had appointed.

The chemist looked around vaguely. 'Well, they were here. I was just asked to help tick the children off.' He chuckled. 'Not *tick* them off, as in annoy them,' he said. He chuckled again. 'Nor as in tell them off. No, I mean–'

'We know what you mean, Roger,' growled Ryan. 'Don't you have something to blow up somewhere?' This last was a nasty jibe relating to an incident in the man's first term and was a gross calumny. There had been some smoke and a little flame – there was never, of course, one without the other; not in Leighford High. And the child's eyebrows had soon grown back, so no real harm done. But it had been said now and the chemistry teacher drew himself up and, with a last injured glance at Ryan, stalked back up to the school.

'That was a little harsh, Bernard,' Diamond remarked. 'Roger hasn't done anything. In fact, none of them have, really.'

Ryan was aghast. Not *done* anything. Overspending. Changing the itinerary. Overspending. Losing a member of staff, not once, but twice.

Driving home with not enough adults to child, ratio-wise. Overspending. What part of over-spending did James Diamond not understand?

Diamond took advantage of the man's temporary catatonia and turned back to the school building. 'I have things to do, Bernard,' he said, mildly. 'I know you want to rip Maxwell's head off and I will of course, when the time comes, hold your coat. But there's no need to get aerated.' And leaving his deputy fuming in his wake, he went back up the drive, through the foyer and into his office to take another of those lovely pills he had got from the doctor.

Hidden in her office, Sylvia Matthews lost no time in catching up with phone calls. She liked to have a plan and often had them, carried in her head, up to and including Plan Z, which was pretty much the one she was using now. Sitting Nolan down with a pad and some pens, she rang Guy first, and told him to take Maxwell home via Happy Paws and then come and fetch her and Nolan. Then she rang Jacquie to ask if it was all right if she and Guy kept Nolan overnight and to tell her that Maxwell would be at home with a more or less irate cat.

That done, she filled the kettle for a nice cup of tea, collared a passing child to fetch Nolan a bottle of juice from the machine in the foyer and finally, for what seemed the first time in a week, sat back and closed her eyes, completely, both of them at once.

Chapter Thirteen

Happy Paws Cattery (or 'Kattery' as the sign had it) was not the place it had once been. That is, the place it had been before Metternich Mole-strangler Sherpa Tenzing Maxwell, to give him his full name, had come to stay. Several of the staff had gone off sick with stress, having approached the rather lovely black and white animal in the Executive Suite believing in the old adage of 'handsome is as handsome does'. Metternich had a technique with his claws of picking up just a thin layer of skin and hanging on for grim death. In the case of an unsuspecting rodent the death was theirs and grim indeed, involving a lot of throwing up in the air and mock escapes – he had in a previous incarnation been thrown out of the SS for being too unpleasant. In the case of cattery operatives, it involved crying and a lot of Germolene.

The owners had taken comfort in the fact that the invoice would be huge, involving extras they rarely had to invoke. When presented with the bill, Maxwell had smothered a small scream. Had he, Jacquie and Nolan actually managed an island break somewhere warm and sunny, the total would have been similar to this, but smaller. He paid and left with Metternich in a cardboard box, from which he escaped while Guy Minter was still reversing out of his parking space. Guy had never had to drive while a stone of irate fur rampaged round and round his car at head height but by the time he reached Columbine he was used to it, and almost missed it as he drove away, waving in his mirror to Maxwell, standing on the pavement while Metternich ripped one of his trouser legs to ribbons. *There will be blood*, Maxwell mused. He hadn't seen the film, but assumed it was about an oil tycoon and his cat.

Jacquie met Guy as he turned out of and she turned into Columbine and they waved to each other in passing. At the kerb outside Number 38, she leapt out of the car and scooped Metternich up and hugged him furiously. The great beast went all limp and purry, turning his head to kiss her on the nose. Maxwell looked on in disbelief; he had known that cat for years, kitten and behemoth, and yet still he could be amazed by him. Putting the cat down, Jacquie turned to Maxwell and hugged him too. Apart from the purring, Maxwell behaved the same as the Count and realised in that moment why Metternich loved her so much. Being enveloped in her hug was like being wrapped in cotton wool, but with a layer round you that the world couldn't break in through. A bit like the velvet hand inside a steel glove.

Finally, she let him go and burrowed under his arm to lead the way to the front door. 'Ooh, that's nice,' she said, snuggling in. 'What a day! Isn't it good to be home? Let's get the kettle on, shall we?' She unlocked the door.

He unlooped his arm from round her neck. 'We're a bit prattly, aren't we, Woman Policeman

Carpenter-Maxwell? Is there something you would like to tell me?'

'No,' she said, her voice a bit muffled as she made her way up the stairs. 'Poo, it's a bit stale, isn't it? Shall we open a window?' She went into the sitting room and cracked open the fanlights. The cool September afternoon air swept in. Jacquie never opened the casement, afraid that Metternich might leap out. Maxwell had tried to tell her that he was more likely to leap out of an open window by mistake than was the cat, but she decided to err on the side of safety. She turned to face him. 'Well? Would you like some tea?'

He flopped into his chair. 'I'm not talking to you until you stop wittering and tell me what's going on. I haven't seen you since this morning and at that point you were about to take Tom Medlicott to report his wife missing to the Island police. So why don't we–?' He looked round. 'Where's Nolan?' A sudden thought struck him. 'Should I know where he is?' Terror, momentarily, clawed at his heart.

'Well, I should hope so, just as a matter of principle. But in fact, no, Sylvia and I did the arranging. He's staying with them tonight – possibly longer. You know how hard it is to separate Sylvia and Nole once they get together. But I must say, I don't envy them. He's going to be totally hyper without thirty kids to bend to his will.'

The same could be said of Maxwell. 'I see,' he said. He sat for a moment, gazing at nothing. 'So this means you'll be working.' It was almost a question, but mostly a statement.

'Not working as in going in to work, no,' she

201

said and bustled off to the kitchen. He could hear her, still waffling. 'What a good job milk has such a long fridge-life these days.' She appeared in the doorway, brandishing a flagon of milk. 'I said, what a good–'

'I know,' he said, shortly. 'Wonderful. Where would we be without it? And don't say "drinking your tea black" because it won't wash. I've known you for ... well, a long time, and you can't fool me. Let me see if I can guess what the problem is... Yes, I have it.' He sat up straight, fixing her eyes with his. 'Something has come up with the case, you've been in touch with Henry and he has said that I'm not to have anything to do with it or your promotion is history. Normally history is no bad thing, but perhaps in this case, not so much.' He tilted his head. 'Am I right?'

'In the essentials,' she said. 'Oh, Max, I don't know what to do!' She took a step into the room and then stopped. 'I actually *do* want a cup of tea. Come and talk to me while I make it.' She went back into the kitchen and he heard a tap running, splashing into the kettle.

'Righty-ho, woman policeman.' His voice was suddenly loud, just over her shoulder. She jumped and slopped water on the worktop. 'Oh, sorry, sweetness,' He ruffled her hair. 'Did I startle you? So, what did Henry have to say?'

She turned to him, brandishing a tea bag. 'Max, do you not even hear what *you* are saying, let alone anyone else? I can't tell you what Henry has to say. I can't talk about this case. For one thing, it involves police forces from other places–'

'Places? Interesting.'

'Max! I might be putting in red herrings, so don't jump to any conclusions. Where was I?'

'Places.'

'What? Oh, yes. It *may* involve police forces from other places and it is still very much a hunch of Henry's. I...' she knew as she spoke that it was a stupid question, but she asked it all the same. 'Did he tell you anything?'

'Don't be a silly billy,' he wasn't sure whether that was Denis Healey or Mike Yarwood *doing* Denis Healey. This was no time to decide. 'I told him something, though, which–'

'Max! You know you're not supposed to talk to Henry about cases.'

'But–'

'Enough, already. Anyway, I don't really know the details myself. Henry is coming round later, for a takeaway and a chat.'

'Is Margaret coming? I only ask, so that I'll have someone to play with while you police beings get down to the nitty-gritty.'

'Margaret is at her mother's. Something about a quad.' Jacquie was mashing the tea bag down in the water with some venom. Maxwell wondered if she had given it a name, as he knew she often did to relieve frustration.

'Margaret's had quads?' Maxwell knew that medical advances were coming thick and fast, but surely Margaret, though as well preserved as all get-out, was a little mature to be having quads.

'Don't be silly.'

'Her mother's had quads?' Now that really was taking science too far.

'Max. Stop it. Her mother fell off a quad bike

and broke her arm.' She suddenly saw the funny side and laughed, poking him in the ribs with her teaspoon.

'Ow. That was sharp and,' he paused and rubbed his side, 'hot. So, I'm up in the loft, am I, making plastic history? Downstairs in the garage rubbing WD-40 on Surrey's lumbago?'

'Anywhere would be good. Because Henry has made it crystal clear that you won't be within earshot. Why don't you take the opportunity to visit Mrs Troubridge? I'll drop you off and you can get a cab back.'

'I'll miss the takeaway,' he whined.

'Point taken. In that case, get a cab there and I'll fetch you. How about that?' She handed him his tea and a packet of chocolate digestives and ushered him through into the sitting room. 'Now, let's go and have a sit-down and not talk about missing people, dead people or anything else like that. Who won the Last Kid Standing pool?'

'No one, I don't think. I definitely saw the parents of our choices there when the coach pulled in, at any rate. What do you mean, dead people?'

She sipped her tea and looked up, all wide-eyed innocence. 'I don't think I did say "dead people", did I?'

'Yes, you did. You said blah blah "not talk about missing people, dead people or anything else like that".'

'What is this?' she asked crossly. 'This conversation may be recorded for training or other purposes?' She always forgot until it was too late that Maxwell had honed his memory for the spoken word on the hard whetstone of Five Zed Nine and their ilk for more years than he cared to remember. He could usually recall off the top of his head at least the last twenty minutes of conversation. If he was really trying, he could do the last few hours. Sometimes the odd bit of editing took place – for example, he could delete any number of expletives without missing a beat – but the accuracy was alarming, as James Diamond had often discovered to his discomfiture, in staff meetings and out.

'Slip of the tongue,' she said, grumpily.

'Slip of the tongue? "Queer old dean", that's a slip of the tongue. "Dead people", that's not a slip of the tongue. That's just you knowing there is a dead person in this case.'

She looked into her cup, as if the tea and not its leaves held news of her future. Then she looked up at him. 'Right. I shall say this only once.' It spoke volumes for her sincerity that she didn't even bother with a Froglish accent. 'Yes, there is a dead person. I don't know the dead person. It may or may not have a bearing on this case. If, when Henry comes over, you let slip, by word or deed or, in fact tongue, that you know, I'll kill you. Is that clear?'

'But who is it?' He thought one more question was worth a punt.

'Is that clear?'

'As crystal, my love,' he said meekly and subsided into his chair, thoughtfully dunking his biscuit. This would take cunning, the very lowest of low cunning and he needed to plan his next move. He glanced up just in time to see Jacquie's half-full mug start to tilt as she finally let sleep take her. With a speed and agility which surprised him and amazed Metternich, watching from his lounging spot on the window sill, he saved it from tipping and watched fondly as she slept. 'Well, Count,' he whispered. 'I hope you've got your thinking cap with you? I think we'll be needing it later on.'

Henry Hall had been beautifully brought up, years before, by his parents, Mr and Mrs Hall. True, they'd named him after a Thirties bandleader, but after that, had hardly put a foot wrong. It was difficult to think of Henry as a child; the Maxwells always imagined that he had probably spotted trains, or mothed, or had some other solitary and pernickety hobby that didn't make him blind. But the side effect was that, invited for a meal, he always came armed with wine, chocolates, flowers and a small something for Nolan. On this particular evening, he had added a catmint mouse for Metternich, because he still felt strangely guilty about putting him in a cattery when it was obvious to everyone, or at least to Metternich, that the correct approach would have been to move in and care for him at home until such time as Jacquie and Maxwell returned. Maxwell took the mouse with trepidation. Like Hall, the Count had been well brought up but had never been very easy to buy for; Christmas was always a nightmare. But tonight, he was feeling magnanimous. Guilt had guided Jacquie's hand when dobbing out the Whiskas and so, pleasantly full, he lay on the hearth rug and tossed the offering between his paws before tucking it under his head and going back to sleep.

'I'm glad he likes it,' Hall said. 'I did wonder after I had bought it whether it might be a bit beneath him.' Jacquie, with the fervour of the adopted parent, often filled Hall in on Metternich's latest when they were driving or had stopped for coffee. The Incident had kept him – silently – amused for weeks.

'No, no,' Maxwell said. 'He loves his catmint. Especially when still growing in neighbours' gardens, unfortunately. It will be nice for him to have some handy without going out equipped with a spade.'

There was a silence. All three of them were willing the takeaway to arrive and fill in the gap for a bit. It was hard to make small talk when Izzy Medlicott was also metaphorically in the room. Jacquie excused herself and went to tinker with cutlery in the dining room.

'How did you find Mrs Troubridge?' Maxwell asked Hall. Asked the same question, Maxwell would have almost certainly mentioned going in at the main gate and turning left. Not so Henry Hall.

'Not very well, Max, to be honest. I haven't seen much improvement, but the nurses say she is a lot better. Fighting them off, that sort of thing.'

Maxwell smiled. 'That certainly sounds like her,' he said. 'She's not one to take things lying down. I hope she's all right, though. It would be a shame if she ... well, you know, didn't make it, just when her sister is starting to really get somewhere with the family research.'

Hall grabbed on to the subject. 'Ah, genealogy. Margaret does a bit of that. Very interesting. Does a lot online. Um...' He looked furtively at Maxwell.

'It's not an illness, Henry,' Maxwell said. 'It's a choice. And anyway, I'm not that bad. I am often online. I just need someone to put me there. But I would imagine that any serious family searches would be very expensive without the computer to help in the first place. Millie – that's Mrs Troubridge's cousin goodness knows how many times removed – has been all over the place, looking in paper records and things. Very pricey. And you have to spend a lot of time sitting cheek by jowl with some very unsavoury chaps.'

Hall nodded. 'Margaret stopped really when she went back before compulsory registration, whenever that was.'

'1837,' Maxwell said, automatically.

'Yes, that sounds right,' Hall said, and because he was still looking at Metternich and his mouse he didn't see the look on Maxwell's face. 'But I think that when she didn't find we were related to anyone exciting, she rather lost interest.'

'Great-granddad not Jack the Ripper, then?' Maxwell asked.

'Possibly, possibly,' Hall said. 'Though looking at the old photos she managed to find, it would be more likely that Great-Granny was Jack the Ripper. She was a very formidable old besom.'

Maxwell smiled. 'Every family has one. In Mrs Troubridge's case, it's Millie. She's built like a brick privy.' There was a ring at the door. 'Oh, here's the food. I'll go down and pay.' He raised

208

his voice to call to Jacquie. 'Food, honeybunch. Shall I bring it straight in?'

'Please,' she shouted. 'Can you send Henry through?'

'Will do,' Maxwell said and held the door open for Henry, ushering him through. 'Won't be a moment.'

He ran downstairs and opened the door. Outside stood an Old Leighford Highena, holding two carrier bags. 'Hello, Mr Maxwell. I thought it might be you.'

'Might be me, what?' Maxwell was puzzled.

'You, ordering the Chinese.' The lad was also puzzled. 'When I saw the name, like, and the address. I remembered you lived out this way somewhere. Still up at the school?'

'Yes, still there,' Maxwell said, squinting at the bill. 'What does that say? There appears to be soy sauce on it.'

'Oh, yeah,' the delivery boy said and wiped it down the side of his trousers. 'Looks like twenty-seven pounds ninety-five. Have you got it exact, cuz I ain't got much change?'

Maxwell gave him a long look. He didn't remember him being quite this sharp at school. Seemed to remember old Dave Hollister, Head of Maths, swearing to rip his bollocks off, that sort of thing. He toyed momentarily with emptying Nolan's piggy and giving the grasping little so-and-so the total to the penny, but then he thought how delivering other people's food for a living probably wasn't up to much and relented, giving him three tenners. 'Keep the change,' he said, taking the bags.

'Oh, cheers, Mr M. You was always my favourite at school,' the lad said. 'Oh, my sister was on that trip to the Isle of Wight. She had a great time. Shame about that teacher. The one what got murdered.' He gave a shudder. ''Orrible. All that blood and stuff.'

Maxwell opened his mouth to put the boy right and then decided against it. Gossip and scuttlebutt will always prevail; why stand in its way? 'Yes, it was, Vernon,' he said, remembering his name in the nick of time. 'Very nasty. Well, thanks for dinner. Bye bye and Fa Choi,' and he closed the door.

As he went up the stairs, he could hear a hum of voices from the dining room; Henry filling Jacquie in on the case, he had no doubt. He tried walking more quietly, but they were onto him and had left the door open. Jacquie was standing back into the room, but positioned so that she could see him coming along the landing.

'Nice try, Max,' she said. 'We're wise to you.' He went through into the dining room and stood there, bags aloft. 'We won't bother with bowls, just put the cartons on the table and we'll pick and mix.'

Soon there was a savoury smell from the plastic boxes on the table, mushroom and beef, noodles, crab, duck. When they had made inroads into the food, Maxwell turned to Hall.

'So, Henry. How's the case progressing?'

His *gravitas* not even dented by the noodle stuck to his chin, Hall answered calmly, 'Nicely, thank you, Max,' and went back to his rice. He looked up again and said to Jacquie, 'Thanks for

210

the forks, by the way. I've never really got to grips with chopsticks.'

'Nor me,' she said. 'Although I always think it looks like fun, the way they eat Chinese food on American cop shows. They have those cartons and chopsticks and never drop anything down themselves or lose the whole mouthful onto the table.'

'And the way they call it *Chinese* food,' Maxwell said. 'Rather than Chinese *food*. There's rather a lot of it in *Stakeout* I seem to recall. Maybe that's why they made *Another Stakeout*, because you feel like another one soon after.'

Maxwell could fill aeons of otherwise silence with junk-food talk from films alone. He regaled Henry and Jacquie with the mountains consumed by Robert Morley in *Too Many Chefs* and the upmarket home delivery of serial loony Rod Steiger in *No Way to Treat a Lady*. In fact, it was the way various ladies had been treated recently that Maxwell really wanted to talk about; but he'd have to bide his time.

'Would anyone like a coffee?' Jacquie asked. 'A beer?'

'No, I'm absolutely full,' Hall said. 'That was lovely. Thank you.'

Maxwell looked at him. What a thoroughly nice man he was, he thought. How sad that he would have to annoy him intensely, yet again, when he started digging in this case. Because it was a case, whatever anyone else thought. And it was a lot more complicated than a missing wife. It was pointless trying to muscle in, though. He would have to winkle it out of Jacquie later, or work it

211

out with a pencil on his own.

'Darling,' he said to Jacquie. 'Did you order me a cab?'

'Yes,' she said. 'It should be here...' She checked the kitchen clock by leaning over and peering through the doorway. 'Anytime now, really. I checked with the ward as well. Because Mrs Troubridge has not had many visitors, except apparently her son,' she smiled as both men's heads spun round. 'Don't get excited. If it is her son, he is you to the life, guv. Because she hasn't had many visitors, they are willing to stretch visiting time a bit, but even so, you won't get long with her.' A distant toot in the road told them that she was right in her estimate of the time. 'There he is. Aren't our taxi drivers wonderful?' She reached up for a kiss as Maxwell got up, wiping his face in case of random noodling. 'I'll pick you up at ... what shall we say?'

'Ten?' he said. 'I'll walk down to the pub and wait in there. Then you won't have to worry about time if you get chatting.' He smiled innocently and left the room.

They waited until they heard the door slam and his distant voice hail the cab driver before Henry spoke.

'I suppose he knows all about it,' he said, resignedly.

'I haven't said a word,' she said, almost truthfully. But they both knew that it was only a matter of time before Peter Maxwell knew all that they did, with probably a little more for luck.

Chapter Fourteen

As Maxwell descended the stairs, he was repeating to himself a mantra he often used when shopping or using public transport. 'No Old Leighford Highenas, no Old Leighford Highenas, no Old Leighford Highenas.' For once, his prayers were answered and the driver sitting in the sagging seat of a Ford Mondeo at the kerb was both unknown to Maxwell and as old as the hills. The fact that the car smelt of an old ashtray was a mystery to Maxwell at first, as there were signs on every flat surface admonishing the passenger not to smoke. As the cabbie turned round to ask Maxwell his destination, his breath was a clue; he could give a person ten years' worth of secondary smoking with a single exhalation.

'The hospital, please,' Maxwell said, trying not to breathe in.

'A&E?' the cabbie asked.

'No, no thank you. The main door, if that's possible.' Maxwell turned round to find his seat belt. This had the added advantage of getting out of the man's breath, which could only be a good thing, health-wise.

'Oh,' the man said, swinging the car up the incline to the main road, 'it's just I pick up a lot of blokes your age, take them to A&E.' He tapped his own chest. 'Heart. The old dicky ticker.'

'Do people get taxis to take them to the hospital

213

with a heart attack?' Maxwell asked. 'I would have thought an ambulance would be rather quicker.' And, he added to himself, rather less likely to give you lung cancer.

The man sucked in his breath, which was a mercy. 'Nah, they don't want the neighbours to see, see. If they get a cab, they might be going anywhere, out, on holiday. But once the neighbours see an ambulance ... well, there's no knowing what they might think, is there?'

If Maxwell had learnt anything in all his years at the chalkface, it was how to tell that your conversation was going nowhere. But the driver had missed that lesson and carried on regardless.

'They start avoiding them, crossing the street, that kind of thing.' He sighed. ''S'what happened to me, when I had my triple bypass. Got a scar down the middle like a zip. Very neat job. But it's always just a repair, like. Never the same again. Oh, yes. I could still go at any time.' He snapped his fingers. 'Just like that.' He sighed again. 'Oh, yes. Any time.' He waited. This was clearly Maxwell's clue to join in.

'Goodness. How terrible,' he said. 'Isn't driving for a living perhaps a bit...?' He wasn't sure how to end the sentence. 'Potentially lethal for your passengers'? 'Of a really stupid idea'? 'Illegal'? They would all fit, but he settled for, 'Stressful?'

'Nah. I keep healthy, see. I was tole, up at the hospital, that it was just sheer bad luck give me my heart attack. They couldn't believe it. Said my arteries was blocked right up, but when I said what I ate they couldn't believe it. No, what with the vitamins and that, I should never have had a heart attack. But still...' he paused briefly whilst manoeuvring into the hospital car park, '...you gotta go of something, aintchya?' He hauled on the handbrake and screeched to a halt. 'That's ten quid to you, then.'

Maxwell handed the note over the back of the seat and was out of the car like greased lightning. 'Well, thank you very much,' he said and was gone, in through the automatic doors. Glad to be alive. Still.

The driver stuffed the note into his shirt pocket. 'Mean bugger,' he said to himself. 'No tip. The quiet ones are always the mean buggers.' He threw the car into gear and pulled out into the path of an ambulance, which blasted its horn. The cabbie made a generic gesture and carried on out of the hospital grounds. 'Bugger,' he muttered. 'Blasting his horn like that. I could have died.' He savoured the thought and almost whispered, as if to remind himself of his own fascinating mortality, 'I could go any time, just like that,' and he clicked his fingers. 'Just like that.' He enjoyed this time in the evening, no one going anywhere much. Just time for a bag of chips and a fag. Humming with anticipation, he drove off into the gathering night.

As soon as Maxwell had gone, Henry had said, resignedly. 'I suppose he knows all about it.'

'I haven't said a word,' she replied. 'I don't know much to tell him, to tell you the truth, except just that there is a dead body in the frame somewhere.'

'Yes,' Henry said, shortly. 'And that dead body

215

is Izzy Medlicott's first husband.'

If his head had suddenly burst open to reveal a flight of doves, Jacquie could not have been more amazed. 'What? I mean ... how on earth did you find out about that? What made you look?'

'You know I said that the story reminded me of something? Well it was that an art teacher had been found dead at the bottom of a ladder. In Northampton somewhere, little village, his name was Paul Masters. Anyway, that doesn't matter. The important thing for us is that his ex-wife is now Izzy Medlicott.' He sat back, imperturbable as always, arms folded.

'Guv ... I really don't know what to say.' She screwed up her face in thought. Something was chewing at the back of her brain.

'OK, Jacquie?' he asked.

'It's something that Izzy said, on the first evening, I think. We were chatting out on the decking and trying not to notice that Pansy was getting seriously pissed. We were talking about old sayings. She comes from Northamptonshire, I'm not sure exactly where, and her granny was full of sayings, funny words for the weather, that sort of thing. Then I said my favourite was my mother's. She always says, when someone is getting married and becomes, say Smith where they were South ... hang on, I want to get this right ... um ... "change the name and not the letter, change for the worse and not the better." And Izzy said something like "too right!" or something like that.'

Hall looked interested, but puzzled.

'Well, guv, don't you see? Mmmmmasters to

216

Mmmmmmmedlicott. She seemed to imply she had changed for the worse.'

'True,' Hall agreed. 'Did you get that impression?'

'No. They really did seem happy. But, if she was still fond of her ex – do you have his date of birth, by the way? Tom said he was older.'

Conscious of his audience, Hall said, 'Yes, he was older. Quite a bit, actually.'

'And I think Tom must be six or seven years her senior, not much, in the scheme of things, but still, it shows a pattern perhaps,' Jacquie added.

'Yes,' Hall said. 'She sounds like a lady who likes to be looked after.'

'Oh, definitely,' Jacquie agreed. 'This makes it all rather different, doesn't it? The ex being dead, Izzy and Tom not necessarily as happy as we thought ... well, everything. I started off thinking this might be a nice straightforward case, but it isn't.'

'No,' he said, shortly. 'It certainly isn't. For a start, we don't know whether we're looking for Izzy Medlicott alive and hiding, or dead.'

'Dead? Why should she be dead?' Jacquie knew the answer, but wanted Henry Hall to say it.

'Suicide. A falling-out with a secret lover, perhaps, if she had help killing her ex-husband. It could be the "someone else" she was seen with the night before husband number two reported her missing.'

'Pardon?' Jacquie was even more puzzled now. 'Where did that bit of info come from?'

'Max. He got it from a kid's notebook. He rang to ... oh, of course. He didn't tell you. Sorry, I thought he would have mentioned it since.'

'Um, no. I think that may have been my fault.'
She reran the conversation in her head and realised that yes, it was *definitely* her fault.

'Well, it's nothing much, really. She might well
have come back in after that, just out for a breath
of air, that sort of thing. It can be difficult, sharing a room if your other half snores, or something. I know Margaret often lies awake in hotels
because of my snoring. She just goes into one of
the other bedrooms at home.'

'Izzy did mention Tom snored, and that he slept
really soundly.'

'There we are, then. So, that might not be a
clue after all.' Hall shifted in his chair.

'I'm sorry, guv. Let's go into the sitting room.
These chairs can be a bit hard on the bum.'

'No, it's just I seem to be sitting on something.'
He reached under his leg and brought out a small
plastic piglet. 'Ah.'

'Sorry,' Jacquie reached over for it. 'They get
everywhere. My mother bought Nolan a farm for
... well, I don't know why, really. Just a present, I
suppose. She's trying to wean him off being a
policeman or a teacher.'

'So she thinks farming would be a good option?'

'Or accountant, but he's a bit young for double-
entry bookkeeping as yet. We will move, though,
shall we? I've been driving for a lot of today and
I could do with being a bit more spread out.'

They picked up their mugs and moved through
into the other room, where Hall made himself
comfortable after finding three lambs, a farmer's
wife and a hen under his cushion. 'I see that he

218

believes in free range,' Hall said.

Jacquie laughed. 'He is a bit of a lad,' she said. 'The farm has more or less given way to card tricks.'

'His granny is rather broad-minded, then,' Hall observed.

'No. Needless to say, that was Max. He thinks busking may be the way forward. He was practising on...' she put her hand to her mouth. 'Oh, dear. Sorry, guv.'

He leant forward. 'It's all right,' he said awkwardly, patting her knee. 'It's all right.' He had no idea what the problem was, but he could wait.

'Sorry.' She gave a sniff and carried on. 'He was practising on Mrs Troubridge and Millie last week.' The mention of Mrs Troubridge reminded her and she glanced at the clock. Plenty of time yet before she had to go and fetch Maxwell. 'I hope she's going to be OK.'

Hall said nothing. He decided to return to the case in hand, as a safer option. 'So, the sighting the night before could well not mean anything. Do we know where Izzy Medlicott was in the week before the trip?'

Jacquie drew herself up a bit straighter and went into briefing mode. 'No, we don't. She is having a career break at the moment, so her time is totally free.'

'Career break? How can they afford a nice new house and a career break?' Henry Hall was bouncing right back.

'Apparently, she has just had a bereavement...' Jacquie slowed and stopped. 'Surely not!'

'No, that won't do. Masters only died a week or

so ago and they certainly won't have sorted out a will or anything. Was it a family member?'

'I remember now. It was her father. Because Tom said she was doing it all because her parents had divorced. There was money from the sale of the house, things like that.'

'So they have no financial worries?' Hall was mentally ticking the usual boxes.

'No. On the contrary, I should say. Tom has an ex-wife and family, two children I think he said, but they aren't in touch. I don't know whether he has to find child support or anything.' Jacquie was trying to remember the details of a conversation which hadn't seemed too important at the time. 'But, why are you asking me this? Don't you have Tom at the station?'

'We did, yes. But the police surgeon took a look at him and said it wouldn't be a good idea to question him tonight. She gave him a couple of tablets to take and the car took him home.' He noticed her expression. 'Don't worry, Florence Nightingale. Fran Brannon went with the car and made sure he was settled before she left him. He'll be OK. But, anyway, until we know the details of the dead man's estate and who benefits, it isn't necessarily vital to know every detail of their finances.' Hall went on to the next point. 'Knowing what you know now, how did they seem to get on? Tom Medlicott and his wife?'

'Well. Very well. They weren't lovey-dovey, but on a school trip, you're not anyway. The kids are always there, watching you like hawks. They don't miss a trick. We didn't know that Pansy drinks, but the kids soon picked it up. They could gauge her hangover to the second and when she came out of it they made sure they were as far away as possible.'

'That's Pansy Donaldson, is it?' Hall was staggered. No one, not police or civilian, got in to Leighford High School without running the gauntlet that was Pansy Donaldson.

'That's right.' Jacquie smiled. 'She likes a splash of gin with her gin.'

'My word.' Hall sat back, steepling his fingers and looking thoughtful. 'Pansy Donaldson, a drunk.'

'So it turns out,' Jacquie said. 'Sylvia and Guy I think you know. You've probably met them here.'

'School nurse. Umm...'

'Yes. Younger husband. That's them.' Jacquie was used to filling in that particular gap. She never quite saw why people had so much more of a problem with their much smaller age gap, because of the way round it was, than the gap between her and Maxwell. That was mainly because she seldom got to hear the things her colleagues said about her and Maxwell – and that was probably for the best. 'Well, they seemed to get on all right with them. We got on all right with them as well, although to tell you the truth, she was a bit – I don't think I want to say snooty, but some people might.'

'I see. Difficult to read?' Hall was trying to get things straight.

'Yes. Even for me. Max couldn't get her sorted either. Nolan didn't even bother and he usually bats his eyelashes at all adults, just to keep his hand in.'

'Aloof.' Hall had brought out a notebook from his pocket, so quietly she scarcely noticed. He jotted something down. 'Right. Do you have a photo of her? I got the uniform boys to ask Medlicott and he could only come up with some wedding shots.'

Medlicott. Surname only could be a bad thing. Jacquie still couldn't believe that he was acting. No one was that good. 'I've probably got some in the camera. I haven't had a chance to do anything with that yet.'

'Could you have a look now? We need to get on to this as soon as possible. It's difficult, of course, because it isn't really our case in any respect. The dead man belongs to Northants police. The misper belongs to Hampshire.' He sat there, writing calmly in his little book, then looked up. 'Could you, Jacquie? It would be a help.'

'OK, guv.' She got to her feet and rummaged in a bag. 'I won't be a minute. I've just got to get this hooked up to the computer. I'll give you a shout, shall I?'

'Lovely,' he said, not looking up.

She went out of the room, a cold hand clutching at her heart. Somehow, being in on the whole thing from the beginning made her less police, more public. She was getting a taste of life from the other side of the fence and she didn't really like it much. She realised, perhaps not for the first time, that this was how it happened for Maxwell.

From a corner of the sofa, Metternich watched events through slitted eyes. Timing was of the essence. Hall continued jotting, checking back a page or two every now and then. Then, Jacquie called from the landing above.

'I've got one, guv, if you'd like to come up.'

That was it. The cat had had enough. First, this geezer had come to mock him in prison. Then, he had given him a poxy mouse to try to make up for it. Now he was going up to where the Boy slept. Never you mind that the Boy wasn't here. Metternich wasn't having that kind of behaviour, oh no. With effortless grace he sailed through the air and landed with all eighteen claws hooked into the back of Hall's leg.

With commendable forbearance, Hall said nothing to Jacquie as he went into the study on the second floor. He just hoped the blood wouldn't seep through his trousers and give the game away. Metternich was curled up again on the sofa, chuckling quietly as only a cat can.

'Sorry, guv,' Jacquie said, looking over her shoulder. 'Did you call?'

'No, no,' Hall said. He would rather no one knew about the scream. 'Just a yawn, you know, one of those loud ones.' He mimed a stretch.

Jacquie was confused. A loud yawn just didn't seem like Henry Hall, but she didn't like to argue. 'Well, here she is.' She pointed to the screen.

'Pretty.' Hall wasn't surprised. He had somehow expected someone like this. Groomed. Perfect. Just a little bit ruthless. 'Can you print this off for me?'

'Of course. Do you want me to email it as well?'

'Good girl. I don't know how I'll manage when you're an inspector.'

'The same way we manage now, guv, I expect,'

Jacquie said. 'I won't be going anywhere. Max is ... well, not too old, I don't think, but too not interested to change schools. Mrs Whatmough has Nolan down for his GCSEs already, so we can't move him.' She tapped a few keys and the printer churned out a photo of Izzy, cropped but still unable to totally remove Pansy Donaldson, looking cross-eyed, Jim the driver and a motley crew of holidaymakers in the background. She tapped a few more and sent the image on its way as a JPEG to Henry Hall's in-box. 'There you are.' She handed him the picture. 'All done.'

Hall looked at the clock on the wall. The numbers seemed to be on backwards and the time looked a bit unusual. 'Has that clock stopped?'

She glanced up. 'No. Why?'

'It says half past three.'

'No. Half past nine.' She smiled at him. 'It goes backwards.'

He patted her on the shoulder. This was the Carpenter-Maxwells' house after all. 'Of course it does,' he said. 'Of course it does,' and limped down the stairs.

'Are you all right, guv?' she asked, anxiously.

'Yes. No problem. Why?'

'You're limping,' she said.

'Oh, you know. Leg gone to sleep. Nothing to worry about. Anyway, I had better be off. Thanks for the photo. I'll let you know if anything comes up.'

'Did you have a coat?' she asked, looking round.

'No,' he said, hurriedly. In fact his coat was in the sitting room, but he didn't want to go within leaping distance of Metternich again that evening. He had his car keys and phone; the coat could wait. 'Oh, one thing. Do the Newport Police have a contact number for you?'

She blushed. 'I gave mine, not his. I know I shouldn't have, but I didn't think he should ... well, you know.'

Hall looked at her and wished he was a more demonstrative person. She was the nicest person he knew and he could never tell her. He would probably have been amazed to find she knew already. He contented himself with a brusque, 'Goodnight, then,' and made for the stairs.

Jacquie was concerned to see he went down them with some care, using only one leg on the down step, then catching up with the other. She didn't ask again if he was all right; if it was gout, or arthritis or similar, he probably didn't want to be reminded of it.

Back in the sitting room, something purred.

Maxwell had been in many hospitals, many times, but had never managed to quite get used to the smell. It had changed over the years, from his early childhood days in casualty with various bumps and bruises, when that nice Mr Lister had swept through the echoing wards and the place smelt mainly of Dettol and cabbage, through to this evening, when the smell was of inadequately hoovered carpets and slightly damp plaster casts. He examined the board by the lifts and found Lady Elizabeth Molester tucked away in the opposite wing, on the fourth floor. Just the thing for all those old ladies visiting their comatose friends; a ride in an overcrowded lift followed by a ten-mile route march along slippery corridors. Perhaps Leighford General needed more patients and that was a very good way to get them. *And* another thing! Who in their right minds would call a ward after a woman whose name, to those not local to Leighford, was Molester? No one further east than Brighton or west than Little-hampton knew that it was pronounced to rhyme with 'holster'.

Finally, the lift arrived, full, as usual, with puzzled people who had got on at the second floor and who had pushed '4' to no avail. Max-well tipped his hat at the surly nurse pushing a wheelchair. It had always been his policy to be nice to medical staff more than twenty years his junior. It would not be good to meet them in the geriatric ward a few years down the line other-wise. He leant across her to press '4' and, despite the tipped hat, got a severe bridling for his pains.

The tide of visitors was much stronger leaving the ward than arriving. Pausing to wash his hands at the dispenser at the door, Maxwell was brushed aside by a large woman elbowing her way in without benefit of hygiene. Maxwell was no great believer in global pandemics per se, and flu, neither bird nor swine, had not alarmed him particularly. But flesh-eating viruses, now there was something he wanted to avoid. He had seen enough horror films to be able to picture their phlegm-dripping fangs emerging from every orifice and thought that getting one of those would probably be quite unpleasant. So he spent a few minutes cleaning all his important little places before he stepped onto the ward. And stopped dead in his tracks. There, in the third bed on the left, as described in detail by Henry Hall, lay Mrs Troubridge. And, looming over her like some prehistoric carving, was Millie Muswell.

Peter Maxwell was not a cowardly man. In fact, there were those who said he was particularly brave in willingly facing, as he did every day, rooms full of children who had driven many staff to the brink of insanity. John Christie had been in someone's class once; so had Ted Bundy, Aileen Wournos and J.T. Ripper. Wonder if their teachers ever had an inkling? But even Maxwell blenched at the sight of Millie, at the thought of sitting opposite her with a comatose Mrs Troubridge between them, making talk which would be small from his direction, incredibly large from hers.

'Pip pip,' came a voice from behind him. ''Scuse me.'

He scooted out of the way as a trolley manoeuvred its way into the ward, pushed by a figure he recognised. 'Mrs B?' he said. 'I didn't know you worked here.' Was there an institution south of the Wash that the woman *didn't* work in?

'Hello, Mr M. You've caught me! I've worked here years. It's a wonder we haven't bumped into each other before.' She gave him a wink and a nudge. 'I just do weekends, as a rule, but Sonia – she's the weeknights trolley operative – she's gone off sick. Well, I say sick. She's just having a bit of a lead-swing, if you ask me. Still, a bit of overtime never comes amiss. Oh, hold on, Mr M.' She held his arm, not that he could have gone anywhere, as she seemed to have trapped him in a corner with her trolley. 'Ming Wai?' she called.

A nurse sitting at the station in the middle of the ward looked up. 'Yes, Edna?'

'Visitor, love. Fiddling with the bedding.' She pointed and the nurse got up and strode over to the other side of the ward.

Trapped by the trolley, Maxwell could feel his right leg growing numb. It probably wasn't a good idea to crash to the ground holding your leg, up here in Lady Elizabeth Molester, so he tried to alleviate it by doing a little subliminal hopping.

'You all right, Mr M? We have to keep an eye, you know, on people bringing in germs. Fiddling with bedding's not allowed. No need, is there, with these lovely nurses about? You're here to see Mrs Troubridge, I suppose? Love her, she's not very well, you know, not well at all.' She made a screwing motion near her temple and mouthed the next phrase. 'Gone a bit mental.' She compressed her lips and folded her arms. 'Still, she's in the best place, in'she? Since she's become institutionalised, she might as well be in one. Must get on, this tea won't pour itself.'

Maxwell felt strange, here with Mrs B in such an alien landscape, but old habits die hard and he knew that he would wake up sweating and confused later if he didn't go through the motions. 'Yes, fine, thank you. I'm not surprised,' he said, taking her stream of consciousness one wave at a time. 'I should say not and they *are* lovely, aren't they? Yes, I am. No, she's not, or so I hear.' He also dropped his voice for the next one. 'Bless,' he mouthed. Then, 'Yes, she is indeed. No, I don't expect it will.'

They smiled at each other, content that the ritual had been played out and that, moonlight though they both might in their various areas of expertise, they were still, and always would be, there for each other.

'Take care, Mr M,' she said, taking the strain as she eased the trolley away from his legs and got it trundling down the ward. 'I'll see you up at the school on Monday. We missed you.'

'And I missed you too, Mrs B,' Maxwell said, and he meant it. She would have injected a welcome blast of sanity in an otherwise rather surreal week. Nobody would have gone missing if Mrs B had been there. Rubbing a bit of feeling back into his thigh, he took a deep breath and joined Millie Muswell at Mrs Troubridge's bedside.

The huge woman looked up as Maxwell sat down opposite. 'Mr Maxwell,' she whispered. It was a strange noise, not so much a whisper as a shout, just really, really far away. 'How nice to see you.'

'I thought you'd gone home,' Maxwell said, quietly. He was confused. If Millie was still here, why had Henry Hall not met her at the house?

'Oh, no, Mr Maxwell,' she breathed. 'I had gone home. Well, not home as such. I had just moved on, for my researches, you know. I think Araminta and I have itchy feet in common, you know. Not like poor Jessica here, content to stay in one place all the time. Anyway, I popped back the other day, just to say hello, you know, as I was in the area. I remembered that you were away and I thought the poor thing might be lonely. So, of course, I found the house empty and asked the neighbours across the way where she might be.' She indicated the woman in the bed, so frail that she hardly disturbed the bedclothes. 'And I found her here.'

They silently contemplated the sleeping Mrs Troubridge. 'Is Araminta planning to visit?' Maxwell asked.

'I don't believe so,' Millie said, disapprovingly. 'You know the story, of course?'

'Well, yes, we do,' Maxwell said. 'But what family doesn't have its little ups and downs?' His Katharine Hepburn was unmistakeable, even in a hoarse whisper, but Millie Muswell, faux historian though she was, was not really into the Plantagenets and so it was all rather wasted.

'Well, I tried to persuade her, but to no avail. But still, I don't suppose it would do any good. Apparently, she is hardly ever conscious.'

Suddenly, Mrs Troubridge's eyes flew open and her head tossed madly from side to side. She fixed her gaze on Maxwell and then on Millie. She tried to sit up, scrabbling at the bedclothes. 'Ninety-nine thousand,' she shouted. 'One billion. Please don't. Mr Maxwell, please don't...' then she fell back on the pillows, exhausted.

The nurse leapt to her feet and came at a run. She elbowed Millie out of the way and leant in close to the sick woman, slipping an arm behind her head. 'It's all right, lovey,' she murmured. 'I'm here. I won't let anyone hurt you.'

Mrs Troubridge let her head fall back against the nurse's arm. She turned her head to Maxwell. 'I think you'd better both go now,' she said. 'She's very hard to settle when she gets like this.'

Maxwell was shocked by seeing his old neighbour in such a state. Somehow, he could only picture her lurking outside the door, clipping invisible shoots from the hedge, waiting to gossip or complain. Toothless, with her hair parted to one side in a way she never wore it, in a hospital nightgown, sizes too big and slipping off her shoulder, she seemed like a stranger. But he was very reluctant to leave this fragile little person here on her own. Even so, he felt he had to deal with Millie, who was flailing her enormous hands about and seemed to be trying to manhandle either the nurse or Mrs Troubridge or both to one side.

'Come on, Millie,' he said. 'I know it's upsetting, but the nurses know best.' He hauled on her sleeve, but nothing seemed to move. It was like trying to shift Mount Rushmore.

'Come on, duck,' suddenly Mrs B was at her other side. 'Let the dog see the rabbit. No good staying here, in the way. Go with Mr Maxwell here and I'll stay with your friend. Mrs Troubridge and I go way back, don't we, Mr M? I'll be finished in a minute and Ming Wai won't mind if I stay, will you, love?'

Without turning round, the nurse grabbed her chance. 'That would be great, Edna, if you would.' Then, mindful of her budget, 'Off the clock, though?'

'Of course!' Mrs B was outraged. 'I'm doing it for a friend.' She met Maxwell's eye around the substantial back of Millie Muswell.

231

'Thanks, Mrs B,' he said. 'Come on, Millie. Mrs B will take care of her.'

A booming noise filled his ears and he shook his head as Metternich did when he had swallowed a fly. He looked around and then realised what it was. Millie Muswell was crying.

Chapter Fifteen

Outside the hospital grounds, Maxwell realised he had given himself a bit of a task. He had to get rid of Millie before Jacquie came to fetch him, otherwise he could see them ending up with a house guest. True, the house next door was, by definition, empty, but it seemed rather ghoulish to put her in there. They had just about enough milk in the house for a cup of coffee and a bowl of cereal in the morning and something told Maxwell that Millie was probably not a frugal eater.

'Are you staying here tonight?' he asked her in a casual tone.

'Here?' She gave an enormous, gulping sob and looked around her. 'Where?'

'No, not literally *here*,' he said. 'I mean in Leighford, in the area in general.'

'No, no, I have a hotel room in Brighton. I ought to think about getting back. Do you know the train times?' She looked vaguely around again, as if a departures board might suddenly materialise against the fence.

Maxwell was not a train user by inclination – he'd never really trusted them since that unfortunate incident with Mr Huskisson and the Rocket's pistons – and he had no idea when the last train was. But by listening carefully to the whispered plans in his classes, he had gathered that it was possible to go clubbing in Brighton and get back on the last train, which was at midnight, fooling parents and responsible adults in general that the whole evening had been spent playing Scrabble at a friend's house. So he assumed the last train in the other direction was of that general time. 'I would imagine eleven-thirty, midnight, that sort of thing. Jacquie is picking me up at the pub at ten. Why don't you wait there with me and I'm sure she would be delighted to give you a lift to the station?'

Millie brayed with pleasure. 'Would she do that? Oh, you are kind, both of you. I must admit, I did wonder how I was going to get back. The hospital is such a walk from the station.'

'Well, it was very kind of you to come,' he said. If the conversation got any more trite, he thought, she would be saying thank you for having me.

'Least I could do,' Millie said. 'The family seems to be getting smaller and smaller and we have to watch out for each other. Poor Jessica. Do you think she will be all right?'

Maxwell was stuck for an answer. It was true that Mrs Troubridge had come through all manner of alarums and excursions in the time they had been neighbours, what with the Incident and everything, but this was Medical. Other people, professional people, were worried about her and somehow that made the outcome less easy to second-guess. 'I really don't know, Millie. She certainly seemed to be rather frail.'

The woman looked at him, faintly surprised. 'Of course she's frail,' she trumpeted. 'A gust of wind would blow her over. She comes from the slight side of my family. It's my mother who gives me my strong constitution.' She slapped him on the back and nearly broke his shoulder. 'Strong bones. That's what we have. Wouldn't snap like a twig just falling down the stairs.'

'That's very fortunate,' Maxwell said. 'But I meant, frailer than usual. The calling-out, that kind of thing.'

'That was very upsetting,' Millie conceded. She gave Maxwell a sidelong glance. 'She seemed rather frightened, I thought. Did you think that?'

'Yes, she seemed a little nervous,' Maxwell agreed. 'But people, when they are on painkillers, morphine, things like that, they can say very strange things. I made advances to the dentist once, and I'd only gone in for a filling.'

'Really? And did that worry you, at all? Make you wonder about anything...' she narrowed her eyes and lowered her voice, so that it seemed to arrive in his brain not through his ears, but up his legs from the soles of his feet, 'subliminal?'

'No,' he said, hurriedly. 'I was just trying to be funny. A little joke, Millie, that's all.' Suddenly the whole week caught up with him in one hit and he wanted to be home, snuggled up with Jacquie, Nole and the Count, watching something mindless on telly, no one missing, no one ill. Just the usual same ol', same ol'.

'I see.' She fetched him a sharp one on the arm. 'Cheer me up. How thoughtful.' The whole speech was delivered in the tones of a sarcophagus lid closing. 'Thank you. But I think what I meant was, she seemed frightened of you.'

'Me?' Maxwell cast his mind back. Taken in one way, he supposed that the old woman's words

235

could be construed that way, but there was no need for Mrs Troubridge to be frightened of him, surely. 'I think you must have misunderstood, Millie. Apart from anything else, I wasn't even in Leighford when she fell.'

'As far as we know,' Millie said, darkly. 'As far as we know.' Then, as if she had not spoken, she said, brightly, 'Did you take Nolan to the zoo, at all, on the Isle of Wight?'

'Not the zoo, as such, no. Jacquie isn't wild about snakes and they rather specialise. On our free afternoon, we went to Amazon World. Ant-eaters, tapirs, sloths, that sort of creature.'

'How lovely. Even sloths are very endearing as babies, aren't they?'

'They have their moments,' Maxwell agreed. It was quite difficult to keep up with Millie's thought processes, but fortunately, they had arrived at the door of the Horse & Collar, an unpretentious pub with the cheapest beer and wine and the most expensive food in town, to allow for the habits of the local influx from the medical professions. The ground outside was carpeted with dog-ends, mostly sucked down to the filter. On fine nights, there were more people outside than in. Maxwell pushed open the door and gestured to Millie. 'Shall we?'

'I don't usually go in to pubs, Mr Maxwell,' she said, looking furtively in through the door, as if expecting an orgy to be taking place in the public bar.

'Well, you're with me,' he smiled, giving her a nudge, which did no good. 'You'll be perfectly safe.'

'Well, just a tiny drink, then,' she said and edged in, shyly. There was a table right by the door and Maxwell pulled out one of the chairs for her. 'You are such a gentleman,' she said. 'Thank you.'

'What will you have to drink?' he asked, rummaging for his wallet.

'What are you going to have?' she asked, a little coquettishly. The effect was not attractive and Maxwell was keen to get away for a minute to the bar, where he could recover.

'My usual drink is Southern Comfort,' he said, 'but...'

'I'll have one of those, then,' she said, 'if I may?'

'Ice?'

'No, thank you,' she said. 'I have sensitive gums.'

'I'll be back in a moment,' Maxwell said and went up to the bar, leaning on it in the time-honoured tradition, one foot up on the rail, a note between his fingers.

'Evening, Mr Maxwell,' a voice said in his ear. He closed his eyes for a heartbeat. He had *specifically* said 'No Leighford Highenas' on his way down the stairs, and yet here was one. 'Not often we see you in here.'

Reluctantly, he turned his head. Praise be – not an Old Leighford Highena, but Donald, the post-mortem technician. Almost unbelievably, he appeared to have put on a few hundredweight. 'Donald! How the hell are you?' he said, shaking the man's hand. 'I haven't seen you since Adam was in the Militia.'

'No,' Donald said ruefully. 'We're very quiet at the moment. Dr Astley's on his holiday and we've

237

got a locum in.' He ran the sentence back and realised it made little sense. 'Not that that's why we're quiet, of course. That's two completely different things.'

'Yes, I do understand, Donald,' Maxwell said. 'I didn't think that even Dr Astley provided his own bodies.' He let his eyes swivel sideways and leant closer, 'Although, I did hear the odd rumour...' and he nudged Donald where he presumed his ribs ought to be. 'Have you ever given any thought to why things go quiet? There must be a reason.' The barman caught his eye. 'I'll have two Southern Comforts, no ice and... Donald?'

The big man downed the remains of his pint and slammed the glass down on the bar. 'I'll have another of these, thanks very much, Mr Maxwell. *Two* Southern Comforts? Is Jacquie ... I mean, Mrs Maxwell with you?' Donald and Angus, the forensics supremo, fought over Jacquie's supposed attentions, in a spirit of brotherly competition. Unbeknownst to Maxwell they both had photos of her, head to foot in SOCO whites, in their respective lockers. Donald turned his head without removing his elbows from the bar; a neat trick honed over the years of solitary drinking. 'Where is she?'

'I hate to disappoint you, Donald,' Maxwell said, picking up his change, 'but I'm not with Jacquie. I'm with that lady over there, by the door.'

This time, Donald turned round completely, spilling a fair bit of his pint in the process. 'Good God, Mr Maxwell. Have you gone nuts?' The technician could scarcely believe the evidence of his own eyes. "What a moose.'

'Now, Donald,' Maxwell said, calmly, picking up the Southern Comforts. 'Millie might not be to everyone's taste, but I am pretty sure she has a heart of gold.'

'Where?' Donald asked. 'How would you know? Blimey, Mr Maxwell, I'm glad I don't have to get that one in one of my fridges.'

'Your sensitivity does you credit, Donald. Anyway, nice seeing you. Give my regards to Dr Astley when he returns. Gone anywhere nice, has he?'

'Huh.' This was clearly a sore point. 'He's come into some money. Somebody died. He and the lush are cruising round the Greek Islands, apparently. For a month.'

Maxwell knew that Marjorie Astley drank a bit. Or rather more than a bit, in fact. Obviously Donald knew as well. Perhaps a month on ouzo and retsina might be a good way of getting her out of the habit. 'Nice. I hope Jacquie doesn't get to hear of it. We were supposed to be going abroad for our holidays this autumn, but something came up.'

'Something nice?' Donald asked politely

'Not ever so, no. It was a school trip to the Isle of Wight.'

'Oooh,' Donald said. 'I didn't know that was *you*. Was it the one where that woman was butchered in the hotel shower?'

'No, Donald,' Maxwell said, with a sigh. Did gossip know no bounds? 'That was Janet Leigh in the Bates Motel and it was *Psycho*. Anyway, as I think I said, nice to see you. I must rejoin my guest.' Donald launched himself off the bar, with

239

the clear intention of following Maxwell to the table. An evening of Donald and Millie, no matter how little time remained, was quite a picture and he knew he must get out of it, if only he could work out how. A small noise worked its way into his brain. 'Is that your bum making that noise?' he asked, pointing.

Donald slapped his pocket and then drew out a pager. 'Oh, bugger. I'm needed. Never mind.' He drained his pint in one and slammed the glass down again. 'My fault for saying we were quiet.'

'You're on duty?' Maxwell asked, surprised. He had always thought that post-mortems tended to be done in the day, to a timetable, strictly nine to five and usually two days after the event.

'Overtime,' he said. 'We have an on-call system for the SOCO and they are a bit short-handed. Also, this locum they've got in for Astley, well, she's a bit green, so I said I would be on when she was, help out, know what I mean?'

'She?' The light was dawning. Donald was a sucker for a pretty face.

'Strictly professional.' The fat man bridled, setting his chins wobbling. 'I don't know if it is SOCO yet, though. It might just be somebody croaked in theatre, something like that.'

Maxwell dropped his voice and Donald leant in to listen. 'My ... companion and I have just come from visiting a very sick friend in the General. So, perhaps...'

'Sorry, Mr Maxwell. Lips are sealed.' And Donald swept through the doors with a jaunty wave at Millie, to his date with Death.

'A friend of yours?' Millie asked, when Maxwell

240

sat down.

'Not as such,' he told her. 'Just someone I have met while ... enjoying my hobby.'

Her eyes shone. 'Hobbies. Yes. Marvellous things. I, for instance, derive so much pleasure from my genealogy. I could tell you some tales! Oh, yes.' And she proceeded to do so until, like an angel of mercy, Jacquie's head popped round the door of the pub.

'Millie!' she cried, somehow adding subliminally to Maxwell, 'What the hell is going on?'

'Darling!' he replied, adding in body language, 'Don't worry. She just needs a lift to the station.' To make things clearer he added, out loud, 'Millie needs a lift to the station, heart, if that is possible.'

'Of course,' Jacquie said, holding the door open for them both. 'Not a problem at all. Oh,' she glanced at the table, 'finish your drinks first. No hurry.'

Millie picked up her glass and chugged back the drink. For a stranger to liquor, she had a hell of a swallow on her. The drunk in the corner all but applauded.

'I won't bother, thanks, honeybunch,' Maxwell said, eyes wide.

'That is very pleasant,' Millie boomed. 'What did you say it was called?'

'Southern Comfort,' Maxwell said, stealing a sidelong glance at Jacquie.

'Lovely,' Millie said, licking her top lip to get the last drop. 'I must get some in for Christmas.'

'Right,' said Jacquie, herding her charges towards the car. 'The station it is.' The first mad

241

bars of 'Flight of the Bumblebee' rang out. 'Sorry,' she said. 'I should take this.' She wandered off away from the car, head inclined and one finger in her ear. Maxwell chased her, ostensibly to get the keys, but also to listen in if possible. Unfortunately, his timing was way off and she was receiving rather than transmitting. He went back towards Millie, swinging the keys around one finger. There was some unseemly struggling with the complexities of the immobiliser and the door had only just sprung open when Jacquie returned and slid into the driving seat without speaking.

Millie got in the car and looked around, perplexed. 'Where is Nolan?' she asked. 'You surely haven't left him at home all alone?'

'No,' Jacquie said, tersely. 'Of course not. He is staying with some friends of ours. The school trip was a little stressful. Max and I needed a break for a day or two.'

'Really,' Millie said, acidly. 'Well, I must say, had I ever been lucky enough to have a child, especially one as lovely as Nolan, *I* shouldn't just leave him with any Tom, Dick or Harry because I wanted a break.'

'Goodness me, Millie,' Maxwell said, mildly. 'Keep your wig on. We are lucky to have Nolan, I especially am lucky to have him, and we don't just fling him at the nearest passer-by. But even if we did, I don't really think it is anyone's place to say so.' He might have been a public schoolboy, but even Maxwell had his limits. Neither David Starkey nor Jeremy Paxman were overkeen to mix it with him.

The sweet Millie was back in an instant. 'Oh,

no, no offence intended,' she purred, making the dashboard vibrate. 'I just feel very strongly about family, as you know.'

Maxwell, who had come as near to hating history as he ever would come in his life whilst listening to her stories of genealogy adventures, nodded, his head lolling tiredly. He almost drifted off as Jacquie negotiated all the short cuts a woman policeman learns and got them to the station in record time. She stopped at the front entrance and leapt out and wrenched Millie's door open, virtually dragging the woman out.

'Well, lovely to see you again, Millie. Where do you need the train for?'

'Brighton, but...'

'Lovely. Far platform. Around every half an hour at this time, I believe. Smashing to see you again. Bye bye.' She leapt into the car and was off, as if Leighford Station was the starting point of a race and she was in pole position.

Maxwell turned and waved out of the rear window as Millie's waving figure grew smaller as the distance between them grew, rather more quickly than the speed limit strictly allowed. Then they turned a corner and she was gone.

'Tom, Dick or Harry?' exploded Jacquie. 'Who the hell does she think she is?'

'Well...'

'Don't say Millie bloody Muswell or you can go and share her hotel room with her, Mister, and no mistake.' Jacquie was an excellent driver, which was just as well, because the phrase 'to cut corners' was seldom as accurate as it was now. She flung the car round as though she was on a crash test circuit and, seat belt notwithstanding, Maxwell was flung from side to side as if he was the dummy of the same ilk. Something had upset her, and it wasn't a bit of lip from Millie Muswell. Experience told Maxwell to just hang on and wait; she would tell him in her own good time.

'Sodding, buggering, sodding bugger,' Jacquie exploded as soon as they got through the front door at 38 Columbine and burst into tears.

'Sweetheart,' Maxwell said, scooping her up, to get a kick on the shin and a thump on the arm for his pains. Plan B. 'Jacquie.' He shook her. 'What is the matter with you? Ever since...' he stopped shaking her and lowered his voice. 'Ever since you got that phone call, you've been like a thing possessed.' A horrible thought crept like cold water up the back of his neck, over his scalp and seemed to settle in the fine skin round his eyes, making it hard to focus. 'What was it? Is it Mrs Troubridge? She seemed very...'

Jacquie shook her head, reached into her pocket and, pulling out a handkerchief, blew her nose hard. 'No,' she said, squaring her shoulders and looking him in the eye, almost defiantly. 'It's Izzy. Some kids looking for a quiet spot for a barbecue, smoke a few joints, generally not get interrupted, found her. She's dead at the bottom of a cliff, with a broken neck.' And finally, she fell into his arms and cried, cried for the dead woman, her husband and everything sad in the world.

244

Chapter Sixteen

Henry Hall was sitting quietly at his desk, full of a Chinese meal, but not so full that he couldn't cheerfully have eaten another, when his phone rang.

'No calls,' he said sharply, then listened to the desk sergeant who was on the other end. 'Is it? Put them through.' He waited only semi-patiently to the series of clicks and whirrs that this instruction set in motion.

'Is that DCI Hall?' A woman's voice, clipped and businesslike came through.

'Speaking.'

'Sergeant Carpenter-Maxwell gave me your number and asked me to ring. This is Hampshire Police.'

'Right.' Henry Hall armed himself with a pencil, ready to take down some numbers, names, case numbers. 'Fire away.'

'Nothing to fire with, really, DCI Hall,' the woman said, flatly. 'I am just ringing to tell you that, pending visual identification, we believe we have found the body of Isabelle Medlicott.'

Hall dropped his pencil and also almost dropped the phone. 'I'm sorry,' he said. 'I thought you were just ringing to ... well, to make contact.' He found his pencil again and pulled a larger piece of paper towards him. 'Where was she found?'

'At the bottom of a cliff, not much more than half a mile from the hotel where the group was staying. As I understand it, they did go out to look for her.'

'I believe so, yes,' said Hall, making notes.

'If you should come across any of the people involved in that search, then I would appreciate if you could make it clear to them that it would have made no difference had they found her. Death was instantaneous.'

After he got used to the feeling that the woman was reading from a script, Hall appreciated her style. 'I assume she struck a rock, or something. With her head?' Without small talk from the other end, not so much as an 'uh-huh' it was like talking into a bucket.

'She may well have done, yes,' the policewoman said. 'In fact, there are contusions on Mrs Medlicott's body, but they are all post-mortem. In fact, our pathologist is of the opinion that her neck was broken at the cliff top.'

Henry Hall felt the world stop turning. His life flashed before him, especially the bit spent sitting next to Mrs Troubridge's bed, looking at all the many and varied bruises on her body. In his memory, it seemed that there were some, around her neck, that had nothing to do with a fall downstairs. 'Strangled?' he asked.

'No. He thinks a chop. She has grass and soil under her fingernails, so we think that it was a push, but she saved herself. Then, the murderer leant over and gave her a karate chop with the side of the hand. He must have been quite powerful.'

'Definitely a man?' Hall had to check, but a

man was beginning to take shape in his mind. Not too powerful in the Arnold Schwarzenegger sense, perhaps, but fit enough.

'I should say so, but, of course, we must never say never, DCI Hall. Anyway, I'm sorry to be ringing you so late and with such sad news. I understand that Sergeant Carpenter-Maxwell was a friend of the family.'

'She knows them, yes,' Hall said. He didn't want to label Jacquie as a friend. It was going to be bad enough trying to tie everything together, what with different forces and only a thread in his brain to link them, without having Jacquie off the case because of conflict of interest.

'She seemed quite upset,' the woman remarked.

'She would be, yes. She ... it's very complicated.'

'I see. Well, apart from keeping you in the loop, DCI Hall, I rang to ask if you could send someone out to inform the husband. Sergeant Carpenter-Maxwell was very insistent that we didn't phone him. She said he is under medication at the moment, is that right?'

'He is, yes,' Hall confirmed. 'He came in to the station, but we took medical advice and our police surgeon gave him a sedative and we took him home.' He sensed the woman's heightened awareness on the other end of the phone.

'He's been in to the station? May I ask why, particularly?'

'We just wanted a chat. We only had second-hand information and I felt that since this had happened on a school trip, we needed extra confirmation, in case this should become a child protection issue.' Hall was proud of himself; he had managed to justify himself without lying too much.

Back in her night-dark office, his caller smiled. Clever. Very clever. There was some other issue here that he wasn't going to share. However, he clearly wasn't going to tell her what his agenda was and, with all the other things on her desk, she didn't really want to know all that much. So she let him off the hook. 'I see. You have his address, then?'

'Yes, we do.' She seemed to have bought it, to his surprise.

'Well, DCI Hall, if I could leave it with you, then? I'm not sure how to arrange identification if Mr Medlicott is too ill to travel, but we can talk that over tomorrow, perhaps.'

'Be glad to,' Henry said. 'Could I have a contact number for you?' She gave it and he wrote it down. 'Thank you. Goodnight.' He put the phone down and rubbed his eyes, which were suddenly feeling rather tired. Then he picked up the phone again and dialled zero for the front desk. 'Do we have a WPC around at the moment?' he asked.

'Yes, guv,' the desk sergeant said. 'We've got...' There was a pause as he turned to look at the duty roster. 'Sorry, guv. My mistake. I thought we had Mel, but she's off sick. Do you want me to call someone in?'

'No, no. Don't do that,' Hall said. Staff off sick could become part of a vicious circle if the powers that be weren't careful and he had seen it many times. Staff off sick means everyone else works twice as hard. Working twice as hard means going off sick, with stress, viruses or just good old fed-upitis. Best not start that cascade off. He sighed and said, 'I'll do it. Just send anyone you've got to the car park and I'll be down there in a minute.'

'Need anything special, guv? Ram, anything like that?' The desk sergeant watched a lot of American TV and was beginning to lose the flavour of life on the streets of Leighford.

'No. Nothing special. A box of tissues might come in handy, though.'

'Oh,' the desk man understood at once. 'One of those. OK, guv. Will do.' And the phone went down with a clatter.

Henry Hall sat for a moment, hands flat on his desk. He took a deep breath and stood up, reaching behind him for his jacket. He hated these jobs, but he was glad he had drawn the short straw. He would be on the spot to see how Medlicott reacted to the news of his wife's death. He had had to shelve one theory – suicide – because surely even the most determined suicide didn't push themselves off the cliff with a well-aimed karate chop. So now he had just the two theories – wandering maniac or conspiracy. He had long ceased to believe in the wandering maniac, so that left him with one theory, which he could put to the test as soon as he got to the Medlicott's house. He checked he had his keys, switched off his desk light and ran down the back stairs to the car park.

Maxwell and Jacquie had settled down in their respective seats in the sitting room with their respective favourite drinks in hand. Metternich stretched out along the back of the sofa and every now and then touched a paw to Jacquie's shoulder. She turned her head and nuzzled his back

'You're an old softie,' she said. The cat, outraged, got up and walked away, his tail high, his pencil sharpener bum swaggering from side to side. You give them an inch…

'Oops,' Maxwell told her. 'You've offended him now.'

'Well, he is,' she said, taking a sip of her gin and tonic, not quite Pansy-style, but pretty near. She curled her feet up under her and sighed. 'Sorry for being so wet earlier,' she said.

'Sweetie,' Maxwell said. 'You had every right. You've had a hell of a day, well, hell of a week, really. School trips are far more stressful than anybody thinks, though I must say the kids this time deserve to be mentioned in despatches. I've never known such a good year group. I thought we had the difficult ones; I think someone must have got the paperwork mixed up.'

'Some of them were a bit strange,' Jacquie said. 'The one with the notebook.'

'Ah, the lovely Jarvis,' Maxwell said.

'I thought his name was Gervaise,' Jacquie said. 'That's what it had on the list.'

'Long story. My favourite was the one who folded everything. Did you notice her?'

'Oh. Do you know, I wondered where all those little pellets of paper were coming from. Which one was that?' She was enjoying this, even if it was just pencil sharpening to stay away from the job in hand.

'It was that tiny little girl, the one with the plait with about three hairs in it. She folded everything, not just paper. She was sitting next to the one with the ears, you know the one.' He chuckled, just picturing it.

'How could you miss? She looked like a taxi with the doors open.'

'Yes, very unfortunate for the poor child. We were coming back from ... Carisbrooke, I think it was. I took a stroll down the bus and there they were, the folder had folded the ear kid's ears right in. They looked like little envelopes. Uncanny, it looked, and then, suddenly,' he was leaning forward, drawing her in, 'they popped out.' He sprang upright, hands in the air.

Jacquie was laughing now. 'Poor kid. What did she do?'

'Just folded them back in. It was like earigami.'

Jacquie was disappointed. 'I thought that was a true story,' she complained. 'But you did it just for the joke.'

'No,' he protested. 'It really happened. I just thought of the joke, just now. Ask Sylv. She took a picture.'

'Talking of pictures,' Jacquie said. 'I've downloaded the pictures from the camera. Henry wanted one of ... one of Izzy.'

Maxwell decided to ignore it for the present. 'Are they good? The pictures?'

'Some are. The problem was we were always with so many people. Not just the kids and staff but holidaymakers, all over the shop. And I would swear there isn't a single one without Pansy in it.'

'Surely not that one of Nole and me cleaning

our teeth?'

She laughed. 'No, perhaps not that one.' She twirled her glass and watched the last shards of ice break up and disappear. 'We've got to talk about it, Max. We can't pretend it hasn't happened, can we?'

'No,' he said, solemnly. 'We can't. But I think we can leave it until tomorrow. You're so tired I don't know how you're still upright. There's nothing we can do tonight. Henry will see to it that Tom is told properly, sympathetically. Tomorrow, when we all feel a bit brighter, you can call Henry and see if there is anything you can do.' It almost cost him an arm and a leg, but he didn't ask her a single question about what she knew about the case. He could feel the words bouncing around in his head, in his mouth, beating on the inside of his skull to be let out. But he knew that this wasn't the time. With his wife, as with good comedy, timing was everything, so he would wait.

Jacquie wasn't so tired that she didn't wonder what Maxwell was up to; why wasn't he bombarding her with questions? Perhaps she *was* too tired. She wasn't concentrating. She put down her glass and yawned, stretching. 'I think I will go up to bed. I'm pooped.'

'Of course you are, heart. I'll come and tuck you in, then I might do a spot of modelling. Is that OK?'

She stood up and reached out a hand to him. 'That would be lovely. Come on, then, up the wooden hill to Bedfordshire.' She pretended to haul him hand over hand to his feet and they went upstairs.

While she was in the bathroom, he turned back the duvet and fluffed her pillows. He turned on her bedside light and turned off the main one, so that when she came back all she could see was an inviting patch of sheet in a pool of warm light, the man she loved standing there with her book in his hand, ready to hand her into bed like a very attentive butler.

'Oh, no reading, I don't think,' she said, turning on her side. She switched her light off and reached up, lips pursed cartoon-style for a kiss. 'Night night. See you in the morning.'

'Night night,' he said, 'Sleep tight. Don't let the bed bugs bite.' He looked down at his wife with a smile, but she was already asleep.

It was not true that Peter Maxwell could only think straight when he was talking to his cat. He had many cogent thoughts when sitting apparently asleep in staff briefings at Leighford High School, as James Diamond could ruefully attest. He could follow a train of thought through the most labyrinthine of A level Politics debates, blowing the arrogant and the ignorant out of the water having apparently been sitting marking in a corner of the room. But when it came to un-ravelling a crime, especially the crime of murder, his favourite sparring partner was definitely Metternich, the cat who thought for himself.

Maxwell switched on the modelling lamp which hung over his work table. A deep pool of shadow was over the basket which had, through long usage, become the Count's favourite seat. It had once belonged in the bathroom, but now, matted with a lightly padded covering of black and white hair, it was generally agreed that the cat could have it. He showed as some white patches in the gloom, which stirred slightly when the light snapped on.

Maxwell adjusted the vintage forage cap which gave him his inspiration till it was at the correct angle. He picked up the partially constructed James Olley of the 4th Light Dragoons and chose a suitable brush and pot of colour. He held his breath as he applied the first delicate stroke and then exhaled gently, so as not to disturb the tiny fragments of paper, the shards of plastic which, in the fullness of time, might well become a vital piece of some other figure.

Metternich was far too polite to begin the conversation. There was a certain protocol which prevailed in these private chats and the cat had indeed known occasions when Maxwell came up to the loft just to be quiet by the simple expedient of not speaking. But somehow, something in the air tonight kept the beast on his perch, though his superfine hearing could detect the scrabbling of bats in the eaves, the swish of tiny feet through the grass at the edge of the lawn. Given the time and the solitude, he could have heard the moths beating their powdery way towards the glow of the street light. All of them were fair game, some tastier than others. Moths, for example, made him sneeze. He'd take a frog if one crossed his path, but preferred not to, because they made him dribble. And if a frog followed a moth, he could be all night cleaning the resultant goo off his whiskers. Bats just tasted of old shoes marinated in wee. Voles made good presents, but there was nothing quite like a nice corn-fed mouse, best at this time of year. Metternich preferred to eat seasonally; he liked to watch Jamie Oliver as well as the next mammal. These mouse-based musings were interrupted as Maxwell turned to him and said something he didn't catch.

He raised his head. 'Murrrhh?' he said. It didn't mean anything in Cat, but the Boy seemed to like it, so he used it now and then.

Maxwell chuckled. 'Sorry, were you miles away?' he asked.

He had no idea. Metternich buried his nose again, but kept one ear up, to denote that Maxwell had his full attention.

'To recap,' Maxwell said, pleasantly, 'I was just wondering who this second body might be. It can't be Izzy's father, because I'm sure otherwise Tom would have mentioned that he had died through foul play. I mean,' he put another dab of paint on Olley's jacket, 'it's the sort of thing you mention, isn't it? Not many people have a murderee in the family, do they? It's a conversation piece.'

There was no reply from the cat, who didn't see what all the fuss was about. Death was a daily routine for him and if he had a mouse for every one of his friends who he had discovered squashed on the side of the road ... well, his maths wasn't great, but he knew he would have more than one mouse.

'So,' Maxwell mused, accidentally putting the

wrong end of the brush in his mouth and spitting. 'Eugghh. Cobalt blue doesn't taste half as nice as burnt umber. So, it must be someone from where they lived before, wouldn't you say? Where was that, can you remember?'

Metternich had no idea.

'Nottingham? No, I would have remembered that because of the sheriff. It began with "N", I'm sure...' He laid down a little more paint. 'Northampton,' he said suddenly, making the cat jump awake and sit up, looking round wildly. 'You agree? Good, because I'm sure that's it. Deene – Lord Cardigan's country pad. Yes, that's the county. The problem we have now, Count, is that I have no idea how I progress that thought, without asking the Mem outright and she has learnt a great deal of cunning over the years and can see a ploy at a thousand yards.' He put down the little figure he was painting, carefully leaning him on an old wine cork so that his wet bits didn't smudge. 'I know what you're thinking.'

The cat was surprised. He wasn't under the impression that anyone not of the feline persuasion knew all the methods for immolating moles. He was impressed, despite himself.

'You're thinking that, if only I were a little more computer literate, then I could look up newspapers and such, to see if anything was reported. And I would reply to you, that there is a box of recycling downstairs holding months' worth of various newspapers, which might well tell us just what we need to know. *And,*' Maxwell held up a triumphant finger, 'the good bit is that the Mem needn't know what I'm doing, because I shall simply pretend I am doing some tidying up. So, brownie points all round.' He chuckled happily to himself, in honour of a job well done.

The cat, who usually let him witter on regardless, couldn't help but give him a withering look. The look said that he, Metternich, had known the Mem, Jacquie, for a much shorter time than he, Maxwell, had. The look also said that if Maxwell hadn't sorted out yet that nothing, absolutely *nothing* – not a whisker, not a disembodied tail, not the tiniest giblet – got past her, then really, he should just hang up his cycle clips and give up. Metternich had had her sussed within the first five minutes, as she had him. Their affection was built on a mutual respect of one expert in the field for another. The enormous feline gave a small snort of amusement and jumped down from his perch.

He walked to the door and looked at Maxwell in a meaningful way, which took a while to take effect.

'You want feeding?' Maxwell asked him. 'Again? Well, I suppose you deserve it, spending your hols in a cattery.' At this point, Jacquie would have fondled his ears, but Maxwell knew better. 'Come on, then. Let's see what we've got. I bet *you've* got some food in the cupboard.'

They crept down the stairs, man and cat, to the kitchen, where Maxwell fed Metternich something from a pouch which purported to be steamed fish. The cat lapped it up and Maxwell, unused to such an empty fridge, almost joined him. It was only lack of bread to sop up the gravy which stopped him. That, and the sudden

257

extreme tiredness which swept over him.

Leaving the cat to find his own way out, Maxwell wended his way to bed and fell asleep almost at once, little caring that the blue paint on his lips would give Jacquie a hell of a turn when she woke up next to him in the morning. Anyway, he thought, as his eyelids flickered for the last time, he would have licked it off by then, so peckish was he – he'd give his right arm for a Kit Kat.

'Do you know where this house is, guv?' asked Phil Smart, the duty sergeant assigned to Henry Hall for everyone's least favourite job.

'I don't know the very one, no,' Hall said. 'But I know the estate and it isn't very big. We shouldn't have a problem.'

'I hate these places at night, don't you?' Smart said. 'Nobody has proper numbers on their doors anymore, they're all fancy carved things with hedgehogs and stuff all over them. You have to practically be in the hall before you know what the number is.'

'True. Anyway, you look out for the numbers when we get there. It's jotted down on that sheet, there, in the file.'

The sergeant turned the sheet to the window to try and catch the light as the car whizzed down the dual carriageway on the outskirts of Leighford. He also tried to get the gist of the notes on the page. He had heard various snippets about this case in the canteen. There had been no briefing, because it wasn't a case, really. Not for them, anyway. There was a body here, a body there. Just no bodies in Leighford. He could see this one coming up to bite the boss in the arse, if he wasn't careful. But then, 'careful' was Henry Hall's middle name.

'Nearly there, Phil. Ready?'

'Yep. Whoah, could you slow down a bit, guv? Small numbers.' Craftcarn Avenue wasn't very long, but of course they had come in at the high-number end, and although the development was quite new, the waters had already been muddied by various 'a's and 'b's added when granny annexes had been built, or gardens sold.

Hall braked and they crawled past the houses, Smart counting under his breath as they went.

'It should be that one, guv, over there. Oh, hang on. I've done that wrong. He's in bed, sedated, isn't he?'

'That's right,' said Hall.

'Well, he must have got up again. All the lights are on, if that's the right house.'

'That's strange,' Hall said. 'It was light when they brought him back. I'm sure they wouldn't have just left them on. Perhaps you've counted wrong.' But, as they got nearer, it was clear that he hadn't. The Medlicott house was ablaze with light. Literally every bulb in the place must have been burning, down to the security light outside and the decorative fairy lights still in the tree since last Christmas.

'What's going on, guv?' Smart asked. 'Do you think he's had some kind of, well, a breakdown of some sort?' Smart was a bit of an amateur psychiatrist He had, after all, watched every episode of *Frasier*, some of them many times, and he could swap Freud and Jung with the best of them. 'He's probably put the lights on so that he can see his wife when she gets back.'

Hall rarely felt a shudder down his spine. But he did now. 'Let's hope not, Phil. I'm sure there's a sensible explanation.' He cut the engine and they got out of the car. 'I just can't think quite what it might be.'

Unconsciously mirroring each other, for comfort, the two men walked up the brick drive and Hall rang the bell. It echoed down the hall but no one came to the door.

'Perhaps he's dropped back off to sleep, guv,' Smart said, hopefully. 'He had a sedative, got up and switched the lights on and then just went back to sleep.' It had sounded lame enough in his head; out loud it fooled nobody. He didn't say the next thoughts at all – that he could well be hiding behind the door with a hatchet. Or lying in the bath in a pool of cooling, watery blood.

'Go round the back, Phil,' Hall suggested. 'The door might be open.'

The sergeant squeezed through the bushes at the side of the house. How they had the nerve to call these houses 'detached', he had no idea. You couldn't swing a cat in the gap. A sudden stench reminded him that cats could do a lot more than swing. When he got to the lawned area in the back, he spent a while cleaning off his shoe before going round the conservatory to the kitchen door, which was locked firmly.

Squeezing round the other side, by the garage, he rejoined Hall on the drive. Hall wrinkled his nose and moved away an inch or two. 'Sorry, guv,' the sergeant said, scraping his foot against the side of the bricks edging the garden. 'Cat shit.'

'Yes,' Hall said. 'So I noticed. No open door, though?'

'No. Locked tight.'

'One last try at something before you break in. There's a phone number in that file. We'll give that a go.' Hall watched as the man made his way back to the car, surreptitiously scraping the side of his foot every few steps. He reached in and pulled out the file. Leaning on the car he got out his phone and dialled a number, following it a few digits at a time from the page. Inside the house, a phone began to ring. Smart let it go on until the answerphone kicked in. A woman's voice said, 'Hi. You've reached Izzy and Tom. Sorry we're out, but we'd love to talk to you later. Leave a message with the beep, not forgetting your number, and we'll get back to you as soon as we can.' Then a man's voice joined hers. 'Byeeeee,' they sang out in unison. He broke the connection before the beep. There was something heartless about leaving a message for a dead woman, and although Phil Smart wasn't the most sensitive tooth in the denture, he just couldn't do it.

'No reply, guv,' he said, raising his voice enough for Hall to hear, but not enough to attract the neighbours outside.

'Right then, Phil.' Hall stepped back. 'Break in. But, can I suggest that before we go in, you take your shoes off?'

'Yes, guv. Sorry.' Phil Smart hated cats. Dogs only pooed where you could see it and scoop it. They didn't hide it in the undergrowth. He stepped into the open porch and slipped off his

261

shoes. Then, he used the non-cat-shit one to tap the glass near the handle. The faux-stained unit crazed but didn't break at first, but a few more taps did the job and the whole thing fell out onto the hall floor. It also fell onto the head of Tom Medlicott, as he lay there at a rakish angle, his legs up the stairs. But he didn't mind. He was quite, quite dead.

Chapter Seventeen

If Phil Smart had managed not to disturb the neighbours earlier, then they were certainly disturbed now. Some twitched their curtains aside and stood concealed in the darkness of their bedrooms. Some came blatantly out into their drives and watched, their dressing gowns clutched tightly round them against the first autumnal chill on the September air. The sirens had been cut and the blue lights doused, but police were not a common occurrence in Craftcarn Avenue and everyone wanted to be in on the act. There might even be cameras!

Henry Hall and Phil Smart had called Leighford nick and the desk sergeant there had done the rest. From all quarters, police and SOCO had descended on the quiet suburbia of Craftcarn Avenue and had choked the road with vehicles and surrounded number 6 with yellow tape. Already, the local moaners were in full cry. Seated at computers or writing desks as their techno-knowledge dictated, they were shooting off letters to the local paper, the Chief Constable and the Prime Minister, by way of the Archbishop of Canterbury and Jeremy Kyle, to protest at the high-handed churning up of lawns, the scaring of children and small dogs and the interruption of their viewing pleasure. The fact that someone who they knew, a neighbour, was dead was something that they chose not to address.

First on the scene had been police backup, to keep the neighbours at bay. Then had come the SOCO team, in a white van. They had jumped out, dressed all in white, and had frightened an overimaginative and three-parts-drunk housewife at number 11 into hysterics. It was unfortunate that she had just finished watching *District 9* and was now on constant alert for the Men in White to come and purge the ghetto of Craftcarn Avenue. They erected a tent against the front of number 6 to shield their comings and goings from the nosy neighbours. Last came Donald and his discreet van. He parked back up the road. He jumped out of the driver's seat and rushed round to the passenger side to help down a woman of such exquisite beauty and apparent frailty that she made him look like something she had run up that afternoon out of spare parts. He guided her to the house and introduced her to the SOCO team, to whom she smiled and nodded. Angus, dressed in pristine white but carrying with him the aura of an old, abandoned squat, nodded at her and shook her hand in both of his gloved ones. His mouth wasn't visible behind his mask but the woman, whose name was Dr Lacey, knew he was leering horribly. She was beginning to tire of Donald's rather overwhelming care and longed to get up to her elbows in a really gory cadaver, without losing her supper, just to show him she was equal to anything that Leighford could throw at her.

She wasn't disappointed exactly when she saw Tom Medlicott, lying upside down on his own stairs, with scarcely a hair out of place, but she sensed that she wouldn't be setting the world on fire at this particular crime scene. She stayed in the doorway, waiting to be invited in. This confused the SOCO team, who were used to Jim Astley barging in, whingeing about being called away from his golf and shedding whatever outside detritus he happened to have clinging to his clothes onto any surface that presented itself. If sentences were to be passed on forensic evidence alone, he would be slogging through an indeterminate sentence, with a tariff of around nine million years rather than sailing round the Peloponnese. A white suit was found which she struggled into, turning back the legs and sleeves so that she could walk and use her hands. Donald stood back admiringly, smiling and nudging everyone. Anyone would think he had invented her.

'Donald?'

The fat man jumped to attention, making the ornaments on the hall table dance and rattle.

'Have you got my bag?' Her Birmingham accent was a disappointment. It shouldn't have been able to survive in the delicate setting of her size-six body; lips so perfect should not have been able to frame the sound. To Donald, it sounded like the sweetest birdsong.

He thrust it forward. He didn't say much when Dr Lacey was around. He seemed to get sweaty teeth and words tended to come out at random, sometimes with no vowels in them, so, rather than risk being sectioned, he kept quiet.

'Thank you.' She rummaged for a rectal

thermometer and most of the men looked away.

All over the house, white-clad men and women were puffing powder at light switches and flat surfaces. Their general demeanour was truculent; it was clear to everyone except Henry Hall that the bloke had thrown himself down the stairs because he had killed his missus. A small nagging thought at the back of every head, which tried to tell the head's owner that, for a grown man in decent health, throwing yourself down twelve stairs onto a roomy and thickly carpeted floor was more likely to result in a bruise at best, was brutally suppressed. The house was full of means of death, pointed out the thought. Knives, ropes, electrical equipment; all the means of slaughter we all possess. Why entrust your suicide to such a dodgy method?

And slowly, one by one, the SOCO team came to see Henry Hall as he stood immobile, waiting for results, in the tent at the front of the house. And one by one, they told him what he already knew. That almost the only fingerprints in the house belonged to Tom or Isabelle Medlicott. There were one or two in the kitchen belonging to Sergeant Carpenter-Maxwell. But not one of them was to be found on a light switch, since all of them had been wiped clean.

His final visitor, in his halogen-lit domain, was Dr Lacey. 'DCI Hall?' she asked.

'That's right,' Hall said. 'Dr Lacey, I assume. Thank you for coming out. Is Donald looking after you?' From anyone else, it would have carried a trace of irony and, had she been there, Jacquie, who knew her boss inside out, would

266

have been able to identify it – just. But to Dr Lacey, it seemed like a serious question.

'Oh,' she said, brightly. 'Yes, very well. Hmm, yes...' Her voice lost its natural enthusiasm. 'Very well. Anyway,' she perked up again, 'first thoughts. The deceased has been...' she had already painted herself into a linguistic corner, '...um, deceased for about four hours. He has no obvious injuries, although the postmortem will tell us more on that, except the one that killed him, of course, which is a broken neck, to put it simply.'

'Would you have expected that after such a shallow fall?' Hall asked, leaning forward, his glasses blank in the spotlight's glare.

'I have seen broken necks when someone falls from a sofa, DCI Hall,' she admonished.

'Have you?' He straightened up, astonished. 'Where?'

She spluttered a little. 'Well, not me personally, as such,' she said. 'There are examples in text-books, though.'

'Ah, *text*books. There you are, then.' Hall turned to Phil Smart, who was making notes in a corner. 'In textbooks, Phil,' he said. Then he turned back to the pathologist. 'No, Dr Lacey. You see, this is the real world, and in there is a real body. What I want to know, Dr Lacey, and make it quick because I have been up for a long time and I'm really tired, is this. Would you have expected a broken neck after such a shallow fall?'

She looked at him for what seemed like a week. His expression didn't change. Then, she said, 'Not really, no.'

'Well then, that's good,' he said. 'Because I don't expect one, either. Can you just pop back in there and see if there are any signs of his having received a blow of any kind to the neck. Any unusual bruising at all.'

She turned on her heel and went back in to the hall, tears pricking the backs of her eyes. She just wasn't being taken seriously. He wouldn't have sent Jim Astley back in like that. She said so to Angus. And although Angus thought she was a bit of all right, he felt he had to tell her. Jim Astley would have noticed the bruise, which was about as plain as the nose on his face. Then, Angus made a mental note to ignore any excess sodium in the facial swabs he would receive later in his lab. It would just be from the tears. But that was fine; it just made her more vulnerable.

Henry Hall didn't go back to the station. He knew that if he did, he would fall asleep at his desk and be found, all gritty-eyed and sweaty, by the Saturday shift when they came on duty, in not many hours time. He went home and poured himself a glass of milk, to fill in the gaps his long-ago Chinese meal had left, and took himself upstairs. He had a wash and stepped out of his clothes, leaving them like a shed skin in a trail from the bathroom door to the bed. Although he had no reason to suppose that any of the fatal falls dogging him this week had been accidental, nevertheless he took each tread very carefully indeed. He drank the milk as though it were medicine, switched off his bedside light and turned on his side, to have a think while he was still just about awake enough.

Tom Medlicott wasn't going to go anywhere where Donald didn't take him. The job of identifying Izzy Medlicott would have to go to someone else. Hall would check through the house on Saturday and see if he could find any addresses. He might need to get the IT boys on to the laptop if necessary. He was annoyed at the silly little pathologist. She was no Jim Astley; usually something he would consider a bit of a bonus, but in this case, when so many other threads were spreading out from Tom Medlicott's body, he couldn't leave anything to chance. He would send Bob Thorogood out first thing to have a word with Donald, who was the real brains in Leighford General morgue, to make sure he helped her find the right things. He was pretty sure the tox screen would come back negative, except for the couple of sedatives the police surgeon had prescribed. This killer was not subtle enough to use poison. This was hit-and-run, the blitz attack.

The man in the clown suit ran past him, heading for the stairs. He tried to call out to him to stop, that he might fall, what with the big, floppy shoes, and the cat and all those seagulls. He climbed up a ladder to see more clearly, but there were too many noodles on the rungs and he couldn't make the light go out, no matter how much he tried, because Peter Maxwell was in the way and... Henry Hall was finally asleep.

There was a strange noise in Peter Maxwell's dream. He seemed to be in an auditorium, full of ginger-headed children, all of whom were scribbling furiously. On the stage, an enormous woman was playing the violin, the instrument dwarfed in her enormous hands, which were the size of oven-ready turkeys. The tune she was playing seemed familiar, but he just couldn't quite place it. Someone was talking as well, but he couldn't quite make it out. Now it was becoming clearer. But it still didn't make much sense.

'Sorry, guv,' the voice was saying. 'He's *dead?* Since when? I mean, when did he die? How?'

Maxwell sprang fully awake and seemed to be standing by the side of the bed with no memory of getting there. He reached over and grabbed his wife's shoulder. Common sense told him it wasn't Nolan or Metternich she was talking about, but, even so; it wasn't every day, not even at 38 Columbine, when you woke up to hear your wife asking how long someone had been dead. She turned and flapped her free hand, both to shut him up and reassure.

'No,' she was saying now. 'He's with Sylvia for the weekend, possibly till tomorrow afternoon. We left it a bit loose, you know, what with... Oh,' she turned and grimaced at Maxwell, 'he's got marking to do, something like that, I expect.' She listened for a moment. 'No, guv. Not a word. I do understand. See you in about an hour, then.' She pressed the disconnect button on her phone and turned slowly to face him.

'Tom Medlicott's dead,' she said. 'That was Henry.'

'I thought it must be,' Maxwell said, absently. 'But ... Tom? That's awful. I suppose he...' It was

270

hard to comprehend, let alone put into words. He had hardly known either of them, but the intensity of the trip, and then her disappearance, had made them seem much more part of their lives than they really were. It struck him that, had things been different, they would have come back to Leighford from the Isle of Wight, shown a few photos to colleagues and then never spoken to each other again, except in passing in the corridor, or if Tom had a particular beef with one of the Sixth Form. And now, Izzy Medlicott had been found dead at the bottom of a cliff and her husband had, Maxwell assumed, killed himself out of grief.

'I didn't get that impression,' Jacquie said. Before her husband could draw breath to ask the next question she held up her hand and continued hurriedly. 'Look, hon. Can you fend for yourself today? There's absolutely no food in the house, except for the Count's stuff; there's loads of that, because of his enforced absence.'

'I'm supposed to eat cat food?' Could this morning get more confusing?

She gave him a cuff round the head. 'No, twerp. I'm meaning you don't have to lug moggie fodder back from the shop. Just something for your lunch and something for us for tonight. Don't know what time I'll be back, though, so get something that will wait for me.' Not for the first time, she wished he could drive. But she knew he never would; she could tell sometimes, on long, dark drives, that he was reliving the loss of his first wife and child in a car accident and she drove more carefully than was natural to her as a

271

result. What he could fit in Surrey's basket would be fine.

'Oh, good,' he said. 'Although it does give you a very glossy coat, apparently.'

'So I believe,' she said, making for the bathroom. 'And how else did you think I got so good at licking my own bum?'

He sat back down on the edge of the bed and rubbed his eyes. What time was it, for goodness sake? He felt as if he had only been asleep about five minutes. After a good stretch he went downstairs to make coffee, tread on some mouse giblets and check the text on the telly – once upon a time the acme of technology in the house. He brought up the local page – nothing. He would have to wait patiently until Jacquie came home and then winkle it out of her. It was going to be a long, long day. Then he remembered; he was going to go through all of the newspapers down in the garage, to look for clues. He sighed. He had been wrong before. It was going to be a long, long, *long* day.

Jacquie couldn't believe she was walking in through the door of the nick again already. She had banked on the weekend between coming back from the school trip and starting back at work to detox and dekid herself and it had been ripped from her; the fact that it concerned someone she knew just made it worse. The week on the Isle of Wight had seemed somehow other-worldly as it was. The weather had been unseasonably hot, and there had been a strange air of being in an episode of *The Prisoner* about the

272

whole venture. Maxwell had the boxed DVD set and every now and then, as he cycled off to the hell where youth and laughter go, she would hear him shout to the world in general, 'I am not a number; I am a free man!' Throw in abandoned towns, theme parks gently sliding into the sea, fossils thickly scattered underfoot and Pansy pissed as an owl every night and you hardly had to have a missing person to make it seem like a dream.

And now she was awake, it was only getting worse. There was a guideline buried somewhere deep in the operating policy of Leighford Police Station which precluded anyone working on a case involving someone they knew, no matter how vaguely, and in general terms Jacquie found that reasonable enough. But in practice, that was difficult. Not only was Leighford a small and closely knit town, but most of the personnel were married to or lived with civilians who worked with other civilians and so it went on, like the fleas having little fleas to bite 'em. She came off worse as Maxwell had a built-in contact list of over a thousand kids at any one time, plus parents and the inevitable steps. Then there were staff. So, before she broke into a sweat, there were close to four thousand people who she knew just a little too much about. And then, of course, in her case, there was Maxwell himself. If Henry Hall had had his way, she would never have had anything to do with anything; but since she was the best sergeant he had, what was a man to do?

She signed in and would have liked to leap up the stairs two at a time and burst in on the briefing, bright-eyed and bushy-tailed. Instead, each step felt as though she was climbing Machu Picchu. She pushed open the door into the ops room. At the far end, Henry Hall had already established a large whiteboard, marked into sections. One for Paul Masters, Izzy Medlicott's first husband. One for Isabelle Medlicott. And one for Tom Medlicott. It was quite poignant, Jacquie thought, to see Izzy sandwiched between her two husbands, looking rather like a monumental brass Maxwell had shown her one sunny afternoon, long ago. The photo of Izzy was cropped from the one she had given to Hall. Tom's disembodied arm was over her shoulder and there were still a few fuzzy shapes in the background which she could probably have identified from the school party. Tom's photo was from the same snap, again peopled with random shapes in the background, his arm disappearing off the edge and just a tiny amount of Izzy's T-shirt showing. Her ex-husband's photo was grainy, clearly blown up from something very much smaller, and she suspected a fax. It showed a smiling man, no longer young, perhaps forty-five, and just a threat of someone's bridal veil blowing in the wind behind his head. It was with a jolt that she realised that the photo was from his wedding to Izzy.

She heard voices coming along the corridor and suddenly the room was full of chatter, chairs scraping, gradually quietening down as Henry Hall took his place at the front. Jacquie sat at the back, with her notebook open on her knee. Bob Thorogood turned round in his chair and

274

beckoned her nearer.

'Sorry this all happencd to spoil your holidays, Jacks,' he said. She hated people to call her that. It reminded her of Marlon Brando in a sub-liminal memory of a film she remembered from Saturday morning film club as a kid. Maxwell could certainly have explained why.

'Thanks, Bob,' she said. The man meant no harm and had probably caught a whiff on the grapevine about her possible promotion and wanted to be in on the ground floor, in the brown-nose club. 'I certainly wouldn't recommend it.'

Henry Hall tapped gently on the board with a marker. Apart from the names and a photo taped to the top of each section, the board was blank. This was the Hall method, to fill in thoughts, facts, ideas as they came, and scc if a pattern emerged. Sometimes, the crime was solved virtually before the bums had hit the seats. Some-times, the boards grew whiskers before a single link was made. 'Right, ladies and gentlemen. Let's get started. As you see, we have three murders up on the board. Strictly speaking, only one is ours, this one,' he tapped on the board behind his left shoulder, 'Tom Medlicott. The one in the middle is his wife, Isabelle, or Izzy Medlicott. She belongs to Hampshire Police, but there are talks in pro-gress as we speak to let us do most of the legwork on this one, as she comes from here and now we have her dead husband on our hands. We might not end up with this case, of course, but this morning I intend to proceed as if we will. The third case, here,' he reached across and pointed to the column marked for Paul Masters, 'has not even been logged by the local police involved as a murder. He was found at the bottom of a ladder and, despite a few strange circumstances, it was put down as unexplained, but most probably accidental.'

'Do we know when that one happened, guv?' someone asked from the centre of the room.

'Good question,' Hall said. 'I've left dates off for a reason. I'll explain. We only know when Tom Medlicott died, of the three. The time of death, given by Dr Lacey...' He knew his men; he paused for the inevitable response.

Jacquie was confused. Who was this person? She poked Bob Thorogood in the back and made a querying gesture. He mouthed back that he would tell her later.

'As I say,' Hall resumed, 'the time of death, given by Dr Lacey, is between eighteen hundred and twenty-two hundred hours last night. She can be more precise after the post-mortem, which she is conducting as we speak.'

'You mean Donald is conducting, I hope,' someone offered.

'As you say,' Hall said, with no emphasis. 'But all we know in the case of his wife is when she disappeared, and even that could be said to be a little moot. At the moment, we are going with late on Wednesday night, possibly very early Thursday morning. Again, precise details will follow.' He turned to the board and jotted down the facts so far, under their photos.

'What about the ex, guv?' Phil Smart was on his second shift with only a few hours' break, but he had asked to be included, having been in at, as it were, the death. 'What have we got on him?'

'We know very little,' said Hall, 'except that he was found dead, that is as in dead and cold, a week ago yesterday. That means, by and large, that he must have died on the Wednesday before last. We assume he died during the day, in that most people don't start doing even the simplest DIY in the middle of the night and his death was caused by a fall from a ladder.'

'So he lay in the garden for two days?' Jacquie asked. She didn't know what kind of house Izzy's ex lived in, but she knew that should she or Maxwell fall from a ladder, they would be discovered almost as they hit the ground, if not by the neighbours on either side, then by the ones across the back or absolutely anyone using the rat run footpath at the end of the Columbine gardens.

'Yes,' Hall said. 'He lived in a small village, gardens very secluded, apparently. I've had a look on Google Earth and I'm surprised he was found at all.'

'Had the local police contacted the dead woman?' someone asked. 'Did she know he was dead?'

'She did if she shoved him off the ladder,' Bob Thorogood suggested.

'True,' Hall said, 'but we have no idea whether she did and also no reason to suppose she would want to. We aren't sure how happy her marriage was to Tom Medlicott, but surely, no matter how unhappy your second marriage is, you don't kill your first husband. How would that help?'

'More money,' said Fran Brannon, from the front row. 'If she was his beneficiary.'

277

'Again, true,' Hall said. 'But we are waiting on that, so we'll have to just put a question mark on him.' He turned and did so. Then he turned back to the small but enthusiastic crowd in front of him. 'I'm sorry to have called you all in with so little to go on. Our task today is to make sure there *is* something to go on. As reports come in, they will need to be entered on the system, cross-referenced and emailed to me as soon as you see any connection, apart from the obvious. Don't worry about how many times you contact me. There are no wrong answers here. But I just know,' and he stopped speaking to rake the rows of faces with his blank stare, 'I just know there is more to this than meets the eye. There is no such thing as coincidence, don't forget.' He turned as though to dismiss them, then seemed to remember something. 'Sorry,' he said. 'There is one more thing and I will have to give this job to someone specific. Umm...' he pointed randomly with the board marker and came to rest on Fran Brannon. 'Fran. I would like you to get in touch with the General and get stats for falls in the past ... what shall we say? ... the past six weeks. Look for anything out of the ordinary or something you would like to call coincidence, should there, after all, be such a thing.'

Fran Brannon nodded, but not very enthusiastically. Having cast herself as Wonder Woman, even though it meant wearing her underwear on the outside, she was rather disappointed. But no one got anywhere by grouching, so she got up to go and start her task.

Hall spoke again, over the sound of scraping

chairs. 'Sorry, everyone. One *more* thing, and this really is it this time. As some of you may know, Jacquie was on a school trip last week with the Medlicotts. She may have some specialist knowledge that you might find useful. She will be working in the out-of-hours duty office, so that anyone who wants to pick her brain can do so in relative peace. Right. Any questions?'

Apart from a random mutter in which the word 'Maxwell' seemed to surface every now and then like a turd in a swimming pool, as Bob Thorogood later described it, there was nothing and soon everyone was bent to their work.

Chapter Eighteen

The Maxwell family garage was, like most garages not used to house a car, a small microcosm of life upstairs in the house. Being part of the building, not a last-minute addition on the side, it didn't suffer from the usual garagey smells, like damp and mould with the intriguing top notes of wellies, paraffin, old sump oil, and metal, which could be sold by one of the more avant-garde perfumeries as *L'eau d'Garagiste*. Instead, it smelt of wood from the shelving, paint quietly drying in inadequately closed tins, optimistically stored on said shelves, mineral oil coating unused tools and, predominantly, newspapers.

Leighford County Council had a Policy regarding Waste Disposal. This was in a file several inches thick, stored in the Policies Office and available for County Hall staff and members of the public to examine, having given twenty-four hours notice. The person who had constructed it was clearly a reincarnation of a medieval alchemist, steeped in the lore of arcane grimoires. He was certainly no good at turning a simple sentence and had also only scant understanding of the desires re rubbish disposal of the reasonable man on the Clapham, or indeed any other, omnibus. Subsection had piled upon subsection, recycling had its own appendix, long since removed, as is the way of such things, and refiled under another category entirely. Bin colours ruled supreme and days for green waste, kitchen waste, garden waste and, for all anyone knew, the Arctic wastes, were carefully annotated and coded.

Sadly, the man responsible for this entertaining work had suddenly rushed into the Register Office attached to County Hall one morning, dressed only in his underpants and brandishing a leaf torn from the Council Leader's cheese plant. The bride and groom had been hushed up with a free honeymoon in Canvey Island and the poor man was never seen again, although there was a rumour that he was sometimes to be seen walking along The Dam, armed only with a stick with a nail in the end.

So the Maxwells, along with almost everyone else in Leighford, put their ordinary rubbish out on a Wednesday, pretty much confident that it would have gone by Tuesday. Newspapers, destined for recycling one day, were simply allowed to pile up in the garage. It was to this pile that Maxwell now addressed himself. Eat your heart out, Colindale Newspaper Library.

He had taken the precaution of popping down to the shop first and had supplies on hand. He had a sandwich in a triangular pack, which he knew he probably wouldn't be able to open, but down in the garage there would at least be some kind of power tool which would no doubt come in handy. He had two four-finger Kit Kats which could cover a double use of snack and something to run down the columns when his eyes got tired. He had a two-litre bottle of Coca-Cola and a thermos of coffee, should his caffeine levels threaten to dip below near-fatal. Ice he had in plenty in the freezer which hummed hypnotically in the corner. Add in a garden chair and a picnic table, a cordless phone, a table lamp pinched from the spare bedroom and his reading glasses and he was all set. He left the door into the hallway open and the front and back doors ajar. This was so that he didn't suffocate in the enclosed space and also, should he be crushed under a pile of collapsing newsprint, Jacquie would know where to look for him. It also gave access and egress to Metternich, the nosiest cat in the world.

Peter Maxwell was by heart a researcher. When he had been at Cambridge he had spent hours in the library, finding out small and hitherto undiscovered sidebars to history. He was obviously fascinated by the big picture, but if he could also find out the colour of Hammurabi's eyes, or what Thomas More's third daughter had called her pet rabbit, he found that he could remember the main facts all the easier and that he could empathise better with his subject. That his lecturers didn't always share his enthusiasm for minutiae was sometimes clear from the grades for his essays, but that and a lifetime of teaching Eleven Pea Queue about the causes of the First World War had not diminished his thirst for the tiny bits of history everyone else might miss. And history, as he was constantly telling his Year Seven classes, is happening all the time. It isn't just hundreds of years ago. It is last week. It is yesterday. It is this morning. It was created just a minute, a second, a millisecond ago. 'Whoops', he would tell them. 'There goes another bit.' Mostly, they just looked at him open-mouthed. But just occasionally, he saw a familiar gleam in someone's eye and he knew that he had just brought into being another historian.

The piles of papers rather reflected this tendency. The Maxwell household didn't have a regular daily paper; theirs was the most confused paper boy in the world. As a politics teacher when the devil drove, the Head of Sixth Form felt he had to have the opinions of all sorts of writers, from the right-wing ranter to the leftest of left-wing polemicists. This, he could see, was going to be a problem. His piles of newspapers, whilst representing every colour of journalism from red to blue, through purple and the occasional issue of the *Fortean Times*, were so random that few stories were followed through in their entirety. The best plan would probably be to pile them up in chronological order, not by publication. Then, although the take on an issue might vary, the facts might still emerge. Local papers only were put on one side. He felt much as the miller's daughter must have felt, destined to spin straw into gold for the evil dwarf Rumpelstiltskin.

He began to sort the papers and was getting on quite well, the radio burbling away in the background, when a noise in the doorway made him jump. Surely, the dwarf wasn't back already? He had hardly made any gold yet. But no, it was just the Count, come to check if Maxwell had found the mouse nest. Metternich was using sustainable hunting methods in the garage and it was working quite well so far, though the population had been given a chance to increase in his absence in the previous week. A quick glance told him that Maxwell had some way to go as yet, so he settled down on the nice, soft top of a bag of potting compost, tucked his nose under his tail and went to sleep.

The sorting went well. Once into a pattern, Maxwell found that what had looked like a dauntingly enormous pile of newsprint was in fact merely huge and as such, very do-able. He made an early decision to cut the papers into months, putting anything older than June to one side, to be looked at if, God forbid, he needed to. July he left as a random, though discrete pile. August was put in sets of weeks. September was put in strict date order. In no time at all the job was done and he sat back and had a celebratory Kit Kat. Usually at this time on a Saturday, the whole family was out shopping and this had to be an improvement, surely. He was dusty, sneezing and ink-smeared, his heart was still beating faster after the unexpected discovery of a mouse nest in a pile of July *Radio Times*, but generally speaking, he was quite pleased with his progress. Metternich had left in disgust, having seen the disposal into the back garden of his midnight snack bar, and was last seen sprawled out on the roof of next-door's shed.

Looking out of the back door, Maxwell was suddenly struck with a pang of regret for the missing Mrs Troubridge. He must nip round later and visit her. He would try and catch Mrs B as well, to ask her how it had gone last night, after he had left. It was an unchanging pattern – and Maxwell liked an unchanging pattern as well as the next man – that as soon as the old woman heard a door open, she would suddenly be working away with clippers or broom in the garden, front or back as required. She didn't always have anything very fascinating to say, usually it tended towards the complaining end of conversational gambits, but she was fond enough of him in her little stunted way, and Jacquie and Nolan she loved. He hoped the old trout would be all right. He sighed and made his way back into what he had decided to call the Peter Maxwell Archive. It made him feel better than to think he was stuck in the garage wading through a pile of old newspapers, looking for he didn't know what. His researcher's spirit was kept buoyant by the unexpected, like the rasher of bacon pressed between *The Sunday Telegraph* and *The Observer* of the last weekend in July. He remembered how that had happened, he mused nostalgically. He had been gathering the papers up to take down to the garage whilst eating a bacon sandwich. When he took the last mouthful he had thought it was a bit bready. Now he knew why. The sun had been shining at the time, it was the beginning of the summer holiday and, although he was not embarking on his expected retirement, things were generally pretty good with his world and that of everyone he knew.

Now, apart from the fact that the sun was shining, everything was different. Whilst his world was still bouncing along quite happily, colleagues were dead and his neighbour was lying in hospital. He would be the first to admit that Tolkien was far from his favourite author, but he suddenly knew how the hobbits must have felt, when the dark wing of Sauron cast a shadow over their world. Leighford wasn't noticeably like Hobbiton, especially now they had built the new twenty-four-hour superstore on the old football field, but the general idea was the same. He gave a little shudder and another sneeze.

'You wanna put a jumper on, Mr M. You'll catch your death.'

Maxwell dropped the handful of papers he had gathered together and clutched his chest. In the doorway, silhouetted against the daylight, was the last person he expected to see. It was as though his thoughts had summoned her. Not Mrs Rumpelstiltskin, come to see why he was slacking; it was Mrs B, fag akimbo, bag of clothes and unguents at her side.

'Good Lord, Mrs B,' he said. 'You could have killed me. What are you doing here?'

'Well, I missed my day, what with not being able to get in. I didn't know Mrs Troubridge was in the hospital then, o' course. I called her a few things, I can tell you. Pore ol' thing.' Mrs B was a kindly soul and sometimes helped lame dogs over stiles which were miles out of their way. 'I thought I'd come and catch up. You'll have washing and things need doing. And what with that murder last night, I 'spect Mrs M's up at the police station. And here's you, front door open, with killers about.'

'How did you know about the murder?' Maxwell said. 'It hasn't been on the news.'

'Not on the *news*, no,' Mrs B retorted. 'But our Brenda's bloke, you know, I tol' you about him, was on that hippodrome stuff, but he's off it now, well he's got a milk round and he was delivrin' out near the airfield and he saw the sirens.'

That was an interesting concept, but Maxwell assumed it must just be a side effect of hippodrome. He knew he shouldn't ask but did all the same. 'So how did he know it was a murder?'

'He popped round, well, he was ahead of time, what with starting the deliv'ry early with some milk left over from Friday mornin'. He saw that Hall and a load of police. In the white things and that. They carried a body out and they don't do that if it ain't a murder. I went online soon as our Brenda texted me and there's nothing yet.' Mrs B as technophile was something with which Maxwell was still coming to terms. 'But I thought to meself, I bet that Hall gets Mrs M in on this, though she's still on her holidays.' She looked around, as if expecting Jacquie to leap out from behind a pile of newsprint. 'That where she is, is it?'

'Yes,' said Maxwell. It was unusual for Mrs B to only ask one question at a time. The world was turned upside down today.

'And little Nolan?'

'With Sylvia Matthews from up at the school. They hung on to him yesterday afternoon.'

'Oh?' Mrs B was on it like a Jack Russell on a rat. 'Something already going on yesterday, was there? I heard there was a murder on that trip. Blood everywhere, I heard. Woman had her head cut off on a roller coaster.'

Maxwell sighed. 'No, Mrs B. No blood. No decapitation.'

287

She spotted his omission. They went back a long, long way. 'But there was a murder, though?' she asked.

'Tell you what, Mrs B,' Maxwell said, getting up from his garden chair and stretching his legs. 'Why don't we go upstairs, you can do your cleaning and I'm sure Jacquie would be more than grateful if you did a bit of washing as well. And I'll make a cup of tea and you can tell me about how Mrs Troubridge got on last night, after we left.'

'Pore ol' soul,' Mrs B said, allowing herself to be ushered out of the garage. 'She was ever so agitated. But the nurses said she was much more with it than she had been. She was ever so pleased to see you.'

'Do you think so? I'm pleased to hear you say that, because her other visitor thought she seemed scared of me.' Maxwell was strangely comforted by the cleaner's words. He leant over at the foot of the stairs and pulled the front door to; despite the fact that he doubted the existence of the wandering killer, it paid to be careful.

'You jokin' me?' How Maxwell wished that Mrs B wouldn't let the kids' speech patterns rub off. He winced and was glad that she had her back to him as she toiled up the stairs. 'Scared of her, more like. Great big thing, mauling her about. Who is she, anyway?'

'She's a cousin of some sort. We met here ... do you know, it seems like months ago, but it was only the beginning of the week before last. She's doing some kind of family research.' They had reached the landing and Maxwell peeled off into the kitchen to put the kettle on. Mrs B followed

him and, extracting a cloth from her bag, began to give the taps a desultory buff. No one could ever accuse her of being too zealous.

'Pfft,' Mrs B was unimpressed. 'Our Glenda's eldest lad, that's Brenda's brother, you probably remember, well, he did a bit of that, but our Glenda made him stop.'

Maxwell knew he shouldn't, but he had to ask. 'Why did she do that, Mrs B?'

'Well, not healthy, is it? Pokin' your nose into that kind of thing. You never know, do ya, what might turn up, if you know what I mean? Even that Jeremy Paxton cried when he found out about his family's past doings.' She looked at him meaningfully, 'And it's especially so with our Glenda.' She paused again. 'And her ways.'

'Oh, I see,' Maxwell indeed did see. He remembered Glenda now. She occasionally helped out at Leighford High in the dining room and she had a predatory gleam which had even discomfited James Diamond, who didn't usually notice such things.

'Now you come to mention it,' Mrs B said, 'I did notice a resemblance. Across the eyes. But I can't say I took to her. She's just so...' It was unusual, but she was actually lost for words.

'I know,' nodded Maxwell, turning as the kettle came to the boil. 'She's just so big.'

'And clumsy,' added Mrs B and turned her brief attention to the draining board.

They were soon sitting opposite one another, sipping tea at the table. They had known each other since God was a lad and there wasn't always need for words. But as always, Mrs B got

straight to the heart of the matter, if with some inaccuracies built in.

'It is terrible, though, innit?' she said at last, 'That Mr Medlicott getting hatcheted like that.'

Maxwell spluttered into his tea. 'Hatcheted?' he said. 'I don't think so. I think he...' And then he realised the stark truth. He didn't know anything. Jacquie had said she didn't get the impression that he had committed suicide. That might mean that he had had a small tap on the head, had been shot, bludgeoned, set on fire, dismembered or all five. He was in no position to argue with anything that his cleaning lady had to say. He just hated this feeling. So, he said all he could say. 'Hatcheted. Well. Goodness. I'll go to the foot of our stairs.'

'Our Brenda's chap said there was blood everywhere. Great pools of it, apparently. That's a shame, that.'

How could pools of blood make death more of a shame than any other method of despatch, Maxwell wondered.

He was about to find out. 'When they come to sell the place, it'll keep coming back, the stain. Seeps into the floorboards, see. Can't get it out,' she informed him. 'Mind you, some people go for that, don' they? You know, murder house, this-way-to-where-it-happened sort of thing.'

Bowing to her superior knowledge, he drank off the rest of his tea and went back to his newspaper dungeon.

Henry Hall had never really believed in the innate goodness of humankind. When he was a

child he had always seen the wasp, not the ice cream, the jellyfish, not the sand. So, when the front desk called up to say that Izzy Medlicott's mother was downstairs, he was ready for more or less anything. He popped his head around the door of the night duty room. 'Jacquie? Are you busy?'

She twisted round in her chair. 'Not really, guv.' She pushed a lock of hair behind her ear. He hoped she wouldn't go all severe on him when she made inspector. He'd never really liked that look, the strained-back hair, looking like Olive Oyl. 'Is there something you need me to do?'

He would have loved to say, 'Yes. There's a woman downstairs who I don't want to see. It's the dead woman's mother, the mother-in-law of both dead men.' But instead he just said, 'There's an interview I'd like you to sit in on, if you would.'

'No problem.' She stood up and swung her jacket off the back of the chair and shrugged it on. 'Who is it?'

'It's...' he stopped. It wasn't like him to be missing vital information. 'In fact, I don't know her name. It's Isabelle Medlicott's mother.'

'She got here quickly,' Jacquie said. 'When did she get a call?'

'I got someone to do it first thing. We'll need to provide someone to do the ID on the Isle of Wight, plus of course, she can do Tom Medlicott.'

'Even so.' Jacquie looked at her watch. Nowhere near lunchtime yet. 'She must have shifted.'

'Where did she have to come from?' Henry asked. 'I didn't know you knew her.'

Jacquie raised her eyebrows, surprised at her-

291

self. 'I don't. I just ... well, I suppose I assumed she came from up in the Midlands somewhere, further north, even. From where Izzy came from. For all I know she might live down the road.'

'Well,' Henry Hall said, setting off down the corridor, 'Let's find out, shall we?'

Downstairs, in one of the nicer interview rooms, with low chairs and a coffee table, with nothing chained up or screwed down, Isabelle Medlicott's mother sat, arms folded, lips pursed. Her age was impossible to gauge; her hair was suspiciously glossy and a uniform black, so dark it was almost blue. Her make-up was immaculate, but no foundation, no matter how much Jane Fonda recommended it, could counteract the bitter expression and the hardness around the mouth and eyes. She looked as though she knew the price of everything and the value of nothing. Her restless eyes seemed to be appraising the rather grubby furniture and deciding she wouldn't give a brass farthing for it. Her handbag, at first glance Louis Vuitton, at second glance a cheap knock-off, stood four-square in front of her on the table. She looked up as Hall and Jacquie went in but decided they weren't worth the wear and tear on her eyes and looked away almost at once, to resume her checking out of the room. The glance had been brief, but she had priced Jacquie's suede jacket and linen trousers to within a couple of pounds. Hall's suit had almost beaten her; it looked like Hugo Boss, but this man was a policeman. It had to be Matalan. She was wrong on both counts. It was Armani. Margaret Hall was a demon on eBay

292

and it had been his Christmas present.

The police persons sat opposite her. 'Mrs...?'

The woman didn't fill her name into the gap, leaving an awkward silence. Eventually, she said, 'Ms.'

'I'm sorry.' In his hatred of the term, Hall and Maxwell became one. The DCI tried again, this time more directly. 'I'm afraid I wasn't provided with your name, Ms...'

'Nelson,' she said. 'I reverted to my maiden name when I got divorced.'

'I see,' Hall said. Jacquie had quietly brought out her notebook and jotted it down. 'May we have your address?' he asked. 'Just for the record?'

'It's 92 Olivier Terrace, Spindleford,' she said. 'I suppose it counts as Gosport. Hampshire. I can never remember the postcodc. PO something, I suppose. I haven't lived there long.'

'Thank you,' Hall said. So, she didn't live far away. Not from either murder scene. He reminded himself hurriedly that this woman was a bereaved mother, but it wasn't easy. 'First of all, Ms Nelson, may I offer our condolences on your loss?'

'What loss in particular are you talking about?' she snapped. 'Would that be my ex-husband? My ex-son-in-law? My daughter? My son-in-law? Which?'

'I beg your pardon,' Hall said, hating the woman so much he wanted to squeeze her throat until her eyes popped out. Jacquie, hearing him hiss quietly through his teeth, knew what he was feeling and would happily have held his coat. But Henry Hall gave nothing away that the woman

293

would have noticed and carried on smoothly. 'I do realise that it has been difficult for you just lately...' but he got no further.

'Difficult?' she spat. 'How can you realise that? First, my husband leaves me for some chit in his office, and takes my daughter with him, shoves her in boarding school, won't let her see me. Then, stupid fool takes to drink when the little tart ditches him, kills his stupid self and leaves everything to Isabelle. Every last stick and stone of the house I used to live in, every last penny he hadn't poured down his stupid throat or gambled away on stupid horses and cards and God knows what.'

Hall and Jacquie murmured sympathetically, but there was no stopping her.

'Then Paul – best of the bunch, if you ask me, not that anybody ever asked me, bit older than Izzy, but steady – he goes and falls off a stupid ladder. I'd been in touch; he was going to see what he could do, financially. In fact,' and she flicked her hair in a simulacrum of coquetry, 'given time, I'm not sure that it might not have grown to something more.' She didn't seem to notice the looks of horror on the faces of Hall and Jacquie, each a perfect reflection of the other. 'Anyway, as I say, stupid ladder stopped that. Then Izzy falls off a cliff. I ask you, who does that in real life?' She looked up as if waiting for an answer to a perfectly sensible question. 'Well, nobody, that's who. She was paying the rent on this poxy little house I'm in, but I thought she might at least buy me somewhere. Wouldn't have to be big. And of course, she would have been loaded, with Paul dead.' She looked at Hall. 'Did she know Paul was dead? You know, before she died?'

'We think not,' Hall said, keeping his voice level with an effort. 'The Northants police did try to find her, but—'

'Right. Well, she would have been. Loaded. He'd left everything to her, you know.'

Hall and Jacquie exchanged glances. That solved that question, anyway. But Jacquie had a question of her own. 'You seem to think that Mr Masters had a lot to leave. As a teacher, I don't quite see...'

'The house, I expect,' she said. 'Izzy didn't go halves when they divorced, because of it having belonged to his parents, childhood home, that kind of thing. But it would come to her when he died, or half would if he had remarried. That was the settlement, or at least the main part of it.'

'I see.' Jacquie made a note. It said 'What a grasping bitch!' She angled her pad so that Hall could see, then thought better of it and turned over the page.

'So, anyway, when the house is sold, she would have got the lot. Well, did get the lot, I suppose, because he died before she did.'

Then suddenly, the Devil got into Henry Hall. 'Well,' he said. 'This is good news for Mr Medlicott's children, isn't it? Nice to have a windfall when you're young. They won't have to worry about student loans, or anything, will they?'

The woman froze. She could scarcely move her lips enough to whisper, 'Pardon?'

'Well,' Henry continued, 'if Isabelle got everything because her ex-husband died first, then

Tom Medlicott's heirs will get everything now, because Isabelle died first. That's right, isn't it, Jacquie?' His face betrayed nothing, but inside he was laughing like a loon.

'I believe so, Detective Chief Inspector,' Jacquie said gravely. 'Lucky children indeed, although not so lucky, having lost their father.'

The woman opposite rose to her feet, but stiffly, as though on wires. 'I'll contest it,' she hissed. 'He killed her, that's what he did. He killed her and then he killed himself. I'll go to the Police Complaints Department. I'll go to the Ombudsman. I'll go to the Supreme Court.'

'I hardly think that this is a matter for the United States to get involved in,' Henry Hall was imperturbable. 'But if they show any interest, we'll be in touch.'

'What?' she screeched like a banshee. 'Are you condescending to me, you ... you condescending git? I'll have your badge, I'll have your job... And you...' she spun round, pointing at Jacquie, 'what do you know about anything, you ... you tart you?' By this time she was out in the foyer and pushing her way through the barrier to the outside. A harmless little old lady stood there with a tin of biscuits, brought in to say thank you for the safe return of her no-longer-missing Yorkshire terrier. 'And you,' the bereaved mother yelled, turning on her. 'What are you looking at? You're a tart as well, I shouldn't wonder.' And with that she threw herself out of the door, spoiling her exit a little by having to turn and free her coat which was caught on the door handle.

The foyer was silent for a moment, before the

little old lady bent to her shopping basket, from which protruded a beribboned head. 'Well,' she said, 'She wasn't a very nice person was she, Keith?'

And all the gathered policemen and women shook their heads. Jacquie patted Keith's head, apologising silently to Metternich for consorting with the enemy. 'She certainly wasn't,' she agreed, then turned to Henry Hall. 'So I gather we're looking for someone else to do the ID?'

'Looks that way,' sighed Hall. 'We'll see who we can come up with in a minute. I don't want it to be you, Jacquie, but more than that I don't want it to be Max. It would only encourage him. What about Sylvia?'

'Well, I suppose she could,' said Jacquie. 'But from a selfish point of view, I'd rather it wasn't, because she's looking after Nole at the moment and I want him kept away from all this as much as possible.'

'I understand,' Hall said. 'It might have to be you, then, I'm afraid. Perhaps we can rig up some kind of webcam so we don't have to send you down there. I'll get Bob on that.' They climbed the stairs in silence and then he said, explosively, 'She was a monster, wasn't she? Had you had any inkling of that? In your chats with Tom?'

'Well, she clearly wasn't close to them,' Jacquie said. 'I had no idea about the house rent, though. Perhaps even Tom didn't know that.'

'It was probably the cheapest way of keeping her at arm's length,' Hall said. 'Is she a suspect, though? I must say, I'd love her to be.' They had arrived at his office and he pushed open the door

297

and waved her in.

'No,' Jacquie said, sitting in the chair opposite his. 'If anything, she is an anti-suspect, because she had so much reason for keeping Izzy alive, or at least alive until all other beneficiaries were dead.'

Hall sat down and frowned at the files which were beginning to clutter his desk. 'Yes, I suppose so. But what if she just took the chance to kill Izzy? She followed her to the Island and they had a row? Then she was going to frame Tom, so he couldn't benefit ... then... Does that work?'

'Possibly in an episode of *Midsomer Murders*. I'm not sure it makes much sense in Leighford, though, guv.'

'Oh, I know,' he said. He looked up at Jacquie. 'Go and have some lunch. Or go home, if you want. We can carry on here.'

'No, guv. I'll stay. Let's set a time, shall we? Till we crack this, or five o'clock, whichever is the sooner?'

'Fair enough.' He foraged about on his desk. 'Look, here's the post-mortem on Paul Masters. Can you give it the once-over and let me know if there's anything interesting?'

Jacquie knew that the PMs on both Medlicotts were on Henry's desk as well, but he would deal with them himself. And she was glad about that; she wasn't really up to knowing the weight of the brain of a man who, not twenty-four hours before, had been crying in her arms like a baby.

Chapter Nineteen

Number 38 Columbine was a much more peaceful place to be than Leighford nick. Upstairs, the intermittent whine of the vacuum cleaner was interspersed with bursts of singing, some from Mrs B and some from the radio. The worst moments came when the cleaning lady accompanied the radio and definitely beat it hands down. But these sounds were muffled by distance and didn't disturb Maxwell, in a world of his own down among the newspapers. The gathered ghosts of trees piled around him seemed to absorb what little sound there was: from outside the occasional car going past, a distant lawnmower; from inside, the soft flap of a turning page, the faint zhurring noise as he ran a craft knife around an interesting article, to remove it to look at later. The quiet motor of Metternich's snoring was the background to it all.

The pile of interesting things was growing taller. At first, Maxwell hadn't known quite what he was looking for, then he seemed to get his eye in. Falls resulting in death, obviously. But that couldn't be all; he then went back and started looking for missing people in general, then, if they were reported found, he went back and threw the article away. This way, he reasoned, the pile of cuttings might stay within reasonable bounds.

He was miles away when Mrs B made him

jump again. 'I'm off now, Mr M,' she said. 'One load is dry and piled on the spare bed. Another load is drying and another load is washing. I've hoovered and dusted but it was a bit of a lick an' a promise today. I'll get back to normal this week coming. Ooh, could I have a key? Mrs Troubridge won't be ... out by next week.'

Maxwell appreciated her delicacy. There were several different endings to the sentence, but she had chosen the least dramatic, which was not like her. 'Ah, now, that's a bit of a facer,' he said. 'I don't have any spares. Hold on, though. We've got Mrs Troubridge's key. It's on a hook in here somewhere.' He looked around and located it above the freezer. 'If you wait in here a minute, I'll nip next door and get our keys from her house and give them to you.'

'That's a good idea,' Mrs B said. 'I tell you what would be nice as well. What if, when I come next week, I give her place a bit of a going-through. Nothing much, just a dust and a wipe. So's it's nice for her when she gets home. Sort the fridge out, that kind of thing. Pick up the post. Water the plants. I can tell her tonight and that will be one less thing to worry her. She was a bit fretful last night about things. She seems to be worrying about money, so I'll make sure she knows it won't cost her anything.' She looked meaningfully at Maxwell.

'Of course it won't,' Maxwell said. 'Just take it out of your time with us.'

She gave him another old-fashioned look.

'Or do extra, of course. Just let me know how much. But you know,' he paused in the doorway,

Mrs Troubridge's spare keys in his hand, 'you surprise me that she is worrying about money. I really think she is all right in that department.'

'Oh, old people are funny like that,' Mrs B said. 'She wouldn't say if she was hard up.'

'No, but really. Her sister, for example, Araminta, she's always gadding off, foreign holidays, you name it. And she just has the family money. Mrs Troubridge has that and the money from her husband. She's quite comfortable, I'm sure.' He tossed the keys in the air thoughtfully. Had he and Jacquie missed that the poor old soul might be in difficulties?

'Well, I say you never can tell,' Mrs B said. 'Does she drink? Gamble? It doesn't take long, you know, with these Internet poker sites, things like that.' She gave a cough and changed the subject. 'I'll just tidy these papers, shall I, while you're next door?'

'No,' said Maxwell hurriedly. 'They're all where they are for a reason. Don't touch anything. In fact, why don't you come next door with me? You can have a look round, see how long you'll be next week.' The hint was heavy but if she took it she gave no sign.

'All right, Mr M. Will do. Have you got *your* front door key? To get back in?'

'Good point, Mrs B.' He rummaged in his pockets. 'Yes, here it is. Shall we go?' He stood aside and they performed the comic turn of walking up the Maxwells' path to the pavement, performing a sharp about turn and walking down Mrs Troubridge's to her front door.

'It would be easier if you didn't have this

301

hedge,' Mrs B observed.

'Easier?' Maxwell asked, putting the key in the lock. 'Why would it need to be easier?'

Mrs B was scandalised. Where she came from, everyone had their neighbours' keys and were in and out all day. A pint of milk here, a slice of bread there, a space on the washing line on a good drying day, everything was there for sharing. The only things you didn't touch were money and spouses, and even they were negotiable in the right circumstances. 'Well, easier to pop in and out,' she said.

'Mrs Troubridge isn't a popper,' he said. 'She's more of a lurker. She'd be lost without this hedge.' The lock had a personality of its own and he was finding it a little tricky. The woman pushed him to one side. Most days she had to let herself in to other peoples' houses and there was often a knack. She crouched a little to Mrs Troubridge's approximate height, pulled down slightly on the key and turned it in two rather jerky twists. The door opened instantly. Maxwell was amazed. 'However did you do that?' he said.

'You just have to behave like the owner,' she said. 'Locks get into a habit over the years, they get ground, like scissors. Coo,' she was in the hall. 'It's not much like your place, is it?'

It was an odd thing to say, as in structure the house was exactly like the Maxwells' house, just in reverse. But even so, she was right. Where next door was light and airy, Mrs Troubridge's house was dark. Pictures crowded the walls and furniture filled every corner. It was very clean, every knick and every knack polished regularly by its

302

owner, memories giving everything a placid gleam. Even after nearly a week, the film of dust had hardly started to settle. There was a small amount of post on the mat and Mrs B scooped it up and riffled quickly through it.

'Not much here,' she announced with the voice of the connoisseur of other people's correspondence. 'No red demands, that sort of thing.'

'It's not really our business, though, is it?' Maxwell asked, feeling awkward.

'It's our business if we can stop the electric cuttin' her off,' the cleaner replied sharply. 'I don't want the pore ol' soul coming back to rotting food and a cold house. It's September. She'll need the heatin' on soon, stop the place getting damp.' She gave a shiver. 'It's a bit cold today, don't you think?'

It was true there was a bit of a chill in the air.

'We'll put the heatin' on low,' she said. 'She got one of them boilers like you've got, has she? In the kitchen, is it?' And she marched up the stairs, shoving the post into Maxwell's hand as she went.

It struck Maxwell that perhaps he ought to say that they were just here to get the key, not to nose around, but he knew that Mrs B, though naturally nosy, was also thinking of Mrs Troubridge and also that Mrs Troubridge would probably not mind. No, that was wrong. She would mind a lot, but she need never find out. He decided to minimise the intrusion, though, and hurried up the stairs, straightening pictures as he went. It occurred to him on the top step that they had probably been knocked crooked as his neighbour had fallen down the stairs and went back and put them all crooked again. He still had a vague thought that this might be a crime scene. Henry Hall was seldom wrong.

In the kitchen, Mrs B was just closing the door to the boiler cupboard. There was a faint popping noise as the jets got down to business. 'I've just set it on low,' she said. 'It will just tick over. When you come in to check the post, just see if it feels warm enough to you.'

'Check the post?' Maxwell felt he was being drawn in a bit far into Mrs B's world of care.

'In case there's any red'uns. Stop her bein' cut off, that sort of thing. It's for her own good.' The woman was adamant and Maxwell knew what she was like when she got her teeth into something. And seeing her every day at school as he did, he also knew his life wouldn't be worth living, should he fail to do her bidding.

'Oh, yes. I do see. I'll do that.'

'Right. Well,' she looked around, appraisingly. 'She keeps it nice. I'll just give it a quick once-over, shouldn't come to more than an extra twenty quid, I shouldn't imagine. That all right?'

'Yes,' Maxwell said, weakly. Not only was he suddenly and inexplicably responsible for Mrs Troubridge's economic well-being, he was also forking out for her cleaning as well. Never mind, he consoled himself, it was probably the least he could do, what with the cat feeding, childmind-ing and the general twenty-four-hour surveil-lance that Mrs Troubridge provided. 'It's the least I can do.'

'Right,' Mrs B agreed with a nod. She glanced

up at the clock on the wall. 'Look at the time! I must be off. Where's this key, then?'

'She keeps it on a hook inside the boiler cupboard,' Maxwell said.

'Oh,' Mrs B muttered. 'Din' see it.' She pulled open the door and looked around. 'No, no key here.'

'Let me look,' Maxwell said. 'It's always here.' He too looked around inside the cupboard. 'That's odd. It's not there.' He stepped back and looked around. He just couldn't imagine Mrs Troubridge being anything other than careful with their keys, seeing that she was so obsessed with security, keeping her outside doors locked at all times. Even when she was outside in the garden, she had to let herself in with a key. Maxwell started to open and close cupboards at random. Where do you start?

Mrs B had wandered into the sitting room and was looking around, the thronging furniture making a search difficult. Suddenly, Maxwell heard her shout. 'Here they are!' He joined her in the other room. Mrs B stood by the fireplace, holding up the keys to his house. 'They were in this pot on the mantelpiece.'

'Whatever were they doing in there?' Maxwell wondered. 'She always keeps them in that cupboard.'

'Bless,' Mrs B said. 'Pore ol' soul probably thought she was being a bit fly. Perhaps she thought somebody as shouldn't knew where they was.'

'That's probably it,' Maxwell said, uncertainly. It wasn't as if Mrs Troubridge's house was lousy with people coming and going. But she had had the gas serviced a while back – perhaps she had moved it then. No matter, Mrs B had her key and he could now wave her off and get the day back on track.

'I'll be off, then,' the woman said, 'or I'll miss my bus. I'll see Mrs Troubridge tonight and tell her you're lookin' after the house. She'll like that. Careful down these stairs. That bit of carpet looks a bit loose. See you Monday.' And with that she was off, up the path and on up to the bus stop, fag miraculously in her mouth now she was outdoors.

'Yes,' Maxwell said, automatically under his breath. 'We don't want that. Thank you. Will she? Yes, I will. Yes it does, a bit. Look forward to it.' He checked that Mrs Troubridge's door was firmly closed and retraced his steps to his own front door. He stood for a moment and looked at the hedge. It needed a trim; it was growing fast without Mrs Troubridge's daily ministrations. He made a mental note to bring the shears through next time he had a minute. He expected that to be any time after Christmas – and surely, Mrs Troubridge would be home by then.

Detective Sergeant Jacquie Carpenter-Maxwell massaged her temples and pushed back from her desk. She just needed a few minutes not wallowing around in someone's insides, so she wandered down the corridor to get a coffee. Fran Brannon was at the machine, looking hopefully at the empty cup in the dispenser.

'Where's my coffee?' she said plaintively to Jacquie.

306

'What sort did you ask it for?' Jacquie asked her.

'Cappuccino,' she said. 'One sugar.'

'There's your problem, then,' Jacquie said. 'This machine is the Mark III Stupid version of this model. It can only do one thing at a time. Cancel and ask it for cappuccino, no sugars or anything fancy. I keep sugar sachets in my bag – I like to feel I have beaten it at its own game.'

'OK,' Fran said and punched a few buttons. On cue, the cup filled up with some greyish-brown liquid on which the froth lingered for all of five seconds, before subsiding into a slight, greasy scum. 'That's better.' She took it and stepped back.

Jacquie chose black coffee and watched it being dispensed, with just a hint of Fran's cappuccino slick floating on the top. She took the cup and moved on to the chocolate machine. 'Hmm,' she said. 'My sugar hit is more than due. I think I'll have a bag of Maltesers.' She put the money in and pressed the keys for the Snickers bar two up and three across from the required chocolate. Before Fran could show her ignorance and correct her, the red bag moved jerkily forward and fell into the chute.

Jacquie smiled at Fran. 'I assume that you don't tend to spend much time in the office,' she said. 'Otherwise you'd know a bit more about these stupid machines.'

'I am out more than I'm in,' Fran conceded. 'I'm enjoying this, though. Makes a change.'

'You might want to rethink the use of the word "enjoy",' Jacquie said. 'Three people are dead, don't forget. That's people, as in human beings.'

Fran Brannon was immediately contrite. She had remembered all of a rush that Jacquie knew two of the three. 'Sorry,' she said. 'It's just that it's difficult not to be a bit excited, working on a big case.'

'Come into my office,' Jacquie said. 'Let's talk this case through, shall we? It will be a change to work with someone who doesn't feel the need to go and smoke every ten minutes and spend the gaps in between farting. Though to be honest with you,' she said, 'I'd rather they smoked indoors and went out to fart.' She pushed open the door and stopped. 'Oh, hello, guv,' she said, blushing a little. Not that she had ever been aware of Hall farting, although she assumed that even he did, sometimes.

'Jacquie, Fran,' he said. 'Come in, both of you.'

Fran Brannon started to back out. 'Oh, no, guv ... sir. I've got stuff...'

'No, no, come on in. Another brain won't do any harm.'

They went in and Jacquie sat behind the desk she had been using, Hall pulled a chair out from the wall for Fran. He held a file in his hand and, leaning forward, opened it on the edge of the desk.

'Now, then, Jacquie, I don't know how far you've got with the PM report on Paul Masters?'

'I'd just finished, guv,' said Jacquie. 'Hence the sugar break.' She held up her chocolate and coffee. 'Want one?' She proffered the bag.

'Thank you, perhaps later.' He bent to the file again. Fran Brannon was left wondering whether she would ever feel confident enough to offer the boss a piece of chocolate. She was guessing that the rumours were true and that Hall and Jacquie were an item. She wasn't sure she would want to go as far as that; she wasn't really that dedicated.

Jacquie crunched a Malteser and then bent her head to her file too. 'It all seems quite straightforward, guv,' she said. 'Fell off the ladder. Quite severe injuries, but all commensurate with the fall; broken bones, fractured skull, various bruises.'

'*Various* bruises?' Hall asked.

She breathed out through her nose and hummed a little as she ran her finger down the report. 'A lot of lividity, that's the trouble. He lay there for a couple of days, they reckon. Bit of nibbling by wildlife; that's what you get I suppose, from living in the country ... umm ... oh, hang on. Broken hyoid. That's odd.' She looked up at Hall, who was looking very smug. 'The pathologist doesn't mark it up as not in keeping, though. Perhaps he fell across something. He probably twisted in the air, trying to save himself. And apparently he lived for a few minutes after he fell. He was in an odd position, re the ladder.'

'What if,' Hall said, steadily, 'he would have lived for another forty years after he fell off the ladder? What if someone moved the ladder and finished him off?'

'What?' both the women said together.

He handed Jacquie the file and Fran stood up to read it upside down; she had attended that lecture, unlike Bob Thorogood. 'Read the highlighted bits.' They did and then they looked up at him.

'Broken hyoids,' Jacquie said. 'And bruises to show it was pre- or at worst peri-mortem.'

'Yes,' Hall said. 'And I'll tell you something else, and the trouble here is that it is just something that I saw myself – there is no report on it.' He looked at Jacquie. 'Any ideas what it might be?'

She looked at him. She hardly dare say it. 'Is it that ... Mrs Troubridge has a bruise on her neck as well?'

'Well done,' he said calmly. 'Totally correct.'

Fran Brannon was confused. Who was this person and why had Henry Hall been looking at her neck?

'The problem is,' he said, 'that because she is alive...' he saw Jacquie's expression and qualified the statement, 'because the blow wasn't fatal and luckily Mrs Troubridge is alive, the bruise is practically gone. The hyoid being cartilage, damage to it doesn't show up on X-ray and an ultrasound isn't really justified at the moment and in her rather fragile state.' He gathered up his file and got up to go. 'Interesting, though, isn't it?' he said and walked out of the room.

There was a silence, then Jacquie also stood up. 'I think I want to go home now,' she said to Fran. 'I'll just OK it with the DCI. If you want to work in here, where it's quiet, then knock yourself out. Bye.' And she was gone. Rules or no rules, promotion or no promotion, she had to talk to Max.

Maxwell was happily ensconced amongst his papers when he heard the car draw up. He looked up as Jacquie's key turned in the door and judged the moment to speak so she didn't die of shock.

'Hello, hon,' he said, from the gloom of the garage. 'You're home early.'

She leapt a mile in the air and came down fuming. 'Good God, Max! Are you trying to kill me?' He hadn't got the timing quite right, it appeared.

'Sorry, sweetie,' he said. 'I tried not to scare you. I thought you might notice the light.' He sounded very contrite and as a rule she would have forgiven him on the spot, but she had had a serious word with herself in the car on the way home, wavering from wanting to tell him every-thing, to never wanting to speak to him about work ever again, and all points in between. So, of course, it was his fault.

'Well, I didn't!' she snapped, standing in the doorway.

He recognised this mood and decided he was too busy for it. 'Well, don't lurk, sweetness. You're in my light.'

She didn't move straight away. He knew his Jacquie and she took the bait. 'What are you doing in here, anyway?' she asked.

'A bit of research. It's like looking for a needle in a haystack, but I had to do something.' He held up his clutch of clippings.

'I assume Nole isn't back?'

'No. For some reason Sylvia and Guy haven't had enough of children so far this week and so they are taking him and Guy's niece to Chessing-ton.'

'He'll enjoy that,' Jacquie said, smiling. 'He and

Lucy always get on ... it is Lucy, isn't it? Not his other niece, the bossy one?'

'No, it's Lucy. They'll be bringing him back to-night or tomorrow if the kids can't be separated, as usual. They'll ring to confirm.' Maxwell was more than ready to have his son back; twenty-four hours without him was plenty. But when he thought of the havoc he would wreak amongst the newspapers, building forts and tunnels with his father's careful filing system, he was glad he was elsewhere.

'Great. That gives us a good while, then. Leave that for a minute. Let's go and get a sandwich – have you lunched, by the way?'

Maxwell shook his head. 'I had a cup of tea and a biscuit with Mrs B.'

Mrs B? Jacquie decided she would delve into that later. 'Nor have I. Just a bag of Maltesers.'

'One of my favourite food groups,' Maxwell said, 'but not really lunch. I've got this sandwich,' he looked around him but there was no sign, 'well, I had one. It's under here somewhere.' He gave up the search. 'I bought some bread and bits. We'll go up and have something to eat. What meal is it? Not brunch, that's for sure.'

'Tunch?' tried Jacquie. 'Lea? Lunch and tea doesn't work so well, does it?' She could never stay mad at him for long.

'I think "tunch" has a ring to it,' he said. He got up, showering bits of paper. He looked rather like Kerwin Mathews as Gulliver, shaking off the Lilliputians. Following her gaze, he said quickly, 'I'll clear up later. I'll bring my clippings. See if anything fits your theories.'

'What makes you think I'm going to talk about the case?' she said.

'Oh, Woman Policeman Carpenter-Maxwell,' he laughed, kissing her. 'When will you learn that you can't fool an old fool? But I like it when you keep on trying.'

She looked at him seriously for a moment. 'I know I say this every time, Max, but please don't–'

'–use any of this information to get involved. Of course not, poppet.' Despite Maxwell's considerable thespian skills, it didn't sound too convincing. 'Now, get that apron on, woman, and make me my tunch!'

Chapter Twenty

The bacon-and-egg sandwiches went down a treat and soon Maxwell and Jacquie were sitting opposite each other across the kitchen table, each with a very welcome cup of tea.

'That was nice,' Jacquie said. 'I had no idea how hungry I was.'

'It's having been on the school trip,' Maxwell told her. 'Having to feed the little dears regularly so they don't turn into something even more unpleasant becomes a habit very quickly.'

'You are always so nasty about them,' Jacquie said, reprovingly. 'They really weren't that bad, I didn't think.'

'I'll tell you what,' Maxwell said. 'If you want to see a school's worth of pupils behaving badly, come in with me on Monday. Legs will announce the deaths in a special assembly. Girls will immediately start to cry and hug each other. Anyone not there will be texted. The boys will start to kick off, knowing that everyone will be making allowances. A large number will bunk off. Flowers will start appearing on the school gates and before you know it, it will be Grief Central. And that doesn't even include the kids who were on the trip. The Ed Psychs will be circling like vultures, kids will be given counselling whether they want it or not. But only, of course, for point-three-five of the week because the County budget

314

won't spread any further. Pansy, Sylv and I will be asked if we would like counselling. We will all tell them to go and do the other thing. That will mean that we need counselling ... but only, of course, for–'

'I get your point,' she said, to try to stop the flow. 'But even so, I don't think they were too bad on the trip. What with one thing and another.'

'I must say, I was glad that Tom found Barton that first day. Otherwise, we would still be circling the Isle of Wight, trying to achieve escape velocity.'

She spluttered into her tea. 'He was a piece of work, wasn't he, Jim? Was he a real coach driver, do you think?'

'I've never known one who takes seven goes to get out of the one-way system in Leighford, I must say,' Maxwell said.

'One-way system? What was he doing there? It's on the opposite side of town to the road to Southampton.'

'Indeed,' Maxwell said. 'I think I rest my case.' He took a sip of tea. 'Barton was a good bloke, though. It seems a shame that he doesn't have a permanent job.' He looked thoughtful. 'I wonder if Legs would consider having him as supply to replace Tom.'

She looked at him over the rim of her mug. 'You can't fool me,' she said. 'You don't want to get him a job because he is a good bloke. You just want him in the vicinity to grill him in case he knows anything.'

'And you think that's a bad idea, I assume,' Maxwell said.

'Not a bad idea, no. But, the way the case is going, it's not what happened on the trip that is important. There are lots of other threads which seem to be more relevant.'

'Such as?'

Now the moment had come, she still felt reticent. It was pointless asking him not to get involved. The sheaf of cuttings on the table between them proved that. But somehow there was a huge difference between letting him tinker about with old newspapers and telling him all she knew. But, and this was a big but, someone had tried to kill a defenceless old lady; an annoying and defenceless old lady, it had to be said, but she was, in the absence of anyone else to care, *their* annoying and defenceless old lady. Which meant the 'zipped lip or no promotion rule' no longer applied. So, she took a deep breath and told him everything she knew. *Plus ça change.*

When she had finished, leaving nothing out, he leant back in his chair. 'Is that it?' he asked.

'It?' She was appalled. 'Isn't that enough?'

'Well, yes and no. There are so many gaps, aren't there? Did Izzy know she was her ex-husband's beneficiary?'

'I imagine so. I got the impression that it was part of the divorce settlement.'

'Right. Do we know where Izzy was when he died?'

'No,' she said. 'And now, of course, there's no one to ask.'

'Her mother no use on that one?' he said, knowing what the answer would be.

316

'Hah! Don't ask me to even think about that woman. She was a nightmare. Tom had said she was grasping, but... I don't think she ever thinks about anyone but herself, anyway. Even if she knew where Izzy was at the time, she wouldn't remember. It gave me the willies when she implied that she and Izzy's ex would have become an item, given time.' Jacquie gave a huge shudder.

'I'll put that down as a no, then, shall I?' Maxwell said, solemnly. As Jacquie opened her mouth to clarify further, he held up his hand. 'Enough, already. Now, have you police people given any thought to who Izzy was with on the Wednesday night?'

Jacquie ran her hands through her hair. 'I think someone is on it, but it's such a long shot. We really need to have a suspect, then see if we can put them there at the time, rather than try and pick someone out of a population of ... what is it now? Sixty-six million, something like that?'

'On the Isle of Wight? That's huge for such a small place. I would have guessed at ... what? A hundred and forty, hundred and fifty thousand people at the most. I mean, I know they used to say that the whole of the world's population could stand on the Isle...' He saw her expression and stopped. 'Sorry. You were saying?'

'I was being frivolous, I admit,' she said. 'But at the moment we have three suspects for Paul Masters, two for Izzy, one for Tom. And the one still standing is Izzy's mother, Mizz Nelson, who wouldn't have done the murders in that order, because she has now lost out entirely.'

'Mizz?' Maxwell said. 'What a nightmare she

317

must be, to be sure.'

'Yes,' Jacquie said. 'Mizz. Henry hates that almost as much as you do. Possibly more. So, long story cut short, Henry is trying to get the other forces to agree that the cases are linked. Hampshire are OK with it; I think they have enough on their hands, what with the Bestival and the thousands of extra people that brings. Northants don't see the Masters case *as* a case, so that's also a problem. Henry wants to bring Mrs Troubridge's fall into the mix, but that isn't going too well. To be honest with you, hon, I was only too glad to come home.'

'I hope you're *always* glad to be home,' Maxwell remarked, rather archly.

She flicked at him across the table. 'Can we have a bit of time off murder and mayhem for a while?' she asked. 'I feel as though I need another holiday already and I'm not even officially back from this one yet.'

'Sweetie,' he said. 'Of course. You must be pooped. Let's go and see Mrs Troubridge...' he held out his hands, 'no, hear me out. We'll just go and pop in for a few minutes to see the old trout, then we'll go round to Sylv's and pick up Nole, peeling Lucy off him if we must. Fish and chips for supper, as if we didn't have enough last week, and then home for a nice bath and bed. And that goes for all of us. Then, tomorrow, we'll go ... you pick.'

'That all sounds good,' she said with a sigh. 'OK, let's go to...' She peeped at him from under her lashes. As predicted, he was mouthing 'antique centre' at her, hoping that it might have a subliminal effect. '... Marwell Zoo.' She looked up at him properly. 'That would be nice. See how all the little babies are progressing, the ones we saw in the spring.'

'That reminds me of something,' Maxwell said, pursing his lips and looking at the ceiling for inspiration, which, as usual, wasn't there. 'Never mind, I'll remember it later. All right, the zoo it is.'

Jacquie mimed extreme surprise. 'No antiques?' she said.

He rifled through his cuttings. Not all of them were to do with the case, it transpired. He found the one he wanted and held it up.

'Otter inner aim cord ize,' she read.

'What? No, no, that's the wrong side. Sorry.' He turned it round.

'Antiques Fair, Winchester, Sunday the ... oh, I see.' She smiled. 'It's a deal. Antiques, then lunch, then zoo. Lunch is your shout.'

'Yes, I must talk to you about money,' he said.

'Why?' It had never been an issue between them. Although they joked about 'yours' and 'mine', it was a case of *mi dinero es su dinero* in the Carpenter-Maxwell household.

'Nothing, really. It's just that Mrs B wondered if Mrs Troubridge is having money troubles. Apparently, she calls out, numbers mostly. Unless she was a bingo caller in a previous existence. The staff wondered if it is because she is worrying about money.'

'Henry mentioned that.'

'That's good,' Maxwell was relieved. 'It's not just a Mrs B-ism then. And of course, with her in hospital, bills will be coming in, and they will need to be paid.'

'Oh, I see. Well, I think there is a way of dealing with that. Sylvia will probably know. If we just sort the bills out as they arrive, there's Patient Liaison, something like that.'

'Oh,' Maxwell said, the light dawning. 'The almoner.'

'Aren't you a sweet old-fashioned little thing?' she said, smoothing his cheek. 'Yes, the almoner. When I was a little girl…'

'Just after they stopped having almoners,' he slipped in.

'…I used to think they were the ladies who gave out nuts to the patients,' she concluded.

'As opposed to most NHS staff now…' he began.

'…who just *say* nuts to the patients.' She kissed the tip of his nose. 'We should go on the stage,' she said, and went off to shower and change. She had worn suede in a fish restaurant with Nolan before and had come to regret it.

'We'd be a riot,' Maxwell said. He also needed to shower and change, if only to get rid of the large black smear down the middle of his face which both Mrs B and Jacquie had found it amusing not to mention.

Jacquie and Maxwell weren't quite sure what they would find when they visited Mrs Troubridge in Bed 7, Lady Elizabeth Molester that afternoon. Maxwell had not told Jacquie quite how bad she was, Mrs B had slightly exaggerated to Maxwell. So it was anybody's guess.

'Which one is she?' Jacquie whispered as she peered through the glass as they sanitised their hands. 'They all look the same.'

Maxwell peered in as well and pointed with a still slightly damp finger. 'There she is, third along. Oh, that's good. She's sitting up. She was flat-out when I was here last night.'

As they walked into the almost silent ward, a nurse looked up and beckoned them over. 'Mr Maxwell?' she asked.

'Mr and Mrs Maxwell, yes,' he said, putting one foot in the stirrup of his high horse. 'Is there a problem?'

Jacquie was turning round from the nurses' station and waving at Mrs Troubridge, who lifted a weak hand in greeting.

'We've had ... a call,' the nurse said, looking embarrassed. 'Asking that we don't allow you to visit Mrs Troubridge. In case she gets upset.'

'But look,' Jacquie said, pointing. 'She's waving at us.'

'Waving at *you*,' the nurse pointed out. 'Not at *him*. Sorry, but I have my orders.'

'From whom?' Jacquie asked, sharply.

'Well ... from the person who rang up, I assume,' the nurse said, looking for the Post-it note which had carried the message.

'And that person was...?' Jacquie was already reaching into her bag and only Maxwell knew what she was searching for.

'They didn't give their name, I don't think. A well-wisher, I suppose you might call them.'

'So,' Jacquie said, keeping her hand below the level of the desk, with her warrant card firmly clasped in her fist, 'an anonymous caller rang in to say that Mr Maxwell, specifically, should not be allowed to visit Mrs Troubridge.'

'More or less, yes,' the nurse said, folding her arms and looking truculent.

'Any reasons?' Jacquie's voice was ice.

'It upsets her, the man said...'

'That's a help,' Jacquie said. 'A man, was it?'

'I believe so. I didn't actually take the call. I think we all assumed that it was the man who has been visiting. A Mr Hall, I think it was. He's a policeman.'

'I know,' said Jacquie. 'And here's a coincidence.' She brought her warrant card up to face level. 'So am I. Now, I happen to know that DCI Hall would have made no such call, that Mrs Troubridge would want my husband to visit and so that is what he is going to do.' She walked away from the nurses' station towards Mrs Troubridge's bed.

Maxwell, glancing behind, saw the nurse reach for the phone, hit one button and speak into the receiver without taking her eyes off them. He was sorry he had made his plea for no Old Leighford Highenas. One would come in useful around about now. He and Jacquie sat one each side of their neighbour and each took a hand. That she squeezed back showed how glad she was to see them. Usually any physical contact, apart from with Nolan, was strictly off limits.

'Hello, Mrs Troubridge,' Jacquie said. 'You've given us quite a fright.'

'I've been so worried,' she said, in a small, weak voice. 'Such dreams, I've had. Flying. Wardrobes.

Showers of money.' She looked at Maxwell. 'Metternich, he was there.' She gave a little shiver. 'I was so frightened,' she said, her voice getting shriller. 'Please, please don't...'

The nurse slid off her stool to come over to the bedside. She was stopped halfway across the room by the entry of some shoulders, dressed in a dark-blue uniform. 'That's him, there,' she said, in the strident whisper specially taught to nurses, particularly those likely to do a lot of nights.

'Right,' said the security officer, shooting his cuffs and making his way over to Bed 7. Maxwell turned round and, lo and behold, an Old Leighford Highena, as he lived and breathed. 'Hello, Mr Maxwell,' the man said. 'They said on the phone it was a Mr Maxwell, but I said to my mate, it can't be *our* Mr Maxwell and he said no, it can't. He went up the school as well; you taught us up to GCSE.' He turned to Jacquie. 'This your good lady?' Jacquie nodded and the man shook her hand, almost wrenching her arm off at the elbow. 'Glad to meet you. "Mad Max", we used to call your old man, you know. T'cha. Old times, eh? Sorry about this little misunderstanding. I'll sort it out.' Suddenly, he struck a pose with one finger in the air. 'Neville Chamberlain was the first British prime minister to fly. I've never forgot that, Mr Maxwell. Won us a pub quiz, that did, last week.' He leant over and shouted at Mrs Troubridge. 'I'll leave you with your visitors, shall I, love? Yes! Nice visitors!' Then, on a rather less volcanic level, to Maxwell and Jacquie, 'Nice to see you again, Mr Maxwell. Nice to meet you, Mrs Maxwell,' and he turned

323

on his heel and strode over to the nurses' station. From her vantage point, Jacquie could see the body language and decided that for everyone's sake, it was as well they couldn't hear what the Old Leighford Highena was saying in support of his hero. 'Ape' would have gone through the shredder for that man.

Maxwell, Jacquie and Mrs Troubridge were all stunned into a mildly catatonic state. Finally, she said, softly, 'Well, that was nice, Mr Maxwell. An old pupil.'

'Yes, indeed,' Maxwell said. 'Always nice to catch up. But anyway, Mrs Troubridge, how are you? It's so nice to see you looking better.'

She leant slightly in his direction and Jacquie leant also, to hear what she said. 'As soon as I saw you, Mr Maxwell, I started to feel better. I knew you wouldn't let her hurt me.'

'Who, Mrs Troubridge?' Jacquie said. 'Let who hurt you?'

The old lady furrowed her brow. 'That's the trouble,' she said. 'I don't know.' She shook her head. 'It's probably part of my dream. It's all so confused. There was so much in it that I don't understand. Two television sets, I remember that. Side by side. And definitely a wardrobe. And Metternich.' Again, she furrowed her brow. 'I've got to feed him, haven't I? He'll be hungry.' She released her hands from theirs and tried to throw back the covers. 'We don't want another Incident, do we?'

'It's all right,' Maxwell said. 'Metternich isn't hungry. You need to stay here until you're quite well. We're looking after the house for you. Mrs B will be watering the plants and so forth. She'll be in to see you, later on, when she's finished her rounds with the trolley.'

'Who?' Mrs Troubridge looked from Jacquie to Maxwell, confused.

'Mrs B,' Jacquie said. 'You know, the lady who cleans our house.'

'Polishing?' Mrs Troubridge asked, her eyes swivelling from side to side.

'Well, yes, and other things. She will be looking after your things as well, while you're in here.'

'Tell her not to polish the wardrobe!' Mrs Troubridge called. 'Don't let her hurt me!'

The nurse wasn't to be stopped this time. She appeared like a genie at the foot of the bed. 'I think Mrs Troubridge has had enough excitement for one day, don't you?' she asked, rhetorically. 'I think it's time you both went.'

It would be a step too far to kiss Mrs Troubridge. So they patted a shoulder each and walked away, turning to wave as they went. But Mrs Troubridge was in the nurse's hands now, and she didn't see them go. They could just hear her, faintly, start to count down from one million.

Pausing only to prise Nolan from the arms of Sylvia and Guy and a sobbing Lucy, and via a fish and chip supper, the Maxwell family had an early night. They had made a solemn undertaking not to discuss the case and so Maxwell was like a pressure cooker that needed its valve adjusting, especially since the visit to Mrs Troubridge. But Jacquie was unshakeable. She had deafness so selective that she only seemed to hear Nolan or comments about food or television. Maxwell's attempts to sneak one in under the wire by asking her how she thought Mrs Troubridge would like one of Jamie Oliver's school dinners, or what she thought Mrs Troubridge would think of the weatherman's jacket were ignored. Finally, he gave in to the inevitable and played a rather one-sided game of Scrabble with Nolan – one-sided because a new rule, invented by his son that very evening, meant that the biggest person only got to play with consonants. Nolan won 703 to 4. A personal best.

Sunday was much the same, with additional antiques, pub lunch and animals. Maxwell had never hated his job, so Mondays held no terrors for him. But he found himself, that Sunday night as he cleaned his teeth ready for bed, looking forward to a Monday more than he had for a long time.

As he watched in the darkness, the LED on the clock rearranged themselves silently to say '00:01:01'. He poked his wife in the back. 'It's Monday,' he pointed out.

'I'm ignoring you,' she said. 'And also asleep.'

'But, technically...'

'I'm *asleep*,' she repeated. 'I'll see you in the morning.'

And finally, he was asleep too, his dreams full of old ladies flying past on leathern wings, chased by Metternich, trying to claw them out of the air.

Chapter Twenty-One

Monday. Monday. Hate that day. Legs Diamond didn't do whole-school assemblies; his doctor advised against it because it was more or less carte blanche for trouble. Put over a thousand kids together in a sports hall with the acoustics of ... well, a sports hall, really, and the inevitable result was likely to be bedlam.

So the Head Teacher did it a year group at a time with the relevant Year Head at his elbow, in the school hall which was altogether more cosy and certainly more purpose-built. He had weighed up over the weekend how best to approach this and there was no good way. So he consulted Maxwell. Even before Surrey's saddle was cool, propped and padlocked in Maxwell's secret place, Uriah Heep was at the Head of Sixth Form's elbow, asking, and not for the first time, for advice.

'Sixth Form first,' Maxwell had told him, 'then the kids on the trip. It's an awful thing to say, Headmaster, but there's a hint of a silver lining in that Tom Medlicott hasn't been here long. Anyone of longer standing and the hysteria would be worse.' Or, Maxwell forebore to say, if it was one of the SLT, the party would be wilder.

'Quite right,' Diamond nodded. 'I'll get Pansy on it. Er ... you don't want counselling, do you?'

'Thank you, Headmaster,' Maxwell smiled, 'but

I keep my own counsel. And I'll tell my Sixth Form.'

'Quite,' Diamond said, after a while. 'Quite,' and he scurried off in search of his office amanuensis.

Maxwell's Own, his Year Twelve and Thirteen, usually had their assembly on Wednesday, so a Monday slot was odd. There was something in the wind, they all knew that, and a book was starting on the possibilities even as Maxwell took his place front and centre.

The usual hush fell. The tutors stood at the back. They knew the score from the staff briefing and knew they had witnessed another nail in the coffin of school trips. First it had been the mountain ranges of paperwork generated by Risk Assessment; then it had been litigious parents and insurance demands – 'Have you been injured on a school trip recently and it wasn't your fault?' Now, it was dead teachers and their wives. The Sixth Form's book was more exotic – Mr Diamond had had the nervous breakdown he'd been negotiating his way towards for years; a Year Seven kid had got stuck in quicksand on the trip and was still there, being fed food and oxygen by a tube; Mad Max was pregnant.

'There's no easy way to say this,' the Head of Sixth Form said ... and all was revealed.

By the time the Isle of Wight party had assembled in the library, Peter Maxwell had hotfooted through the school to join them. Legs Diamond hovered near the juvenile fiction and didn't understand the mimed shorthand when Conan the Librarian offered him a cup of tea from across the room. Her name wasn't really Conan, of course, but then she wasn't really a librarian either, so what the hey?

'Mobile phones,' Maxwell said to the horde. 'Where do I want them? Here, on this table. When do I want them? Now.' They looked at each other like the returning survivors of the Donner Party and one by one came out and laid the offending beasts in front of Maxwell. Sixteen; not a bad haul. Nobody queried the command. Nobody challenged it. Nobody so much as hinted at the infringement of a human right. They already knew Mad Max too well for any of that nonsense.

The Head of Sixth Form drew aside and left the podium to his boss. Diamond surveyed the serried ranks. Was it him or did they look younger than ever?

'I hope you enjoyed your Getting To Know You Week,' he said, 'but now I'm afraid I have some rather bad news.' He looked at Maxwell and never felt so alone in his life. It went with holding the top spot, picking up the biggest cheque, but it wasn't much consolation now. 'Mr Medlicott, your Art teacher, has died. So, unfortunately, has his wife.'

Conan had not been at the staff briefing and all but dropped her cup. She stood as open-mouthed as the kids. Diamond looked at Maxwell who nodded. 'You will hear all sorts of stories in the days and weeks ahead,' he said. 'I want you to ignore them. Because of the ... unusual nature of all this, it is possible that the police will want to speak to you...'

The sudden hubbub was like a tsunami around the room, but it ebbed when Maxwell raised his hand.

'If that is the case,' Diamond went on, 'you have the right to have your parents present. In fact, I insist that you do.'

'Please, sir.' One little boy did his Oliver impression. He hadn't put his hand up since Year Three, but in his shock he had reverted.

'Yes ... um...?'

'What happened to Mr Medlicott? Was he murdered?'

'Memories,' said Maxwell to shield his Head Teacher from the onslaught that would surely follow. 'Your memories of this week will last for ever. Think of the good times. Don't let the bad ones spoil it for you.'

'Photographs,' Diamond said suddenly. 'Who's got some photographs of the trip?'

Virtually every hand shot skywards. Most of the piccies lay in the phones in front of the teachers now.

'Well,' Diamond felt inspired. 'Why not print them out? I'm sure the library staff can help you with that.' He raised a questioning eyebrow at Conan, who shook her head frantically. 'Excellent,' he nodded at her. 'Thank you. Print them out and then we'll have a little memory corner, shall we, right here in Mrs Wantage's library.' The woman glowered at him, but the deed was done.

'Is that like when someone puts flowers at a roadside accident?' Jazmyn wanted to know.

'That's right, um ... yes. It'll be a little reminder of Mr and Mrs Medlicott.'

Some of the hands had not gone down from the previous question. Others were in the air for the first time. They were like First Formers again, a wriggling, squirming Reception Class bursting to know more. Maxwell read their minds. 'There's no more we can say at the moment, people. Take a little time, if you want to, then back to your classes. You can start the picture gallery at lunchtime. It's the best way.'

One or two of the girls began to cry. There were even trembling lips among the boys. Solemnly they came forward, the sixteen, to reclaim their phones and to find a picture of Mr Medlicott, whose face was already fuzzy in their imagination.

The day had been very difficult, one thing taken with another. The staff had been rather more reticent than the kids, generally speaking, but even so Maxwell, and, he was sure, Sylv and Pansy, had spent the day fending off questions. Pansy was rather better built for fending, but they were all feeling a little frayed by the end of the day. The rumour mill had been grinding well, and beheadings, dismemberments and various other atrocities loomed large in the questions coming at them from all directions. The photo gallery had grown apace and the atmosphere there was surprisingly unmaudlin. There were lots of pictures of staff looking less than their best, one corner being given over almost exclusively to Maxwell asleep, with various kids pointing at his open

331

mouth. He was not too surprised to see that there was at least one when Jacquie was the culprit; she had fitted in well, but it wasn't until now he had realised just *how* well. He would have to have words.

Maxwell had enjoyed the ride home; Surrey had decided not to squeak, wobble or otherwise show signs of age and for that, Maxwell was grateful. The sun was warm but the breeze was showing signs of autumn chill as he swept round the curve into Columbine and up the path. As he tucked his faithful steed away in the garage, he saw Mrs Troubridge's key hanging on its nail. He really just wanted a cup of tea and a think, but now he had reminded himself of his responsibilities, he thought he might just as well check next door now as later.

Jingling the key in his hand, he walked down and then up the path again; he would have to carve a hole in that hedge if he was going to be doing this much, he could see. He opened the door carefully and stepped over the few items of post that were on the mat and turned and picked them up, shuffling quickly through them. Two circulars, a phone bill and a postcard. The circulars he binned and then peeked in through the window of the phone bill, checking for the prevailing colour of ink. Black, so that was all right. He'd wait for the red one; it wasn't likely to be huge, after all. The postcard showed a rocky coastline and some rather attractive castles. Maxwell the historian was immediately intrigued and he tried and failed to persuade himself that he really shouldn't turn it over to find out who it was from and where precisely it was. The writing on the reverse was quite spidery, but easy to read. He let his eyes drop to the bottom right of the message area and saw, to his surprise, the name – Araminta. He put it in his pocket to take with him when he visited next; it would cheer the old trout up.

He did a whistle-stop tour of the rest of the house and all was clearly in order. Perhaps the thinnest of a thin new layer of dust had fallen, soon to be moved randomly around by Mrs B, but that was all. He let himself out through the back door, checked the garden, then out through the front door, up the path, down the path, through his door, up the stairs and was finally standing in front of the kettle; it still seemed strange to think that he had been inches away through the wall not ten minutes before and was now standing in his own kitchen, knackered. Ah, the miracles of modern town planning. While the kettle boiled, he checked the postcard again and filled the time by soaking up the architecture of what turned out to be Rhodes. Oops, he had better not let Jacquie see it – it might be a sore subject, especially with what had happened in the previous week.

Accidentally on purpose, he turned it over and read it. He didn't know whether Miss Troubridge was a drinker, but her writing style was certainly a little strange. 'Dear Jessica,' it said, 'HEre i am Like a bad Penny, sending a postcard hoME. i know you say I never HAVE thought aBout sEnding thEse Nice cards FrOm the Unusual Nooks anD crannies And memoRiEs of me and

'YOU Are Lingering Longer these days. wRITE when you can, your loving Araminta.' There was no other reason for it, the woman must be drunk. He put the card down on the table and made his tea. He sat in his favourite chair, staring at nothing much. The day had gone more or less as expected. Diamond had done a difficult job well, the picture gallery in particular being inspired. It had really brought back the week, seeing everyone milling around, in the background. Pansy Donaldson in particular had been hard to miss. The dark glasses were always in position in the morning shots and it was almost possible to tell the time of day of the photo by whether she was wearing them or not. Maxwell sipped his tea and let his mind wander. Something wasn't quite adding up and he couldn't quite put his finger on it.

He reached down by the side of his chair and felt for the phone. He dialled with as little fuss as possible, not wanting to interfere with his train of thought. The phone he had called rang for ages and just as he was about to give up, it was answered.

'Leighford High School.'

'Who is that?' Maxwell asked.

'Who is that?' the voice retorted.

'Oh, Bernard,' Maxwell said. He couldn't think of anyone else who would ask him of all people who he was. 'Are you going to be in school much longer?'

'I rarely leave much before six-thirty, Max, as I thought you knew. Why?'

'Well, I was rather hoping I might come back

and look at something important.'

'The school is locked and alarmed, Max, I'm afraid,' Ryan said, pompously. Any school with Bernard Ryan in it had every right to be alarmed.

Maxwell was puzzled. 'I'm assuming you can get out, though, Bernard, can't you?' he asked, wondering briefly whether the kids were right and that Ryan *did* actually live in a cupboard.

'Of course.' It was obvious that the Deputy Head was not going to make this easy for the Head of Sixth Form.

'Well, why can't you let me in, if you can let yourself out?' he asked, patiently, having long ago grasped the fundamental workings of a door.

'How will I know when you get here?' Ryan said, as if laying the ace.

'I could ring you from outside,' Maxwell said. 'I do have the technology, Bernard, whatever you may have heard. I'll only be about twenty minutes or so. Would that be all right? For you to let me in?'

There was a silence, then Ryan said, in his usual curmudgeonly fashion, as though every word was going to have to be accounted for one day, 'All right, then. Ring me when you're outside and I'll let you in. Don't let this become a habit, though.' And the phone went down with a crash.

Maxwell rang off himself and put the handset down carefully in its rest. A good response to that was that he didn't make a habit of chasing murderers, but since that would be patently untrue, he didn't even bother to think it. He could still remember the good old days, when he had his own key to the school and came and went as he pleased; a time before the Age of Paranoia. He swigged the last of the tea and stood up. Being occasionally of a tidy disposition, he took his cup into the kitchen. Straightening up from putting it in the dishwasher, he saw the card on the table. He glanced at the clock. It was Nolan's day at Tumble Tots with Plocker and his mother. It was Jacquie's first day back at work and the middle of a murder enquiry. It looked as though he was probably a more or less free – or as a more self-pitying person would see it, neglected – man. He would have time to pop in and see Mrs Trou-bridge and give her her postcard. She would be cheered up hearing from her twin and he might be able to catch her on the mother planet for long enough to find out why Araminta was writing like some kind of mad person. He popped the card in his pocket and went to wake up Surrey.

He swept up the rise to the main road, swore colourfully, making a lone pedestrian blench, turned round and went back for his phone.

He swept up the rise to the main road and turned off in the direction of Leighford High School. It felt odd to be doing the journey at this, the wrong end of the day. He often stayed late himself, but he seldom went back once he had made his escape. The traffic was different at this time; too early for what passed for a rush hour in Leighford, too late for the school runs which clogged roads with a swarm of four-wheel drives – all, it seemed to Maxwell, driven by very tiny, very inadequately trained women.

Soon, he was standing outside the school doors, waiting for Bernard Ryan to answer the

336

phone. Maxwell did the small jig that is the lot of mobile-phone users waiting for a reply. He muttered the usual mantra, 'come on, come on, come on' to himself and finally the magic worked.

'Leighford High School.'

'Bernard. It's me. I'm outside.'

'Who is this please?' Ryan said, annoyingly.

'For heaven's sake, Bernard. It's me, Maxwell. Can you let me in?'

'It's been longer than twenty minutes,' the Deputy pointed out.

'Possibly,' Maxwell conceded. 'But not by much. And it's still me. Can you let me in, please?'

'I suppose so. How long are you going to be?' Maxwell could see Ryan through the glass doors into Reception, holding the phone as if it might bite and looking straight at him.

'Look, Bernard, can we have this conversation inside? I could be halfway to where I want to be by now.' Maxwell only just stopped himself from pulling a face at Ryan through the half-glazed door.

'All right,' Ryan said. 'I'll let you in.' And he put the phone down and started his pedantically slow progress to the front doors, unlocking, locking, unlocking, locking, like an astronaut returning to the mother ship after making repairs out in space.

'Come on, come *on!*' His careful timetable would only work if no one messed him about and Bernard Ryan was definitely messing him about. Finally, the Deputy Head docked with the main doors and, infinitely slowly, shot all the bolts and unhooked all the chains, before tapping in a code on the electronic pad next to the lock.

Maxwell was amazed to find that the doors didn't swing inwards with a shrieking howl like those of Castle Dracula. Instead, they just caught on the carpet halfway through their arc and fetched Maxwell a nasty one on the shoulder, just as they normally did.

'Ouch, Bernard,' Maxwell remarked. 'Thank you for letting me in. Are you here doing anything particular?'

'There's always something to do,' Ryan said. 'But as it happens I am trying to find a replacement temporarily for Tom Medlicott.'

'Have you thought of Barton Joseph? I know he works in a different authority as a rule, but the kids from the trip know him, which might be a help, and he is a really good chap.' Maxwell crossed his fingers, trying to forget the pick-pocketing incident.

Ryan's eyes lit up. 'Do you have any contact details for this man?' he asked.

'They're in the file I gave to you when we got back. It might even make it easier for you to pay him, if he works here for a while.'

'Pay him?' Ryan was always nervous when paying out was involved.

'Yes. For the work he did on the trip.'

'Ah. Does this cause a problem, though?' Ryan asked. 'Is he a suspect at all?'

'Suspect?' Maxwell feigned surprise. 'In what?'

Ryan looked at Maxwell closely. Could it be that the great murder hunter had hung up his magnifying glass? The Deputy Head decided to put it to one side. A supply teacher is a supply teacher, when all was said and done.

'Anyhoo, Bernard,' Maxwell smiled. 'Time's a-wasting. Is there a possibility that I might get to the library without the keys to the kingdom?'

'Oh, the library,' Bernard said. 'I was expecting you to be going up to your department.'

'No, the library is what I want,' Maxwell said, holding on to his temper by the slenderest thread.

'That's quite a good thing, actually,' Ryan said, with a trace of disappointment in his voice. 'Because you wouldn't have been able to get to the Sixth Form Corridor. It's been alarmed.'

It was entirely to Maxwell's credit that he let that wonderful chance go by. It was to Ryan's credit that he didn't let his disappointment show. He had spent the last half an hour crafting some wonderful ripostes, which must now remain unsaid.

'Library?' Maxwell said. 'Do I need keys?'

Bernard Ryan was far from sensitive, but what synapses he had fired now. 'Just go in,' he said. 'No keys. No alarms.'

'Excellent. Nice to know there is no barrier to education in this great country of ours. You won't lock me in, will you?' Maxwell made it sound like a jokey remark, but in fact he meant it. He knew his Bernard of old.

'Of course not,' Ryan was aghast. 'You might tinker with my keypads.'

'Highly unlikely, Bernard, but you may keep on hoping if you like,' said Maxwell, patting his shoulder and half-running, half-walking down the corridor. His timetable was now very, very close to breaking down. If his suspicion could be easily confirmed in the library, it might yet work.

He pushed open the doors and, as might be expected, they opened without a sound. Maxwell flicked a light switch and nothing happened. Ah-ha, a timer. Bernard Ryan was as cunning as a fox, it had to be said. But Maxwell wasn't beaten. Once, what seemed like long ago, he had been forced by Jacquie to get to know all his phone had to offer. And so he knew, that by pressing buttons, more or less at random, he could make it into a not-terribly-bright torch. The combination of that and the daylight coming through the high and grubby windows would probably suffice.

He peered at the corner given over to the Medlicott photos. He scanned some, looked closely at others and finally, with a cry of triumph, removed two from the display. Feeling rather like a grave robber, he slid them into his pocket along with Mrs Troubridge's postcard and slipped out of the library, along the corridor and out of the double doors, with a merry cry of farewell to Bernard Ryan.

It was only as he was straddling Surrey and riding off down the drive that the sound of sirens wailing from the school building reminded him that he should probably have done something esoteric and secret with one trouser leg rolled up before he left the building. Or at the very least tapped a number into a keypad. He skidded to a halt at the bottom of the drive and turned back, just to check that it was unlawful egress that had caused the brouhaha and not twenty-foot flames.

Bernard Ryan was standing at the top of the low

flight of steps up which generations of reluctant children had traipsed, day after day, year after year. He looked as though he was shouting something which Maxwell, whose lip-reading skills at a distance were a trifle rusty, couldn't make out. And the sirens drowned out Ryan's voice entirely. He was shaking his fists in the air, though, which gave Maxwell quite a strong clue. The Head of Sixth Form had to admit to himself he thought people only did that in the old *Beano* and *Dandy* comics, not in real life. For self-preservation, he hopped on Surrey and was pedalling furiously in the direction of the General before Ryan could chase him down the drive. His journey was made all the more colourful by the sight of so many police cars, ambulances and fire engines all racing in the opposite direction.

Chapter Twenty-Two

Jacquie's day was not much better than Maxwell's, but she had to put up with rather less hysteria. The case, if case it were, was not going anywhere fast. It was not like Henry Hall to flog dead horses, but he was having extreme difficulty in pulling every-thing together and seemed doomed to spend the day in meetings, arguing his point of view. Most of the people pulled in on Saturday had now gone off to other duties, leaving Jacquie, Fran Brannon and Phil Smart working on the board, adding data as it became available. There was little more by the fag end of the afternoon than there had been on the first morning of the case and they all sat in the front row of the seats in the briefing room, legs out, chins sunk on chests, gloomily staring at what little they had.

They had been there so long that the conver-sation had turned general. 'Apart from the obvi-ous,' Phil Smart said to Jacquie, 'did you have a good time?'

'I did, actually,' Jacquie said. 'Nolan loved every minute. You wouldn't think he lived by the sea-side to see him gallop along the beach every night before bed. And he loved the little zoo we went to and the theme park. He wants a baby sloth as a pet, now. We were lucky, they'd only let it out into the enclosure that day.'

'At least a sloth wouldn't be able to run away

very fast,' Phil said. 'My nipper has lost I can't tell you how many guinea pigs that way.'

'Tortoises, that's the answer,' Fran said. 'I've got one. It's as good as gold.'

They all half-sat, half-lay across their chairs, mulling over the relative virtues of sloths versus guinea pigs versus tortoises. It was a tough one to call.

'It was quite busy, though,' Jacquie said, making Phil, who had started to nod off, jump. 'You can see all the people in the background, look, in the photos.' She waved an arm to the pictures of Tom and Izzy Medlicott.

'That big one,' Fran said. 'You particularly can't miss her.'

'Oh,' Jacquie said. 'She's not a tourist. That's Pansy.' Phil Smart interrupted with a snort. 'She's with us. She runs the office at Leighford High School.'

'Oh, right,' Fran said and let her chin sink onto her chest again. Suddenly, she stood up. 'Are we allowed to go home?' she asked Jacquie.

'Christ, Fran. This isn't infant school. 'What are you rostered for?'

'I'm not rostered at all. This is flexi.'

'Flexi? What, paying back or accruing?' Phil Smart said. He was the king of flexitime and gave in time sheets so labyrinthine that sometimes even he didn't know what they meant.

'Accruing,' the girl said. 'I've got seventy-three hours outstanding.'

Jacquie and Phil Smart both woke up fully at that. 'You can't accrue that much,' Jacquie told her. 'You're only supposed to have a day or so at most. Clear off home now, before it gets worse. Go on. Shoo.'

'You're sure?' the WPC said, edging over to the door.

Jacquie just flapped a hand at her. 'Off. Go.' As the door flapped to behind the girl, Jacquie turned to Phil Smart. 'How are you for flexi?' she asked.

'Don't know till I fill in the sheet,' he grinned. 'OK though, I expect.'

She nodded towards the door, eyebrows raised.

'I'll race you,' he said, and was gone, through the door and down the backstairs, like a guinea pig up a pipe.

Like the good housewife she would have liked to have the time to be, Jacquie went through the room, picking up abandoned coffee mugs and turning off lights. She went out the front way, signing out and walking to the car, savouring the September afternoon. She couldn't decide whether to collect Nolan early and put up with the wails as he and Plocker were separated, after only a whole day together, sitting at the same desk, playing with the same football, tumbling with the same tots, or to go home and have a few minutes with her feet up, chatting to her husband. About the case. Or, rather, about not being able to talk any more about the case, because it was complicated enough, with other forces and Henry's problems with the powers that were.

She decided on Plan C – she would nip in and have a word with Mrs Troubridge.

Maxwell poked his head around the door of the

ward, warily looking out for the nurse of the previous day, but she was nowhere to be seen. Instead, he was welcomed aboard by an Old Leighford Highena, who he remembered as a rather nervous boy, scared of the sight of blood, his own or anyone else's. They stood chatting in low tones at the bottom of Mrs Troubridge's bed and Maxwell could feel the shade of James Robertson Justice as Sir Lancelot Spratt start to settle like a cold mantle over his shoulders. They were just getting into their stride, when a peevish voice came from the business end of the bed.

'It's rude to whisper,' it said. 'I would have thought that you, Mr Maxwell, would have been better brought up. I can't vouch for *you*.' This was directed at the charge nurse, who shot her a glance in which the venom was barely concealed.

'Mrs Troubridge is so much better, Mr Maxwell,' he said. 'Quite her old self, I would imagine.'

'Mr Maxwell is allowed to judge if I am my own self,' Mrs Troubridge snapped, 'having been my neighbour for a great number of years. *You* on the other hand, I have never met before you attempted to wash bits of my person to which only Mr Troubridge was allowed to be privy.'

Maxwell turned to the nurse. 'You're right,' he said. 'She is certainly much better.'

Mrs Troubridge patted the bed invitingly. 'Come nearer, Mr Maxwell,' she said. 'I really don't have the strength to shout.'

He pulled up a chair and went to sit close to her. 'You did quite well then, Mrs Troubridge, if I might say so.' He knew that Neil would never

345

take it out on her, but his policy of being nice to nurses had never let him down thus far and he thought Mrs Troubridge would do well to follow his example.

The old woman's voice dropped to only just above a whisper. 'It takes it out of me, Mr Maxwell,' she said, 'but I don't like to lower my standards. I won't be mauled.'

'Quite right, Mrs Troubridge,' Maxwell said. 'I've got a nice surprise for you, here.' He pulled the postcard out of his pocket with a flourish. 'It's from Miss Troubridge.'

'Araminta?' Mrs Troubridge repeated. 'A postcard? It's been ages. The last time I heard she was in ... oh, I can't remember. Marseilles, I think. She was always rather,' she dropped her voice even lower, 'louche as a girl. I hope she has been behaving herself.'

The concept of Miss Troubridge sashaying along the esplanade at Marseilles not behaving herself made Maxwell feel quite queasy. However, this may explain the writing, he thought.

'Can you pass me my spectacles, Mr Maxwell?' Mrs Troubridge asked. 'They are in that drawer. *Not* that one, Mr Maxwell. That contains ... personal items. The one on the right. That's the one.' Maxwell handed over her specs. He had known she wore them, but she was never seen in public with them on, as she was far too vain. She perched them on the end of her nose and held out the postcard at arm's length. 'Rhodes!' she said. 'The nerve of the woman. She knows that that was the favourite holiday destination of Mr Troubridge and myself.' She dropped the card.

'She is just trying to twist the knife, Mr Maxwell. She knows I am stuck in this bed and so she gads,' she fixed Maxwell with a glare, 'yes, *gads* to my favourite place. Cruel. Very cruel.' She looked down and brushed the card aside, revealing a photograph that had got stuck under a corner of the inadequately licked stamp.

Maxwell reached for it, but she was already examining it. 'Oh, this was a kind thought, Mr Maxwell,' she said. 'A photograph of Nolan! He is really enjoying that ice cream, isn't he? Goodness, that is a very large lady he is standing near, isn't it?'

'Yes,' Maxwell said. 'That was one of our helpers, Pansy. A very good-hearted soul.' He didn't see why he should ruin her rose-coloured view of his holiday.

'Does she suffer from migraines, poor thing?' Mrs Troubridge asked.

'Why? ... oh, the dark glasses. Yes, she does, rather.' It was true, Maxwell thought; Pansy definitely looked rather strained.

'And Jacquie! She looks as though she is enjoying herself as well. Who is that pretty woman she is standing next to? Now she *doesn't* seem to be enjoying herself. She looks very ill at ease, Mr Maxwell. Perhaps she doesn't like children.' Mrs Troubridge was examining the picture minutely. Suddenly she dropped it on the bed. Quietly, she said to Maxwell, 'I wonder if you could call a nurse; a proper one, not that man. I won't be mauled.' Her eyes were suddenly wild and Maxwell jumped up and beckoned to a nurse at the far end of the room, who came scurrying over.

'Has she gone again?' she asked Maxwell, as though it wasn't obvious. Mrs Troubridge was plucking at the covers and crying out in a high voice, 'Mr Maxwell, Mr Maxwell. Don't let her hurt me.'

The nurse glared at him. 'We had her nice and calm. What have you said to her?'

'Nothing,' Maxwell said. 'She was looking at this photo, that's all.'

The nurse gave it a cursory look, followed by a shrug. 'We really never know what might set her off,' she said. 'I'll give her something to calm her down.' Seeing Maxwell's stricken look, she reassured him. 'It's not your fault,' she said. 'She had a trifle for dessert at lunchtime and she was off as soon as she saw it.'

Maxwell had a sudden Road to Damascus moment, but he had to be sure. 'Trifle,' he said. 'Was it decorated?'

'I expect so,' the nurse said. 'They're not exactly Heston Blumenwhatsit in the kitchen, but they usually do a dash of hundreds and thousands...'

'Nine hundred and ninety-nine thousand,' trilled Mrs Troubridge on a rising scale. 'The wardrobe at the top of the stairs. Don't...'

Maxwell slipped silently away, his mind whirling. He needed to be at home with Metternich, or failing that, Jacquie. He needed to talk this case over, because it was a case and everything was related, if only he could work out how. So perhaps Metternich would be a better bet than Jacquie, if the embargo on discussion had been reimposed, as he suspected might be the case.

Deep in contemplation he turned a corner and walked into something solid and yet bouncy, which smelt instantly familiar. As he bounced off it, it said, 'Max? What are you doing here?'

Recovering quickly, he formed his right hand into a gun and shot at her, the murder mystery fan's immediate reaction to those words. 'I've popped in to see Mrs Troubridge.' He ran through the events of the day so far and took out and filed the visit to Leighford. He could tell her later, depending on how the rest of the evening went. 'I was at a loose end.'

Jacquie was suspicious. Maxwell was never at an end so loose that he would cycle halfway across town to visit someone he could visit with her later on. But she decided to let it go. 'I bunked off early,' she admitted. 'This case, these cases, whatever they are, aren't going too smoothly.' She caught his alert look, the pricking up of the ears, the slight flaring of the nostrils. 'Don't get your hopes up, sunshine,' she said. 'I've recovered from my attack of loose-lipitis. And don't sulk,' she added, as he slumped extravagantly. 'How's Mrs Troubridge?'

'Not too good again,' he said. 'She was fine; I took her a postcard from Araminta which came today.'

'That was nice; of you and of Araminta,' Jacquie said.

'You'd think so, wouldn't you? But she got a bit steamed up, because apparently Araminta has hijacked Mr Troubridge's favourite romantic destination. Then I showed her a picture of us on our hols and she suddenly went.'

'Don't tell me the Isle of Wight was Mr Tr–?'

'No, Araminta is in Rhodes.'

'Lucky,' Jacquie said, with only a trace of bitterness.

'Oh, ha. Anyway, I don't suggest you go in. She really is in a bit of a state right now. Although...' he paused.

'What?' She felt the sinking feeling she always felt when he started to nibble at the edge of a case. She knew that Henry Hall thought there might be a connection and she felt a pricking of her thumbs.

'I just think you might benefit from perhaps seeing her tomorrow, during the day when she's fresh, see if you can get to the bottom of what's worrying her. Because something is, definitely, worrying her. Pore ol' soul,' he finished, with a perfect Mrs B.

'I'll speak to Henry,' was all Jacquie would say, then she linked her arm in her husband's and turned to go back to the car park. 'You're on Surrey, I take it?' she said.

'Stabled round in the bike racks. Race you home?'

'You'll beat me. I'm picking up Nole from Plocker's.'

'See you there, then. I'll start supper, shall I? What had you planned?'

'Anything that doesn't have a side order of fries and a pinch of mixed salad will go down a treat,' she said.

'I'll do my best,' he promised and they returned to their vehicles and soon were on their way home.

Maxwell unearthed a cottage pie from the bowels of the freezer in the garage and it was soon bubbling away quietly to itself in the oven. As he put it in, he chuckled and rechristened himself Heston Blumenwhatsit. He knew he had a while before Jacquie was back, so he whistled his cat who, though within earshot and clear sight, took absolutely no notice, and went up into the loft, where the soft evening light filled the room. Just being at his desk seemed to organise his thoughts and before he could lose them altogether he pulled a piece of paper from the top drawer, switched on his modelling light and began to write. A soft chirrup and a thump signalled the arrival of Metternich, so he began to talk as he made his notes.

'Evening, Count,' he said. 'Thanks for dropping by.' He didn't mind talking to himself but that always seemed a bit too close to the 'mad' bit of Mad Max for comfort; it could only be a matter of time. Talking to the cat was something else entirely – it could class as being friendly. 'Park your bum,' he said, pleasantly, 'and listen up. I shall need your input later, when the going gets a bit tougher. I've numbered these points for my convenience; I know you're not a number person, but bear with me.'

The cat extended a leg and chewed between his toes.

'Thank you. Right. Number One – while we were away, Mrs Troubridge was pushed down the stairs by person or persons unknown. Only Henry Hall and I think this to be the case, and presumably Mrs Troubridge does as well.' He looked across at his favourite feline. 'I know what you're thinking, Count, and I have no idea about the wardrobe and the numbers. I think that might be because the poor old trout is in fact losing it a bit. Any comments so far?'

Metternich was now licking behind his knee and Maxwell took that as a no.

'Just to underline the point about next door, I think someone had tampered with our key. I had a look round and as far as I can see nothing has gone from in here, so it is a bit odd. Anyway, I digress. Number Two – and I suppose this should be Number One, really, but I don't want to confuse you, so we'll leave it – just before we went on holiday Izzy Medlicott's ex-husband was pushed off a ladder.' He paused for effect, but the cat didn't react. 'I notice you don't argue with the "pushed" bit, and I can't agree with you more. It would be too ridiculous if he just fell, don't you think?' He took the chomping noise as the cat's grooming teeth reached his back to signify assent. He took a moment to admire the cat's dexterity; it was all Maxwell could do to scratch his own back, let alone chew it. 'I'm assuming, Count, that you have started to see the pattern.'

He paused to write down the next point before reading it out. 'Izzy Medlicott goes missing – twice – while we are on holiday. She is seen by a moderately dim but unimaginative, and therefore trustworthy, child up late with the runs. She is later found dead ... would you like to fill in here? It's an easy guess.' The cat looked up at him, mouth open in mid-cleanse. 'Correct. Got it in

352

one. At the bottom of a cliff.'

'Number Three ... is it Three, by now, or more? Let's not bother with numbers, eh? Next – Izzy's husband, Tom Medlicott – there should be some word, shouldn't there, for the various husbands of one woman? Husband-in-law would be a good one – Tom is found dead at the bottom of the stairs. Not butchered and hacked as rumour would have it, but just as dead as if he had been. Now, you've seen me fall down the stairs in my time, Count, I know. That one time when I caught my foot in the Hoover lead, you were lucky I didn't fall on you, if you remember. And yet, here I am, to tell the tale. So I will have to mark this one as also very dodgy.'

Maxwell sat pensively, tapping his pen on the paper. 'Then, things get less tidy, so you'll excuse me, I'm sure, if I witter quietly to myself and don't make sense.'

Metternich looked up at him. Make sense? When was he going to start? But he was a comforting old bugger to have around and it was very soporific to be up here, in a twilight pool beside the desk, hearing his voice droning on and lulling him asleep.

Maxwell jotted some disjointed words on his sheet of paper, then reached into his pocket and lined up the two photographs and the postcard in front of him. If staring at something gave the answer, then it should be written in ten-foot-high neon letters in the air, but that wasn't how it worked. He jotted some more, crossing things out and muttering. 'How can there be two?' he asked the cat under his breath. 'It certainly scared Mrs

Troubridge. Izzy's father is dead, and her mother is horrible. Does Araminta drink?' He picked up the postcard again and read the message once more. It seemed rather oddly constructed. It must mean something more than the words, but he–

'Hello, the house!' his son's voice floated up the stairs.

'Up here, darlings,' he called back, making the cat flinch. There wasn't usually shouting up here in the Sanctum. 'Sorry, mate,' he said to the animal, risking a swift pat. 'They're back. I must go and feed them or they will turn, and you know what that means.'

And he went down the stairs, to be enveloped in the bosom of his returning family. 'Cottage pie all right?' he asked.

'Is it with chips?' Nolan wanted to know.

'No,' Maxwell and Jacquie chorused.

'Ohhh. I want chips,' the boy whinged. Holiday habits are hard to break.

'If you want chips,' Maxwell said, 'it will have to come with salad. And liver.' As a deal clincher it was inspired, and soon the evening was swinging along its usual track, with no murders, no sudden death, just good food, a quick and inequitable game of Scrabble followed by bath and bedtime story.

Jacquie came down from the final tuck-in to find a drink waiting along with an almost preternaturally relaxed husband.

'How was your day?' he asked, formally.

'Much as yours, I would imagine,' she said, taking a long swig from her glass. She waited, but nothing came. 'Is that it?'

354

'I understood that you weren't to talk about it,' he said.

'Of course,' she said, puzzled. 'But since when have you let that make any difference?'

'We have your career to think about,' he said, picking up a magazine and leafing through it.

'Max?' she said. 'You're scaring me. What are you planning?'

'Nothing,' he said. 'You're so suspicious,' and he turned back to his magazine.

Jacquie had not been expecting this and she found herself desperate to talk over the case so far. As reverse psychology went, this was working well, she thought. Two could play at that game. After a while, Maxwell put down the magazine and said, 'I just have to pop up into the loft for a moment. I've left some glue drying. Won't be a minute.' He got up and went out of the room, walking at, if anything, a slightly slower than normal pace.

Giving him a few minutes start, Jacquie followed him, not knowing really what to expect, but as she poked her head into the loft space, all there was to see was the cat asleep on the ex linen basket and Maxwell, screwing on the lid to a tube of glue. The page of notes, with several vital additions and Maxwell's passport, was hidden under a sketch of Private Olley's horse furniture.

'Hello, sweetums,' he said, without turning his head. 'Be with you in a minute.'

'Urn, yes,' she said. 'I just came to ask if you wanted anything. Hot chocolate, snack, you know, anything.'

'Hot chocolate would be lovely,' he smiled.

355

'What a marvel you are. I quite fancy an early night and a nice milky drink will be just the job.' When he judged she was safely in the kitchen, he turned to the cat. 'Until she remembers that dodgy board outside Nole's bedroom door, she'll never catch us at anything, will she, Count?' he said with a wink.

Jacquie Carpenter-Maxwell lay in the warm cocoon of her bed and cursed her neighbours. They weren't generally a noisy lot, but a car door had just slammed and the vehicle had driven off up the road with little regard for the fact that it was half past two in the morning. She listened for a while longer and her police person's mind snagged on the fact that she hadn't heard a door closing, which was to be expected if someone had been seeing guests off the premises. Then it also occurred to her that it was the early hours of Tuesday morning, not the standard dinner party night, especially not in sleepy Columbine. She was too comfy to get out, but she was sure that the noise would have woken her husband, and as he was naturally nosy he would think getting out of bed to have a look would be a reasonable price to pay. She reached out with her leg to give him a gentle nudge, known as a kick, to speed him on his way. Her leg just hit cold bed. Oh no, don't say she had been snoring again and driven him into the spare room. She snuggled down for a minute but the feel of that cold bed niggled at her and she knew she had to get up to look. She padded along the landing, automatically looking in on Nolan, who was, as usual, asleep under a pile of various stuffed toys essential to his well-being. She eased open the door of the spare room; it was bad enough that her snoring had driven him out into a cold bed, without waking him again by barging in.

Then, her heart stopped. The cold moonlight coming in through the window showed an empty bed, with the covers neatly pulled up as they always were. Maxwell was not in this bed and had not been near it this night or any other since she had changed it after her mother's last visit. She fought down panic. She didn't know why she was so frightened; he was probably in the attic. He often went up there when he couldn't sleep and his unnatural reticence on the case had probably made him restless. She looked up the stairs but there was no light. Perhaps he had just gone up for a think, without putting the modelling light on, but more likely he was in the study. The few steps to the study door felt like miles and her legs were like lead. She pushed open the door. No one. Nothing was different from when she herself had been in there last, to print out the picture for Henry Hall, years ago, or so it seemed.

Running now, she checked the rest of the house, but everywhere was silent, just the small noises of a house settling down as it cooled in the night disturbing the deafening silence. With her blood roaring in her ears, she forced herself to check the attic. She told herself she was looking for a living man; Maxwell wasn't the sort to go somewhere and just stupidly keel over. He wouldn't go with a whimper. She snapped the loft main overhead light on and suppressed a sob.

Chapter Twenty-Three

'Henry! Henry, it's me, Jacquie.'

'Jacquie?' Henry Hall sounded more than half-asleep. She heard him speak to someone and she imagined Margaret, up on one elbow, asking who it was. 'What's the matter?' She almost heard him spring into wakefulness in a second.

'Henry, it's Max.'

'What's wrong?' Hall was always ready for Maxwell to do something unfortunate when a case was ongoing; he had been expecting something for days. It was like waiting for the other shoe to fall and now he was strangely relieved. The waiting was finally over. 'What's he done?'

'I can't find him,' she said, trying to keep the wobble out of her voice.

'Where have you looked?' he said.

'Everywhere in the house. Literally, from the garage to the attic. He isn't here. He has just disappeared.' Hall was totally silent, so much so that Jacquie thought she had lost the connection. 'Guv? Are you still there?'

'Yes. Sorry; I was thinking. I assume you've been talking about the case.' It was a statement, not a question.

'No, guv. We had a bit of a chat over everything on Saturday, but I haven't told him anything he can act on here in Leighford. I just told him about Paul Masters, about Izzy's horrible mother. I

358

thought that was fair enough – he knew these people.' Her voice rose as she became more defensive.

'Will he have gone to ferret anything out? Gosport? Northampton?' Hall was just trying out all the options.

'In the middle of the night? Why would he?' Then Jacquie remembered something. 'Guv. There was a door slamming. And a car driving away. That's what woke me up in the first place.'

'A cab?'

'It may have been. But where would he be going at this time of night?' She was getting really frightened now. She could hear Hall talking quietly to Margaret, then he came back on the line.

'Jacquie, look, I don't want to overreact and I don't want to scare you, but there have been too many apparently random occurrences over the past weeks and I don't want Max to be another. I'm coming over and bringing Margaret. She'll stay with Nolan and get him off to school in the morning if we need to be elsewhere.'

'No, guv, she's just got back...' Jacquie wanted to be polite, but she also wanted help from any quarter; Henry and Margaret Hall were the first quarter she would choose.

'Nonsense. She's already up and getting dressed. We'll be with you shortly. While you wait, have a look round, see if you can find anything that might give us a clue as to where he's gone. And Jacquie...'

'Yes, guv?' She was close to tears, but knew she had to hold it together.

'He'll be all right. Max bounces, you know

that.' What Henry Hall did not add was that bouncing depended not only on the height of the drop, but also whether anyone had given you a karate chop to the neck before you started on the way down. 'See you in a while. Chin up.'

When telling the story later, Jacquie would always miss out the next bit. That Henry Hall's 'chin up' had been the last straw and she wasted at least ten minutes good searching time while she put her head down on the kitchen table and cried.

Searching a house whilst trying not to wake a sleeping child is not easy, but Detective Sergeant Jacquie Carpenter-Maxwell and DCI Henry Hall were old hands. Margaret was soon ensconced in the spare room, and Henry agreed that he would leave her a note on the kitchen table if they had to leave as well. She just gave him a kiss and Jacquie a hug and quietly closed the door. She had been a policeman's wife for too long to take this in anything other than her stride.

Hall stood on the landing for a moment, then turned to Jacquie. 'We're lucky, aren't we?' he said.

'I hope so,' she said. She took a deep breath. 'Let's go.'

'All right,' the DCI said. He recognised the signs; she had just officially become police, not public. 'Shall we search together? I think that would be best. I'll perhaps spot things and you can tell me whether they have been there for ever.'

'Good plan,' she said. 'With Mrs B as a cleaner the dust layers are quite a good guide, but you can never be sure. We'll start in the garage, shall we? He was going through some old newspapers on Saturday – he might have left something there.'

'All right,' Hall said. 'Lead on.'

The garage didn't look very promising from the beginning. The piles of newspaper were still there, one having been pushed over by Metternich in a more vigorous than usual mouse hunt. The keys to next door hung on their hook over the freezer, the dust motes spiralling quietly down in the harsh strip light. A cursory look was all it took; even Surrey's basket was empty.

The sitting room also had nothing for them. The magazine Maxwell had been reading that evening was shaken out, riffled and tweaked, but there was nothing between the pages. The dining room, likewise, had nothing to tell. In the kitchen, the little pile of cuttings sat forlornly half-under a sugar jar. Hall flicked through them and quietly congratulated Maxwell; he had been attempting, in a civilian sort of way, what Hall had achieved working with police reports and two officers. Maxwell just hadn't had the breaks. One cutting was separate from the others, but it involved an antiques fair. Typical Maxwell.

Upstairs, they had to be quieter, so as not to disturb Margaret and Nolan. Jacquie had decided to assume that Maxwell would not have left anything in Nolan's room. He was punctilious about not involving his little boy in any dark doings which might cross his path. With the experience of the Medlicotts in mind, Jacquie searched their bedroom. It was a given that Maxwell would not have left a message in any electronic format, but

Jacquie kept a pad by the bed, for night calls, and she checked every page of that. Nothing.

They had high hopes of the study, but there didn't seem to be anything amiss. Henry noticed Jacquie's passport on the desk; she was still obviously hoping for a break in the sun. The computer was off and cold. Although Hall knew, unlike most of Maxwell's colleagues, to whom he was still *the* dinosaur, that Maxwell was fairly computer-literate, he would not have expected him to have left a message on the thing. He would have needed Jacquie to get him past the home page, for one thing. Even so, they waited for it to grind into life so they could check. The Maxwells had been saying for ages that they needed a newer model; Jacquie had never wanted a faster computer so much in her life. Eventually, the screen lit and she could search for new documents. Again, nothing.

Only the attic remained. They went up the stairs and Jacquie switched on the light. Hall had visited this room before, but never failed to be amazed at the *trompe-l'oeil* achieved by the ranks of tiny soldiers arrayed on the sand-painted board. The valley was laid out in front of him, the doomed riders almost seeming to shift in their saddles as their horses rattled their bits and stamped their hooves in anticipation.

'Guv,' Jacquie whispered. 'Over here.'

Carefully skirting the diorama, Hall joined her at the modelling table. She had switched on the light over it and the surface sprang up in extreme detail. Among the shavings of wood and plastic, daubed at one corner with some cobalt-blue paint, were two sheets of paper.

362

On one were the words in Maxwell's writing, clearly copied from somewhere. Ah, 'Araminta'. Jacquie realised these were from the postcard, then. Underneath, in single capital letters spaced apart, Maxwell had written HELP/ME/I/HAVE/BEEN/FOUND/ARE/YOU/ALL/RITE. Hall read it through a couple of times. Then he turned his attention to the other piece of paper. On this, Maxwell had made a list, with numbers at first, but then he had scratched them out, as though he had decided the order didn't matter. The list of items was: Mrs T down stairs; ex off ladder; Izzy off cliff; Tom down stairs; dead dad?; otter?; two pansies; sloth; key; Araminta.

Hall turned to Jacquie. 'Does any of this mean anything to you?' he asked her.

'Well,' she said. 'Some of it does. The first...' she ran her finger down the list, '...four do, of course. Then, Izzy's father has recently died. I'm not sure if Max is thinking that might be linked as well. That would fit in with her mother as suspect, if she still is a suspect. Otter is ringing a bell. I've seen it written down somewhere. I'll remember it shortly. Two pansies. That must mean two Pansies, as in Pansy Donaldson. Can't think what that means. Sloth – Nolan wants a sloth as a pet. We saw one on the Isle of Wight. Key. Don't know. Araminta – that's Mrs Troubridge's twin sister. She sent a postcard. There's the message, there.' She pointed to the other piece of paper covered in Maxwell's writing. 'Max took it to Mrs Troubridge at the hospital but she got a bit worked up about it so he had to come away.'

'Where did she send the card from?' Henry

363

asked the question to fill in time.

'Er ... Rhodes, I think. Yes, Rhodes.'

'Does she have any psychological problems?' he asked.

'Well...' What could Jacquie say? 'She's a Troubridge.'

Hall pointed to the first piece of paper. 'It's just that this is a rather odd message, don't you think? Even for a Troubridge?'

Jacquie clutched Henry's arm. 'I think I know where he is,' she said. 'Oh, no, guv, I can't believe that even Max...' She made for the stairs and hurtled down them, missing the last few altogether. Going down more circumspectly, Hall found her in the study, with her passport in her hand. She waved it at Hall and held up a piece of paper and a photo that had been underneath it. 'Our passports are always kept together in a drawer. His is missing. He left me this.'

Hall took it and read, 'Woman Policeman Carpenter, I know you will find this because you are a whizzo detective, straight from *Boy's Own Paper*. Sorry I couldn't tell you where I was going, because you wouldn't let me go, not least because I am having to spend the holiday fund to get there. With luck, by the time you find this, I will be at least in the air, if not actually landing at my destination, which you have probably already worked out. Don't follow me, I'll let you know as soon as I have found out what's going on. Taxi's here, must dash. Love you always and for ever, Agapi mou, M xxx'

'Where the hell is he, Jacquie? Has he gone nuts?'

'No, he's not gone nuts, guv. He's gone to Rhodes.' Even as she spoke, Jacquie could hardly believe her ears.

'But...'

'There are at least three flights a day,' she recited, from memory, having pored over more travel brochures than a reasonable person could stand. 'He will be on...' she looked up at the clock, 'the one which is probably taxiing as we speak.' Suddenly, it was as though all of her strings had been cut and she flopped into the chair at the desk.

'Get up,' Hall said. 'Two can play at that game. Would you rather drive or shout at people over the phone?'

'What?'

'We are going to be on the next plane,' Hall said. 'If he is trying to find Araminta Troubridge, then so can we. And a good deal quicker, or we don't deserve to be in the job.' He hauled her to her feet. 'Up for it?' he asked.

'I'll drive,' she said. 'Do you have your passport, guv?'

He patted his pocket. 'I never leave home without it. I find I sometimes need it to prove my age when I buy alcohol.'

Now Jacquie was really scared. Henry Hall had made a joke.

Going to the airport without any luggage was a peculiar feeling. Driving through the gathering dawn with Henry Hall shouting down his mobile phone was even more peculiar. Drives to the airport in Jacquie's normal world meant being in a

365

taxi, Nolan going hysterical and Maxwell reading a history book on their destination. She personally would keep checking passports, tickets and resort information, round and round, as though they were stations on a prayer wheel.

'I don't care,' Hall was saying. 'We'll sort out accommodation later. What we need is for you, yes, *you*, to make sure that when we get to Gatwick,' he covered the phone and turned to Jacquie, 'When?' She held up three fingers and then made a zero. 'When we get to Gatwick in half an hour there will be a man standing by to drive my car to secure parking. There will also be someone standing just inside the door with two tickets to Rhodes. You will also arrange VIP lounge facilities, breakfast and an international call to the British Consul on the Island. Clear?' He listened and appeared appeased. 'All right, then.' He closed his phone and sat back.

Jacquie tried to beat down the lump in her throat. If it were Maxwell sitting next to her, that last phrase would have been via Jim Carrey. To fill the silence, she said, 'It's terribly good of Margaret, guv...'

'She'll love it,' he said. 'She misses the boys. Empty nest, that sort of thing. Did you leave all the instructions? Not that she'll need them. She has boys off pat.'

Jacquie didn't mention that her boy had been brought up by Mad Max. Let Margaret find out in her own good time. The slip road to Gatwick was the next turn and Jacquie took it as if she was at Brands Hatch. Hall furtively clung to the edges of the seat and closed his eyes.

All too soon they had gone through security and were in the VIP lounge, with an uneaten breakfast in front of them. Hall had gone into the security office to make his call to Rhodes, and as he sat back down, he patted his breast pocket. 'I have the address here,' he said. 'She's staying in a little villa just outside Lindos. It will be about three-quarters of an hour from the airport and if we don't beat Max to her, we'll be right on his tail.'

Jacquie breathed a sigh of relief. 'He won't stand a chance of finding her, though, will he?' She couldn't believe it would be as easy for a random member of the public as it had been for Henry Hall. 'He's still in the air and will be for around another hour and a half.'

Hall watched her carefully. Her mood was very brittle and he didn't think he ought to shatter it. So he kept to himself the fact that a nice English policeman had already rung the consulate, very, very early. He was searching for an old lady, the same old lady, and was coming out to bring her some bad news. The consulate had laid on a car. Henry Hall had been rather terse with the very nice consulate official, but had been unable, when push came to shove, to prove over the phone that he and not the other very nice, very well-spoken policeman, was the real policeman in this case. So, Peter Maxwell would be swept, in consular splendour, to the doors of Araminta Troubridge's rented villa. So he said, 'I'd like to see his face when he gets there after a three-hour journey on a busload of goats to find us sitting there drinking a nice cold drink with Miss

Araminta Troubridge in handcuffs.'

'Oh,' Jacquie said. 'It isn't Araminta we're going to catch, guv.'

'It isn't?' he said.

'No. Don't you remember what I said? Araminta is Mrs Troubridge's twin, you know, the tiny little thing. She couldn't push Nolan downstairs. No, the person we're after is someone else altogether. I'll show you a photo if you like. Let me know when you have it sussed.' She reached into her handbag and got out the photo of the trip which Maxwell had put under her passport. She smiled to see Hall examine it closely, ticking off the people on his fingers and leant back in her chair and, rather to her own surprise, dropped off to sleep.

The heat, as he stepped off the plane, hit Peter Maxwell like a wall. He had not really stopped to consider the weather and so was wearing what he had taken off, very briefly, the night before. He had lain in bed for long enough for Jacquie to go to sleep and had then slipped out of the room and away in the waiting taxi. He was wondering now whether he should have left her the clues and where he would be, but surely, the budget of West Sussex Police wouldn't run to tickets to Rhodes. It wasn't a huge amount, as his credit card had been delighted to discover, but he remembered the fuss last spring when someone had claimed for a parking ticket which he only got because he was pinned down by some loony with a gun in the Botanical Gardens. It had gone to three tribunals.

He looked around, but mostly at the blazing sky, the blue so deep it was almost cobalt. He could check; he still had a fleck of the paint under his thumbnail from painting Private Olley's jacket. He wasn't a fearful man, but he had a bad feeling about this showdown he was about to have. He knew that the murderer had killed at least three people, almost certainly four, and had tried to kill five. And these were just the ones he knew about. With luck, he would prevent the sixth. With a following wind, he would not become the seventh. He took off his jacket as he left the terminal building. It was at least fifteen degrees hotter than it had been at home, and the sun was still climbing. He hoped this car they were sending would be air-conditioned.

'DCI Maxwell?' A uniformed driver was standing in front of him. He almost sidestepped him, not having expected the rank, but realised in time.

'Yes, yes, that's me.' He suddenly was aware how little he knew of police procedure. Was he supposed to salute? Was this man a policeman, or just amazingly well turned out? If truth were told, Mad Max had impersonated policemen before. He'd flashed his NUT card, split his infinitives and hoped for the best, but that was at home, on his own turf, where he could bluff his way out of anything, more or less. This was different. 'Abroad was a bloody place' as some long-dead Englishman had said. Interpol. There would at least be forms to fill in, probably in triplicate.

'You wish to go to the Villa Arcati?' the man asked.

With the dear, dead shades of Rex Harrison and Margaret Rutherford for company, Maxwell nodded and climbed in to the back of the car and went off to meet his own Colossus of Rhodes.

'We will have to go the pretty way, Chief Inspector,' the driver said.

'I'm sure it will be lovely,' Maxwell beamed. 'I am in your hands.'

'Yes,' the driver shoved a wad of paper at him, almost as thick as the Yellow Pages used to be before it went online, 'and these are in yours.'

'Thank you,' Maxwell was still beaming. 'What are they?'

'Authorisation papers,' the driver said. 'You must read and initial each page before I can let you out of the car. You have done this before?'

'Oh, of course,' Maxwell bluffed, 'Anything new since 2004?'

'Page 6, Clause 38b might amuse you,' the driver said. He wasn't smiling and behind his shades he was as inscrutable as Henry Hall.

'And do I have to sign these in triplicate?' Maxwell asked him.

'No. Just three times,' the driver said.

The drive was beautiful, and he tried to drink it all in, to tell Jacquie and Nole about it later. He concentrated on the later, it was the best way. In the meantime, he thought he'd better actually read the paperwork. It wouldn't do to have the driver become suspicious.

He had rehearsed what he would say when he got there, over and over on the plane, to the irritation of the man in the seat next to him. He had watched the film to try and relax, but as the credits rolled he realised he had absolutely no idea what he had just watched. It might have had Matt Damon in it. At least that would mean he could watch it again, with Jacquie when he got home. He began to feel a little like Dorothy in Oz; he wasn't sure where he was just now, but he sure as hell wasn't in Kansas anymore. The dreamlike state continued when the driver pulled up at the end of a long, pot-holed drive. The entrance was marked by two tumbledown posts, which had once been stately Grecian columns, but were now so weathered and worn that only shallow grooves running down the more sheltered of the two gave any clue to their past glory.

'Here we are, DCI Maxwell,' the driver said. 'I am afraid I cannot take the car up the driveway. It is, as you see, too small, too rough. But I will wait there,' he pointed down the road to where a rough-tiled roof was just visible, 'where I can get something to eat and drink. If you need me until tonight, I will be there.'

That settled that question, then. He was a policeman. On overtime. 'Thank you,' Maxwell said.

'And the papers?'

'Of course,' smiled Maxwell, handing them over, 'every eye dotted, every tee crossed. It's been a pleasure.'

'Παρακαλώ,' the man said. 'You're welcome.' He got back into the car and it purred away. Maxwell threw his jacket over his shoulder and looked up the drive, as it snaked away up the hill. He checked his watch. To his amazement, they had left the airport nearly an hour ago. He took a deep breath and took his first step. Then the next. Then the next. It was the only way to tackle the incline and prevent his legs from carrying him down the road to the rough-roofed inn and telling the driver it had all been a horrible mistake and please take him home.

With every turning, he thought the villa must certainly appear and just as he thought it never would, there, suddenly, it was in front of him; low, white with green shutters closed against the heat of the day. The door was of thick, grey olive wood and looked as if it had grown to fill the space of the doorway. It was as hard as iron and the hinges had sunk into it, with years of shrinking in the heat and swelling in the rain. He knocked on it and the sound of his knuckles seemed to be soaked up into the fabric. He tried again, but thought that if Miss Troubridge was anything like her sister, she would be lurking somewhere, having been aware of his approach for the last three twists in the path, secateurs gripped in her bony fingers.

He set off round the side of the house, pushing past stunted olive trees until he reached an open space at the back The door on this side of the house was open and the inside beckoned, cool and black against the heat outside. Calling, 'Miss Troubridge? Araminta?' he walked into what appeared to be the kitchen of the villa. There was a huge wood-burning stove which was, unbelievably in this temperature, belching out heat. A pan of something was mumbling away to itself on the top and he could smell the aroma of lamb and garlic. He realised how hungry he was and sniffed appreciatively. On the table was a glass of lemonade. He felt rather like Goldilocks.

Above the soft bubble and pop of the stew, he thought he could hear another noise, a faint mewing, like a distant seagull. He remembered Metternich had made the same noise when he was a kitten, missing his mother. He pushed open a door on the other side of the room and the sound grew louder. Another door and he was in the room from where the noise came. Sitting in a chair by the mercifully empty fireplace, her eyes like marbles, sat Araminta Troubridge. Across her mouth was a piece of sticking plaster. Behind her, like an enormous temple deity, toying lightly with the old woman's fluffy white hair, stood Millie Muswell.

'Mr Maxwell,' the huge woman rumbled. 'What a totally delightful surprise. How is Mrs Maxwell? And your lovely son? And of course, dear Jessica?'

'All well, Millie, thanks for asking.' Maxwell was amazed that his voice was working so well. He was thirsty and hungry and scared out of his wits. He knew now that she hadn't just murdered three people. She had murdered as many people as had crossed her in her entire life. It was the Millie Muswell Way. 'Fancy bumping into you, all the way out here.'

'I could say the same,' Millie said. 'Come to chat about Jessica and her broken hip, have you? About how she is as mad as a hatter. Not got long, so I hear.'

'Actually,' Maxwell said and knew he sounded both desperate and pompous. 'She is much better. I showed her Araminta's postcard and it perked her up no end. I also showed her the picture someone had taken of you on our school trip. You were often in the background, but rather stupidly I didn't really look closely. I just saw a – large person in the shot and assumed it was a colleague. And then I saw you both in one photo and it began to click into place.'

'Ah, yes, the drunk,' Millie laughed and the windows shook. 'She came in very handy. I'm a bit cross with myself, though, for ending up in one picture with her. I was very careful. Digital cameras, I suppose. Panoramic shot, was it?' She laughed again, unpleasantly.

'Then I started thinking. You mentioned baby sloths being sweet. But the sloth was only out in public for the first time when we were there, and unless you had seen one somewhere else, and they are not exactly ten a penny in England, then you must have seen it then. Then, Gervaise saw Izzy talking to someone outside the hotel, and I think it was you.'

'Well done, Mr Maxwell. You really have done splendidly. Little woman know all this, does she? Right behind you with the handcuffs?' Millie looked behind him, miming extreme concentration and shading her eyes with a hand like a small suitcase. 'No. I don't see her. Any other clever clues, Mr Maxwell?'

'Yes, as a matter of fact. Mrs Troubridge, bless her, cried out quite a lot when she was on a morphine drip and after, in her sleep. She kept going on about a wardrobe, which, unflattering as you might find it, Millie, is what you had

374

become to her in her delirium. She kept counting as well, but I only worked that out last night.' It came to him with a sudden shock how recently he had been in his own house and how far he had come, so quickly. He lost his thread.

'I made a bit of a bosh shot with Jessica,' Millie mused. 'Of all of them, I thought I could snap her like a twig. Ironic.'

'We thought you had gone home,' Maxwell said.

'I had,' the woman said. 'I know you all thought I got about by train, but for heaven's sake, how can anyone do that these days? Online time-tables? Ha!' So she and Maxwell had that at least in common. 'I kept my car parked in the station car park, so I could come and go as I liked. I had already palmed your keys from the cupboard in the kitchen, so I got into your house, used the keys you so cleverly hide...' she paused to snort, 'in your garage and let myself back in. Jessica had no idea I was there and came whiffling along the landing like a little shrew. I went for her neck but she beat me by fainting and I only got a glancing blow. I put the keys...' she looked at Maxwell. 'I put them in the wrong place, didn't I?'

He nodded.

'Drat. I remember now. That's where *Mirabell* kept his keys.' She looked at him and smiled. 'It gets confusing, you know, Mr Maxwell, after a while. Never mind. Where was I?'

'The keys,' said Maxwell, trying to be helpful.

'Yes. The keys. I put them ... down, went to the front door. Put on one of her slippers, so it looked as if she had fallen down the stairs, and

375

went out, slamming the door behind me. Then I went back into your house and hung the keys back up. Simple. I can't work out why she was found so soon, though. A while longer and she'd have been dead for certain, with the gap under the door.'

'It was my cat,' Maxwell said, proudly. 'He was calling outside her door.'

'Damned animal,' she said, pulling Araminta's hair in her annoyance. The little woman winced and put her hand up to her head, only to have it slapped down.

'Also, you started one of Jacquie's police colleagues thinking by putting the slipper on the wrong foot. You obviously don't know your own strength.' As soon as the words were out of his mouth, he knew it was a mistake.

Millamant Muswell pulled on Araminta Troubridge's hair until the woman was on her feet. Then she pulled some more, making her scream behind her plaster. The old woman's eyes were full of tears and she reached up to try and stop the pain. The murderess held both of her wrists together in one hand and yanked on those as well. 'So, Mr Maxwell, why don't you come and watch me throw Araminta here over the edge of the cliff? It's not high, not that much higher than, say, an upstairs window, but she's old, and quite frightened now, I think.' She turned her round and poked her in the chest, holding her face nose to nose. 'Is the old heart beating a bit faster, dear?' she asked. 'Dearie me, I might not have to chuck you off the cliff, after all.'

'Don't hurt her,' Maxwell took a step closer.

'She hasn't done anything to you.'

'Well, yes and no,' Millie said. 'Nosy old besom was looking into the family history – oh yes, that bit was true – and she noticed that the numbers of an unclaimed EuroMillions prize were exactly the birthdays of my brother, me, his daughter, our parents ... you get the picture. She told me all about it, in a wide-eyed,' and she poked the little woman viciously again, 'sort of way. She didn't know, of course, that Mirabell would bet on anything, so the lottery was definitely his sort of thing. I went to see him, but the stupid man was so drunk he couldn't remember where he had hidden his ticket.'

'So you pushed him down the stairs,' Maxwell said. 'An accident at home, I think you called it.'

'Mr Maxwell, you have excellent recall,' the woman congratulated him. 'Well, I had to work fast, but I wasn't fast enough. First that daughter of his was round, going through his stuff. Then that grasping wife of his. They had the house cleared like locusts. I didn't know quite what Isabelle – isn't that sweet, Mirabell and Isabelle? – would have done with his things and I didn't know where she had gone to live, exactly. But I had visited her at her real house, with her real husband, and so I thought I would ask him. He was a sharp one.' She shook her head and laughed, making Maxwell's teeth buzz. 'He knew I wasn't just there for a chat. I could see that he was suspicious. So I killed him and then threw him out of the window.'

'A slight change of method, then,' Maxwell said. He looked at Araminta, who had gone pale

377

and limp. 'Please let her go. She's fainted. Or...'

'Oh, is she dead?' Millie said, releasing her grip. The old woman slumped back into her chair and lay there, horribly still.

'When you mentioned the school trip I knew you'd be away and that's when I thought I would polish off Jessica. This one,' she kicked a limp leg with her toe, 'had already taken off. I thought I'd just watch to make sure you went – what with wifey being in the police, I couldn't be sure – and I saw Isabelle with you. Perfect. Kill Jessica, kill Isabelle. Couldn't decide what to do about the husband. But then he made it easy for me. I mistimed your coming home and I was in the house when your lovely wife delivered him back. I was trapped upstairs with him weeping and wailing in the front room. And then ... guess what?' She leant forward.

'You found the lottery ticket.'

'Mr Maxwell, you are so clever! The things that Jessica says about you are mostly untrue in my opinion. Anyway, I was just making my way out of the door, when he came out into the hall. He tried to stop me. I, well, I just sometimes hardly know my own strength, as you said. I just–' she made a chopping motion, 'and there he was.'

'But why did you have to kill anyone?' he asked, stepping one pace nearer.

'Pardon?' She looked puzzled.

'Could you not have just told Izzy about the lottery ticket and shared the money out?' He might just as well have said 'elephant chocolate pencil' for all the sense it made to Millie Muswell.

'Share? Why should I share?' she said. Anyway, it was only a single rollover. The top prize was only something like twenty-five million euros. And how far does that go these days?'

'I see,' Maxwell said. 'So what are you planning to do with it?'

'I haven't decided,' Millie said. 'Do you know, Mr Maxwell, it's a shame you're spoken for. I think we would have got on, if we had met when you were a single gentleman. But I don't believe in breaking up families, so I'm afraid it has to be over the cliff with you.'

'Won't that break up my family?' he asked. 'Nolan fatherless, Jacquie a widow.'

'I'll send them a little anonymous something from time to time,' Millie promised. 'They'll want for nothing.'

'Except me,' Maxwell persisted.

'They'll soon get over it,' she said, reaching forward and grabbing his wrist. 'People do.'

He leant back instinctively, trying to use his weight to stop her but she was too strong for him. The slick, tiled floor didn't help matters and soon he was outside, and being dragged to the edge of the garden, which was over a sheer drop. Millie looked over and smiled.

'It's a bit further than I thought. The fall would probably do it, but it's best to be certain,' she said and raised her arm for the final blow.

Maxwell struggled and flailed around as he had witnessed Nolan do when he met the hard place that was his mother at bedtime, and to as little effect. He wasn't making headway but at least he had stopped her progress.

'Mr Maxwell,' she said. 'Don't make me angry. You wouldn't like me when I'm angry.'

Unless she actually turned green, Maxwell thought, she couldn't get more like the Incredible Hulk if she tried. And the thought of Millie Muswell bursting out of her clothes was more than he could stand. He gave another mighty wrench and suddenly, he was free. Flying through the air, to the rock-strewn sand below.

Jacquie and Henry Hall were younger than Maxwell, in Hall's case not much but he tried to keep himself in trim. Even so, he was sweating and panting and way behind Jacquie as the Villa Arcati came into sight. Jacquie still seemed to have the breath left to yell as she ran round the back of the building.

'Max! Max! Where are you?'

Henry was a little more measured as he got to the back door and went inside to look around. He had nothing to worry about. Millie Muswell had been picked up by the local police as she was getting into her taxi at the bottom of the drive. The powers that be had believed Henry was a policeman to the extent of sending out a patrol. It had taken four policemen to subdue her, but she would say nothing. She denied that Maxwell had even been to the villa. Araminta wasn't saying anything either. Still alive, but only barely, she was out for the count in Rhodes Town hospital, with two huge bald patches on her scalp and two broken wrists to show for her Dodecanese adventure. There was only Maxwell to account for now.

Jacquie's yelling stopped. But there was something in the silence that made Hall's short hairs prickle. He went outside. Jacquie was kneeling on the edge of the little cliff, her hands to her eyes. And down below, spreadeagled face down in the sand, lay Peter Maxwell, legend and dinosaur. And he wasn't moving.

Chapter Twenty-Four

The room was in darkness. It was silent. Years Twelve and Thirteen, Maxwell's Own, sat in serried ranks, looking towards the front. From the darkness, music played, then fell away, diminuendo. The darkness lessened as images appeared on the screen, ancient buildings, modern guns, superimposed on each other, changing, shifting. It was as if Peter Maxwell, Mad Max, was encapsulated there in front of them, in all his fossil glory.

The woman standing at the back lowered the music a little more ... a little more. This had been planned in advance. It had to go right. Peter Maxwell deserved that it should go right.

A voice spoke out of the darkness. 'Right, my little dears. As you know, I have a broken leg.' The classes gathered together heard a dull sound as a board rubber was banged against plaster, to prove the point. 'So instead of assembly, Mr Diamond has allowed me to use this digital device to show you an excellent film instead.' He gestured to Nicole, the IT girl at the back of the room. 'Clara, music please!'

And, as if in celebration of Peter Maxwell and his island adventures, the music rose above the scattered applause of his Own.

'On an island, green and beautiful, green and beautiful, stand the guns of Navarone...'

And in the darkness, Peter Maxwell smiled.

The publishers hope that this book has given you enjoyable reading. Large Print Books are especially designed to be as easy to see and hold as possible. If you wish a complete list of our books please ask at your local library or write directly to:

Magna Large Print Books
Magna House, Long Preston,
Skipton, North Yorkshire.
BD23 4ND

This Large Print Book for the partially sighted, who cannot read normal print, is published under the auspices of

THE ULVERSCROFT FOUNDATION